BAGMEN

Also by William Lashner

The Barkeep
The Accounting
Blood and Bone

The Victor Carl novels:

A Killer's Kiss
Marked Man
Falls the Shadow
Past Due
Fatal Flaw
Bitter Truth (Veritas)
Hostile Witness

Writing as Tyler Knox:

Kockroach

BAGMEN

A VICTOR CARL NOVEL BY

WILLIAM LASHNER

THOMAS & MERCER

This is a work of fiction. Names, characters, organizations, places, events, and incidents are either products of the author's imagination or are used fictitiously.

Published by Thomas & Mercer, Seattle
www.apub.com

Cover and book design by Stewart A. Williams

ISBN-13: 9781477822838
ISBN-10: 1477822836

Library of Congress Control Number: 2013922352

Printed in the United States of America

For Barry,
who, like an old stick shift with a rust-ridden chassis,
always comes through in the clutch.

Every time I hear a political speech or read those of one of our leaders, I am horrified at having, for years, heard nothing that sounded human.

—Albert Camus
August 1937

CHAPTER 1

PARTY SHOES

Politics, stripped of its masquerade of policy, is an exercise in pure personal ambition. Right up my stinking alley, you would think. But the shoes gave me pause.

"You've got to be kidding me," I said.

"I never kid, Victor, about five-hundred-dollar shoes."

"Five hundred? For a pair of slippers? I'd sooner go barefoot."

"You might as well, if you intend to wear those . . . those clodhoppers you came in with."

"They're my normal work shoes."

"What kind of work, Victor, exterminating? Because I've no doubt they're lethal on cockroaches, but they just won't do with a tuxedo. Now this fine pair of Guccis would be just perfect."

"They have bows on them, Timothy."

"You'll be the belle of the ball."

"That's what I'm afraid of."

I was seated in the shoe department of Boyds, the finest clothing store in Philadelphia if price is any indication, and isn't price always an indication? Amidst the rustle of fine fabric and the whispered ejaculations of the staff—*Oh, yes, that's perfect. Oh, no, that just won't do*—I was buying myself a tuxedo with all the accoutrements, pronounced in the French manner because this was Boyds. In the past, on those rarest of occasions when I had needed a tux, I rented the thing, picked old prom tickets out of the inside pocket, and looked snazzy enough. But a political opportunity had fallen into my lap and I was running with it. Suddenly I had impressive people to impress and impressive places to go to, including a formal ball that would be packed with everyone who was anyone in Philadelphia politics. A rental tux would no longer do.

And, get this: I was on an expense account.

"Look at the lines, Victor," said Timothy, now caressing the shoe as if it were some shiny body part sensitive to the touch. "Look at the taper of the toe. One could say, if one were being naughty, that it is quite louche."

"It looks like it was made for a ballerina."

"With that heel? No, this is a piece of pure masculine elegance. You will be noticed, I promise you."

"I'm not sure I want to be noticed in a ballet slipper."

Timothy looked down at me with lips pursed and shook his head in sad disapproval. Timothy was one of those people you meet in this world with a brilliant piece of specialized knowledge. Tall and emaciated, with pale skin and a wary, toothy smile, he knew how the upper crust dressed and how those of us in the soggy bottom layers might best pretend to fit in. I had let him pick my tuxedo, my ruffled shirt, my gold-and-onyx studs, but I was balking at the shoes.

"Tell me, Victor," he said. "Where are you going?"

"To a black-tie ball with a bunch of political hyenas."

"I don't mean your little party. I mean in the big picture of your life. Where are you going?"

I thought for a bit. This was the second of three questions that Timothy, like the troll beneath a bridge, would posit during my political adventure, each more insoluble than the next. Where was I going?

"Anyplace," I said, "so long as it's not where I am now."

"And that is why you are here at Boyds, correct?"

"I'm here because of a misguided notion as to a link between price and style."

"And that is why you have asked for my help."

"I didn't quite ask; the moment I walked through the door, you glommed on to me like I was a walking sack of money."

"Oh, Victor, you can buy a tuxedo anywhere. You can pick one up at Men's Wearhouse, or even, and I shudder to think of it, on Craigslist. But you have come to me, at Boyds, because you want to go someplace new and bright and full of rakish promise."

"I do?"

"I don't believe clothes make the man, but they are a signifier of where that man intends to travel in his life. You can wear your lawyer shoes and look like every other lawyer at the party, and everyone will know exactly where you are going—to the island of pickpockets. Or you can wear the Guccis with the bows so that others, noticing the details of your dressage, will see you as a pirate, swashbuckling his way to virgin lands."

"I always wanted to be a pirate."

"The men will beckon to know your investment strategies. The serving persons will hand you goblets of champagne without your having to ask. The women will have the urge to take you into the broom closet and bite your chest. You will end up in places you never before imagined, and only you will know the reason why."

"The shoes."

"Precisely."

"Wrap them up, Timothy."

He bowed his head submissively. "If you insist."

"I'm lucky you don't sell insurance."

"I did. This pays better. Now, may I show you something you simply must have in hosiery?"

All of which serves to explain why two days later I was wearing a pair of the daintiest little patent-leather slippers with neat black bows in the crowded ballroom of the Bellevue in Philadelphia, and why, surprisingly, they instilled in me a strange and wondrous confidence. As I made my way through the dollops of influence floating across the ballroom floor, as I was jostled by this congressman and that councilwoman, as I smiled at the pretty young aides and watched with surprise as they smiled back, I was certain I was headed someplace splendiferous. The world of politics and power was a tasty little oyster, and these ludicrous shoes would be my shucking knife.

Just the tools I needed to survive the horror of the Governor's Ball.

CHAPTER 2

STATE FLOWERS

Oh, the ball, the Governor's Ball, mounted by some political action committee in honor of our governor, as if being governor wasn't honor enough for a hack from Allegheny County. How to describe its exquisite awfulness?

The band on the stage was swinging brassy and manic; vodka from some second-rate Scandinavian country was flowing out of a fountain made of ice; there were rivers of balloons, and clouds of sequins, and, scattered across the scattered tables, meadows of mountain laurels, our lovely state flower, each beautiful branch slaughtered in midbloom just for this event. Men were dressed like waiters, and waiters were dressed like concert pianists, and spilling out of the designer frocks of emaciated wives were great sets of bountiful breasts, seemingly there to be sampled like the hot hors d'oeuvres wending through the crowd on silver salvers.

Can I tempt you with a little something? Oh, yes, absolutely.

And all about the room were little electromagnetic fields of power and money, for that was what kept this whole intricate dance spinning, the sparks that tingled your flesh as the chosen, with their snapping auras, brushed you by. That billionaire options trader, that cut-rate city councilman, that blonde aide who was nightly flinging her long tan legs over the shoulders of that gouty state senator, all of them trailing licks of power that could be felt in the bone.

And there I was, humble little Victor Carl—legal lemur, low man on anyone's totem pole, the pride of, well, nothing and no one—sipping champagne amidst this gaudy display, wearing my ruby slippers painted black, with an inexplicable force field of my very own.

"The mayor just toddled in," said Melanie Brooks, leaning close and speaking right into my ear so that I could hear her over the horn section that sounded like a murder of crows. "I've been told he wants to meet you."

"Me?" I said. "Why would he want to meet me?"

"All the good things he's heard."

"Have you been pimping me out again, Melanie?"

"That's what I do, dearheart. Oh, look, there's Simpson," she said, indicating a squat, jowly man with a shining pate. "He wanted to meet you, too."

"I'm suddenly so popular."

"You're now a man with skills. Come along, hip hop. We mustn't leave the senior partner waiting."

Melanie was dressed to kill in something tight and red. That was her color, fingernail red, from her delicious lips to her shiny spiked heels. I'll tell you about Melanie's stunning transformation later, but for now it is enough to know she was strikingly beautiful without exuding any sexual heat whatsoever. It was Melanie who had snagged my invite to the ball, who had handed me an American Express card to purchase my tuxedo, and who now clucked in my ear like a mother hen as she clutched my arm and steered me about the room.

"Victor Carl, let me introduce you to our senior partner, Simpson McCall," said Melanie.

"The McCall of Ronin and McCall," I said.

"Someone has to balance out Ronin's sharp edges," said Simpson McCall, a Pillsbury Doughboy in a bespoke blue suit. "I used to be on the front lines, like you and Melanie, and I loved every minute of it, but those days are past. Now I just have lunch with rich people."

"Client development," said Melanie.

"It must be done. I think I single-handedly keep the Union League in business. But I miss the excitement."

"No, you don't, you old fraud," said Melanie.

"Oh, yes, I do. The intrigue, the battle of wits with everything on the line. Those were the days."

"You like your lunches too much, Simpson."

"True. And the Union League makes a wonderful salad."

"You should try it sometime," said Melanie.

"Part of my job is appearing well fed. Are you a member of the club, Victor?"

"My gosh, no," I said. "Even the Union League has standards."

"Is that Norton Grosset over there?" said Melanie.

I turned to spot a hunched, fleshy-faced man laughing, his arm around a girl young enough to be his daughter's daughter. "Yes, I think that's his name," I said. "I met him at one of the Congressman's fund-raisers."

"Look at the beady eyes set in that fat face," said McCall. "They give me such a shiver. He's a vicious animal, absolutely heartless, but he's richer than Croesus and he pays his bills on time. The perfect client. Grosset has plans to privatize the state's prison system. He says it's finally time to put the profit back in crime. We can make it work for him, if only we can get the right people on board."

"Which means you're looking to buy a politician or two."

"Do you know anyone in this room who isn't?" said Melanie.

The three of us laughed and laughed.

"I like you, Victor," said McCall. "Your future in the business is undoubtedly bright. You know what you've got? The common touch."

"I come by it honestly."

"Just the kind of man we're looking for at Ronin and McCall. Phone my secretary and we'll nail down a luncheon date. Now I must be off. There is always work." And then he was gone, waddling after his client, ever ready to glad-hand.

Melanie leaned close. "You impressed him," she said.

"He liked my common touch."

"Grew up in a log cabin, did you?"

"I was jealous of the kids in log cabins. They had dirt floors, all we had was dirt."

As the band played on, exhibitionist couples flashing dentures made spectacles of themselves cheek to cheek on the dance floor. Kisses were airmailed and hands were enthusiastically shaken and sly smiles were flashed and false laughter fell like tinsel from an aluminum Christmas tree. And above us all, presiding over everything, were two great chandeliers, perfectly round, with thick aureoles of light surrounding protruding crystal nipples, the fixtures like symbols of the great public teats that financed all the strut and merriment.

"Oh, there you are, Victor," said still another woman, taking hold of my other arm, so that I was flanked now by beautiful politically connected women. This second woman was Ossana DeMathis, sister to Congressman DeMathis of the Thirteenth Congressional District. "Our new miracle worker. Are you enjoying yourself?"

"Does anyone enjoy these things?" I said.

"That's not what they're for," said Melanie.

"Oh, I don't know," said Ossana. "Sometimes they have a little spark to them." She gave my arm a slight squeeze. "Like now. I've been looking for you."

"Me?"

"Do you dance?"

"God, no. And I'm not sure this is the place for it anyway."

"There's a band," she said. "There's a dance floor."

"That's what I mean."

Ossana DeMathis was tall and whippet-thin, with eyes so wide apart they gave her features a fetching hint of derangement. Derangement, I have found, is a deceptively attractive quality in women. We say we want soft and sweet, we say we want grounded, and then derangement walks in the door. Normally, Ossana was as washed-out and cold as a ghost, yet now here she was holding on tight to my arm with a flush to her cheek, a rising of temperature—I could feel the heat of her through the woolen fabric of my tuxedo—and was I crazy to think I knew why? I tapped my toe, and the skin on my chest twitched.

"May I interrupt?" said a tall, drawn man, who looked like a mortician in his tuxedo. Ossana and Melanie each let go of an arm.

"The mayor wanted to meet Victor," said Melanie.

"That can wait," said the man. "I need a moment, Victor."

"Go on," said Ossana. "The master calls."

I gave a wink for only her to see before I walked away with the mortician to find a more private spot to talk. Tom Mitchum was Congressman DeMathis's chief of staff. DeMathis had a seat on the House Ways and Means Committee; if you wanted to talk to DeMathis—and what lobbyist didn't?—you had to first talk with Mitchum. He was one of the most powerful gatekeepers in the capital. Somehow I had been taken up by these people.

"Apparently, the decision has been made," said Mitchum.

"Decision?"

"About who we're going to face in the fall."

"Isn't there a primary for that?"

"In our district, the primary's for show. The committee came to a decision a while ago, they just wanted word from their candidate of choice. Someone overheard them getting that word tonight."

"Who were they waiting on?"

"Bettenhauser," he said, as if expectorating a gristly piece of veal.

"Bettenhauser?"

"Tommy Bettenhauser." Mitchum indicated a man standing on the balcony above us. Broad-shouldered and handsome in his white dinner jacket, he leaned on the balcony's railing with his hands clasped, staring down at the crowd with a cold, appraising look. "He's a former Marine. He won a Bronze Star in Iraq and then came back to teach public school. Eleventh-grade civics, imagine that. He's an upstanding community leader, a good family man, has three of the cutest kids."

"That son of a bitch," I said.

"He's been grooming himself for this run from the start. It's why he joined the Marines after he graduated from Penn. I mean, who does that? He's just been waiting to sense weakness before making his move."

"And that's now?"

"With the hints that bastard Sloane's been putting in his columns about the Congressman, yes, of course. We're going to have a fight on our hands with Bettenhauser."

"What are you going to do?"

"Whip him."

"With what?"

"With whatever we can find. That's where you come in, Victor."

By the time I rejoined Melanie, she was talking to some slick-haired business type. She leaned forward and whispered in his ear, and they both burst out in conspiratorial laughter. Once again I was amazed at how changed she was. When she disengaged, she turned to me.

"What did Mitchum want?" she said while coolly looking about the room.

"He had an errand for me."

"Be careful, dearheart. Don't ever forget they're all a bunch of vipers."

"And you, Melanie, are you one too?"

"That's for you to find out," she said, a sweet smile on her hard face. "But don't doubt the pit is deeper than you can imagine."

"In deep is where I want to go. What happened to Ossana?"

"Whatever happens to Ossana. She has—how should I say it—her own sense of priorities. You and she were mighty chummy."

"Weren't we, though?"

"Be careful with that one, especially."

"I think, dear Melanie, the one I need to be careful with is you."

"At least you're learning."

A woman with a tray full of champagne goblets swerved my way without my having to call her over. I took two, handing one to Melanie.

"There's just something about me tonight," I said. "Do you like my shoes?"

Melanie looked down and stared for a moment. "Won't your sister miss them?"

"I don't have a sister."

"Let's go find the mayor."

We made our way toward the mayor and his entourage, trying not to spill our drinks as we edged through the glittery, clattery crowd, bright-eyed, working and whirling, washing down skewers of meat with gouts of champagne. Above us were those great chandeliers, each a glistening galaxy of evening stars, and around us spun the orbits of the city's political and financial elite, making deals, dealing revenge, drinking and spluttering, slipping surreptitious passes at the sunny young things looking to rise.

Which only begs the question: What the hell was I doing there?

I'll tell it all later. For now I'll just say it was like anything else in this world: part luck, part desperate scheming. But when I think back on my soaring career in politics—when law firm partners sought to buy me lunch, and mayors clamored to meet me, and congressional sisters with pale-green eyes laid hands on me—the absolute zenith must have been that very moment, at that dreadful ball. I was being introduced, my services were in demand, my arms were being grasped by beautiful women; I was finally a man on the make. Well, to be truthful, I've always been a man on the make, but just then I was feeling almost made. And I thought—God spare my innocence—that I had finally found my place in the world, a place among these wonderfully appalling people, in a role that fit my talents and proclivities and would give me the exact rewards I had always sought. I was heading toward the heights, and I had the shoes to take me there.

What could go wrong?

It was at first just a rise in the hubbub surrounding us and I thought, for a moment, that maybe somebody truly important had entered the ballroom. The governor? The vice president, who was rumored to be making a quick stop to give his regards? Or could it be, oh my God, one of the "Housewives of Philadelphia"? Maybe that saucy number with all the work done to her face? We all craned our necks to see what brilliant personage had entered our midst, and then the hubbub quieted, and the music died, and the crowd pressed back and parted like the Red Sea before Moses's staff. And that's when I saw them.

Two uniformed police officers, a tall man and a squat woman, made their way through the crowd, followed by a plainclothes detective in a snappy blue suit.

You want to see a school of puffed-up blowfish turn into a mass of spineless jellies, send a couple of uniformed cops and a detective into a sea of politicians and their spouses. As the cops made their way into the middle of the room, the only movement in the crowd was of men and women turning away, pulling out their cell phones, speed-dialing their lawyers. It was like a game of politician roulette: spin the wheel, ladies and gentlemen, and see where the indictment will land.

I was in the process of wondering what poor sap they had come for when I realized that everyone around me, Melanie Brooks included, had shrunken away, leaving me alone in the center of the once-crowded dance floor. And the three police officers were aiming my way.

Could I have ever expected anything different? The poor sap they were coming for was me.

"Victor Carl?" said the detective.

"That's right."

"The name's Armbruster, Detective Armbruster. Would you mind coming with us, please?"

I lifted my drink. "I'm in the middle of something," I said as the uniformed officers slipped behind me, just in case I had the notion to bolt, which I admit had crossed my mind. I looked to my right, and the mayor, who just a moment before had wanted to meet me, stared at the scene with the frozen expression of a figurine on a Grecian frieze. To my left, Simpson McCall was pretending not to know who I was. I suppose I had suddenly become a bit too common even for him.

"Detective McDeiss told me I could ask you nicely," said Armbruster, "but that if you said no, I was authorized to brain you with a nightstick and drag you by the cuff of your pants."

"Cuffs on a tuxedo? McDeiss's idea of style is no style."

"So you know him."

"Yeah, I know him. Am I under arrest?"

"Not yet."

"Well, at least there's that." I downed the drink, felt sweetness fill my nostrils as the bubbles massaged my throat, and handed the glass off to some councilman's wife who had gotten too close to our little scene. I leaned toward her and whispered in her ear and watched her face collapse in shock.

"All righty then," I said to the detective. "Lead on, Macduff."

"The name's Armbruster," said the detective.

"Close enough."

As I followed Detective Armbruster out of the ballroom, the uniforms trailing after us, I tried to make it look like I was an important personage being called to some important duty, but from the looks sent my way everyone could see through my facade.

Whatever jig I had been dancing was up. Whatever could go wrong had. Because McDeiss was a homicide detective, which meant somebody was dead and they thought I had something to do with it.

And it turned out they were right.

CHAPTER 3

RED CARPET

The squat female uniform sat next to me in the back of the police cruiser, keeping her gaze forward, as if I had a horrible mole on my face and she was trying not to stare. Detective Armbruster peered out the passenger-side window while the uniform who was driving relayed our position on the radio.

"Hold the son of a bitch at the tape until I get there," crackled a voice over the speaker. The voice was thick and hoarse, and I recognized it from its utter unpleasantness.

"The big bear's in a mood," said the driver, looking at me in the rearview.

"Isn't he always?" I said.

"True. But tonight he seems to have a hard-on for you. When he bellowed your name, he sounded like he had been gutshot. I wouldn't want to be in your shoes."

"You couldn't handle my shoes."

I spotted the woman looking at my little bows. When she glanced up and caught me catching her, she said, "Really?"

"Quite the shindig you was at, hey?" said the driver.

"If you like those things," I said.

"Cash bar?"

"Open."

"Sweet."

"Where exactly are we going again?"

No response.

"If you won't tell me where we're going," I said, "could you at least tell me what this is all about?"

"No," said Armbruster.

"You just can't drag me out of the stinking Governor's Ball without telling me anything. I have rights."

"You have the right to shut up."

"What about at least telling me who was murdered?"

"Here's the thing, Carl," said Armbruster, turning around and giving me the glare—you know the glare, the one they teach at the police academy and test for on the detective examination, the hard-eyed squint that makes you feel all of two feet tall. "We were hoping you could tell us."

We ended up on Twentieth Street, not far from my office. A pair of cop cars with their flashing red-and-blues narrowed the northbound traffic to one lane. A pair of police officers kept a small crowd on the civilian side of the double band of yellow tape stretched across the mouth of a narrow alleyway. As I was escorted to the tape, I saw an old beater sitting in the alley. Set up beyond the car was a rack of arc lights focused against a brick wall, giving the crime scene, with its bright, washed-out colors, its clutch of neck-craning onlookers, its uniformed police acting like ushers at Grauman's, the feel of a movie set, which seemed about right. It was the same heightened sense of reality I felt at the Governor's Ball. It's all confused these days, news and fashion, crime and entertainment and politics, it's all of one piece. In my tuxedo, it felt like I was on the red carpet.

"Keep him here," said Armbruster to the two cops before he ducked beneath the tape. I watched as he headed around the old parked car and toward a hulking man in a plaid jacket and a pork-pie hat, standing with his back to us under the lights.

"The Governor's Ball," said the tall cop. "I should get myself invited to a party like that. I always appreciate an open bar. They got it made, those stinking politicians. Maybe after a few more years on the force, I'll run for something myself."

"A pork chop?" said the woman.

Detective Armbruster approached the hulking figure and started talking. The hulking figure stayed motionless as the detective gestured toward me.

"A council seat or something," said the tall cop. "I mean, you want to make money, that's the way to make money. And their pensions—forget about it—they make ours look like little pink piggy banks filled with nickels."

"What makes you think you could get elected?" said the woman.

"What's so hard about it? Shake a few hands, kiss a few babies, tell them anything but the truth. You tell the truth, you're screwed, but anything else is fair game. Lower taxes, better schools, more police. And once you get in, Boot, let me tell you, it's like a license to steal. One for you, and ten for me."

"You couldn't get elected bathroom attendant."

The hulking man handed something to Armbruster, turned around, and headed toward us. With his forward slouch, the jut of his hat, and the angle of the lights, his face was a fierce smudge of shadow.

"I don't know about that," said the tall man. "I was talking to this guy the other day at the bar—"

"A cop?"

"No, you know, just a guy. Big fat fellow with a name like a rock, some politico or something. And he told me I got possibilities."

"Was he drunk?" asked Boot.

"Drunk enough to do the buying. And right there at the bar, he told me I could go places. He told me I had the common touch. How do you like that?"

"Is there anything more common than the common touch?" said Boot.

"It got me thinking, you know. What do those guys got that I don't got?"

"You mean other than a clue?" said Boot.

The hulking man came closer and then stopped about ten feet away from us as the red and blue lights washed across his face in waves, exposing his sour, mashed features. He was staring up at me from beneath his great protruding brow.

"Hey, Cinderella," rasped McDeiss.

"You talking to me?" I said.

"Who else you see dressed like they're in some stinking fairy tale? Get the hell over here."

I looked at the two cops standing beside me, still jabbering back and forth.

"You guys ought to find yourselves a room and get it over with," I said before ducking below the tape, heading to the bright lights of the crime scene, and being hit in the face with a stench that sent me staggering.

It smells sweet and coppery, like a rotting ham-and-cheese on toast, smothered with foul. It's hard to describe but easy to recognize, because deep in the rat's tail of our brain stem we have evolved a revulsion to it that sparks a chain reaction right into our guts. It affects us like no other aroma in the world; Limburger cheese may set us to gagging, but the cloying scent of human death coats our nostrils, and clings to the backs of our throats, and drives its inevitable nausea straight to our souls.

Or maybe it was the sight of McDeiss that was roiling my stomach.

"Whoa there, Carl," growled McDeiss, catching me midstagger and saving me from an embarrassing face-first dive. "Take it easy there, boy."

I looked behind me. "Damn crack in the asphalt."

"I understand," he said, and I suspected he did.

Detective McDeiss was a bear of a man, with catcher's mitts for hands, a face like a boiled potato, and a taste for ugly in sport coats and hats. We had worked more than a few cases together, on opposite sides, and he had made it clear that he didn't like me much and trusted me even less. But while we hadn't become pals, I liked to think we had developed a mutual respect, though maybe it was only that he respected my utter shamelessness and I respected that he could pound the stuffing out of me if I ever pulled a big enough turkey out of my ass.

"How was the bash?" said McDeiss.

"You yanked me out before I had a chance to find out."

"I did you a favor. Stinking flock of vultures."

"I think I saw your chief there."

From where I stood now, I could see where the arc lights were aiming, at something covered with a bright-blue tarp, slumped against a brick wall. I turned away from the thing and toward the crowd, but it didn't help with the smell. "How'd you find me anyway?"

"Your phone."

"I didn't get a call."

"I didn't say I called. Just a few weeks ago you were scouring the courthouse for pity cases and now here you are, fresh from hobnobbing with the elite, wearing a full-blown monkey suit. Who did you kill to rise so quickly?"

"Is that an official query from the Homicide Division?"

"That tux a rental?"

"Detective, please. I have standards."

"I know you do, and I know what they are. You go to the party right from your office?"

"I went home first, but not from the office. I was at a meeting."

"When did it end?"

"About five thirty."

"Where and with who?"

"It was about a legal matter. That's all I can say."

"And then you went home to change?"

"That's right."

"Anyone see you there?"

"There hasn't been much of a crowd in my apartment since I sent away the Chinese acrobats. Do I need an alibi, Detective? Do I need a lawyer?"

"You tell me."

"I always advise my clients to say nothing without a lawyer."

"That's because all your scum clients are guilty as sin."

"Let's not let the truth get in the way of things."

We stared at each other in a game of blink to decide which of us was going to volunteer something of interest first. I actually didn't know anything of interest, so I had the upper hand. As I stood there marinating in the stench, I wondered if the reek of death was going to sink into the fabric and ruin my tuxedo. Maybe that explained McDeiss's horrid sport coats; garments that ugly are easy to toss.

"We have a corpse without any ID," said McDeiss, finally. "No license, no phone, no shoes."

"No shoes?"

"No shoes."

"There's nothing like a good pair of shoes."

"We need an identification."

"And you think I can help."

"We do."

"Why?"

"That's confidential for the moment."

"How bad is it?"

"I've seen worse."

"Have I seen worse?"

"No," he said.

"Oh."

"And if you have to throw up, make sure it goes in your pocket and not on my crime scene."

What is it about dead people? We can pass scores of live humans without a second thought, with nary even a first. Whole universes collide about us, each thick with history and insight and wondrous perversion, uncharted territories ripe for exploration, and we barely notice. We are surrounded by the living, and amidst the crowds we think about them as much as fish think about water. But then we come face-to-face with the dead, and our breath catches. Something in the dead stills our unending internal monologue. Something in the dead has its call on us all. Now, standing there as the tarp was about to be pulled away, I would have thought I'd be silently contemplating the mysteries of life and mortality and the void, but I wasn't. I suppose such questions are better left for those moments when vomit isn't surging up your throat.

"Easy now, Carl," said McDeiss as he put a hand on my shoulder and nodded to Detective Armbruster.

Armbruster leaned down, reached for the corner of the tarp, looked up at me with a filthy little smile on his face. "You ready?"

"No."

I stood between the bright lights and the thing beneath the slick blue oilcloth, my shadow ominous on the brick wall where the lifeless thing leaned. I shrugged off McDeiss's hand and stepped forward, into a puddle I hadn't noticed. The smell was stronger than what had assaulted me before, fresher, almost predatory.

A snake uncoiled in my gut as Armbruster pulled away the tarp.

CHAPTER 4

MEET THE PRESS

A moment later I was leaning against the old car in the alley, throwing up in great heaving spasms.

"Did you recognize her?" said McDeiss when I'd reached a lull. He was wisely standing behind me.

I wiped my mouth with the back of my hand, wiped the back of my hand on my black pants. "There wasn't much to recognize."

"They killed her with some sort of tool, apparently a hammer, and then kept going."

"Did you find the weapon?"

"No. Whoever did this cleaned the field up nicely."

"That was considerate of them. And no one saw anything or heard anything?"

"The car abandoned in the alley blocked it off from any onlookers, giving our killer enough privacy to slam away."

"Why would somebody do that to her face?"

"That's what we're trying to find out. You recognize her?"

I had caught a glimpse of what remained of her features before I turned, just a glimpse, but it was enough. It was like a jigsaw puzzle with half the pieces missing, and the missing pieces were an eye and a cheek and the left side of the forehead. But what remained was specific enough for me to guess the picture on the box top. Yes, I had known the woman. I had just that day sat down in a bar with the woman. And in some pathetic part of my brain I'd believed that

I had helped the woman in ways large and small, and I had felt so smugly good about doing it.

"Her name was Jessica Barnes," I said, still searching for a draft of clean air. "She lived out in Lancaster."

"How did you know her?"

"I can't tell you."

"What the hell, Carl?"

"It's privileged."

"We have a woman with half her face bashed to pulp and a killer on the loose and you're talking about privilege?"

"I met with Ms. Barnes this afternoon on behalf of a client. I had a confidential discussion with her. That's all I can say."

"Did she give you anything?"

"Detective."

"Did you give her money?"

"Don't."

"How much?"

"I can't."

"Do you want to see Ms. Barnes again to refresh your memory? Do you want me to shove your ugly face into what is left of hers?"

"I have to go."

"Back to the ball?"

"Sure, why not?"

McDeiss sighed. It was a loud, emphatic sigh, world-weary and well practiced, a sigh of resignation to all the stupid lawyers in the world, of which I was just the latest to cross his path.

"You make my kidneys hurt," he said finally. "We found an empty manila envelope at the scene with the outline of a stack of something that matched the size of a brick of money. If it was full when she left you, then we have a possible robbery motive. Be clever enough not to tell me what you talked about or why. Just tell me this—was there money in the envelope when she left you?"

"Yes."

"How much?"

"I've told you all I can."

"Was it enough money for someone to kill her for it?"

"Kids are killed for pocket change."

"Yes, they are."

"This was more," I said. "Are we done here?"

"I suppose that's all we're going to get out of you tonight, but we are not done, not by a long shot."

"How did you know to call me?"

McDeiss gave me the up-and-down, like he was examining a dead shark hanging on a fishing pier. "Look at you, frilled up like a little girl's doll. You best take care of yourself, Carl. You're swimming with the nasty now."

"I can take care of myself."

"Not against them, you can't. You're out of your league."

"You don't know my league, Detective."

"It's a shame about the shoes."

"Hers?" I said, glancing at the tarp.

"Yours."

I looked down. My shiny tuxedo slippers were smeared with filth, the bows slopped with vomit and blood. "They'll clean up."

"That's not what I meant."

He turned away dismissively, like only a cop can, and headed back to his corpse.

I stood there for a moment, thinking about the sense I'd had earlier that night of having found my place in the world. I thought about the dead woman whom I had tried to help, and the now-missing money I had tried to give her. And I thought about what I was going to do about it all.

Sometimes a man's got to take a stand. Sometimes a man has to yank away the curtain of deceit and reveal the truth of things.

Sometimes a man needs to step out of his own little prison of greed and desire and do what he knows to be right. And that's when I decided, right then and there, what to do about the murder of Jessica Barnes.

Nothing. I was going to do nothing.

I wasn't some savior out to salve some deep public wound, I wasn't some knight errant out to right some grievous wrong. I was in a different game now, the political game, in which every sap was out for himself. See what I mean when I said politics was right up my stinking alley? I couldn't have been more of a natural if my last name had been Kennedy or Bush.

Warmed by my decision to let the investigation into the murder of Jessica Barnes flow on without my involvement or interference, I flipped up the collar of my jacket, jammed my hands deep into its pockets, and headed out of the alley. I was just ducking beneath the tape, trying hard to appear as incognito as the tuxedo allowed, when a flash of something hit my face.

"Victor Carl, what a pleasant surprise."

Through the miasma of my light-burned vision, I searched for the owner of this hiss of a voice, and felt my stomach plummet even further when I found it. Short and pug-like, with bad hair, bad teeth, and rubbery brown orthopedic shoes, he was as unimpressive a specimen as could be found outside of a microscopic slide.

"What are you doing here, Sloane?" I said to the political reporter for the *Philadelphia Daily News*. "This isn't your usual beat."

"It surely wasn't until you showed up. Smile." He raised his camera. Flash flash.

"Take another picture and you'll be digging that camera out of your dentures."

"When I heard the call on my radio, I was just sitting at home, twiddling my thumbs."

"Twiddling something."

"I thought I ought to check it out, for the good of the public. They do have the right to know. And then, imagine my delight when you showed up. Hard work is so rarely rewarded. Who's dead?"

"No one you need worry about."

"I'm not worried, just curious."

"About what?"

"About why the police called Congressman DeMathis's bagman to a murder scene."

"He's here? Where?"

"Don't get cute, Carl, you don't have the face for it. What's the connection between DeMathis and the victim?"

I took a step forward and wagged a finger. "Careful what you print, Sloane, or we'll sue you and your paper both into a barrel."

"I'm a reporter for a print newspaper; what could you do to us that the iPad hasn't already done?"

"Then I'll cut off your dick, and stick it up your ass."

"Can I quote you on that?"

"Just get it right."

"Oh, Victor, I always strive to get it right."

"Then tell it true. I'm nobody's bagman."

"You're not?"

"No."

"Then what exactly are you?"

I didn't answer. Instead I gave the ink-stained wretch a threatening sneer, which I fear came off more like a fit of gas, before heading south on Twentieth Street, away from Sloane's camera, away from McDeiss, from the dead woman, from the whole stinking ball of mess. And all I had was Sloane's final question ringing in my ears.

Knock knock. Who's there?

That's the way every good story begins, and the joke was on me, because I didn't anymore have an answer. Something foul had washed over me, or I had fallen into a pit, or I had fallen into my future, I couldn't yet tell. All I knew for certain, other than that I wouldn't come out unscathed, was how it started and where.

It started for me in the criminal courts building in Philadelphia, at the lowest moment of my lowly career.

CHAPTER 5

MELANIE BROOKS

Just a few weeks prior to the ball, before ever I entered the blighted realm of politics, my career was neck-deep in the crapper. To say my legal business just then was fallow was to insult fields all across the Midwest. My roster of clients had deserted me, my billable hours had dwindled, my practice was going south so fast it was already playing shuffleboard in Boca. You can blame it on the recession; I surely did.

The legal world is as riven by caste as the most hidebound outpost in the Hindu Kush. There are the top dwellers in their office towers, cruising the lush feeding grounds of the high-powered corporate world. These denizens of Big Law are slow and fat on the proteins of their prey, but I learned long ago that you underestimate their predatory viciousness at your own peril. In the depths of the Great Recession, with their feeding grounds thinned, they were forced to dive lower to satisfy their insatiable hunger, snatching smaller fish from the mouths of second-order predators. And so these lower-level meat eaters, lesser firms with lesser reputations but no less hunger, plunged ever deeper to grab what scraps remained, reducing their fees and taking clients and cases from the jaws of even lesser firms. And so on, and so forth, and so it went.

As a lawyer, I was a cheerful bottom-feeder, used to crawling through the muck of society, surviving on what leavings had fallen from the flashing jaws of those above. My practice was a desolate territory of bounced checks, lying clients, and lost causes, but it was mine, and within its bounds I could find enough scraps to hammer out a living. Imagine my surprise, then, when amidst this debris of failure that I called home, I sighted in the distance other suited carnivores sifting through the garbage. First one, and then four, and then scores, flashing me abashed smiles before they went back to foraging what before had been exclusively mine.

And so it was that, like a Jewish peddler in the Old West, I found myself calling out my wares as I traveled from courtroom to courtroom: *"Plea agreements, motions to suppress, trials of any stripe, DUIs half-price."* Let me assure you, begging for work in the criminal courts is not why you lock yourself in the law library for three years and bury yourself in debt. What you're after is a cushy job in some huge law firm with an expense account, a handcrafted suit of the finest New Zealand wool, and a silken-haired secretary named Mimi with hips that knew what they were all about. What you're after is everything and a cigar. But there I was, sitting in some random courtroom, hoping to put a pitiable amount of change in my pocket, which meant what I had was squat.

"Do you have a case before me today, Mr. Carl?" said old Judge Winston. Ruddy-faced and arrogant, he had spied me sitting in his courtroom as he scuttled in, sans robe, to speak with his clerk.

"No, Your Honor."

"Just here for a hope?"

"Yes, sir."

"Well, from what I understand, our defendant this afternoon is well represented, so you might try fishing in another pond."

"Thank you for the advice, sir."

"And don't look so hungry all the time," said the good judge. "It makes my stomach twitch."

If it wasn't for the humiliation, I might have laughed along with the rest of those in the courtroom as I slunk out the door, but the humiliation was real and my feigned chuckle died like a butchered frog in my throat. It is one thing for your career to hit an all-time low, it is quite another for it to become such a public jibe that judges feel free to crack jokes, and smarmy assistant district attorneys, with their steady government paychecks, laugh with impunity.

I fled Judge Winston's courtroom and slumped red-eyed and desperate in the hallway, wondering about the opportunities for rug salesmen in the city: *"How about a lovely Berber for your rec room? It is such a sturdy weave."*

"Victor? Victor Carl? Is that you?"

I pulled myself out of Carpet City and saw a woman calling to me whom I was sure I had never seen before. Dressed in scarlet, she was thin and sharp with long legs, spiked heels, and a look in her eye that was hard and predatory both. You know the look, you can see it in Realtors and exotic dancers on the prowl. And she was flat-out gorgeous, model gorgeous. If I had seen her before, I would have remembered her absolutely, yet even as she approached, with golden bangles jangling, her sharp chin and raised cheekbones drew a blank.

"It's me all right," I said.

"How are you doing, dearheart? It's been so long."

"It certainly has."

"You look . . . good."

"That's a lie," I said. "But you, you look fabulous."

Her hard smile turned girlish. "Why, thank you, Victor. That's so sweet of you."

"So how have you been?"

"Just marvy, I must say. And you?"

"Dandy. Dandy randy roo."

"You don't remember me, do you?" she said.

"Not a whit."

"I guess I should be flattered. I'm Melanie. Melanie Brooks. From law school."

"No, you're not."

"Yes, I am."

I tilted my chin and looked closer and, yes, there she was, something soft and earnest encased within that hard, stunning exterior. "Melanie?"

"Present and accounted for," she said, laughing.

"Melanie, my God, look at you."

"The new me," she said, posing for just a moment. "All pressed and pleated. Do you like?"

"Oh my, yes. What the hell happened?"

"Life."

"Well, I must say, it's been a darn sight better to you than it has to me."

Melanie Brooks was in my study group our first year of law school. She was pudgy and somber, quite serious and committed to the cause, with her tight mouth and Angela Davis afro. More than anything, she was sincere, tooth-achingly sincere. Every case was analyzed for its sociopolitical implications, every discussion was about race or class or the rape of the poor, or about rape itself. Save the homeless, save the whales, equal pay for equal work, civil rights, gay rights, dolphin rights. No beef because of the methane; no eggs because of the cages; no McDonald's out of sheer principle. I can still hear her preaching in our group as I tried just to get through Torts. "*You can make a difference. We all can. Life is all about making a difference.*" She was the best of us in many ways, yet her sincerity always felt like a nail being rubbed across your eyeball. That was what made it so hard to recognize her in this red-clad predator-eyed incarnation with the straightened hair and glossed lips. Yes, physically she had changed, thinned and hardened and polished up in a way I could never have imagined, but even more than that, her sincerity had somehow been battered to death like a baby seal.

"I've read all about your exploits in the papers, Victor. I'd say congratulations are in order. You've made a name for yourself like you always wanted."

"Notoriety is not the same as success."

"Oh, give it time."

"I've given it plenty of time."

"Good things are on the way, I've no doubt. I'd love to catch up and chat about the old times but I'm due in court with"—she opened her bag, took out a document, gave it a quick scan—"Judge Winston, apparently. I have a criminal matter."

She pulled me aside and nodded toward a man in a long leather jacket standing a bit down the hallway. He was tall and bearded, stick-thin and mournful, and he stared at me with pale eyes as cold and flat as winter slate.

"Colin Frost," said Melanie. "The poor man is up on a heroin rap and we've got a motion to suppress, but I have no idea what I'm doing. I hate making a fool of myself in court, and I was so hoping someone would cover it for me, but here I am."

"It doesn't matter who covers it. Clarence Darrow would be at a loss in Judge Winston's courtroom. He's an old-line puss, and death on defendants."

"What am I going to do?"

"Go down with dignity. What are you doing in the criminal courts anyway? I thought you went to Legal Aid after graduation."

"I did—landlord-tenant, welfare, child custody cases—but eventually I found something a little more suited to my personality."

"A big firm?"

"Not that big. I'll tell you about it sometime, but right now I have this thing I don't want to do." She started looking up and down the hallway as if she were Diogenes with his lantern. "Do you happen to know someone with a clue about criminal matters who might be able to cover this for me?"

"Without preparation?"

"It won't take much. We'd be willing to pay."

"P-pay?" I said, trying to slow the stutter of desperation that had slipped onto my tongue. I made a show of checking my Timex. "You know, Melanie, if I push some things around, I could maybe squeeze an appearance before Judge Winston into my schedule."

"Really, Victor? You would do that for me?"

I tried to hide the wolf in my smile. "Old friends."

"That is so decent of you."

"That's me, decent to the core."

"Now tell me, how much do you charge?"

I cocked an eye, made a quick calculation of the level of my bank account, divided by my greed, multiplied by the square root of my desperation. "What about seventy-five an hour?"

"Victor," she said sternly, like I had been caught at something.

"Is that too much?"

"We're professionals, we deserve to get paid commensurate with our training and experience. I won't allow you to take a penny less than two-fifty an hour for this."

I looked at her for a moment, wondering what had happened to Melanie Brooks, but I didn't look too long. Gift horses are rare enough in this world as it is; I don't give a crap about the condition of their teeth. "If you insist."

"Oh, I do. Let me talk it over with Colin first to make sure it's okay with him, and then we'll brief you on the case."

CHAPTER 6

SELMA

It was with a sense of vindication that I found myself back in Judge Winston's courtroom with an actual honest-to-God paying client.

Commonwealth v. Frost—as common a case as ever there was. Colin Frost had been driving recklessly, weaving across the road with a busted taillight, when State Trooper Trumbull pulled his vehicle to the side. Out of the car, my client, his eyelids so heavy they were bricks, nodded off during questioning. Trumbull subsequently found drug paraphernalia in the front seat and enough scag in Colin Frost's pocket to charge him with possession with intent to distribute. At issue today was a motion to suppress the evidence by claiming the stop-and-search was unreasonable and illegal under the Fourth Amendment of the Constitution.

I didn't yet know how Melanie ended up with a dog case like Colin Frost's defense, or why she was so eager to palm it off on me, but truthfully, I didn't much care. All I really cared about was the two-fifty per I had been promised. If I had my druthers, it would be a long hearing, but that was unlikely. Judge Winston was a former prosecutor who thought the Fourth Amendment was tacked on to the Constitution by some bleeding-heart liberal do-gooder out to destroy the moral framework of the country. The case was doomed to a quick death, I figured, even with the strange piece of magic Melanie had slipped into my pocket outside the courtroom. But even so, I could feel the tingle of the magic's power in my bones.

Before any hearing, I always like to get a sense of my audience; a trial is nothing if not theater. Melanie was sitting in the back, by the door, trying to look as inconspicuous as possible, which was hard with that body and all that red. Along with Melanie, scattered about, were the usual assortment of courtroom characters, old guys passing their retirements, lawyers killing time before their next appearances, clots of folk who looked like they were lost.

There was one woman I couldn't help but notice, even as I tried not to stare. Pale and quiet, with copper hair and green eyes heavily mascaraed and set wide apart, she was unaccountably lovely, without any of Melanie's newfound real-estate-agent hardness. There was a moment when Colin Frost turned and nodded at her and I saw the connection and felt a stab of disappointment. Lucky bastard, although something was driving him to the needle and, with those wide green eyes, she seemed a likely possibility.

And then I saw a sight that gave me pause.

He was sitting toward the front of the peanut gallery, his thinning hair awry, the knot of his tie thick, his jacket ragged, with a bulge at the inside pocket. He leaned back with his arms over both sides of the bench, nodded at the prosecutor, scrunched his face, sniffed in a way that caused his whole body to heave, sucked his teeth.

Reading over what I have just written, I realize I've made him sound like a two-bit thug. He might have been two-bit, but he was not a thug. A thug I could handle—I had been threatened over the years by the lunkiest thugs in the city—but the sniffer was something far more dangerous. I had seen his ugly mug on the television, talking inside baseball about this election or that vote, spilling the dish on the city's most prominent politicians. Harvey

Sloane was the political reporter for the *Philadelphia Daily News*, filling the tabloid with all the city's dirty little secrets. I looked at Sloane, looked at Melanie, looked back at Sloane.

"I've been advised by a reliable source," Melanie had said to me privately before we entered the courtroom, speaking in a voice as confidential as a kiss, "that if the judge starts giving us any trouble, any trouble at all, we're supposed to just mention Selma."

"Selma?"

"That's right."

"And that should take care of everything? Like some sort of magic spell?"

"Exactly."

"And what is your reliable source?"

"Victor, I'm surprised at you. Some sources are a matter of privilege. But the authority, I can tell you, is impeccable."

"Selma."

"Trust me here, Victor."

"What kind of shady business have you fallen into, Melanie?"

She only smiled in response, a dark, clever smile that never would have flitted across her lips in her sincere youth. What had happened to Melanie Brooks?

"So it's Selma," I said.

"Yes, it is."

"Are we talking the city or a woman's name?"

"Does it matter?"

And now I was thinking about Selma as I saw Sloane sitting there. What could be about to happen in the courtroom that would tickle the fancy of a hack political reporter? And was whatever prompted his presence the same thing that had prompted Melanie Brooks to dump this case on the nearest dupe? I wondered at it all for a bit, but not too long a bit. If I am destined in this life to be a dupe, and I have learned over the years that I am, at least this time I'd be a well-paid one.

"Oyez, oyez," called out the clerk. I turned around just as Judge Winston clambered into the courtroom and up to the bench, like a grumpy old man heedlessly wading through a sea of pigeons.

When he lifted his head and noticed me standing at the defense table, an unpleasant shock washed across his face. "Mr. Carl, what in the blazes are you doing back in my courtroom?"

"I'm here to represent Mr. Frost."

The judge looked at Assistant District Attorney Fedders, the very ADA who had snickered at me in that same courtroom just a few minutes before. Fedders shrugged back at him.

"I thought Mr. Frost was represented by a"—the judge looked at the file—"a Ms. Brooks, from the firm of Ronin and McCall."

"Ms. Brooks asked me to handle the case," I said, "based on my long experience in criminal matters. I have filed my notice of appearance with the clerk."

The clerk stood and handed the judge my notice. He looked it over, still puzzled. "Is it acceptable to you, Mr. Frost," he said, "to drop down and have Mr. Carl as your counsel?"

"Yeah, sure. Why not?" said Frost.

"I don't know how you pulled this off, Mr. Carl," said the judge, "and I'm not happy about it. You better not pull off anything else in my courtroom."

"My shirt is well tucked, sir."

"Now as I understand it, we have a frivolous motion to exclude the drugs and drug paraphernalia that are the basis of this case, is that right?"

"I object, Your Honor, I believe our case is—"

"Spare me your outrage, Mr. Carl. Are you handling this on an hourly basis?"

"My fee arrangement is—"

"That means yes. All right, Mr. Fedders," the judge said to the prosecutor. "I'm sure Mr. Carl has more important places to be than my courtroom—they're giving out free cheese this afternoon by the homeless shelter. Let's get him on his way. Call your witness."

CHAPTER 7

TROOPERGATE

"Now Trooper Trumbull," I said in my cross-examination of the arresting officer, "you testified today that the car you stopped with Mr. Frost driving was swerving wildly across the road. Is that right?"

"That's right."

"Back and forth and back again?"

"That's what swerving means."

"And the pronounced swerving, which you described on the stand just now, was reason enough all by itself to stop the car, isn't that right?"

"I believe so, yes."

"But according to your testimony, that wasn't the only reason you stopped the defendant's car."

"No," he said with a smile. "There was more."

Trooper Trumbull was in full uniform, his shoes polished, the brass on his uniform shined ready for a parade. There is the sloppy cop, the disinterested cop, the overweight cop, the corrupt cop, the earnest cop, the creepy what-the-hell-is-she-doing-with-a-gun cop, but the polished cop is a species all his own. Every answer is as perfect as the shine on his shoes, and that's his flaw; there is nothing so brittle as someone else's perfection.

"You also stated that the car's rear taillight was out, isn't that correct?"

"That is what I wrote in the report."

"And that's what you testified to here, in this citadel of justice. And, of course, you also believe that an unlit taillight would have been reason enough all by its lonesome to stop the car, isn't that right?"

"Yes, sir."

"And yet you put them both in the report just to be sure that no one could object to the legality of the stop. One after the other. First the light and then the swerving, like a dollop of insurance. Are you wearing a belt on that shiny uniform of yours, Trooper Trumbull?"

The prosecutor stood to object, but before he could get out a word, the judge said, "Sustained."

"You're not even going to wait to hear what objection Mr. Fedders had to my question?" I said.

"I didn't need to wait," said the judge. "I know a bum question when I hear one. Whether or not State Trooper Trumbull is wearing a belt has no bearing on this case."

"I was just curious if in addition to his belt he's also wearing a pair of suspenders, just to be sure his pants don't fall down."

"Are we done here yet, Mr. Carl?" said the judge over the gratifying laughter from the spectators.

"Just a few things more, Your Honor," I said. "Let's talk about this taillight, Trooper Trumbull. You say you noticed it was out as you followed Mr. Frost's swerving car?"

"That's right," said Trumbull.

"And that was the reason you stopped Mr. Frost's car."

"That and the swerving."

"And all you wrote in your report was that the light was out."

"That's correct."

"But when the car was taken into the impoundment garage, it was noted that the taillight wasn't just out, but that the bulb was broken and the glass was cracked."

"That's the way it was when I stopped it."

"When you stopped it? Are you sure?"

"That's what I said."

"Now, after Mr. Frost pulled the car over, you checked what you needed to check about his license plate on the computer, right?"

"That's routine."

"And you found nothing of interest, because there was nothing in your report."

"That's right."

"And then you got out of your car, put on your hat, took your nightstick, and headed to Mr. Frost's car."

"That's the procedure."

"And on the way, you gave the light a tap with your nightstick just to indicate that it was out."

"No, sir, I did not."

"Well, maybe it was more of a tap then, maybe it was good swift crack, enough to break the glass and shatter the bulb and give yourself a pretty good talking point if ever you had to defend the stop in court, just like you're defending it now."

"That's not correct, sir."

"Just in case the swerving wasn't swervy enough to pass muster with the judge as providing reasonable suspicion to warrant a stop."

"If you're not going to listen to my answers, then why ask the questions?"

"Indeed," said the judge with a nod of his head.

"Then maybe you broke the light walking back to your car," I said. "Gave it a shot after you realized you had a live one, and you wanted to make extra sure you got the conviction, like you make extra sure to spit-polish your shoes each morning."

"Objection," said Fedders. "Asked and answered."

"Sustained," said the judge. "You asked your question, the witness shot down your theory. You're done, Mr. Carl. Sit down."

"I'm entitled to ask further questions, Your Honor. I'm making progress here."

"Not with me. I'm ready to rule. Sit down."

"That's neither right nor fair," I said. "Selma have I had my questioning cut off in such a prejudicial manner."

As soon as I said it, I could see the judge's head turn swiftly toward me, as if I had yanked on a chain connected to his chin. "What did you say?"

"I said, seldom have I had my questioning cut off in such a—"

"Okay, fine. And I note your exception for the record. Now sit down, Mr. Carl, I'm ready to rule."

"Your honor, Mr. Frost has rights in this courtroom. From Bunker Hill to Omaha Beach to that bridge in Selma, Alabama, Americans have given their bodies and their lives to protect this nation's constitutional rights. I can't stand idly by while you shred the rights that were won in these sacred places. The blood shed in these battles for freedom calls out to all of us. From Bunker Hill to Selma—"

"Mr. Carl, what are you—"

"Selma, Your Honor. They're calling out from Selma. And they're telling us that attention must be paid."

The judge stopped trying to speak over my speechifying and stared at me instead, his eyes narrowed, his jaw loose and misaligned as if he had been punched. He stared at me like he was seeing me true for the first time and what he was seeing was green and scaly.

"Your Honor, this is ridiculous, all of this," said ADA Fedders. "I move that this motion be denied forthwith and we begin the trial immediately."

Judge Winston ignored the protestations of the assistant district attorney as remembrance spread across the judge's face like a stain. It was coming back to him, all of it, whatever he had done to Selma, or in Selma, some travesty of lust or greed, some transgression that he had stuffed down into a forgotten crevice of his consciousness to wilt and die. And now it was all about to be dragged into the raw light of day and slapped across his face by some third-rate lawyer in a cheap suit who had fallen so low he had no choice but to hustle for clients in the judge's very courtroom. I almost felt sorry for him, but only almost, because, really, my emotions just then were so full I didn't have any left to squander on old Judge Winston.

I had just exercised a dark piece of political sorcery. Melanie had whispered to me a word and I had pronounced it like a magician as he waved his wand, and the effect was shockingly apparent. I had no real idea what demon I was calling forth with the incantation; wherever it came from, and whatever its true purpose, remained opaque to me. All I knew was that after a soggy period of utter helplessness I was suddenly imbued with a true and shocking power.

And I liked it, the silvery taste and electric charge that flicked my nerve endings and sent my blood surging. I liked it too damn much.

CHAPTER 8

WINNER, WINNER, CHICKEN DINNER

Selma have I seen such a brilliant display of lawyering," said Melanie over drinks at the dark wooden bar of McCormick & Schmick's. "It was all I could do to keep from falling on the floor, laughing."

"I almost felt bad for the old guy," I said.

"Don't. I know things about Judge Winston that would make your hair turn white, the old reprobate."

"So who was Selma?"

"You don't really want to know, do you?"

"Maybe not."

"Limited information is a beautiful thing in our field. Limited information keeps us all happy and safe and smiling, serene in our ignorance. All you needed to know was how to use the word. I would have thought you'd whisper something in the judge's ear."

"The ADA would have wanted to be part of any conversation. And with Sloane in the courtroom, I had to figure out how to say it in open court in a way that wouldn't get a reporter suspicious. Why was Sloane there anyway?"

"Oh, Colin has some political connections. And he helps us now and then."

"Us?"

"My firm, Ronin and McCall."

"Never heard of it."

"You're not supposed to have heard of it. But I told the partners about you and everything you did. They were impressed. And I'm impressed, too. Every step you made was right. It's like you're a natural."

"A natural what?"

"Another drink, Victor? It's a celebration. We won."

I lifted up my Sea Breeze. "Yes, we did."

It hadn't taken long for Judge Winston to decide how to properly deal with me. Even as ADA Fedders objected to my oratory, I could see the calculation play out across the judge's face. "Sit down, Mr. Carl," said the judge, finally, caution suddenly in his hoarse voice. "I'm ready to rule."

"Your honor, I still have—"

"Sit down, Mr. Carl," he said. "Do as I say."

And in truth, despite my protestations, I knew it was over even before I sat.

"In this case, pursuant to the report and testimony of State Trooper Trumbull, there was apparently more than sufficient reasonable suspicion to stop the defendant's vehicle, which is the current requirement in this commonwealth. And normally, this motion would be down quickly because of that."

The judge looked down at me, something sharp and dangerous in his eye.

"But there was an element in the officer's testimony that gives me pause, a discrepancy regarding the condition of the rear brake light between his official report and the report from the garage that impounded Mr. Frost's vehicle. There is in this a gap enough to raise doubts for me about the full scope of State Trooper Trumbull's testimony. At this point, I am not certain what to believe, and that uncertainty is enough for me to rule for the defendant. I find that reasonable suspicion for stopping Mr. Frost's vehicle has not been sufficiently evidenced and therefore, pursuant to the Fourth Amendment, I'm excluding all evidence gathered as a result of that stop."

"Your Honor," said Fedders, "we object."

"Of course you do, Mr. Fedders. But with the evidence excluded, will you be able to proceed with this trial?"

"No, sir."

"Very well, this prosecution is hereby dismissed. Mr. Carl, will you please approach the bench."

When I stood before Judge Winston, alone in the well of his courtroom, the judge looked down sternly at me and I expected a bout of righteous anger, but that's not what I got. "You made a fine case for Mr. Frost at this hearing, Mr. Carl. I was surprised and impressed."

"Thank you, sir."

"I'll certainly consider you for appointment to other cases. But we're done, aren't we? This thing is over?"

"You dismissed the case, Your Honor."

"Yes, I did. But I want you to understand that I have no regrets. That I would do it all again. That there are imperatives beyond our own pathetic powers that hold sway if we are to be more than mere pawns in this life. Do you understand love?"

"I like to think so."

"If that's the best you can do, Mr. Carl, then I feel sorry for you. And next time, have no doubt, I will throw your bony ass straight into a prison cell and you won't see the sun for a year. Now get the hell out of my sight."

As I hustled my way out of the courtroom, a figure short and bulky stepped in front of me and put out a hand like a traffic cop. "Slow down, there, counselor," said Harvey Sloane. "What's the rush? I'd like to get a statement."

"How about this," I said. "No comment. And the name is Carl. Victor Carl."

"Oh, I know your name. I remember when you were gob-smacked by your own witness in the Jimmy Moore case. Quite a little victory today, hey, Carl? A win against all the odds."

"Sometimes truth actually triumphs."

"And sometimes the fix is in."

"There was no fix, just good lawyering. You can write that if you want, anything else will result in a lawsuit. And make sure you spell my name with a *C*."

"Don't worry," he said as I walked past. "When I publish, I always get my facts right. And from now on, Victor, I'll be looking out for you."

"What kind of firm, exactly, is Ronin and McCall?" I said as Melanie and I splashed down another round at the restaurant bar. "And why am I supposed to never have heard of it?"

"We try to keep a low profile," said Melanie.

"Why would a law firm in a market like this ever try to keep a low profile?"

"Maybe because it has an exclusive clientele that would rather remain nameless."

"Are you a criminal firm?"

"Oh, some might say. But basically we're more like jungle guides. On one side we have our clients, often well known and powerful. On the other side are the things that they want done in the world. And in the middle is a dark wood filled with the thorny thickets of law and regulation, as well as with competitors holding no good intent. Our clients need someone to guide them, someone to help them avoid the cliffs and traps, someone to navigate across the rivers and around these thickets. That's what we do."

"So you're legal fixers."

"Of a type, yes. But if you want something achieved in this world, you need someone like us. Ronin and McCall: *We Get It Done*. That's our motto, or maybe it's *Pay Up*. I sometimes get them confused"

"My God, Melanie, just listen to yourself. How did you fall into something like that? I mean you were all about justice and causes and power to the people."

"I was young."

"But still."

"Well, maybe I realized that nothing was as powerless as the people. And here's the thing, Victor. When I was in law school and even after, I think I enjoyed my powerlessness. Did I really believe I was going to make the world more just by fighting within the system for the dispossessed? Did I really believe I could defeat the Man with his own laws? I knew I would fail, and it warmed me. Nothing is easier than failure—all you need to do is open your arms and let it swamp you mercilessly. Every day you get in deeper, until it sinks into your bones, and it's all you know, and deep down, no matter what you tell yourself, it's all you really want."

"I think I know what you mean."

"I accepted my failure, embraced it, actually, so long as it was wrapped in a cloak of good intent. I allowed myself to be defined by it."

"But things have changed."

"I grew tired of losing."

I leaned forward, concentrating a little too intently. "But how did you do it? How did you stop being a loser?"

"I decided to do whatever it took to win. I embraced my inner Machiavelli."

"You've become a power-mad schemer?"

"No, Victor. Our Italian friend has been misunderstood. I've become a patriot." Her phone vibrated; she kept speaking even as she picked it up and wheeled through her messages. "You'll be glad to know that a spot in the rehab facility opened up unexpectedly, which happens when you represent the facility's major charitable donor. Colin is being ferried there in a Town Car as we speak."

"Good."

"You were right to insist we get him to rehab immediately. Sloane's been sniffing around like a rabid dog, but anything we say now might compromise Colin's rehabilitation. We have a ready-made answer to any of Sloane's inconvenient questions."

"That's not why I did it. He was my client, even if just for a couple of hours. He needs help, and now he's getting it. My job isn't just to acquit, and it doesn't end at the courtroom steps."

"How noble of you. I can almost imagine you mean it. But even so, the partners were quite pleased with your performance all around. Don't wait to send in your bill."

"Don't worry."

"You have good instincts, Victor. The way you handled the judge, sending Colin right to rehab. It's just . . . for us, losing Colin so suddenly is a bit inconvenient."

"How so?"

"He does some work for us, independent contractor stuff, you know the drill. Limited knowledge, limited responsibility. He was very useful, but now he's tied up for a swath of time. We had other errands for him and now we need to find someone else."

"Oh," I said, with as much ingenuousness as I could put into my voice.

Melanie glanced up from her phone, raising her brows like an idea was rising unbidden. "You wouldn't have some free time, would you?"

"I have the feeling you already know the answer to that question."

She laughed, lifted up her chin, flipped her hair like a cheerleader. "I always liked you, Victor. You have a certain charming smarminess about you. Why didn't we ever date in law school? You tried to horn in on everyone else, but never me."

I looked at my drink, gave the ice cubes a rattle. "You were too damn sincere. You made my teeth hurt."

"I was sincere, wasn't I?" she said, laughing and showing her canines. "And now?"

"Now you scare me."

"That's progress. So let's talk tacks. Have you ever been to Chicago?"

"As a matter of fact."

"Good, then you'll know your way around."

CHAPTER 9

THE OPERATIVE

I flew into O'Hare with only a briefcase and a question.

Off the plane and through security, I spotted my driver holding his little sign. I didn't break stride as I nodded and followed him to the exit. The car was black and plush and hummed like a cat. All the way down I-94 I felt like a ninja in a navy-blue suit.

The driver had been advised of the address where we were headed, I was simply along for the ride. I expected to end up in one of the great granite buildings on Michigan Avenue or in a modernist skyscraper smack in the Loop, but I found myself instead on the west side of the highway, in a shabby business district with a nail salon, a blues club, and a storefront selling "Energéticos Hormonas." The driver told me the man I was meeting was on the second floor of the boxy brick building that held the club. The greasy scent of Cuban food from the restaurant next door followed me up the stairs.

A woman sat behind a desk in front of a frosted glass office door, leaning on her elbows in an almost Zen-like stillness. From the size of her, I figured she was part-time receptionist, full-time bouncer. With those forearms, she could have tied me into a pretzel.

"Victor Carl," I said. "Here to see Mr. Flores."

She didn't respond; she simply blinked and stared at me as if I were just another cockroach scuttling across her floor.

"I have an appointment," I said.

"Mr. Flores has no appointment today with a Carl or a Victor," she said. "So whichever one you are, sorry, but no."

"I'm both," I said.

"Two first names?"

"Yes."

"Usually one is enough."

"You would think."

"Mr. Flores is no taking appointment today with no one who has no appointment. In fact he never takes appointment with no one who has no appointment. It is a rule as firm as a fist."

"Tell him I'm the man from Philadelphia."

"Philadelphia? I have cousin who live in Philadelphia. Her name Adalia Martinez. Maybe you know her."

"It's a big town."

"She's a witch."

"Oh, I'm sure she's not that bad."

"I mean a real witch. Dead chickens, charred corn."

"Sounds like dinner."

She reached over and picked up a phone, pressed a button, waited. I heard a muffled sound from the other side of the door.

"El hombre de Philadelphia está aquí," she said. *"Su nombre es Carl Victor. Sí. Carl Victor."* A chuckle. *"En serio. Improbable. Sí."*

She put down the phone and nodded toward the door.

I hesitated outside that door as the woman stared. Melanie had given me the assignment, and I had jumped at the hourly pay—ten hours of travel and this meeting would bring in enough to cover my rent for the next month—but I didn't know who I was representing, or why I was asking the question I had been given to ask. There is a myth that lawyers tell themselves about their service to client and community and the rule of law. And in representing Colin Frost, making the state prove every aspect of its criminal case, including the constitutionality of the stop, I could believe I was working within the proud tradition of the profession, despite Selma's help. But walking through this door, I could no longer sustain such illusions. Melanie Brooks had made of me a tool, handy and expensive, yes, like a premium wrench from Sears, yet a tool nonetheless.

And how did I feel about that?

Evidently Craftsman tough and Craftsman shiny, because though I hesitated a moment, a moment was all. I knocked twice, pushed open the door, and walked into my future.

The office was dark and spare, full of shadows. It smelled of aftershave and tobacco, of thin ties and secret deals and a generation long gone. The desktop was clear, the shelves in the bookcases empty, the walls bare, the lock on the file cabinet depressed. I had walked into a Hopper painting. Standing behind the desk, his back to me, was a tall, thin man in a brown checked suit.

"So you're Carl Victor from Philadelphia," said the man, in a gentle voice with only a trace of an accent.

"Close enough. Thank you for seeing me."

"It is nothing," he said. "Do you want something to drink?"

"No, thank you."

"A cigar?"

"No."

He turned, a glass filled with amber in one hand, an unlit cigar in the other. His face was thin and handsome, his hair was gray, and his eyes were surprisingly kind. "Perhaps, then, a plate of empanadas from downstairs."

"Tempting, but no."

"Your loss. I own the restaurant, and the chef is marvelous." He stepped around the chair and sat down, leaned back, took a sip of his drink, put the cigar in his mouth. He stared at his glass for a moment, as if appraising a jewel.

"I don't know you, Carl Victor," he said, his voice just as gentle as before. "Normally, I have a rule that I will not meet with someone

I do not personally know. It is a rule that has well protected me over the years."

"And yet here I am."

"I was told by someone that I must see you. There are only a few people in this world that I trust enough to cause me to break such a rule. Whether fortunately for you or not is still to be determined, but he was one, and so here you are. What can I do for you, Carl Victor from Philadelphia?"

"I have a question," I said.

"No request, no favor, no point you want to get across? Just a question?"

"Just a question."

"Go ahead and ask your question and we'll see if I will answer it."

"What do you want?" I said.

"What do I want?" He laughed. "You're the one who came all this way. What do you want?"

"I want to know what you want."

"What does anyone want? Wealth, sex, a fine Scotch and a Cuban cigar. Peace on earth, goodwill for all men, the White Sox to win another pennant."

"Let's not get carried away," I said. "But I didn't ask what anyone would want. What do you want?"

"Me."

"You. Specifically."

"And you will grant my every wish, is that the idea? Make me rich beyond my wildest dreams?"

"Is that what you want, money?"

"Who doesn't want money?"

"I look at this office, and I look at your secretary, and I doubt very much that what you want most is money. Oh, you like your Scotch and your cigars, and I assume they're both premium—we all want to maintain a certain lifestyle. But this office tells me that money is not what you are about."

"Your eyes are sharper than your tie, Carl Victor. So maybe what I really want is power."

"Power."

"Who doesn't want power?"

"And why do you want all this unlimited power? So you can stand with senators and governors and have your picture snapped? I figure you can already do that, or I wouldn't be here. And yet, your walls are bare of trophy pictures. No smiling pols, no glowering moguls, no evidence of a single lever of power."

"I am maybe discreet."

"You are definitely discreet. And you are also cautious. Even with all the power you have, you sit in this spare little office and refuse to meet anyone you do not personally know. How much more power do you want? Enough so you would be unwilling to meet with your own brother?"

"It is a conundrum, is it not? If you were faced with such a question, Mr. Carl Victor, what is it that you would want?"

"Money and power, or maybe for someone to get my name right, but it is not a question for me."

"I see. It is my question only."

"Yes."

"And what will I have to do in return for having my most secret desires filled?"

"Nothing."

"Excuse me, Carl Victor, I don't see fairy wings on your back."

"I have been assured that there is no quid pro quo here."

"No quid and no pro. A freebie."

"To the extent there is such a thing," I said.

"Who sent you?"

"Even I don't know."

"And I am to give you an answer with no idea of who is asking the question and with what motive?"

"Yes."

"Why would I do such a thing?"

"Because I'm from Philadelphia, the place where dreams come true."

"Is that your city's slogan?"

"No, I just made it up, but in your case it might be true."

The man looked at me, looked at his cigar, looked at me again. He took a long silver rectangle from a desk drawer, something that looked like a pistol clip. He flicked the top, and a flame erupted. He took a moment to light his cigar. He leaned back, puffing away. The smoke settled between us like a shifting curtain of motive. I sat before him as calmly as a tick on a blade of grass waiting for a fat golfer to pass by.

Finally, he took the cigar out of his mouth, leaned forward until his clasped hands rested on the desk, and shook his head with deep resignation.

"I have a daughter," he said.

About half an hour later I called the information into Melanie from the curvy bar of some steak house just south of Division Street. It was an expensive meat market in more ways than one, but I had time to kill before my flight and I had developed a sudden hunger for a slab of animal flesh, well charred. Fortunately, Melanie had given me an American Express card to cover my expenses. After I downed a quick Sea Breeze, and after a waiter showed me a tray of aged cuts of prime beef and I pointed to something round and red, I made the call.

"He has a daughter who started a catering business in Miami," I said into the phone as a woman a few seats down eyed me with something more than mild interest. "He wants it to be a success."

"The doting father," said Melanie. "I'm surprised."

"That he loves his daughter?" I said, smiling back at the woman. She had thin wrists, and her lipstick was candy-apple red, and she was not the kind of woman who would usually eye me with interest in a bar, but there she sat and there she eyed.

"No," said Melanie. "I'm surprised that he said anything to you at all. The read we got on Flores was that with strangers he was as close-lipped as a clam. Nice job steaming him open. The partners will be pleased."

"And I aim to please the partners." I waved a finger in an oblong circle, letting the barkeep know he should refill my Sea Breeze and buy the woman whatever it was she was drinking. "I got the sense, based on the level of his concern, that it's going to take a lot of weddings to make his daughter's business work."

"Let us worry about the weddings. You just get back here."

"My plane leaves in two hours," I said as I nodded in acknowledgment of the woman's mouthed thank-you. She was tall and lush and blonde, as tasty and well marbled, no doubt, as the rib eye I had ordered. And she smiled as if I were exuding some sense of newly won authority. "Before I depart, I'm going to have a steak and three more drinks and nuzzle the earlobe of the woman four seats down from me, and then I'm going to sleep like a narcoleptic on the flight home."

"Good," said Melanie. "So you'll be well rested when you land."

"Don't."

"There's a hysterical woman in Fairmount who is threatening to kill herself. You need to talk her down."

"Get a psychiatrist."

"We need someone we can trust, someone with tact and absolute discretion."

"Boy, do you ever have the wrong man."

"I'm betting not."

"But if she's threatening to kill herself, what can I do? I won't be back for four hours."

"Trust me, she'll wait."

CHAPTER 10

SHAKE AND KISS

"That lying bastard. I love him so much I swear I'll stick a knife in my throat and watch the blood spurt."

Amanda Duddleman, barely old enough to order a beer in a bar, was sitting on her couch with her bare legs curled beneath her, naked inside a white terry-cloth robe stolen from some high-priced adultery hotel. Her tearstained face was dramatically aimed at the ceiling, a knife the size of a Chihuahua in her hand. We were in her town house by the art museum, quite the tidy love nest, with hardwood floors and comfy furniture.

"And you know what hurts the most?" she said, absently patting the back of the blade against her neck. "The part that makes me really want to kill myself, beyond even the betrayal?"

"Let me guess," I said, sprawled in a chair, my tie loosed, the flatness of exhaustion in my voice. "It's the lying."

"How did you know?"

"Because it's always the lying."

I had been wrong about what I had told Melanie on the phone in Chicago. Yes, I had eaten the steak and downed the drinks and nuzzled the ear, but I hadn't slept an ounce on the flight home, and I was neither fit nor in the mood to be part of a scene where I played the straight man for some love-crazed sweet thing. And yet there I was, supposed to fix whatever it was that had driven Amanda Duddleman to feign suicidal distraction. There wasn't enough glue in Kentucky. I didn't know who the lying bastard she was referring to was, but I figured if I didn't let on to all I didn't know, I'd find out soon enough.

"I just can't take the dishonesty anymore," said this Amanda Duddleman. "I know it's built into the bones of what we have. I went to Barnard, I studied Derrida, I know how to deconstruct the text of our relationship. He's married, which means that every bottle of champagne, every kiss, every hump on the kitchen floor is a lie to his wife, and ultimately to the people."

"How will they ever survive?"

"I am nothing but his lie, and I can handle that. Truthfully, I'm not sure I would want to be anything more. His little helpmeet? A bauble on some congressman's arm? His wife can have that honor. I went to Barnard, for Christ sake. But when he starts lying to me, that's the part I can't abide. Lying to his lie, my God, where will it end?"

"Exactly what I was wondering," I said.

She tilted her head down to stare at me for a moment. Her eyes lost their desperate wobble as she pointed the knife at me. "Some questions are rhetorical."

"I thought I'd help move things along."

"I'm sorry if my trauma is keeping you awake." She was unaccountably lovely, Amanda Duddleman, young and tawny, with perfect skin and healthy teeth. She must have been quite the sight cutting across the Columbia campus, legs flashing, sunlight glinting off her hair, the very perfection of raw youth. She must have destroyed the hearts of all the mad young boys.

"You don't mind if I doze off here, do you?" I said.

"You're not being very sympathetic. I'm in crisis here. I love him. I love him so much I want to rip out my heart and serve it to him on a silver platter."

"With fava beans and a nice Chianti?"

"But when I call him with sobs and pleading and the worst kinds of threats, instead of coming himself to kiss my tearstained face and make sweet love to me, he forces me to wait for hours, and then you show up. And you're no prize, let me tell you. Who are you, anyway?"

"All you need to know is that for the time being, as long as you're putting on the crazy, I'll be the guy you'll be dealing with."

"Where's Colin? Colin knows how to calm me down. We talk, share a joint, listen to some tunes."

"Colin's in rehab."

"Oh."

"Yeah."

"And you're Pete's new errand boy?"

"Something like that."

"I suppose you don't have any weed."

"No, sorry, I'm straighter than a crossing guard in a back brace. But enough about me. Let's go back to the lying."

"Yes, let's. The lying." Her chin tilted up as she lifted her hand so that the handle of the knife was on her forehead. "I just can't take the lying."

"What was he lying about?"

"Is that important?"

"Always."

"Isn't the lying itself enough?"

"Never."

"Really?"

"No one gets upset when someone lies about a surprise party. Or in a deposition. Or about their mother-in-law's hair. But, just to grab an example, when someone is upset that her lover is lying about cheating on her, I've generally found that, no matter what she says, she is more upset about the cheating than the lies. So what is he lying about?"

"He's cheating on me."

"Well, blow me over and call me Kip."

"I had a fish named Kip."

"A salmon?"

"Of course he's cheating on me, Kip, he's a politician. But to be so obvious about it, and then to lie to my face. What must he think of me?"

"Maybe that you went to NYU. So what was the giveaway, the tell? Let me put it in my book of things not to do when I'm cheating on my mistress."

"Do you have a mistress, too?"

"Not yet, but we all have aspirations. Was it lipstick on the collar? A strange perfume?"

"Lipstick or perfume could just be from his wife."

"Who he's cheating on with you."

"Right. No, it was the condoms."

"Ahh, the condoms." I nodded sagely. "You'd be surprised how often it is the condoms. What did he do, write the wrong name on them?"

"Do men do that? I mean, really?"

"No."

"Good, because that would be creepy. I have to buy them for us—he can't very well go into a store and pick up a box, now can he? I mean it would be all over the front page of the *Daily News*."

"I can imagine the headline."

"'Congressional Party Hat,'" she said.

"'Political Rubber Match.'"

"I counted the number in the box I bought and there were too many missing. I counted twice to be sure. The son of a bitch is using my rubbers to screw someone else. Can you imagine?"

"I'm actually impressed. He got you to buy his rubbers for him. Maybe I should put in an order, too. Two boxes, extra large."

"Really?" One eye squinted in disbelief. "What's your shoe size?"

"Ten," I said, and then after a slight pause, I added, "and a half. So that's why you want to kill yourself, the condoms?"

"You don't seem so concerned that I'll go through with it."

I stood up and spread my arms. "It's late, I'm tired, and you're too smart to be counting condoms. Give me the knife."

She looked at me a moment, looked down at the knife, and placed it on the coffee table. I leaned over, picked it up, whirled, and tossed it for effect at her wall. I wanted it to stick in with a thud and then twang back and forth with that ominous sound, but it didn't stick. It just sort of slammed against the wall and clattered on the floor.

"I'm going home," I said. "I'm going to sleep for a week and forget that I was ever here. You don't want to kill yourself, you just don't want to be ignored. Try the rabbit and don't forget to tip your waiter. How'd you meet the Congressman anyway?"

"I write for the *City Weekly*."

"The free rag? Nice gig."

"I majored in journalism."

"At Barnard."

"Well, I took advanced courses at the Columbia School of Journalism. And I was assigned to write a profile on Congressman Peter J. DeMathis, and I was impressed with what I saw. He seemed to really care about things."

"A politician who seems to really care? Boy, that's a new one. And to prove how much he cared, he screwed you in his socks."

"Why would I be wearing his socks?"

"Good night," I said.

"Nothing happened while I was writing the article, I'll have you know. I'm a journalist, I have my standards. But after my profile came out, he called to thank me and we ended up having drinks, and things sort of—"

"I get it."

"—happened."

I looked around at the town house. "Does he put you up here?"

"That would make me a whore. No, this is mine."

"I didn't know the *City Weekly* paid so well."

"I get some help."

"Are Mommy and Daddy tired of supporting you?"

"Not yet, but they're getting there."

"Can I give you some advice, Amanda, good serious advice?"

"Please, God, no."

"Men don't like crazy, especially married men. They want sane and fun and young and beautiful, and you're already three out of four."

"You don't think I'm too fat?"

"If you're too fat, then I'm too smart, and we both know that's not true, because I'm here. If you want him to stop cheating on you, then don't give him any of the crazy. No more phone calls threatening to kill yourself, no more wild scenes about missing condoms, no more showing up at campaign rallies in the shake-and-kiss line."

"How do you know about that?"

"No matter what he's told you about love and the future, he's simply screwing around with you. Nothing wrong with that, but treat it like what it is, a stupid fling with a stinking politician, and have fun with it. Call him tomorrow, apologize, promise him it won't happen again, and then wait for him to call you. He will, and soon, too. You're pretty enough to infect his dreams. But in the meantime, find yourself someone your own age to play with when you're not with him. Get your life together. Don't forget what you are."

"What is that?"

"You're a Barnard girl."

"Who the hell are you, really?"

"I'm a nobody and a nothing, a suit who does what he's told. I'm your friendly neighborhood fixer."

"You're actually pretty good at it, Kip. How long have you been doing this?"

"About a day and a half," I said.

CHAPTER 11

THE CONDOM THIEF

I have a secret to tell you," said Congressman Peter DeMathis, the great condom thief. He spoke softly, intimately, and leaned forward, as if he were about to bare the dark root of his soul. He was a decade older than me, tall and handsome in his navy-blue suit, fit as a gymnast, the very image of exactly what I wasn't, a serious man on the rise. "And this is my secret, as embarrassing as it might be: I still believe in America."

There was a smatter of applause in the dreary hotel reception room from the troop of fine people who had ponied up to drink cheap zinfandel, eat greasy spinach squares, and shake hands as they got their pockets picked.

"They slop this crap right up," I said softly to Melanie in the back of the room.

"Like pigs in a sty," she said.

I reached toward a tray of sautéed pork bits being passed around by a waitress and grabbed two little skewers. "You want one?"

"God, no," said Melanie. "If I ate at every one of the events I'm forced to attend, I'd end up a blimp. But help yourself."

"Don't worry, I will."

"I know it's not popular or cool to believe in America," continued the Congressman. "I know all the smart, clever folk will tell you that America's best days are behind it and that we have no choice but to take our place behind the likes of China and India and Singapore." A round of boos poured from the crowd, as if he were talking about the New York Mets and not a trio of sovereign allies on the other side of the globe. "But I don't believe any of this, not a bit, because I believe not just in this country but in its people. Because I believe in you."

"I can't believe you work for this guy," I said.

Melanie turned and looked at me. "I don't work for him, Victor. Why would I ever want to work for a backbencher like DeMathis?"

"I just thought—"

"Don't think so much, it doesn't pay. He couldn't afford me anyway."

"Then why are you running his errands?"

"I'm not, you are."

"I see so much energy just in this room, so much raw ability and desire to make a difference," said the Congressman. "Think now about all the potential boiling across this land, from sea to shining sea."

"Somehow this speech is making me hungry," I said. "Is that shrimp over there?"

"Sure, we've taken some shots," continued the Congressman. "But when I look at this great country of ours, and I see its people ready to saddle up and bring this nation back, I know no barrier is too high, no challenge is too daunting, nothing can get in our way—except maybe ourselves. Which is why I'm in the House of Representatives, and why I'm asking for your support as I prepare to run for reelection."

The applause rose like a wave out of the paying crowd to wash over the Congressman and he rose on tiptoes to greet it. It was a stirring sight as I stirred a prawn in a beaker of cocktail sauce. The shrimp was as bland as the speech. I took two more.

"I've seen government regulations stifle innovation. I've seen government interference kill progress. And I've seen government-imposed taxes take the profit out of a small business and drive it into bankruptcy. We can outwork, outproduce, outcompete anyone in the world if can we just get the gorilla of the federal government off our backs. That was my purpose in running for Congress in the first place, that's been my mission during my first three terms in the House, and that's what I pledge to continue to fight for if the people of the Thirteenth Congressional District see fit to send me back to Washington for another round of battle."

When I returned from my fishing expedition, Melanie was with a tall, serious man in a dark suit, who stood beside her with his arms crossed, staring with a mournful intensity at the man on the platform waving his hands like a carnival barker.

"Victor," said Melanie, "I'd like you to meet Tom Mitchum, the Congressman's chief of staff."

Without uncrossing his arms or turning his gaze from the Congressman, he said, "So you're the one I've been hearing so much about. The Congressman asked me to thank you personally for your efforts. That's why we invited you here today."

"She's quite the package, that Duddleman."

Mitchum's head snapped my way at the name. "We're all grateful for your tact and discretion."

"Mostly my discretion, I assume."

"Be advised, Victor, that Congressman DeMathis intends to change this country."

"Imagine that," I said. "I have enough trouble changing my sheets."

"It won't be easy, and he can't do it alone. We need team players, Victor. Are you a team player?"

"There's no *I* in team," I said.

Mitchum nodded in satisfaction. "Good," he said before turning back to gaze at his boss.

"Then again, there's no *I* in oyster," I said, "for whatever that's worth."

"You can trust Victor, Tom," said Melanie. "I've known him since law school. He's smart and effective, and he can keep his mouth shut. He'll be an asset."

"I hope so," said Mitchum.

"There's no *I* in law school either," I added, "which is peculiar, because I was there with Melanie."

Melanie elbowed me in the ribs, but Mitchum's attention was already back on the stage. He nodded at the Congressman's words as if listening to a favorite old pop song. I figured he had probably heard the speech enough times that he could recite it in the shower.

"You know I've gone up against the tax-and-spenders," said the Congressman, "the big regulators, the bureaucrats, and the entrenched interests that have tried to stifle our voices every step of the way. It's been a hard road, but we've made progress. I've introduced scores of bills to knock down the size of the government octopus, and with every bill I get more of my colleague's votes."

"Are they serving calamari?" I said, looking around, searching for a tray. "I have a sudden hankering for squid. Perhaps with a bright marinara?"

"Don't they feed you at work?" said Melanie.

"Where some might see an example of grassroots politics at its most basic, I see dinner."

"We're getting closer. Success is at hand. We can do this if we work together. We can make a difference, we will make a difference, and America will rise stronger, wealthier, more influential than ever before. We owe it to ourselves, to the world, and to our children. Thank you for your support, thank you for your vote, thank you for sharing my unabashed love for this country. Thank you, and God bless the United States of America."

As the crowd applauded and the Congressman stepped down from the stage to be dramatically engulfed by the people, at least the people willing to put up a quick five hundred smackers, Mitchum turned to us once again.

"Why don't you both come up to the suite after the event. Generally, we only invite our biggest contributors, but the Congressman would like to speak to you personally, Victor."

"Will there be dessert?"

Mitchum tilted his head quizzically.

"Something sweet yet tart would nicely set off the shrimp."

"Thank you, Tom," said Melanie. "Unfortunately, I have an event across town, but Victor will be there. He so looks forward to meeting the Congressman."

"I do?"

"He does," said Melanie.

"Splendid," said Mitchum. "I'll tell him to expect you, Victor."

"You're not coming?" I said after Mitchum had left us to grab DeMathis's arm.

"An appearance is all they really want from me," said Melanie. "Just enough to show I care, not enough for anyone to wonder why I'm hanging around. You'll do fine on your own."

"I don't think Mitchum likes me."

"Tom doesn't have a sense of humor."

"Boy, did he ever pick the wrong career."

"Politics can be amusing in an absurdist way, true. But don't ever forget, Victor, that no matter how ludicrous the whole thing seems from afar, these people take themselves quite seriously. It helps if they think that you take them seriously, too. And it's safer, to boot. Now wipe the grease from your mouth and grab a stiff drink; you're about to meet the Congressman."

"I'm all atwitter."

"We want him reelected. Do what you can to make that happen, dearheart. But don't ever forget who you work for."

"And who's that, Melanie?"

She smiled like a cat. "Enjoy yourself, Victor, just not too much."

CHAPTER 12

THE STARE

I was in a fine hotel suite, drinking a sherry way too good for me, chatting as an equal with a clot of the upper crust and, remarkably, I felt not one whit out of place. It was as if these were my people, with their dandruff, their locked-jaw self-satisfactions, their dry-to-the-point-of-drought senses of humor. Hadn't I struggled all my life to be in just such a room, to drink just such a wine, to chat uncomfortably about nothing with just these good and ripely bejeweled folk, to laugh at exactly that bad joke and nod at that not-so-sly insinuation? And wasn't my obsession to join their ranks what created their ranks in the first place? In the midst of it all, as one dowager was complaining about the type of people at Mount Desert Island these days, I had the urge to spread my arms wide and shout out, "Lucy, I'm home!"

"It's about time we had someone to stand up and tell the truth," said one desiccated old woman, her throat a chicken's neck strangling in pearls. She was bent like a wire hanger at the waist, but her hair was dark brown without a speck of gray and she smiled with a strange sexual certainty, her bright dentures stained red with lipstick. "That's why we love Pete so much—he's our truth teller."

"Hear, hear," I said. "And it helps that he's not too bad-looking either."

"I should say not," said the woman. Her lips twitched as if her medicine had just kicked in. "He is a magnificent animal."

"And it's not just his position on taxes that makes him such an attractive politician, yes," said the hunched, fleshy-faced man with shiny skin and beady eyes. His voice was slow, his tan was deep, he wore a red plaid jacket, and his shirt collar was open to reveal a thick golden chain.

"What is his position on taxes?" I said.

"Against," said the man.

"Hear, hear," I said again.

"But it's also that the Congressman recognizes that government regulations are strangling us all."

"You're right, Norton," said the woman. "You're so right."

"Why, in our bank," said a rotund man in a three-piece suit, his face so soft and round he resembled a constipated baby, "we have divisions of clerks toiling all day just to keep us from running afoul of their silly regulations."

"It's a crime," I said.

"We know what we're doing," said the beady-eyed man. "They just need to leave us alone and let us do it. Unleash us all and hear us roar."

"Growl," I said.

The woman with the pearls laughed and put her hand on my forearm. "Don't be naughty," she said with her naughtiest smile. "I'm Connie."

"Victor."

"Do you dance, Victor?"

"Not very well."

"Well, who cares about that?"

And here is the mystery of the whole event. I agreed with each and every one of them about everything, and not just out of my normal sycophantic politeness to the wildly wealthy, but wholeheartedly and emphatically. When they complained about their taxes, in my heart I complained too, even though I paid less in taxes than Connie paid for pedicures. When they mocked those on the public dole, I too mocked away, even though the bulk of my income last year was paid by the state for my court-appointed cases. I might not be the one percent (well, the upper one percent) but, by God, I aspired, and in that room, among those people, I let my deepest aspirations guide me.

"Mr. Carl, what a pleasant surprise," came a soft voice from behind. When I turned and saw her, my heart lurched. It was the thin wide-eyed woman from the courtroom at Colin's hearing, pale and serene, wearing a soft blue dress that fell from her narrow shoulders and over her breasts like a gentle waterfall.

"A last-minute invite," I said.

"Do you really like sherry?"

"Who doesn't adore a good sherry?"

"Come along and I'll get you a real drink," she said, softly placing her hand on my forearm.

I excused myself from my new best friends with some false intimacy, a mild quip, and an embarrassing bark of a laugh, before I let the woman lead me to the little bar in the corner, where she ordered me up something with vodka.

"I was in the courtroom for Colin Frost's hearing," she said. "I didn't get a chance to tell you how impressive you were."

"Sometimes the law works as it's supposed to."

"But sometimes it's the lawyer, and I think that was one of those times. You were wonderful. I told my brother all about it."

"Your brother?"

"Pete. The Congressman. I'm Ossana DeMathis."

"The Congressman's sister," I said, nodding, like it all made sense. "I thought you were somehow related to Colin."

"He's just a friend. He's doing well in rehab, actually, if you're interested. I don't have much experience in these things. Does it ever work? I mean really, or is an addict always an addict?"

"An addict is always an addict, but rehab can get him off the drugs and save his life. I've seen it work and I've seen it fail. It usually depends on what the patient has waiting for him on the outside."

"Oh," she said flatly, as if she meant *Poor Colin.*

Oh, I thought with a pleasing sense of possibility. *Poor Colin.*

She took a sip of her drink and looked around. "Don't you just hate these things?"

"Free food, free drink, all these swell people?"

She laughed, which was both gratifying and strange, because I wasn't trying to be funny.

"You're not giving my brother gobs of money like the rest of them, are you?"

"I make it a point never to give money to politicians."

"Oh? And why is that?"

"They'll just spend it to buy my vote. I figure it pays to avoid the middleman."

"In a room like this, keep such impeccable logic to yourself. You can't imagine the carnage if that idea spread. See that man over there in the terrible plaid jacket? Norton Grosset. He made his money in drugs, or finance, or something."

"Does it matter?"

"Never. What matters is how much he has. It is astounding."

The hunched old man seemed to morph in front of my eyes; he grew taller, stronger, smarter, younger, his hair grew thicker, his soul washed clean. Astounding indeed.

"Norton is one of my brother's biggest supporters. He alone pays for every other commercial we put on the air. Apparently, he owns everything."

"Including your brother?"

"Don't be impertinent. My brother can't be bought." She took a sip of her drink. "Only rented. So if you're not here to throw your money into the pit, why the appearance?"

"Apparently, your brother wants to meet me."

"Yes, I would think so. Especially with Colin out of commission. Colin was so useful. Oh, speak of the devil." She waved her drink to the side. "And Mrs. Devil."

I turned suddenly and there he was, Congressman DeMathis and a stately woman, slightly older than he, the two glad-handing their way toward us.

"He must have been a precocious child," I said.

"You don't know the half of it."

"I need a drink," said Mrs. DeMathis, reaching us before her husband. She was a pretty yet formidable woman, with clenched teeth and upswept hair. On her black dress she had clasped a brooch of a lizard with ruby eyes. "And who is this, Ossana, one of your pets?"

"It's Victor Carl," said Ossana. "The lawyer who represented Colin."

"Oh, Victor, of course. Yes, we heard all about the court case. Good work, that. Thank you for coming. And you've already been snatched up by Ossana, so you're in sure hands. Splendid."

"Can I order you something?" I said.

"Just a touch of bourbon, dear. Neat. Maybe more than a touch."

"The more, the merrier."

When the drink was in hand, she lifted it lightly. "To a new friend of Ossana's," said Mrs. DeMathis. "She has so few. And a clean-shaven one to boot, how refreshing. One gets so bored with the literal. Oh, Pete dear," said Mrs. DeMathis as the Congressman approached. "Do you know the lawyer Victor Carl, the one who sprung Colin? Is that the correct word, Mr. Carl? I do like to get my jargon right."

"Close enough," I said.

"I know Victor by reputation only," said Congressman DeMathis, advancing energetically and grabbing my hand. "Thank you for coming. This is a pleasure."

"Thank you, sir."

"I'm glad you're here," said the Congressman, stepping ever forward, so close I had to resist the urge to step back. He tilted his head so that he was staring right into my eyes. "We have much to talk about."

"Do we?"

"Oh, yes," he said, staring all the while.

I need to stop here and discuss the political stare, employed in various levels of success by politicians of every rank. There must be a course they take. Maybe taught by Charles Manson.

Imagine a drunk at a bar, spying a strange woman across the way who inflames his sodden soul. Imagine he gazes unblinking at her as he pounds his bourbon and builds within his derangement a castle of desire. Within this castle is the perfected life, shared with this strange woman at the bar. She is no longer flesh and blood, she is a symbol of everything he ever wanted and never could have. After one drink too many, with a courage born of his alcohol and her objectification, he rises from his stool and staggers to the woman, bores in closely, and stares. His foul breath washes over her, he's so close she recoils, her discomfort is unmistakable. And all the while he stares. And stares. As if in the very act of staring he can capture her whole.

This is the stare that comes closest to the political stare. At a fund-raising event, or a rally, or just at the local soft-serve shop, the politician will swoop in close and stare so intently your breath is snatched away. The purpose of the stare is to make you believe, if only for a moment, that there is nothing more important in the world to this politician than you. It is not true—other than your vote or your money, the politician doesn't give a damn—but its falsity makes it all the more potent. You can feel within its intensity the desire for it to be true, the abject need to grab hold of you and make you believe the lie, the sweaty desperation of it.

If you've never been pinned by the intensity of a politician's stare, like a butterfly pinned to a lepidopterist's display, consider yourself lucky. In the depths of campaign season, in the middle of the night, all across the land, citizens rise from their dreams with shouts of horror. As their significant others shake them out of their nightmares, all these poor souls are able to say, amidst gasping breaths, is, "The stare, my God, the stare."

"I want you to know I'm not proud of myself, Victor," said Congressman DeMathis. "My marriage these last few years has devolved into something I could never have imagined."

The fund-raising gathering had broken up and the two of us had repaired to a small office in the suite. I expected cigars and more of the sherry, but all I got was another dose of the stare. Better than some doses I have contracted in the past, but not by much.

"My wife and I are little more than a convenience to each other now. That was not what I ever wanted, but circumstances and my position give us little choice but to maintain the facade. And so I have gone outside my marriage to satisfy my natural masculine needs."

"I suppose the strip joints were all closed," I said. I was sitting as far back in my chair as I could manage. He was sitting in a chair set up just across from me, leaning forward, a hand uncomfortably set on my knee. "Congressman, you don't have to explain anything to me."

"But I feel as if I do."

"Truth is, and you shouldn't take this the wrong way, but I really don't give a crap."

He pulled back a bit, startled, and then continued as if I couldn't be serious. "I just want you to understand how I became involved with Ms. Duddleman."

"I understand as much as I need to understand. I'm sure it was slowly at first and then in a rush."

"She is quite stunning, isn't she?"

"She's that, all right."

"Okay, you don't want to talk about it, fair enough. But I do want to thank you for the way you handled her. I was beside myself when she called that night, terrified that she would do something crazy."

"You know her better than I do."

"And with Colin in rehab, I was at a loss. That's why I phoned Melanie. Now, I don't know what you did or what you said, but Amanda called me after your visit and apologized and promised never to behave like that again. And more importantly, she had a serenity in her voice that was startling. Can I ask you how you calmed her so?"

"You do know she went to Barnard, don't you?"

"She's made that clear."

"Just take it from there, and buy your own condoms." I slapped the chair, stood, and prepared to flee from his stare. I could feel it in my eyeballs like an itch. "I was glad to help."

"I must say, Victor, it is rare to find such professionalism and competence."

"You must spend too much time on Capitol Hill. Any two-bit attorney in Philadelphia could have done just as well. But don't hesitate to call me again if you need someone two-bit—I could use the work."

"There's a party for the governor coming up, a black-tie ball at the Bellevue. I'd like you to come. As my guest. A little thank-you. Everyone will be there."

“Thank you,” I said. “I guess now it will be everyone and me at the ball, as long as I get my chores done first.”

“Yes, well,” said the Congressman, suddenly standing with me. “I didn’t ask you up just to invite you to a party. I have further need of your services. You see, I’m in the middle of a situation.”

“With Ms. Duddleman?”

“No, thank God. You’ve taken care of her, for the time being at least. I’m going to have to break it off with her, if I could just figure out how.”

“In private,” I said. “And after the sex. But this doesn’t concern her, then?”

“No, it’s something else, something that might need your especial talents.”

“And what talents are those?”

“Discretion. Trustworthiness. I’ve been told I can trust you.”

“By whom?”

“Is it true, Victor?”

“Of course it’s true,” I said. “I’m a lawyer.”

“A sense of humor helps, too, I suppose.”

“And don’t forget avarice. I rate very highly on avarice.”

“What is your normal rate, Mr. Carl?”

“Lately it’s been two hundred and fifty an hour.”

“I’ll double it for this, plus expenses. And I’ll pay you in cash.”

“Cash is good,” I said. “Cash is handy.” I sat down again and leaned back. “Handy as a third hand. So what is your situation there, Congressman?”

He stared down at me for a moment before looking away. It’s a bad sign when a politician breaks off the stare. It either means the Apocalypse is nigh or he’s about to actually tell the truth.

“It seems,” he said, “I’m being blackmailed.”

CHAPTER 13

THE BAG

I needed a bag for the job, and my usual briefcase wouldn't do. An old battered black thing with hard sides, it wasn't expandable enough to shovel in mountains of cash. Worse still, in a more optimistic time in my career I had paid to have my initials embossed between the locks, as if to announce my imminent arrival at the broad wooden doorway of success. *Knock knock. Who's not there?*

Now, for the position in which I had somehow found myself, I needed something new, something absolutely noninitialed; I needed a bag worthy of the work. And I knew exactly where to get it.

"Welcome to Boyds, sir. My name is Timothy. How may I help you?"

This was the very first time I met Timothy, a few days before I bought my tux and those horrid shoes. Boyds wasn't far from my office and, with every intention of taking utter advantage of the Congressman's offer to pay my expenses, I thought I'd just poke around on my own and discreetly see what they had available. But the moment I stepped through the wide glass doors under the blue canopy and into Philadelphia's grand emporium of high taste and higher prices, Timothy appeared, conjured as if by magic. He took his place close by my side, making it easier, I suppose, to slip his hand into my pocket.

"I'm looking for a briefcase," I said.

"Anything specific?"

"Something plain, no designer labels, nothing that stands out."

"Sort of like yourself, I presume?"

"Is that an insult, Timothy?"

"I am only here to help you, sir."

"My name's Victor."

"Good, so we're friends already. Do you have a color in mind, Victor?"

"Brown."

"Of course."

"Something big and brown, with soft sides."

"Are we thinking of a saddle-style bag, with all kinds of masculine belts and buckles? Are we planning to ride out on the range with our spiffy new case, Victor?"

"No buckles, no belts."

"Good choice, sir. I'm going to like you. Tell me, is that tie a Dolcepunta?"

"No."

"Somehow I didn't think so. Follow me, Victor. We don't specialize in the nondescript, but I'll see what we can do."

Timothy ushered me up the stairs to the Boyds luggage department and spread his arms wide to indicate the selection.

"Let's talk about details now," said Timothy, "because one thing I've found in this world is that the details oh so matter. How brown do you want it?"

"Brown as bark."

"And you're adamant about that."

"It only seems proper."

"Not black, which is ever more stylish in a professional setting? Not alligator, which has a predator's aura? Not something with a splash of color?"

"Brown as mud."

"Fine."

"Brown as bourbon."

"Yes, I get it. Brown as a june bug on a banyan tree. What about our other details? Do you want this to be a portfolio style with zipper top or do you want an overhang to protect the documents? Do you want it to be single or double clasp? Do you want your initials embossed or burned into the leather?"

"I need a clasp that locks securely, I want no initials of any kind anywhere on the bag, and as for a closure—maybe I'll leave that up to you."

"Excellent," said Timothy, his eyes brightening. "So tell me, Victor, just so we make the right choice: What do you intend to put into your new bag?" This was the first of Timothy's three queries, and the only one for which I had a ready answer.

"Money," I said. "Other people's money, and lots of it."

"Oh, very good. Other people's money is always the best kind. I think you need a bag with jaws, Victor. Something with a mouth wide enough to swallow whatever you place into its gullet but then one that snaps closed with such force you inevitably fear for your fingers."

"Sounds charming, Timothy."

"Doesn't it, though? A bag as hungry as a shark."

"A brown shark."

"Oh, yes. And it just so happens we have exactly such a bag in stock."

And so it was that while I stood before the imposing front door of a grand old estate in the tony town of Devon, listening to a scrum of dogs howling on the other side, I gripped in my palm a lovely brown diplomatic bag from some Italian manufacturer whose name I couldn't pronounce. The bag, handcrafted from the finest leathers in Florence, had broad, sloped shoulders and clean lines and well-tanned sides. Its skin was burnished with oak and chestnut tannins. It felt solid in my hand, personal and perfect. It felt like an extension of my very self, except with better breeding. And what Timothy had assured me as he described the bag's features with loving detail had turned out to be true. With the bag in my possession I was stronger, swifter, more clever, more sly, my smile was wider, my cock was thicker, my possibilities had grown exponentially.

When the door opened, a pack of wild dogs, each the size of a hobbit's foot, swarmed out of the entranceway and yelped with utter savagery at my ankles. And in the gap from where the dogs had rushed, a blond man in a tight double-breasted suit gave me an appraising look, taking in my scuffed wing tips, my tie, my sterling designer bag.

"I suppose you're the one," he said, his prim voice twisted to the east with just a hint of the British Isles, letting me know I might as well have been something left on the doorstep by the dogs themselves. The way his face scrunched at the sight of me, he looked like the wrong end of roast squab.

"I suppose I am," I said. "I'm looking for Mrs. Devereaux. I believe I'm expected."

"Oh, you're expected, all right. But I'll let you know right here and now that I don't approve of any of this. And you should be warned that I'm a lawyer."

"A real honest-to-God lawyer, with a certificate and everything? I haven't been so frightened since I last visited the urologist."

"Oh, Reginald, who is there?" came a scratch of a voice from the inside of the house. The dogs, at hearing the voice, jumped and yapped and rushed away from me, streaming past Reginald's glossy black shoes like a mischief of rats. "Oh, hello, you darlings," cooed the scratch. "You wonderful naughty darlings. Yes. Yes, you are. Yes."

"It is a man with a briefcase," said Reginald.

"Then let him in, dear. What are you waiting for?"

"You know how I feel about this," said Reginald. "I have made my opinion clear."

"Oh, clam up, Reginald," I said, giving him an intended unintentional jab with the bag as I brushed by. "This is just a social visit, and I've been tested and cleared. By my urologist."

Through the doorway I entered a huge center hall with an arched wooden ceiling and a black-and-white marble floor. It was a Gothic church of money, with paintings of fox hunts on the walls and a great wrought iron chandelier threatening from above. Presiding over the congregation of the leaping and yelping toys was the same old woman I had met at the cocktail reception after the Congressman's speech. Her unnaturally brown hair covered her face as her bent back bent ever further so that she could reach down and scratch one after the other of her vile little dogs. Connie her name was, I recalled, and from that posture, she looked up at me and smiled mischievously.

"Oh, so it is you," she said. "I was wondering who he would send, with Colin out of commission. It is so good to see that you have joined the cause. Victor, wasn't it?"

"Yes, that was it. And it's nice to see you again, Mrs. Devereaux."

"The nice young man says it's nice to see me again," she said to her dogs. "Isn't it funny, my darlings, that whenever anyone is pumping me for money, they are ever so happy to see me?" She looked up again, straightening her spine as much as she was able. "And how is our dear friend Peter?"

"Grateful that you can help him in a time of need."

"I find him so invigorating. He understands our travails and our value to this country, and he is quite good-looking, too, don't you think? Did he say wonderful things about me?"

"Only the most wonderful."

"That jaw of his, I just want to devour it with my teeth. Don't you just want to devour it with your teeth?"

"Let me send him away," said Reginald, still standing by the still-open door. "There are ways to do this properly and legally, and filling this man's bag is not one of them."

"Quiet down, dear, and shut the door. The draft is not healthy for the dogs. Victor and I have ever so much to discuss. Be a darling and call in Heywood, please."

"It is a mistake."

"But it is my mistake to make, Reginald, and my money, and you are in my employ, so fetch Heywood before I grow impatient."

Reginald held his ground for a moment, staring at me with something pinched on his arrogant face, before he slammed the front door shut and stalked out of the center hall in an officially snitty huff.

"Friendly guy, that Reginald," I said.

"He's a bit territorial for a lawyer," said Mrs. Devereaux, reaching out and taking hold of my arm. "But Peter knows he can always depend on me. We have so few champions, we must take care of those who step up for us. It is not easy being envied so."

"Yes, it must be difficult."

"You can only imagine our burdens, Victor. The backbone of the country, and still subjected to so much scorn. Everyone needs their protectors, even us. But enough politics. Come and talk."

Slowly she turned and slowly she led me toward a room off the back of the hall. "So what is the problem this time? I was told you needed a substantial sum of money, and in cash. Is that right?"

"That is correct, Mrs. Devereaux."

"Oh, Victor, call me Connie—all the best people do."

"Connie."

"Lovely. So tell me, Victor darling. What is this cash for?"

"You don't really want to know, do you, Connie?"

"Dear, you must have me confused with someone else, someone older, with fairer sensibilities and far more tact. I have no tact, and my sensibilities have been hardened over the years. Did you know my husband?"

"No, ma'am."

"Charles Devereaux the Third. An absolute brute. The things he made me do. My God, Victor, whatever squeamishness I had was burned out of me quite quickly, and without preliminaries, I must add. I could tell you stories, but I won't, because even if I have no tact, I do have discretion."

Just then a tall slab of a man wearing nothing but a short silk robe approached, his exposed chest hairless and gleaming, his long dark hair shining, his jaw like a fist. Mrs. Devereaux reached out a hand until it cupped a mighty pectoral.

"Heywood dear, I am having a business meeting. Please fill the crystal bowl in the drawing room with the usual."

"As you wish, Connie."

"Maybe twice the usual. And give me a kiss, dear."

Heywood leaned over and slobbered into Mrs. Devereaux's mouth.

"Now be gone, you savage. I'll take care of you later."

Heywood gave me a look much like Reginald's look before taking off. I felt like the new member of a harem.

"Now come, Victor," said Mrs. Devereaux, patting my hand. "Spill the messy details. I just adore messy details. It is a matter, I assume, that our congressman wants to keep under wraps, is that it?"

"Actually, yes."

"He is such a naughty, naughty boy. I should spank him, don't you think, Victor? I should put him over my knee and spank him until he cries."

"I'd like to see that."

"I think I'm going to like you, Victor. Come along, dear. Perhaps I can get you something to drink. How do you like your liquor?"

"Strong."

"Oh, I am going to like you," she said.

CHAPTER 14

THE PAYOFF

My job was to keep the dirty little blackmailer on a string, to keep him waiting for the next payment and the next, all the while keeping his mouth shut. My job was to hide his truth under a pile of the Devereaux fortune. Not so hard, actually. Give me enough cash and I could bury the *Encyclopædia Britannica*.

"I have a package from Washington," I said into the pay phone when I had dialed the number with a 717 area code.

"Who? Oh, yes. Right. Yes." A woman's voice, quick and nervous. So that's what it was about, simple and tawdry. And right away I could feel the weakness in her. Good, that would make everything easier.

"I'll bring it to you," I said.

"No, I don't want that. Please, you can't. Not here. Where are you?"

"Philadelphia."

"I'll come to the city, then. Do you have an office?"

"All I have is a bag. But there's a bar on Eighteenth off Chestnut. It's quiet in the early evening. A basement joint called the Franklin. Tomorrow."

"I have to work tomorrow. But I can get off Friday afternoon."

"Friday will do. Five o'clock."

"Thank you. Who am I looking for?"

"The name's Herbert, Jack Herbert," I said, picking out a false two-first-names name to stay as anonymous as possible. "You'll recognize me. I'll be the guy in a navy-blue suit with the bright-brown bag."

In the Devereaux drawing room I had picked up the money cleanly enough, stacks of bound hundreds laid out in a crystal bowl like after-dinner mints. But no matter how much Connie plied me with drinks and compliments, no matter how cruelly she rubbed my thigh with her bejeweled claw, I didn't reveal the root reality the Congressman was trying to smother in its crib. You could say it was just another example of my sweet discretion, but I simply didn't know. Congressman DeMathis had enough discretion of his own not to tell me his most shameful truths. All I had was an address from which I was to pick up the money, and a phone number with which I was to make arrangements for the payoff.

I didn't recognize her right away when she entered the bar. I was sitting at a small table in the middle of the room, my bag on the seat next to me. I nursed a Scotch, neat; my usual Sea Breeze didn't fit the role I was playing. The Franklin was a long, low-ceilinged joint with leather banquettes and the bar at the back. It was a dimly lit place to conduct adulterous affairs over handcrafted drinks. When she came through the door, hesitantly, clutching her own big brown bag and looking around, lost and nervous, I thought she was stumbling into something wrong with a senior partner at the firm where she typed. But when she saw me in my suit, the only suit in the bar at that hour, she gave a nervous smile.

I was expecting someone hard and venal, I was expecting a corrupt little blackmailer. What I got was Jessica Barnes.

"What are you drinking?" I said.

"Nothing, thank you."

"It's a bar. We're trying to look convivial. Order a drink."

"Okay, yes. Just a little something. A white wine spritzer?"

"I said a drink."

"Anything then."

"Let's go mai tai," I said. "Everything's cheerier with a mai tai."

Jessica Barnes sat stiffly in the chair across from me as I gave the order to the waitress. Whatever I thought about the Congressman personally, I was impressed as hell with his taste: first Duddleman and now this. Jessica was a sturdy woman in her late twenties, wearing a pressed print dress with a flat white collar, and a pair of stolid low pumps. Her shoulders were broad, her hair was fair, her face was round and pretty, her eyes were narrowed as if she were peering at me not across a small marble tabletop but instead across a wide-open plain of dust. Arrange a pea sack around her head like a bonnet and she would have been a Dorothea Lange photograph. I liked her right off.

What would I have said to poor doomed Jessica Barnes if I could go back in time to that moment in that bar? What would my advice have been?

Run.

"You're not what I expected," I said.

"What did you expect?"

"Someone harder, someone proud of her own slick cleverness."

"I'm not proud of myself for this, Mr. Herbert."

"Okay."

"This is not anything that I ever wanted to be doing," she said, twisting one rough red hand in the other. "But when the agency called and gave me the number, and then I found out whose number it was, the idea just came. Desperation, it does things to a person. It's like a disease. It spins you around until you can't tell right from wrong, and even if you could, you don't much care."

"And here we are."

"Yes." She looked around nervously and spotted the waitress bringing her drink, bright and fruity and totally out of place in that hard joint. When it was placed before her, she spun it on its coaster before she took a sip. She tried to fight a smile and failed. She hadn't had enough mai tais in her life, that was clear.

"Tell me about yourself," I said.

"Is this part of it? Is this the way it works?"

"It's the way it works with me."

Everyone has a lesson to teach if you just listen, and Jessica Barnes was trying to teach me the last lesson of her life. But as usual, I was too wrapped up in my own damn self to catch it full. And what was I thinking about, just then, as she hesitated and meandered before getting to the spoiled meat of her sad story? What emotion had suddenly wrapped itself around my shriveled little heart? A strange and perverse sense of possibility.

"It wasn't pancakes and roses even before Matthew lost his job," she said, eyes focused on her drink, "but at least we could keep her fed and pay for the medicine. But when they closed out Matthew's shop, the unemployment wasn't enough to make a go of it, and when that ran out, what with them cutting back on my factory job, we were good as dead."

"What kind of medicine are we talking about?"

"My daughter has a liver thing, something about too much copper. Dr. Patusan says she can't eat mushrooms or dried fruit, chocolate, shrimp. She's covered by the state, but the insurance only pays for a piece of the medicine even when we cut back. I don't get benefits, and the COBRA for Matthew was too high."

"Has your husband found any work?" I asked.

"It's not like he hasn't tried. They just aren't hiring men who can do what he can do."

"Has he tried retraining? Has he looked into programs at the community college?"

"Matthew is a good man, Mr. Herbert, and he wants to do right. But it gets hard even getting up every day with that knot in your gut. And then you drink to ease it just for a bit, until the only thing that gets you out of bed is the easing you're going to get with that first drink. So you can ask the questions everyone asks and blame him if you want, but I don't. I see the hurt in him. It's these times. It drives us to things. Which is why we're here, I suppose."

"Yes, it's why we are here," I said.

"I brought the proof like I said I would." She rummaged in her bag and pulled out a sealed dull-brown envelope the size of a greeting card. She looked both ways, like a kid about to cross a street, before she handed it to me. It was light but not empty; there was something thin inside, a photograph maybe. I could imagine all the twisting of phallus and limbs that the picture would show. It hurt her to pass it on, and I decided I didn't need to look.

"Does anyone else have a copy?" I said.

"I wouldn't do that, Mr. Herbert."

"An honest blackmailer."

"Please don't."

"Okay. You're right."

"I don't really want to say anything."

"I can tell that."

"And I've got nothing against him. You can let him know that, the Congressman. He gave me a gift and I'm ever grateful. But the times, they force you to do what you need to do. Maybe you're too lucky to ever know about that, Mr. Herbert, and then good for you. But here I am, trading on the one thing I have left, feeling ashamed and relieved at the same time. I guess I'll learn the price of it after all's said and done."

I tapped the envelope on the tabletop. "How much do you want, Mrs. Barnes, to keep your secret?"

"It's hard to say. Just enough to get by." Her mouth tightened, her jaw jutted slightly. "Ten. Ten for now, maybe."

This was the moment I had trained for, in school and in my practice. You can sense weakness in a person, sense the way a tiny bit of pressure here or there can change the contours of an entire deal. One thing lawyers can spot a mile away, in addition to an ambulance or a hundred-dollar bill on the ground, is weakness. I had the proof in my hand and the money in my bag. This was my moment, why the Congressman had called on my talents in the first place. Jump the weakness, win the day.

"Ten?" I said.

"Ten would get us through to the next year."

"And after that?"

"I don't know."

"Then you'd be coming back for more, I assume."

"I don't want to, Mr. Herbert. Maybe things will turn around."

"Maybe," I said, "but that's a hard word to use when planning the future. Maybe the lottery will hit, or maybe a meteor, or maybe life will just go on like it's been going on. Let me ask you, Jessica, and think carefully now. Would twenty be better than ten?"

Her head tilted in confusion. "I guess."

"Then maybe you should ask for thirty. How long would thirty last you and your family?"

"I don't know. I do earn some. And we could take out another loan if property values rise."

"And maybe with thirty, your husband could find it in himself to get to a school. Learn something technical."

"He's always talking about HVAC."

"He could find a place to get a certificate in HVAC. Use some for tuition and take out a loan for the rest. One thing we always need is air-conditioning."

"I don't know."

"If he can wake up in the morning with possibilities, he might be able to do something more than drink."

“Maybe, Mr. Herbert, maybe. Thirty would do it, yes.”

I told you she was pretty, and young, and I admit to being a sucker for the young and the pretty. And there was something about that dress, the primness of it, and those shoes, that struck a chord, like she had dressed for church. And, yes, there was an attractive weakness in her, a softness at the core, that made me want to take raw advantage. But not advantage of her.

“Then let’s say fifty,” I said. “Will that do it?”

“Mr. Herbert?”

“Fifty it is.”

I opened the bag, tossed in the proof, and then reached an arm into the bag’s now-gaping jaw. Within the protection of the leather, I picked up one, two, five stacks of hundreds and put them one by one into a plain manila envelope. I folded the envelope around the stacks, pulled off the strip, and sealed the envelope into one sharp, compact package that I placed gently on the marble tabletop.

She leaned back, her arms crossed now, her wary eyes ever warier. “And what do I have to do to get all this, Mr. Herbert? What are you going to demand of me?”

“Only this,” I said, leaning forward, smiling like a shark as I pushed the envelope toward her. “Go home and take care of your family. Buy your daughter her medicine, get your husband back to school, find yourself a job with benefits.”

“That’s it?”

“That’s it.”

“And the Congressman?”

“Don’t call him again, and don’t spill the beans you were about to spill. Not even to me. This blackmail thing is not the racket for you, Jessica. What would happen to your family if I was wearing a wire? What would happen to your daughter if you ended up in jail? This time you ran into me; next time who knows. I’ll keep the proof to keep you safe. You take the money and go home and make your life better. You're too damn good for this."

"Mr. Herbert, I don't know what to say."

"Don't say anything, to anybody," I said. "Ever."

She reached out one of those worked-to-the-bone hands and placed it atop mine, and for a moment there was something in her eye other than wariness. Then the envelope disappeared into her own big brown bag and she was gone. And I sipped my Scotch in satisfaction.

And that was what the sense of possibility I had felt before was all about. Here I was taking cash from a perverted old biddy who thought the world owed her its adulation because she had married some loaded bastard who liked his stuff rough. And here I was giving it to pretty Jessica Barnes, with the scaly red hands and the sick daughter. This wasn't any longer a blackmailing payoff to save DeMathis's career; this was a simple redistribution of wealth from the rich to the needy, and I was Robin Hood. Here I was, finally on the side of the angels. Who could ever have imagined such an improbable thing?

With a bag full of money, what couldn't I achieve?

The satisfaction was destined to drown in my throat a few hours later, but it lived in that young moment. I finished my drink, and left a tip, and left the bar, and took a shower, and put on the tuxedo Timothy had sold me a few days before, and slipped on my patent-leather slippers. And with a whistle on my lips and a song in my heart I headed out to find my rightful place in the political world at the Governor's Ball.

And all the while Jessica Barnes was headed for . . . Yeah, right. So much for my pallid dreams of Robin Hood. *"What exactly are you?"* Sloane would ask me at Jessica's murder scene that very night. I could imagine myself a hundred ways of noble, but the answer was there for anyone willing to see it plain.

You know what a bagman is. He's the scurvy errand boy for some corrupt fat-faced pol. Quiet as a cat, he lugs his bag full of black cash and dirty tricks through the city night, bringing in teetering stacks of crisp bills from those lusting to do business with power, and later passing out those same crisp bills as street money to grease the electoral wheel. He is a dark, malevolent figure in a shady fedora and long leather jacket, and when he whispers in your ear you shiver, because he holds the shiv of his boss's clout at your throat.

I was a bareheaded lawyer, a credentialed member of the bar, lank and weedy and as threatening as a chipmunk. I was nothing like I imagined a bagman to be. But hadn't I become an errand boy for some power-mad congressman? And hadn't I agreed to get the goods on that congressman's next opponent? And hadn't I indeed carried illicit cash through the city streets in a brown leather satchel? I could frame it any way I chose, pretty it up with flowers and bows, deny it to an army of reporters, but that didn't change the truth of things. I had fallen face-first into the worst of all rackets.

Call me bagman.

CHAPTER 15

COVER BOY

The morning after the trauma of the Governor's Ball, still shaken from the blood and the death, I emerged from my office stairwell to find my waiting room stuffed full as a Thanksgiving turkey. It is hard to express the strangeness of such an occurrence. In the last year, physics students from Drexel University had taken to using my waiting room to examine the peculiar properties of a vacuum. And yet there they were, filling my chairs and leaning against my walls, the washed and unwashed alike, men in suits, women with scraggly teeth, young and old, the haggard, as well as slicks in Haggar slacks, all waiting for a chance to speak to . . . to . . .

"Mr. Carl, do you have a moment to . . . ?"

"Mr. Carl? Can I perhaps . . . ?"

"Before you go, Mr. Carl . . ."

I lifted a hand to quiet the calls as I edged my way through the throng. My secretary, Ellie, sitting at the desk that guarded the route to my office, stopped her typing, looked up, and gave me a happy smile. Pretty and young, with a wide freckled face, my secretary normally read romance novels to while away the hours when I didn't have enough work to keep her busy, which was most of the time. But she was sitting tall at her desk when I came into the office that morning, tap-tapping on the computer keyboard, giving the fraudulent appearance to those in the waiting room that my practice was thriving. She was a gem, that Ellie.

"What are they doing here?" I said softly.

"They came for you, Mr. Carl."

"Me? Why?"

"Because of the paper."

"Paper?"

"I tried to call you."

"It was a tough night," I said. "I turned off my phone."

"Then you didn't see the *Daily News*?"

"No."

She reached into a drawer, pulled out the tabloid, dropped it onto the desk. Staring up at me from the front page was a smarmy man in a tux stooping beneath yellow police tape. His face, washed pale by the flash, looked up with an expression of unadulterated guilt. **SHOELESS JOAN** blared the headline, and then, beneath the pale, guilty face, the subheading **BAGMAN SNAGGED IN MURDER WEB.** When I realized the smarm staring up with a face full of guilt was me, I quickly turned the paper over.

"What do they all want? Are they here in protest?"

"No, Mr. Carl, they're here to hire you."

"Hire me?"

"I've made a list of the order they arrived and gave them client intake forms. I'm creating file folders for each of them."

"Thank you, Ellie," I said. "Just give me a minute before you send anyone in."

I snatched the newspaper off the desk, fled to my office, shut the door behind me. The article was short—the *Daily News* is not known for its in-depth reporting. Under the byline of Harvey Sloane, it offered some fuzzy facts about the murder, relayed a statement from McDeiss that described the victim's condition and the missing shoes without giving a name, and then got to the meat of it, as far as I was concerned.

> Victor Carl, an attorney and reputed bagman for a powerful local politician, was brought to the scene by a detective and two uniformed officers to aid in the identification of the victim. Carl made no statement other than threatening this reporter's life and limb. He did leave, however, the contents of his stomach at the crime scene. McDeiss stated only that Carl was a person of interest in the investigation.

I snapped the paper closed, rolled it tight, stuck it in a drawer. How nice of Sloane to include that bit about my weak stomach, and how nice of McDeiss to rope me in as a person of interest. We all know what a person of interest is: he's the guy they intend to arrest right after their appointment at the nail salon.

Could I be in a finer mess?

Just then, with my stomach still roiled from the sight of poor Jessica Barnes, I wasn't in any state to deal with all these people in my waiting room. I would have to send them away; I needed time to plan things out. I put my head in my hands and drew a deep breath to settle my nerves when there was a knock.

"What?" I said.

The man who came through the door was in his thirties, quite short, squat, and poorly shaven, carrying a paper lunch bag and a blue file. He swung around with surprising grace as he closed the door.

"The lady at the desk—pretty damn cute, I might add, well done—she said I should give this to you."

He tossed the blue file onto my desk before he hopped into one of the client chairs.

I opened the file. Inside was one of our client intake forms, filled out with a name, Anthony Pelozzo, a South Philly address, two phone numbers, and a work location listed as Pelozzo Meats. Under "referral attorney" he had simply written "The Daily News."

"So, Mr. Pelozzo is it?"

"Call me Guy."

"Guy, then. How can I help you today, Guy? You left the space for your legal issue blank."

"Oh, I got an issue. Issues, actually. First, can I get personal for a moment? Your secretary . . . She's kind of . . . I was wondering . . ."

"No," I said.

"Okay, good. No offense meant. I'm just recently divorced and it's been a long time since I been looking and, I got to tell you, it's like a Golden Corral out there. You know how it is."

"I know how it is. So, your issue, is it matrimonial?"

"What, the divorce? Nah, that was easy. Her attorney took care of it for us both. Saved a hell of a lot in legal fees. She got everything and I got out, so in the end we both got what we wanted. Now my best friend is stuck with her, the sap. This is like a different thing. I saw your picture in the paper and I suddenly thought that maybe you could help me out here."

"Go ahead."

He took the lunch bag off his lap and placed it on the desk. This was not a new and shiny bag, this was old and wrinkled and well stained, like it had been carrying ham-and-cheese for six months straight. He shoved it toward me; I backed away as if it held a ripe piece of Limburger.

"What's the matter?" said Pelozzo.

"Is that your lunch?"

"Are you trying to be funny? It's my issue. Look inside."

"Do I have to?"

"What kind of operation you running here?"

"Yes, you're right," I said. "Courage above all."

I took hold of the bag, opened it slightly, peeked inside. No moldy lunch, just stacks of paper slips. I pulled one out. A parking ticket for a Chevy Impala. I took out another, and then another.

"To be truthful," he said, "I don't got no explanation or excuse, they just keep piling up."

"That happens when you park illegally."

"How the hell can you not in this town? The only legal place anymore is the middle of Broad Street and they'll be ticketing that next. And the meter maids they got working, my God, what a bunch of vultures."

"How much are we talking about?"

"Including late fees and penalties?"

"The whole ball of wax."

"Maybe seventy-five hundred, give or take."

"Which means more like nine thousand."

"Ten, actually. Which is why I'm here. Vic, you're the bagman, right? You got clout with them downtown big boys—that's what the papers said. You think you can fix them things for me?"

"You want me to fix your parking tickets?"

"Why else do you think I'm here?"

"Okay, I see." I put the parking slips carefully back in the bag, closed it up, leaned back in my chair, considered Guy Pelozzo for a moment.

He thought I had clout with the downtown big boys, but I had no clout with the downtown big boys. He thought I could fix his parking tickets, but I couldn't fix a loose screw with a screwdriver. The rules of professional responsibility and basic standards of ethics required that I disabuse him of his addled notions and send him on his way. And yet . . .

What was a parking ticket, actually, but an opening demand in a negotiation between a car owner and the parking authority?

And who better to handle such a negotiation than a card-carrying member of the bar association? And taking care of this bag of citations sooner rather than later could only adhere to Guy Pelozzo's benefit.

Where some in law school specialized in criminal law or copyright or environmental affairs, I specialized in raw opportunism. I had fallen into something, and, like a drunken tourist in Pamplona, I was going to run with that bull until it gored me through the liver.

"I'll need a thousand-dollar retainer," I said without an ounce of waver in my voice.

"Will cash be okay?" said Guy, pulling out a wad the size of a fist.

"Cash is always okay, Guy. Leave the bag, get a receipt from my secretary, and I'll be in touch."

"Vic, I appreciate this."

"It's what I do, Guy, it's what I do. But can I ask a question? With that wad, you could probably pay the whole thing off and still have enough left for new tires. Why go through me?"

"I didn't just fall off a boat here, Victor. I know the way the city works. You know someone, right?"

"Yes, I know someone."

"Well, in this city, you got to know someone who knows someone to get anything done, you know what I mean?"

"Yes, I do, Guy. And I suppose, today, that someone is me. On your way out, please tell my secretary to send in the next on the list."

CHAPTER 16

STONY MULRONEY

There was a real-estate developer from Mayfair in a shaggy suit who had run into a zoning problem for the apartment building he was trying to renovate. There was a woman who wanted to cut her tax assessment by 50 percent. There was a strip-club owner who was getting hassled by the Department of Licenses and Inspections. There was a Pakistani restaurateur who wanted help getting her liquor license. There was a sea of folk who were anxious to throw their money at me so I could grease for them the grinding wheels of government, all because a slimy political reporter had written that I carried a bag filled with cash all about the town. And to each of them I gave a warm and comforting smile, and from each of them I received a retainer, and I told each of them I would do what I could to make the city bureaucracy work for and not against them.

Is this a wonderful world or what?

"Hello, friend. Do you by chance have a minute for a few words off the record?"

The man in my doorway with the sharp, high-pitched voice, a voice like a grinding siren, was fat. I could use all kinds of politically correct terms to describe him, like stout or portly, but his very fatness precluded their utility. He was a series of circles—head, belly, thighs—a walking snowman in a black suit. His features were squashed flat by the fat in his face, his fingers were like overstuffed sausages. In one hand he held a soft-sided black satchel, in the other a gray fedora placed over his heart.

Ellie came running up behind him, a yellow slip in her hand. "I'm sorry, Mr. Carl," she said. "He got right by me before I could stop him. He refused to fill out an intake sheet."

"Now why in the wide world," said the man, "would I want to fill out a silly piece of paper?"

"Because it helps the process," I said. "Go back to the reception area with my secretary and fill out a client intake form like everyone else. After that we can talk."

"You have the wrong impression, Victor. I'm not a client, and I hope never to be one."

"Then what are you?"

"I'm a colleague. Of sorts."

"You're a lawyer?"

"No, I'm not a lawyer, thank the heavens. I'm a professional man. I just want to have a word, you know, as a fellow member of the Guild." He lifted his bag and rapped the doorframe with a fat knuckle. "You might find it worth your while."

I thought about it for a moment. This whole day was about unlikely opportunity. "It's all right, Ellie," I said. "I'll take care of this."

"I also took a phone message for you, Mr. Carl," she said, stepping past the man and placing the message slip on my desk.

I took a quick look. Ossana DeMathis. *"Wants to meet for drinks."* I felt my blood rise just a bit, even though I figured it was probably just that she had parking tickets of her own.

"Thank you, Ellie," I said. "Call her back and tell her anyplace after six will work."

On her way out, Ellie gave the man with the fedora a warning look that would have frightened a bear, but her stare just rolled off the man's hide like so much drizzle. He smiled at her courteously as she passed, stepped inside my office, and gave me a quick wink before closing the door behind him.

"The name is Stony," he said, after he managed to squeeze himself down into one of the client chairs. The armrests creaked as he settled in. "Stony Mulroney. Yeah, yeah, I know, like a double Dutch rhyme, but trust me, it's better than the real thing. My father was Briggs Mulroney—maybe you've heard of him?"

"No."

"'Tis sad the way all the legends are fading. But they still whisper my father's name with reverence in the stairwells of city hall. Briggs Mulroney: he made strong men weep." The man put his hat back over his heart and raised his gaze to the ceiling. "May the son of a bitch rest in peace. My father, when he passed on to greener pastures, he passed on his responsibilities to me, including this one. So here I am. And what I came to say, Victor—I can call you Victor?"

"Sure, you can call me Victor."

"What I'm here to say, Victor, is welcome."

"Welcome to what?"

"The Gang, the Guild, the Order of the Sazerac, the Club of Kings, the Brotherhood. You're one of us now."

"Is that good?"

"My father used to say we are the princes of the street."

"That sounds good."

"Yes, sure it is, but give my father a half a bottle of Scotch and he'd sing 'Danny Boy' so loudly even the walls would weep. Now, as a friend and as a colleague, I want to give to you a gift of some advice that my father gifted on to me. It kept him in good stead, so long as he listened, and it's been doing all right by me over the years."

"And you came by my office just to give me some advice."

"As a colleague, you know, friendly like. My father, he told me over and again, he said, 'Stony, always use a rubber.'"

I looked at the man and blinked twice.

"Good advice, don't you think? I mean my father, he knew something of what he was talking about, though if he followed his own advice, I wouldn't be here, since my mom was just something he had on the side. And beyond that, if he followed his own advice, he'd still be carrying the bag, he would."

"What did he die of, syphilis?"

"He was too hard a man for that. Syphilis was afraid of catching Briggs Mulroney. He no longer walks among us because he violated a second piece of advice that I'm giving you here and now—and all for free."

"You're like a cornucopia of wisdom there, Stony."

"Scottish, actually, on my father's side. But see, this is what he told me, this is the specific advice I wanted to pass on. As a colleague. And if my dad had followed his own advice, he'd be the one sitting here, welcoming you to the club, and shooting the breeze. Are you ready for this, Victor? Are you ready for a bracing piece of truth?"

"Fire away."

"Keep your fucking face out of the papers."

Stony Mulroney said this with just the right amount of humor to cut the harshness, and just the right amount of harshness to make sure I knew it was less an avuncular piece of advice and more an admonition that I had better take seriously.

"My father," he continued, "thirty years he made his rounds and no one outside of the business knew his name. He used to tell me that half the job was keeping your fucking face out of the papers. Then he made the front page of the *Inquirer* and two weeks later he was gone. And the thing was, he was shocked as hell. I'll always remember the expression on his face as we bid him adieu.

Briggs Mulroney, looking as if a broad with tits like great mounds of taffy had just jumped out of his cake. You see, he forgot himself. Don't you be forgetting yourself. It's not just bad for you, Victor, it's bad for all of us."

"Us?"

"There aren't many of us left, so we need to take care of each other. That's why I'm here, giving you my father's good and sound advice."

"It sounded a little like a threat, Stony."

"Yes, well, he was that kind of guy, my dad. Listen, we meet up every Thursday, five o'clock, over at Rosen's. You know the place?"

"On Twenty-Third?"

"That's it."

"Who's we?"

"The Club, the Guild, the Order of the Sazerac, because that's what we drink, the Brotherhood."

"The Brotherhood?"

"The Brotherhood of the Bag."

"Ahh, yes," I said, as understanding suddenly dawned, like the sun rising on the rocky outcrop of some dim lunar landscape. "How come I've never heard of your . . . your organization?"

"We work hard not to be heard of, something you need to learn. Stop on by at Rosen's, pal, and I'll introduce you around. It'll do you good. And if you need any help with anything, you just let me know. Anything. Except I can't get you a taxi medallion—that's Maud's turf—and I don't work north of Ogontz Avenue, 'cause Hump would have my liver. And criminal courts are too corrupt even for me; it's like the judges each have six hands. But anything else, you let me know."

I stared a bit and processed it all and rubbed my jaw before saying, simply, "Anything?"

"That's the word."

I opened a desk drawer, took out Guy Pelozzo's soiled brown paper bag, and tossed it to Stony.

He opened the bag, took a whiff, and smiled, as if instead of stacks of creased and soiled parking tickets, it was filled with freshly baked bread. "Now we're talking."

CHAPTER 17

THE POLITICS OF HATE

Do they know who she is?" said Ossana DeMathis, wide green eyes shining in the dim light as she rubbed the tip of her finger along the rim of her cosmo.

"Yes," I said.

"Then why don't they give out her name? Calling her Shoeless Joan is abominable."

"Abominable is the way the press likes it. The more they splash the nickname of a corpse on the cover, the more papers they sell."

"That's filthy."

"News is a filthy business," I said before downing a slug of my drink. It would have been more impressively hard-boiled, the whole act, if the drink weren't a Sea Breeze. But, as I like to say, I'm man enough to drink a prissy drink. At least there wasn't an umbrella in it.

Of all the surprises that came my way the day after the Governor's Ball, getting the message from Ossana DeMathis asking me out for a drink was the most surprising. And why, when I was still shaken by all I had seen in that alley the night before, had I agreed to have a drink with a woman I barely knew and wasn't sure I even liked?

Why the hell do you think?

"How did they find out her real name?" she asked.

"I told them."

"You knew her?"

"A little."

She leaned forward, lowered her voice, locked her eyes on my own. "How?"

"I can't tell you."

"Why not? Is it some rule or something?"

"Yes, it is some rule or something."

"Was it . . . ? Did it . . . ?" She lowered her eyes and ran her finger up and down the stem of her cocktail glass. "Did it have something to do with . . . ?"

"Your brother?"

"Yes."

"I can't say anything, Ossana, one way or the other."

"Fine," she said, leaning back now, tilting her head with calculation. "You're being quite admirable, I suppose. Most people are not so discreet when it comes to gossip."

"This is not gossip, this is a murder."

I took another swig of my drink. We were in a large dark lounge on the nineteenth floor of the Bellevue. Yes, that's right, the very same hotel where I had been shanghaied by three cops the night before. Even with its lofty dimensions, it was an intimate place, with high trappings and soft lighting, a bar designed for seduction. The question was: Whose? Well, maybe that wasn't the question. Maybe the question was: Did it matter?

"Why did you call me this afternoon?" I said.

"I wanted to see you."

"So you could pump me for information about a dead girl?"

"Of course. Why did you agree to come?"

"I like your eyes."

She smiled, looked down for a moment, lifted her cosmo and took a demure sip, licked her red lips with her pale tongue. "I've been told that green eyes are a mark of incipient insanity."

"Who told you that?"

"My psychiatrist. So what are you going to do about her?"

"About your psychiatrist?"

"About our Joan."

"That's not her name. And what do you mean 'do'? The cops are looking into the murder. They think it's a robbery. Whatever they think, I'm going to stay out of their way."

"You're sure that's wise?"

"Why wouldn't it be?"

"Because they called you to the crime scene and labeled you a person of interest."

"That's just Detective McDeiss's way of wishing me a good morning."

"And now they're probably doing what they can to link you to what happened to her. We all know how easy it is for the police to influence statements, to create false identifications, to manufacture evidence. Do you think it's wise to sit back and let them build a frame around you without your trying to figure out things on your own?"

"I think it's wise to stay out of McDeiss's way. Always. Especially when there's a buffet involved. I'm going to sit back and hope for the best."

"How has that worked out for you in the past?"

"What's that on your wrist?"

"My watch?"

"No," I said. I gently took her right hand and turned it over. On the sweet flat of her wrist was the tattoo of a flock of birds in flight, tiny *v*'s diving and swirling. I rubbed my thumb across the swarm. Her skin was cool and dry.

"Do you like it?" she said.

"I have the urge to kiss it."

"I was young when I got it. I thought it was an expression of my startling individuality. But have you been to the beach lately? A tattoo is now as individual as a seagull. Do you have one?"

"Yes."

"Where?"

"On my chest."

"Let me see."

I tossed my tie over my shoulder, opened the middle buttons of my shirt, pulled down my white T-shirt. She smiled when she saw it and rubbed her fingers gently over the heart.

"Who is Chantal Adair?" she said.

"She was just a girl, another girl who was murdered."

"Did you know her?"

"No."

"Then why did you get it?"

"I didn't," I said.

She looked puzzled.

"Somebody gave it to me when I was drugged and passed out," I said.

"No."

"Yes."

"And you didn't get it removed?"

"I've grown to like it."

"You keep a tattoo you didn't ask for to remember a dead girl you never met." She pressed her full palm against my flesh; my whole chest froze for a moment from her touch. "You've turned your body into a memorial. Deep down, Victor, you're actually one of the noble ones."

"Whatever I am deep down," I said as I buttoned my shirt, "it is not noble. Did you see the way all the politicians looked at me when the police pulled me out of the ball last night?"

"Like you had suddenly developed leprosy." She examined the pink of her drink for a moment. "What is it like to be stared at like that, as if you've suddenly crossed some unforgivable line?"

"I sort of liked it."

Her green eyes lit up at that. "I don't understand how."

There is always the question of how to play it with someone new. Do you act the part they want you to play, the good-guy part or the bad-boy part, the intellectual part, the awkward-as-they-are part? It's easy enough; the movies have given us all the right lines. Or do you do something radical and tell them one of the truths at the root of your soul, not because you only want to be loved for what you truly are—I don't want to be loved for what I truly am, my whole life is a sprint from what I truly am—but because telling a foul truth is just a perverse enough strategy in this world of mendacity to spark an interest. And if you go with the truth gambit, which is just as manipulative as the play-a-part gambit, there remains the question of which truth to tell, since there are so many. We are, all of us, like Whitman in containing multitudes. We are, each of us, sad and angry and optimistic and hapless and sweet and sour and innocent and depraved. Which of these truths to expose?

"Do you want to know a truth about me, Ossana?"

"I don't know," she said, with a slight smile. "Can I handle the truth?"

I had thought she was a bit stiff, a bit proper, Ossana, the Congressman's sister, but there was a streak in her that was catching me off guard. Okay, it was time to see how the rawest of my truths worked with green eyes.

"You know all those people at that little masquerade party we attended last night?" I said.

"The Governor's Ball wasn't a . . . Yes, okay. All the people in their glittery costumes."

"The rich and powerful and their wives and their husbands and their lovers and their beards and their lackeys? The truth of the matter is I hate them, all of them, and they can sense it on me like a stink. It's nothing personal. I happen to hate everyone more successful than I am, which is pretty much everyone. You know what Gandhi said, 'If you don't hate something, you end up hating nothing.'"

"Did he say that?"

"If he didn't, he should have. Well, I hate them all, the posers and the flunkies, the players and the pawns, the baldly self-serving puffed up with their self-righteous senses of entitlement. I want to be them, too, I want all their perks and powers—their cars, their houses, their illicit lovers—I want to be them so badly that sometimes I piss blood at night from all the wanting. I want to join their clubs and laugh at their jokes and play golf on their courses and have sex with their daughters and broil like a lobster on the lounge chair right next to their lounge chairs at their swim clubs on the Vineyard. But all of that doesn't mean I don't hate them, too. So to have them look at me like I'm a danger to everything they hold most dear, like I'm a leper, well, that's fine. That's more than fine. It feeds the soul."

She took in a breath, as if I had just touched some intimate part of her. "All that hate, my God. It must be poisonous."

"Not really. It's a cheerful hate."

"Does it include my brother?"

"You bet."

"And me?"

"Were you there with diamonds dripping from your ears?"

"Why do I find all of this thrilling? Why do I suddenly want you to ravish me with your hate?"

"Because you understand the power of it, the way it nourishes the will and fires the spirit and engorges the flesh. My hate is hard and relentless, stiff and thick and unyielding, charging like a stallion across a fertile green meadow. And do you want to know a secret, Ossana?"

"Oh, yes," she said.

I leaned forward and she did too. Our faces were close and our lips were closer. "It lasts a damn sight longer than four hours."

CHAPTER 18

UNEXPECTED GUEST

This is a complete disaster," said Melanie Brooks to me on the phone after I returned to my apartment, still tipped from the waves of alcohol and lust that had flooded through me at the Bellevue. I sat down casually on my battered red couch, crossed my legs, loosened my tie, winked. I wasn't alone.

"Can we talk about this later?" I said.

"No, we can't, dearheart. Colin worked for us for years and never had so much as a mention in the press, and here you are, with us for just days, and already you're on the front page of the *Daily News*. Don't you know the first rule of this business?"

I looked up at my guest and said, "Always use a rubber?"

"Victor, I'm serious."

"Then it must be: Keep your fucking face out of the papers."

"Yes, exactly, and put so succinctly, too."

"I received this selfsame advice just this afternoon, so you're not telling me anything new. But I didn't ask to end up looking guilty as sin on the front page of the paper. It just sort of happened."

"It is unacceptable."

"It wouldn't have happened if Sloane hadn't been in court that day, and he was only in court that day because of Colin, so it's not all on me. And, I must say, it has paid some dividends. My waiting room was full this morning and I have a boatload of new clients."

"Because you're connected to a murder?"

"No, because they think I'm connected, period."

"Victor, Victor, what are we going to do with you?"

"Pay me, that's what you're going to do. You're going to pay me."

"Well, at least you're learning. Tell me the truth now: Are you involved in the murder? Have you gotten in that deep with these snakes?"

"No."

"But you knew her."

"I met her once."

"Because of the Congressman?"

"Maybe."

"Maybe? Did you give her something?"

"I gave her what you'd expect me to give her."

"And what did she give you?"

"I can't say anything more."

"Don't give me that privilege dance. I invented that privilege dance. Remember who you work for."

"And pray tell, Melanie, exactly who is that?"

"It sure as hell is not DeMathis. He's a politician, for God's sake. We don't work for politicians. You might as well be hauling mounds of manure for a dung beetle."

"Then maybe it's time for you to tell me who we really report to."

"There are levels to everything, and all you need to know is your own level. You're working for me. Now Sloane will be looking for every opportunity to link you with the Congressman and we can't have that. But there is still work to be done that will require your special talents. Mrs. Devereaux has more donations to make, there are places those donations must go, and there is still the matter of digging the dirt on Thomas J. Bettenhauser."

"You know about that?"

"I know my business, and you, dearheart, have become my business. From now on you'll receive your instructions regarding the Congressman from another source."

"You?"

"God, no, I have standards. Patience. But once you get your instructions, no freelancing. Follow your instructions to the letter unless I tell you otherwise."

"You sound sexy when you're in charge. What are you wearing?"

"Stop it."

"There used to be a heart beating in there."

"I'm not in the mood."

"Are you ever?"

"Not anymore. And what a relief that is. You should try it, Victor. I could get you a dose of Depo-Provera, it would do wonders for your disposition. We have a supply on hand to give to candidates who can't stop their peckers from sabotaging their electoral chances. But I want you to be clear on one thing more. Under no circumstances are you in any way to get in the middle of that murder investigation. You steer clear of the papers, you steer clear of Detective McDeiss, you steer clear of the entire mess."

"Is that an order?"

"Remember where I found you, desperately clutching the courthouse wall, hoping to stop your spiral into financial ruin."

"I remember."

"Make sure you do. Now be a good boy, Victor, and do as you're told."

When I hung up, I took a moment to straighten the pleat that should have been in my pants. That last line of Melanie's had stuck in my throat like a bone. Telling me to do as I was told was one of my mother's favorite admonitions. The disappointment on her face when I failed her was as close as I would get to a declaration of her love. Since then, not doing what I was told has become as much a habit as a matter of principle. Yet I surely did enjoy the money train I was on since hooking up with Melanie. I took a moment to try to reconcile my dual inclinations.

"Trouble?" said my guest.

"There's always trouble."

"I suppose next you'll be telling me Trouble's your middle name," she said.

"More like Shelby."

"Really?"

"No. My parents didn't love me enough to give me three names, I've only got the two. How many do you have?"

"Five."

"That figures. Now what again are you doing here?"

Amanda Duddleman leaned forward and clasped her hands together as if she were praying to me, or trying to sell me insurance, one or the other. "I came here tonight, Kip, because I desperately need your help."

CHAPTER 19

BLIND AMBITION

Duddleman had been waiting for me outside my apartment building, sitting on the steps, smoking a cigarette. Black boots, black tights, black leather jacket, looking like an existential dream, all pretty and pouty and fresh enough to make Sartre squint from the brightness. She was the kind of girl you drank wine with on La Rive Gauche and discussed with utter seriousness Céline and Nietzsche and the effervescent genius of Jerry Lewis, the kind of girl with whom you fought bitterly over obscure political parties in Argentina because the make-up sex was so sparkling, the kind of girl who let her hair grow ratty and developed the sexy paleness of a tubercular patient as she toiled on her dissertation and you ended up loving her all the more. She was an adolescent fantasy for shy intellectual boys with weak eyes and gangly limbs. If I were a different kind of guy and she were a different kind of girl, she would have made my heart skip in that getup. But we weren't and it didn't; her pose just made me feel weary.

"You couldn't have called?" I said.

"If you saw it was me on caller ID, would you have answered?"

"No."

"Can I come up, Kip?"

I thought about it for a moment. Crazy is crazy, but she wasn't hard to look at. And there was a mark of sanity on her features, as if the craziness had passed through a piece of machinery and been pressed into something shiny and pure. With the carelessness of one too many drinks, I had nodded toward the door. Now she was sitting across from me, leaning forward, pleading for my help.

"I think you need more help than I can provide, Amanda," I said. "I could recommend a therapist."

"Be nice."

"Then how about a beer?"

"Yes, please."

I pulled a couple of Yuenglings out of the fridge, yanked off the caps, handed a bottle over. "So, Amanda, Amanda, Amanda. What are you here for, really? How can someone like me, with only two names, possibly help someone like you?"

"I've decided to take my career up a notch."

"Set your sights on a senator, have you?"

"I'm a journalist, Victor." She took a sip of the beer and then a gulp. "It's just my personal life that's a mess."

"Don't sell it short."

"So you're not going to be nice. Tell me something then—when the hell did neatness become such a virtue? Everyone is always going on and on about how my life is such a mess. Well, thanks for the tip, but I don't need the bleating of the sheep in the chorus to know that. I can read my life like a text."

"That's right, you went to Bernard."

"Barnard. It's not a hair salon in Queens. And yes, I know the Congressman's a creep and I'm debasing myself with him just to plug some sort of pathetic gap left over from my childhood. Daddy didn't show me enough attention, so I sleep with a powerful man who fills me with his milky adoration. If it wasn't so sad, it would be comical. Yet the emotions I feel are as real as if this wasn't a pathetic stopgap solution to an immature childhood yearning. And so I go with it. You think I shouldn't?"

"I don't think."

"Well done. How much better would the world be if all men followed your example? The time will come, Victor, when my life will be so well ordered that I'll bore myself to sleep each night, but does it have to be when I'm twenty-three? Can't I make a hash of things first?"

"I'm certain you can."

"Thank you."

"And that's why you want my help, to further hash up your private life?"

"No, thank you, Kip. I can do that on my own. This is on the journalism side."

"Uh-oh."

"I've been at the *City Weekly* for eight months now. It's time to move on, but to do that I need a story. Something big enough to shake the temple pillars. Something that will get me noticed by the higher powers."

"God and country?"

"More like the *Times* or MSNBC."

"So it's rise-and-shine time for Amanda Duddleman, and you've come to me to help you find your story."

"Oh, no, I've got a story. It has everything: sex and politics, money and murder."

"Sounds like a slow afternoon in the nation's capital."

"The story's not there, it's here."

"Please, no," I said, awareness dawning. "Tell me you're not talking about—"

"I've already lobbied my editor and gotten the assignment," she said. "Full-time for as long as it takes. No expenses spared, which for the *City Weekly* means they'll reimburse my subway tokens. For the time being I have a new beat: Shoeless Joan."

I sat down and stared at her flushed and eager face. It had done something to her, the hunt and the excitement and the sense of possibility. It had calmed down the crazy and brought out her undergraduate earnestness. I liked this Amanda Duddleman; she had places to go and I had no doubt that she would get there. Too bad it wouldn't be this way.

"You're going to have to tell your editor to give it to someone else," I said. "Isn't there a convention you could cover, or a new brewpub to review?"

"I need to make a splash, Victor, I need to light up Twitter. Puff pieces on the new trends in urban footwear aren't going to do it."

"Does your editor know you're sleeping with Congressman DeMathis?"

"Why the hell should that matter?"

"Oh, don't play naive, it doesn't become you. Did you order a side of conflict with your interest? For example, why do you think politics is involved in her murder?"

"Because the paper said you were at the crime scene and that you're a bagman."

"A bagman for whom? For the Congressman. Who you're sleeping with."

"He didn't do it, Victor. He's ambitious and horny, but he's not a killer. My God, he cries at movies."

"So did Ted Bundy."

"Really?"

"I don't know, I never saw a chick flick with him. And what about sex? How do you know that's involved?"

"Her shoes were missing."

"What does that have to do with anything?"

"Oh, Victor, come on. Who do you think did it?"

"I don't know who did it. I'm happily leaving the whole mess to McDeiss. But what I do know is that for you to take this assignment is a violation of every journalistic integrity thing."

"It's all been done before. Someone once said that every journalist knows deep in his heart that what he does is morally indefensible."

"Who? Nixon?"

"Close enough. Kip, I need this."

"You need to go home and forget about it."

"There's a guy at the *City Weekly*, he's been there twenty years. He's overweight, his teeth are rotting. Twenty years writing the same pseudocounterculture claptrap for a market that never grows older and never grows up. I can't do that. This is my way up and out. Of everything."

And I saw it, just then, the truth of it for her. This wasn't just a story, this was a route out of all the insanity, a way to maybe grow up.

"What do you want from me?" I said. "Permission?"

"I don't know where to start. I could just hang out at the Roundhouse and wait for Detective McDeiss to make his pronouncements, but that isn't going to catch the attention of anyone. I need to do my own investigation. And for that I need leads."

"What do you think I know?"

"More than you're telling."

She was right about that. I looked at her flatly, pretty Amanda Duddleman. Her life was a mess, absolutely, but she was trying to rise out of it, and who could admire that more than me? I am unaccountably drawn to troubled women. Some of them I want to screw, others I want to help. Amanda Duddleman, despite her youth and loveliness and, yes, innocence—or maybe because of them—was in the latter category. I thought about maybe helping her like she asked. But I stepped back a bit, pulled myself out of myself, and remembered I had felt the same way about Jessica Barnes.

"Here's my advice, Amanda. Run away. This thing we've both fallen into is as foul as a sewer. I'm stuck here, in the middle of this. I have no choice. But you have nothing but choices. Say good-bye to this story, good-bye to your lover, good-bye to the whole damn city. Head back to New York and make a new start while you can."

She looked at me, her face blank as she was absorbing it all, and then the corner of her lip turned up into a sneer. "Thanks, Dad. It was heartfelt and all, your little plea, but I'm a reporter and I have a job to do. Are you going to help me?"

"No."

"Then fuck yourself."

"Attagirl," I said.

CHAPTER 20

SMEAR JOB

They came for me a few nights later, hushed, in the dark. I woke to the sound of ripping, of slashing, of a horror movie being played with the volume low in the very next room, and I knew, right away and without doubt, they had come to slit my throat and steal my shoes.

As the realization hit me, I, quite sensibly, quailed and whimpered in my bed. But then I gathered my wits, what precious few were scattered about me, and rolled off the mattress until I thumped onto the floor as quietly as a bear falling out of a tree. On my stomach, facing the door, I considered my options.

Grab a weapon and attack like my hero, Ulysses S. Grant? It sounded right, except I had always avoided guns—yank one out and the next thing you know it might actually go off—so the closest thing I had to a weapon was my pillow. Grant could have taken Fort Donelson with less, but I wasn't Grant.

Hide? I considered the bedroom closet, the space under my bed, behind a bureau. I had behaved with admirable stealth so far with my whimpering and rolling and thumping. What was the likelihood of actually making it to the closet without being detected? How do you say "nil" in Portuguese?

Flee? That was the ticket. My window was four flights up, a killer drop, but I could do it, without shoes and not knowing what was in the alley below me. I could leap. What was a compound fracture or two among friends?

But in the middle of all this flipping of options, I suddenly stood and, without weapon or plan, charged to the bedroom door and flung it open. It was a demented move born of righteous anger. What the hell were they doing in my apartment? What the hell were they doing to my stuff? I don't have much in this world, sadly, and the stuff I had was mostly crap, but it was still my crap, dammit.

The less we have, the more bitterly we fight for it.

The living room I saw through the flung-open door was an utter shambles: books scattered, the cushions of my red couch slashed, the whole floor littered with my things. And in the middle of the room, a thin, weaselly, sparsely bearded kid in jeans and a loose-hanging flannel shirt, more junkie than mob flunky, was rustling inside my fancy-assed bagman bag. No more than twenty, the kid turned his head to stare at me in fear and surprise, like my appearance in my apartment in the middle of the night was some sort of astounding occurrence.

I stepped forward and said, "What the crap are you doing with my—"

I stopped in the middle of my exclamation when his eyes darted from my face to something behind me. I didn't have time to turn around before the something behind slammed me in the shoulder blades, driving me to my knees. I can just remember kneeling in pain and inexplicably reaching out, as if to some divinity, when I got slammed again, this time in the head.

Then the reception got fuzzy and the television blinked into a test pattern with an Indian's head in the middle. Everything didn't so much go dark as disappear, and the world and my presence in it ceased to exist.

SSSSSSSSSSSSSSSSSSSSSSSSSSSSSS
SSSSSSSSSSSSSSSSSSSSSSSSSSSSSS
SSSSSSSSSSSSSSSSSSSSSSSSSSSSSS
SSSSSSSSSSSSSSSSSSSSSSSSSSSSSS
SSSSSSSSSSSSSSSSSSSSSSSSSSSSSS
SSSSSSSSSSSSSSSSSSSSSSSSSSSSSSSSSSSSSSSSSSSS

When I came to, I was alone.

I sat up with difficulty, my head a bowling ball rolling fiercely down a waxed alley. I tried to stand but, halfway up, the rolling ball rammed into a triangle of pins and I sprawled back down onto my hip. I took a moment to hold my head in my hands before I looked around.

My apartment was a fouled mess, like some revival meeting had ripped through it. And in the center of the disarray my brown bag was flopped on its side, its mouth open like the jaw of a dead fish.

I crawled to it and looked inside. It was scrubbed empty, of course it was. There had been a couple thousand dollars of the Devereaux money, and that was now gone, along with everything else I had stashed there. Maybe I had been targeted because of the newspaper headline, maybe a clever thief would have correctly assumed that a bagman would surely have cash in his bag, maybe this was a simple robbery.

And maybe frogs speak Hungarian.

No, my initial impulse had been correct; they had not come for the money, they had come for me. But not to murder, as I originally suspected, instead to deliver a message, the same message Melanie had given me, but this time with all the subtlety of a forearm shiver.

And they had come not only to deliver a message. They must have known Jessica Barnes would have brought some proof backing her blackmail threat to her meeting with me. They must have searched her after they killed her, and not finding it on her they assumed correctly that she had given it to me. And they had come to me to find it.

I hadn't looked in the envelope when Jessica Barnes gave it to me, discretion being a crucial part of my new job, and I hadn't looked in it after I was shown Jessica Barnes's corpse, because I assumed it to be just another piece of porn and to look on it then, I somehow thought, would be to dishonor a dead woman. But the time for hiding my head in the sand was over.

I hadn't looked inside the envelope, sure, but I hadn't left it in the bag either—I'm cleverer than that. It was in a square brown envelope, like a greeting card, and so I had taken it out of the briefcase and put it in a kitchen drawer with all my other greeting cards: from aunts and cousins, from a few married lawyer-types with bright-eyed children, and from my mother. You may accuse me of being a sentimentalist for keeping such things, but my mother sent me a yearly holiday card and that was pretty much it; putting them in a drawer when they came saved me the burden of reading the damn things.

The kitchen lights were like cocktail forks jabbed into my eyes. The drawers had been left open, the floor was littered with cutlery and towels, spare batteries, loose pens, screwdrivers. And greeting cards, scads of greeting cards, still in their envelopes. I crawled over to the scatter of cards and pulled them into a pile.

Mom. Mom. Aunt Gladys. Mom. The law firm of Talbott, Kittredge and Chase, those stuck-up bastards, wishing me a prosperous New Year. My former partner, Beth, all the way from India. Mom. Mom. (Notice, none from Dad: we don't communicate with greeting cards; we communicate by not communicating.) Mom.

Aunt Gladys again. And then a blank brown envelope, no name, no address.

I leaned against the kitchen counter, closed my eyes for a moment to stop the cocktail forks, and then took a knife from off the floor and slit open the envelope, readying myself for a sordid slice of someone else's sex life.

But it wasn't porn. It wasn't even a photograph.

Inside was a card, but not a greeting card, nothing with sweet sentiments and timeless virtues. It was just a blank card, white, with a broad, thick swath of something painted onto the paper. Something dried and dark maroon, something very much like . . .

I was out of my league, I needed help, I needed backup. And I was thinking I knew where to get it when I heard a banging on my door.

Knock knock.

"Open up. It's the police."

CHAPTER 21

ROSEN'S

In the midst of crisis, the heart yearns for brotherhood.

Rosen's was an old-style steak joint on Twenty-Third Street, infused with nicotine and trimmed in red leather, with a surly barman in a plaid vest and a menu that hadn't changed in decades. While other restaurants threw themselves into each new style of modernist cuisine, with their organic produce and sous vide cooking baths, Rosen's had kept to the basics: meat, potatoes, a sprig of parsley, all of it doused with butter, accompanied by a mouthful of smoke to dull the taste, and a lowball of hard liquor to wash it down. It was so retro it had burst into style a few years back as a hipster hangout, before all the young hip things realized that Rosen's wasn't trying to be clever, it was simply preserved in amber. Since then, the younger crowd had found its way to craft-cocktail lounges and upscale bowling alleys, leaving Rosen's to the same clientele it had served for half a century: the stiff and the drunk, the blue-haired, the red-nosed.

Above the bar was a sign, SMOKING PROHIBITED, but that was obviously for the benefit of the L&I examiners when they came in for their yearly inspections, because the law it represented was being roundly disregarded. And why not? If it was good enough for the '50s, it was good enough for Rosen's.

"Victor, my friend, over here," said Stony Mulroney, waving his cigarette in the air as he gestured to a large round table surrounded by a red banquette. "You're just the man what we've been talking about."

"That's a frightening thought," I said as I stood before them, bag in my grip. Along with Stony sat three others, two men and a woman, the four of them with their own bags set by their sides, the men's hats on the table. They were a strange, hard-boiled crew, with their cigarettes and their squat, ruddy drinks, enveloped by a veil of smoke as if it were a cloud of their own plots and schemes.

"Victor," said Stony, "this here is Hump."

Hump was tall and slim with close-cropped hair, and ears that stuck out like plane wings. He stood as if to politely greet me. I reached out a hand and he took it, but didn't shake it. Instead, he squeezed it tight and twisted it around my back as he slipped behind me and roughly patted me down.

"What the hell?"

"Just a precaution, friend," said Stony.

"I'm not armed."

"We're not looking for no gun," said the third man at the table, a scrawny piece of gristle with a spectacularly bad comb-over and a sour mouth.

"You don't think—"

"We don't get paid to think," said the gristly little man, and in his case I didn't doubt it. Small as a child, he had a sparrow's chin, a pinched nose, a broad forehead. His leather jacket fit him oddly, as if he hadn't taken the hanger out before putting it on. But beyond all that was that comb-over, a sparse swoop of thin strands that barely dimmed the shine off his oversized dome. His comb-over was less attempted fraud and more a piece of performance art. It deserved an ovation, enshrinement in some hall of fame of self-delusion.

"He be clean," said Hump behind me in a deep baritone with a Southern twist.

"I told you he'd be clean," said Stony. "Victor doesn't work for anyone but his own damn self, like the rest of us."

"Stony tells us you're the new Colin Frost," said the woman. Her eyes were coldly blue, her blonde hair was hacked short, her face was pockmarked, her body was all sharp edges and angles. There was something rangy and old-fashioned about her, something of the prairie; she was a straightened piece of rusted barbed wire. "What happened to the old one?"

"Rehab."

"About time he started stepping," said the comb-over man. "Twelve steps off a pier."

"Take a seat," said the woman. "Have a drink."

I sat down next to Stony, setting my bag on the bench beside me like the rest of them.

"Sazerac okay?" said Stony.

"I never had one."

"You'll like it," said Hump.

"Hump is a transplant up from New Orleans," said the woman, fiddling with a new and unlit cigarette.

"I started working for a fellow named Pampy," said Hump. "We was in the parking lot business. Later I covered the Ninth Ward for a host of them aldermen."

"Till the water covered it better," said the little man.

"When he came up north after Katrina," said the woman, "Hump brought along his favorite drink, the Sazerac, a New Orleans specialty. We've taken a fancy to it."

"Nothing not to fancy," said Hump.

"What's it like?" I said.

The woman tapped her cigarette on the table. "Close your eyes and think of the woman who haunts your dreams. You know who she is. Imagine now she's smoking a cigarette, menthol, and drinking a rye whiskey stirred with a licorice twist. And then she leans forward and kisses you long and soft, swirling her tongue across your teeth." The woman lit her cigarette, inhaled deeply, let the smoke out in a slow, narrow stream. "That's a Sazerac."

"Yes, please," I said.

"Aubrey," shouted Stony to the barman. "Two Sazeracs for the guest, and another round for the rest of us."

"Two?"

"Before he entered the business, my daddy was a Marine," said Stony, "and he taught us never to leave a soldier behind."

"Nice bag," said the woman, nodding to my briefcase. "Italian?"

"Yes, actually. I figured if I was getting in the game, I'd do it in style."

"I knew a man carried an Italian bag that pretty, once," she said. "He was so proud of it, showed it off like it was a rosy-cheeked baby. He went on endlessly about the quality of the workmanship, the softness of the leather. He got six years."

"You'd be better off ditching the bag and picking up a sledge or a saw, something useful," said the little man.

"Why's that?"

"It's going to hell is why, the whole business. The money is passing us by, but the feds sure as hell ain't. We used to have twenty at every meeting, with armies trying to get in. Now there are more behind bars than at the bar. It's just us left. We're a dying breed."

"Don't mind Miles," said the woman. "He's a pisser and a moaner."

"Sure I piss and I moan, I got what they call a weak stream, but that don't mean I'm wrong about the business."

"Well, I sort of fell into this new line," I said, "and so I'll take whatever advice I can get. I still have no idea what the hell I'm doing."

"As soon as we saw your mug in the paper, we knew that," said the little man.

"Yeah," I said, "that was unfortunate."

"Indeed," said Hump.

When the drinks came, I lifted up the rosy-red lowball with a twist of lemon peel sliding across the bottom and admired the richness of the color.

"Wow," I said after the first sip. "What's that taste?"

"It's the Peychaud's," said Hump. "That there's the bitters. I have it shipped up from home special, so Aubrey won't be putting that Angostura crap in it."

"A cube of sugar," said the woman, "a dash of Peychaud's, two jiggers of rye, the whole thing stirred and then poured in a glass rinsed with a little Duplais Verte."

"That there's the absinthe," said Hump.

"No," I said.

"Indeed," said Hump.

"Take my word for it," said Stony. "Nothing settles the digestion like a good distillation of wormwood."

As I drank my first Sazerac, wincing with each sip, Stony made the introductions. Hump handled the wilds of North Philly, hauling his bag from shop to shop, taking the envelopes all through the year and then passing out street money on Election Day. And Hump was the one to see if anyone was messing with the salad.

"Salad?" I said.

"The payload," said the comb-over man.

"Ahh, yes."

"Anyone helping himself to the salad, you see Hump," said Stony.

"I take care of things for a price," said Hump.

"You and me," I said to Hump, "we need to talk."

"And this beautiful rose," said Stony, "is Maud."

The woman, looking more like a thorn than a blossom, smoked impassively.

"Maud handles the city administration. If you want anything zoned, anything cleaned up or knocked down, anything cleared or shut down by Licenses and Inspections, anything from the Sheriff, the Prothonotary, the Register of Wills, anything anywhere in city hall, no matter how high up, she's the one you want to talk to. And she's a great friend of the mayor's."

"I introduced him to his wife," said Maud.

"It's a good thing," said Stony, "that His Honor doesn't hold grudges. And this sour grape, this bite-sized piece of municipal corruption, is the one and only Miles Schimmeck."

The little man bowed at the table so that the top of his head under his comb-over glistened in the light.

"Miles handles all levels of the courts: Traffic, Municipal, Family, Common Pleas, Commonwealth, all the way up to the top. If you want influence in a custody battle, in a sentencing, if you want your DUI dismissed or your driver's license reinstated or your appeal looked upon with favor, Schimmeck is your man."

"It sounds like something, but truth is, it's not so hard," said Miles Schimmeck.

"You don't need to tell us that," said Maud. "Buying a judge in this town is as tough as buying a tomato."

"Cheaper too," said Schimmeck. "But they're so ungrateful when you do it. Hey, if you don't want the salad, don't go to the salad bar, I always say. I don't need the griping. But even them judges, the greediest clan in all creation, are closing down on the likes of me. The game's changing."

"The Big Butter's come to town," said Hump.

"Big Butter?" I said.

"Big money," said Maud. "There's too much of it now."

I rubbed my hands together. "And that's a problem?"

"When you have the only canteen in the desert, everybody's your friend," said Maud. "Not so in a flood."

"It's Noah time," said Miles, "and none of us now need a fool horning in on our territories."

"A bagman's territory is more than just a spot on a map," said Hump. He took a closed blade from his jacket pocket, flicked it to life, scraped at his thumbnail with the long, shiny blade. "It's his lifeblood and it needs to be protected. I learned that from my two best teachers, first Pampy and then Katrina."

I looked around at my drinking companions. Schimmeck was smiling unpleasantly. Maud's face behind a rising line of smoke was as impassive as the glass in her hand. Hump was staring at me with eyes black as coal. Stony, my new friend Stony, was looking down at the table.

"I guess I know what herpes feels like," I said.

"It ain't nothing personal, you understand," said Hump.

"Actually, it is," said Miles Schimmeck.

"We can't afford to have someone like you involved in our business," said Maud, "taking pieces of our routes, messing up the game for everyone."

"Someone like me?" I said, my umbrage antennae bristling. "And what exactly is that?"

"A fool with a bag," said Maud.

"I tell you, he's okay," said Stony.

"He's a lunkhead," said Miles. "I know a lunkhead when I see one and he's a lunkhead. No offense."

"Offense taken," I said.

"Let me get this right, just so we're clear," said Maud. "Out of nowhere, you show up with some overpriced bag and a single client, and you think you're a member of the club. But already after only a week on the job, one of your payoffs is dead, you're in the middle of a murder investigation, your picture's on the front page of the paper, and then you get your home invaded and your apartment trashed and your salad eaten and your own numbskull knocked unconscious."

"How do you know about that?"

"I cover the Roundhouse," said Stony.

"You called the police," said Miles, shaking his head.

"I didn't," I said. "A neighbor or somebody did."

"Does it matter?" said Maud. "There's always a fed trying to make his bones by making an example of us, and here you come, waltzing down our street, whistling like an idiot. You don't know our rules, you don't know our game. You're just a fool with a bag."

"We're better off with you not around," said Hump.

"Consider this a polite warning," said Maud.

"You call this polite?" I said.

"Just know that next time we won't be so well mannered," said Miles.

"So that's that," I said.

"That's that," said Maud. "From here on in, know that it will be safer for all of us—"

"Especially for you," said Miles.

"—if you leave the bags to those who know how to carry them."

Hump spun the knife in his fingers until it flipped down and stuck straight through the tablecloth into the wood with a solid thwack.

"Sayonara, lunkhead," said Miles Schimmeck. "It was a pleasure not knowing you."

So much for brotherhood.

"You don't look upset," said Maud, an interested tilt to her head. "You don't even look surprised."

"What did Stony call you? The Order of the Sazerac? The Club of Kings? The Brotherhood?"

Hump pulled the knife out of the table, slapped it closed, slipped it back into his jacket. "Briggs always liked his fancy names."

"So you're rejecting me. Big stinking deal." I looked around at the four of them. "I've been rejected by better, though I don't think I've ever been rejected by worse, and I'm counting here the chess club in high school. I came here because Stony invited me. I thought I'd get a little companionship, a little advice, maybe a chance to learn from your experience. But when I look around, I figure I'd be better off getting advice from the hookers on Spring Garden. At least they smile when they screw you."

"Anyone want another drink?" said Stony.

"Can't," said Miles Schimmeck. He looked at his watch, snatched up the last of his Sazerac, grabbed his hat, a large-brimmed checkered thing. "I'm due in Municipal Court."

"And we have that thing," said Maud to Hump.

"That's right," said Hump, snapping down the rest of his drink, grabbing his own hat, short-rimmed and black. "That thing."

"Another drink for you, Victor?" said Stony.

"I think I've had enough."

"Stinking lightweights, all of you," said Stony. "When my father was around, we would close this place, and head out to the street roaring." Stony downed the rest of his drink, lifted his hand, snapped for the barkeep's attention, raised one finger.

"Don't take it so hard, Victor," said Maud. "We're not much on companionship, and our experience is too hard earned to give it away on a piss and a string. But you want some advice?"

"Not anymore."

"Here it is anyway. Duck."

After the others had laughed and left, I moved to sit across the table from Stony as he finished his drink.

"They'll come around," he said.

"Fuck 'em."

"They just get so damn territorial. But my father always told me, he said, 'Son, you keep reaching out a hand, no telling whose pecker you'll end up grabbing hold of.' I spoke to Schimmeck about them tickets in the bag you gave me. Four thousand."

"That's pretty steep."

"Stop the presses: greedy judges."

"Does the figure include your cut?"

"Let me tell you how it's played down here, Victor. No one wants to know the details. Thanks, Aubrey," he said when the barman brought over his next drink. Stony waited for him to leave before lowering his voice. "If there's a deal to be made, you just give the price. Flat. Your cut's part of that price, and you don't never tell a soul what it is. Now Schimmeck, he talked it over with his boys at Traffic Court and gave me a price. He doesn't even know it's for you. I'm taking that price and giving you a different price. That's all you get. What you do with that is your choice, take it or leave it—I don't give a crap." Stony lit a cigarette. "Word is you're taking a hard look at Bettenhauser."

"Is that the word?"

"The political world may be a sewer, but it's our sewer. I'm just saying, if you're looking at a guy, I do that."

"You do that?"

"Among other things. You need to remodel your bathroom, give me a call. You need business cards, I can get you a thousand for twenty bucks. You need a cop in your pocket, I got a pocketful. And, yeah, I can follow a husband and take pictures of him ramming his secretary in the Alimony Arms Motel. I took a course. Private investigations for fun and profit. Saw the ad for it on the inside of a matchbook. My daddy always said, 'Don't put all your eggs up one chicken's ass.'"

"How much for the full whammy?"

"You talking bathroom or investigation?"

"Investigation."

"Whatever I'd charge, it won't be enough." He lifted the drink, downed it like it was a lowball of iced tea, and slammed the glass back on the table. "But I can't do anything without the okay from the rest of 'em. And they're not wrong. I mean, what do you know about the business? Nothing. You don't even know the most basic of my father's rules, the Briggs Mulroney Rules for Aspiring Bagmen. Sometime I'll elucidate them for you, but not right now. Right now I've got me an appointment." He gave his bag a pat. "Someone's got to keep this damn city running."

I didn't watch him go, I just sat and stared at my glass as I swirled the remaining liquor, the twist of lemon peel floundering at the bottom. I had fallen into something, whether rich or deadly I couldn't quite figure, but something all right. And for good or for ill, it looked like Stony Mulroney was all I had to serve as my Virgil. And every level was proving more venal than the next, which was just the way I liked it.

I looked up and there was the barman in his plaid vest, Aubrey, bringing me something on a tray. At first I thought I would have to wave off another drink, but there was no glass on the tray, only a small leather folder.

Those sons of bitches, first they cut me and then they stuck me with the check. Somehow it only made me smile.

CHAPTER 22

BOOTY CALL

There was a cop car sitting outside Rosen's when I hiked out the entrance with my bag. The cruiser was idling at the curb, and the sirens rose within me even before the car's front door opened and a uniform stepped out calling my name.

"Oh, come on," I said. "You cannot be serious."

"Serious as scabies, Mr. Carl," said my old friend Officer Boot, as short and squat as an artichoke.

"What did I do now?"

"Knowing that is above my pay grade."

"McDeiss again?"

"Yes, sir."

"Don't you have something more important to do, Boot, than ferrying me to some overweight, undersexed detective?"

"I wouldn't call Detective McDeiss overweight," she said, "at least not to his face."

"Tell him I'm busy."

"No, sir."

"Tell him I have an important meeting that I simply cannot miss."

"No, sir."

"You're more afraid of him than I am."

"Yes, sir."

"And how the hell did he know I was here?"

"You'll have to ask him that yourself." Boot leaned over and opened the rear door of the car.

"Don't you have to cuff me or something?" I said.

"If you insist."

"And you'd like that, too, wouldn't you?"

"I'd prefer a muzzle."

"I ought to sue someone."

"How about whoever sold you that tie?"

Boot drove me down to the Roundhouse, kindly escorted me to a bathroom, where I peed while she stood guard outside, and then brought me to a sickly green interrogation room, where she locked me inside. I put my bag on the table and started pacing. This was a violation of some sort of constitutional protection, I was sure, but just then I was fretting too much to figure out which. Something had gone wrong, something had gone kaboom, and I needed to know what it was so that I could duck away before a wide chunk of hurtling cement took off my face.

I waited for a bit, and a bit longer, and when I grew tired of waiting, I stepped to the mirror and starting picking my teeth with a fingernail. Such a lovely sight, it even made me sick to see it. It was but a moment later that McDeiss and Armbruster walked into the room.

"Did you have me followed?"

"No," said Detective Armbruster, who crossed his arms and leaned against the wall beside the door.

"If I'm not being followed, then how did you know I was at Rosen's?"

"Maybe you're not the one we were following," said Armbruster. "Can we look in your bag?"

"Not on your life."

"Then maybe we'll just have to get a warrant."

"On what grounds?"

"On your refusal to let us search your bag."

"Do you hear that?"

"Hear what?"

"The Fourth Amendment weeping."

McDeiss tossed a file onto the table, pulled out one of the hard metal chairs, and scraped it loudly on the floor before sitting, clasping his hands together, and leaning forward. This was his sincere pose; I had seen it before. McDeiss doing sincere looked like a constipated car salesman on the pot.

"Sit down," said McDeiss.

"I'm fine."

"Sit the hell down."

I sat down.

"I brought you here, Carl, to give you an opportunity to climb out from under the muck."

"Out of the goodness of your heart."

"I advise you to take advantage of it."

"We received a report of a violent home invasion in Center City, called in anonymously from a pay phone," said Armbruster. "And imagine our shock when we saw the home that was violently invaded was yours. What happened?"

"They took money and crapped up the place."

"And knocked you cold while doing it."

"Are you okay?" said McDeiss.

"Are you concerned for my health and welfare?"

"No."

"Then I'm okay."

"You need to be careful here, Carl."

"I'm trying."

Armbruster pushed himself off the wall, stepped to the table, leaned forward, and placed his knuckles on the tabletop. "Not if you're suddenly palling around with one Mulwood Mulroney."

"Mulwood?"

"The fat tub of lard who prowls the alleys behind our divisions with a bag of treats for dirty cops provided by bookies and drug dealers and corrupt pols. There isn't a soul he wouldn't sell out for a nickel and a half, and yet there you are, swapping drinks with him and his pals at a dump like Rosen's."

"I'll have you know Rosen's happens to be quite the venerable institution."

"You're up to your neck, Carl," said Armbruster. "You're mixing with foul company, and you're obstructing a murder investigation."

"I guess I'm on a roll," I said. "Is that all?" I looked at one and then the other. "Am I free to go?"

McDeiss stared at me for a moment, something unkind in his eyes, and then opened the file in front of him. "We know that Jessica Barnes was blackmailing Congressman DeMathis," he said. "And we know you paid her off with money you personally picked up from one Connie Devereaux out in Devon."

Like I had been slapped. All the secrets I had been trying to keep from McDeiss had just poured out of his mouth like a half-digested hot dog from a drunken frat boy. Someone had spilled the beans on my lucrative and underhanded political enterprise. I riffled through all the possibilities like a deck of cards, until I came up with an answer that clenched my teeth in hate.

Reginald, that mealymouthed fake-Brit son of a bitch.

"What we need from you," said Armbruster, "is the what. What was she blackmailing the Congressman with?"

"The way we see it," said McDeiss, "there are two possible motives for the Jessica Barnes murder. One is that this was a simple robbery, which is still the most likely. Someone saw you give her the money, followed her from the rendezvous, and cashed her in. But see, that's a hard thing to pin down. We can't check the pawnshops for specific merchandise as if it were diamonds that were stolen, or a luxury watch."

"And the other motive?"

"Something to do with the secret this Jessica Barnes was holding," said Armbruster. "Blackmail is a tough game; there is always the urge just to end the threat. If we knew what she was threatening to expose, we could figure who might have determined it was safer to kill her than to keep on paying."

"And you're looking there because the light's better."

"Exactly."

"I'm not saying who or what was involved, or even if your blackmail theory is correct, but if I told you I didn't know her secret, would you believe me?"

"No."

"Well, there we are."

"How much cash did you give her?" said McDeiss.

I didn't say anything.

"We're talking to Congressman DeMathis next week," said Armbruster. "He'll be lawyered to the max, out to protect his hide at any cost. If he tells us something that you know and that is not privileged, we're going to pick you up on obstruction. It's tough to run a law business from a jail cell."

"Isn't one of you supposed to be the good cop?"

"How much did you give her?" said McDeiss.

"Enough to get her killed twice over," I said.

"It must have been a hell of a secret she was carrying."

I thought about the card and the dark swath of maroon that could only be blood. McDeiss was right; there must have been a hell of a secret in that blood to incite a murder, but I still had no idea what the secret was or to whom it so mattered.

"If there is a secret," I said, "I don't know it. I gave her what I gave her because she needed the money."

"I bet that made you feel good."

"Until I saw her corpse."

"And what did she give you?" said McDeiss.

Another slap. "What makes you think she gave me anything?"

"Because we're not blind," said Armbruster. "Our murder victim's body had been searched, as if the killer was looking for something beyond the cash. And you're too low-rent for anyone to want to rob you for your money, so we figure they came to your apartment to find the very same thing. They take anything not in the police report?"

"No."

McDeiss slipped a sheet of paper from the file and offered up a pen. "Do us a favor and write your phone number."

"You know my phone number."

"Just write it."

As McDeiss stared and Armbruster leaned his face in closer to mine, I wrote.

"I'd say you're smarter than you're acting, but then again you'd have to be," said McDeiss as he put the paper with my handwritten number back in the file. "You asked before how we knew to call you in for an identification of our murder victim. It wasn't too hard because your phone number was scrawled on the envelope we found at the scene, the envelope that held the cash they stole."

I lowered my jaw, letting my face go slack. It's a courtroom lawyer's trick. In the course of every trial, something will go desperately wrong. The crucial trick, when every gesture is scrutinized by that omnivorous creature with twenty-four eyes, is to make it seem as if nothing untoward had happened at all. As if that devastating piece of evidence that skewered your case were no more devastating than a fruit fly. So when McDeiss told me about my number being scrawled on the envelope they had found on the dead Jessica Barnes, I didn't react with surprise or fear. Instead, my face went slack as old meat.

And I would have pulled it off, too, if not for an involuntary twitch of the eye.

"That's right," said McDeiss. "Now you see it."

CHAPTER 23

HAMMER TIME

I tried to keep myself under control for as long as they might be watching from their upper-floor window. I tried to walk away from police headquarters with a calm and confident step. But there is only so much acting a man can do when he is falling into a pit.

From the very first, I had been chained to the Jessica Barnes crime scene; her blood had not even stopped flowing when they started setting me up for her murder. That it wasn't my handwriting on the envelope wouldn't mean a jot, the link itself was enough to wrap the crime around my neck. I wasn't just a bagman, I was a fall guy too. That crowd at Rosen's had been right to cut me off at the knees. I was nothing but a fool with a bag.

I wandered aimlessly into Chinatown, a few blocks west of the Roundhouse. I walked into a restaurant with a name that I forgot as soon as I entered the doorway and headed straight for the bar. I drank a bottle of Tsingtao while still standing. I was too scared to sit; I was too scared to piss.

All I had wanted was to keep my train on the gravy track. I liked carrying a fancy bag filled with cash. I liked the office waiting room filled with people, and the escrow accounts filled with retainers. I liked being full. Like every working stiff, my job was to keep my job. But it was no longer enough to sit back and let the facts pile up without my worry, not when they were piling up like a prison cell around me.

And then I remembered the pressure Melanie had put on me to stay out of the investigation.

Sure, stay out of the way and don't muck up their work as they construct their frame. She must be up to her eyeballs in the whole bad ball of wax, murder included. Machiavelli indeed. But if I was a fall guy, they wouldn't stop with a number scrawled on an envelope. They would keep applying the pressure, step-by-step, until something snapped. And they already had, hadn't they? Breaking into my apartment and searching for the blood swath of proof that Jessica Barnes had given me. What else had they done? What else would they do?

I gulped down my beer, let the heady brightness of the lager mute my terror and clear my thinking, ordered another to clarify my thinking even further. What else?

I began to wonder who had called the cops right after my attack. A concerned neighbor was what I had thought. But then McDeiss had said the call was anonymous. Why would a concerned neighbor go to a pay phone to remain anonymous? I didn't even know there still were pay phones. You had to go quite a ways in this town now to find a pay phone. So it most likely wasn't a concerned neighbor. It most likely was the unconcerned asshole who had brained me in the first place. Why would he want to call the police?

Maybe because—

I slammed down the still unfinished beer, fished some bills out of my wallet, rushed for the door, and then, thinking better of it, went back to the bar and downed the rest of the Tsingtao. I sensed I would need it.

After a frantic and messy search of my apartment, I found it in a bureau drawer, within a pile of T-shirts I didn't much wear anymore, one of those drawers you wouldn't know I didn't use unless you were me. Beneath something blue, atop something white, there it rested, like an undetonated bomb.

A wooden handle, a rusted metal head, the entire tool smeared thickly with dried blood and sprinkled with horrid bits of gunk.

It was the hammer that had battered the face of Jessica Barnes. The hammer the police were supposed to find in my apartment when the anonymous tipster rang. The tipster had thought we would search the whole of the apartment together to make a list of any missing items. We hadn't—I had signed the report without a search because I don't have anything worth stealing and wanted the cops out of there as quickly as possible. The hammer had escaped police attention once, but I had no doubt that they'd be called back to find it a second time, this time with more detailed information. And they'd be coming quickly.

I reached down to grab hold of it and stopped myself just in the nick of time. Then I paced, and muttered expletives, and slammed a fist into my head repeatedly, and all the while I tried to figure out what the hell to do. I couldn't destroy it; it could lead directly to the killer. I couldn't call in the cops, because they would link it straight to me. What the hell could I do? And then it crashed over me like a wave of crazed inspiration, a brilliantly cockeyed solution to an intractable problem.

I mailed the damn thing to Duddleman.

I shouldn't have brought her into it, I can see that now from the vantage of time. I should have said, "No. Fuck, no." But I needed to do something, anything, something to protect my ass, and I didn't just then see an option other than Amanda Duddleman, with her scrubbed and eager face. My phone number had been scrawled on an envelope belonging to a murder victim, the killing weapon had been planted in my apartment, and they had these convenient flat-rate boxes at the post office.

A few days after I sent off the hammer, I went to the Walmart on Columbus Boulevard, bought a prepaid phone, registered it to one Jack Herbert, and sent a text to Amanda Duddleman:

IT'S KIP. DID YOU GET MY PACKAGE?

She responded: OMG!!

WE NEED TO MEET.

K ?

SOMEPLACE HIDDEN

?

AIRPORT, GARAGE D, LEVEL 4, 3:30 TODAY.

K

"Did you touch it?" I said to her as we leaned against a cement pillar in the long-term parking garage at the airport.

"No," she said. "I kept it in the box."

"Good. Do you know what it is?"

"Is it . . . ?"

"I think."

"My God, Kip. What am I supposed to do with it?"

"Take pictures for your article, it will be a hell of a scoop, and then take it directly to McDeiss. But tell him you can't say where you got it from."

"Okay."

"Can you protect your source?"

"We studied that."

"It's a little different in the real world."

It was quiet where we were speaking, deserted, real Deep Throat territory. Anyone who passed by was more concerned with catching a plane than catching co-conspirators. Amanda was dressed in jeans, a dark jacket, and glasses that made her look collegiate and made me regret bringing her in, but not enough to do anything about it.

"Whatever prints McDeiss finds will lead him to a murderer. I only touched it with gloves when I put it in the bag. But, Amanda, he can't know it's from me."

"Okay."

"Now has McDeiss announced anything about the victim? Has he released the name?"

"Not yet. He says he's looking to notify the family before he releases it to the press."

"Okay. I can help you there."

"I'll quote you as an anonymous source."

"You won't quote me at all."

"Then what good are you?"

"I don't know as much as you think I know, but maybe I can give you prods that will send you in the right direction. Leads that will lead to bigger things. But if I do this, you won't be coming to my apartment anymore and I can't be summoned to pay you a visit, so no more acting crazy with the Congressman."

"I'll try."

"Amanda."

"Yes. Okay. I'll turn off the crazy."

"And you have to tell me everything you find."

"It will be in the paper."

"Before the paper."

"Fine, that's a deal."

"Good. But no Internet, no e-mails. I sent you that text from a new phone that can't be traced to me. I'll check it a couple of times each day. If you find something, text me a time and place to meet but nothing specific about the information. The same thing goes if I want to talk to you."

"Cloak-and-dagger."

"In a world lousy with information, we're going to leave a clean slate. Whatever you're going to discover, someone wants to keep hidden in the worst way, as Jessica Barnes learned. Wherever you go, leave no footprints. And don't tell anyone what you've found until it's printed in the paper."

"Except you."

"That's right, except me. Okay, let's start with a name."

"Whose?"

"Shoeless Joan's."

I gave her name to Amanda Duddleman, along with the rest of Jessica Barnes's sad story.

And so it began.

CHAPTER 24

MONKEY'S PAW

At about six o'clock in the evening I grabbed a spot at the window of a coffee bar where I could suck down a jolt of espresso while keeping an eye on Eighteenth Street.

"I need to see you," Ossana DeMathis had said over the phone that morning. "When can you shake free?"

"I have a couple of meetings this afternoon. Maybe six?"

"Okay, where?"

I thought on this a second, and let a flame of suspicion rise to lick my jaw. "There's a place called the Franklin on Eighteenth. Do you know it?"

Perhaps I imagined the slightest hesitation before she said, "No. No, I don't."

"South of Chestnut. It's just a small place. Let's say six fifteen to be safe."

"Okay, yes. To be safe. See you then, Victor. And thank you."

No, I thought. *Thank you.*

Why did I find Ossana DeMathis so enthralling? Of course there were her sharp aristocratic looks, her lithe hard body, her skin pale as an acquiescence, her deranged green eyes that haunted the soul. But the allure of a woman always goes beyond raw physicality into the land of self-transcendence. I'm not looking for a woman to complete me; my God, just the thought of it horrifies. Why would I ever want to become a complete me when I could be something new and shiny? And that's what the most attractive women promise.

With a thin waif with tight black pants spackled with paint, I could become bohemian Victor. With a saintly earnest type with long legs and arms full of pamphlets, I could become dedicated-to-a-cause-greater-than-myself Victor. With a laughing woman at a bar with the big drink and breasts like twin gerbils ready to spring from their cages, I could become hedonistic Victor, sucking the very marrow of life right through her nipples. And with Ossana—connected Ossana, red-haired and distant Ossana, dressed-to-the-max Ossana, haughty and naughty Ossana—I could become political Victor, rising, rising.

But no matter how much I wanted to rise with Ossana, I wasn't going to be her sap. Somebody had spied on my meeting with Jessica Barnes, and I wasn't ready to exclude anyone. My time for being less than utterly careful had passed.

At precisely a quarter past six, there she came, checking the street addresses with a piece of paper in her hand. She looked good walking up the street, her body slim, her copper hair glossy, her eyes mascaraed to within an ounce of their lives, her outfit formal enough to make it seem she had dressed for the occasion, but still kicky, with a pair of shocking-red fishnets scissoring out of a flat black skirt. She stopped in front of the bar, looked left and right, hesitated a moment, glanced down as if she had never before considered that a bar might live down that stairway.

Was her uncertainty real? Was it an act? Did it seem slightly staged, as if she knew I was somewhere watching? Did it matter? Just the sight of her blurred my suspicion into something else, a fizzle and pop of possibility. I drained the espresso and waited a moment to make sure no one was following her. I hitched up my pants in eagerness when I hit the street.

She was sitting at one of the small tables in the middle of the room, right next to the table I had shared with Jessica Barnes. When she saw me, her mouth twitched just enough so that I felt it in my chest, at the exact spot, in fact, she had placed her hand at our meeting before.

"Thank you for coming," she said. "Is this one of your regular spots?"

"No, but my regular spot is a bit regular." I pulled out a chair and joined her at the table. "You've never been here before?"

"No, never."

"You found it easy enough."

"I got the address from the Google."

"Handy, that thing. They don't serve much food here, but they're pretty clever with their drinks."

When the waitress came amidst the smallest of small talk, Ossana ordered herself a cosmo, and I asked for a Sazerac.

"I thought your drink was a Sea Breeze."

"A harder cocktail fits the new line of work I'm trying."

"What line is that?"

"Upholstery."

She laughed and then grew quiet. "I've been thinking about you."

"Is that why you needed to see me?"

"No, but still I have."

"Good, then whatever I'm doing, it's working."

When the drinks came, Ossana thanked the waitress and lapped at her reddish liquid like a cat. My Sazerac was brilliant enough to make me think of taking hold of Ossana's wrist and licking off her flock-of-birds tattoo.

"It was something you told me the other day," she said. "How you welcomed the way all the people at the Governor's Ball stared at you like you were a leper."

"Aren't you sick of it all?" I said. "Dressing right, acting right, minding your precious manners."

"My God, yes."

"Then stop."

Her lips slipped into a sad smile with a hint of wistfulness. "I don't have your courage. But just once I'd like to watch them shrink away like leeches from salt when they see me."

"Your time will come."

"Victor, you're sweet. But there's a reason we all wear our masks. Except for you."

"Oh, I wear mine, like any opportunistic striver in this foul little world. Did you see the shoes I wore to the ball?"

"They were darling."

"See, I try. I'm just not very good at sucking up, thus my fall-back position. As the man said, 'There is no fate that cannot be surmounted by scorn.'"

"I don't think Camus meant the scorn that others feel for you."

"You know the quote? I'm impressed."

"I majored in French literature in college."

"I'm sure that was useful in the job market."

"I wasn't very good at making café au laits, but my pronunciation was sterling. Do you like being the new Colin Frost?"

"It pays well and sure beats what I was doing before."

"And what was that?"

"Wallowing in poverty."

"You?"

"Oh, yes."

"I can't imagine it. You're such a go-getter."

"Is that what I am?"

"Like a regular Sammy Glick. Has anyone told you that before?"

"Yes," I said.

"And you don't like it."

"No."

"I meant it as a compliment. That reminds me, I have this for you."

She reached into her bag, an expensive one, I could tell, because it was a gaudy advertisement for itself, and pulled out an envelope, which she slid across the table. The Franklin was getting to be quite the place for envelopes. I opened hers, took out the paper, gave it a quick scan, put it back into the envelope. It was a list of names, each followed by a figure. I supposed it was time to start spreading the love for the Congressman's reelection campaign, which meant that Ossana was my new contact. Somehow I didn't like that. Somehow, along with the Sammy Glick crack, it made me feel like the help, which, to be honest, was exactly what I was. But still.

"Last time I was in this bar," I said, deciding to shake things up a bit, "I was having drinks with a murder victim."

"Here?" She looked around, her expression a bit theatrical. But then everything she did was a bit theatrical. "This very bar?"

"That table right there," I said, tapping the marble next to us.

"What did she tell you?"

"The story of her life."

"Was it captivating?"

"No, it was just sad. And then it ended."

"Do they know who killed that woman yet?"

"No. Nor why."

"What do they think?"

"That it was robbery. Or maybe something else. They're still at sea."

"Then what do they know?"

"They know that I took money from Mrs. Devereaux and gave it to the woman and that the money wasn't on her when they found her body."

"My God, where did they learn all that?"

"Not from me," I said.

"There's a leak."

"Yes, there's a leak. But I'll take care of it. That's what I do for my dollar, take care of things."

"Yes, that's what you do," she said, putting her hand on mine. "And we're all so grateful."

"So let's get back to the darkness at the base of your soul that you are sick to death of hiding."

"Can we please not?"

"Maybe it's time to show someone."

She pulled her hand away. "Trust me, Victor, you don't want to see."

"But I do. You've whetted my appetite."

Her bright lips twitched. "You're like the little boy saying he wants to go to the horror movie. 'Please, Mommy, I can handle it.' And if she relents, he's the first one to run out screaming."

"Are you saying you think your darkness is darker than mine?"

"No, I'm not saying that at all. Listen closely, Victor. What I'm saying is that my darkness eats your darkness for brunch with a lemon hollandaise and a flute of champagne."

"Oh, Ossana, you're a sunny day in Spain."

She laughed. "Are we really fighting over which of us is more vile?"

"I guess we are."

"Why do I find that so stimulating?"

"Because it's as twisted as we are."

"We might both be twisted, yes, but not similarly, and not to the same degree."

"Want to bet?"

"Now you're just being silly."

"Oh, no," I said. "I'm serious as sin."

"All right then, if you insist. We'll bet."

"What stakes?"

"Something small and mean, I would think, something as abominable as our worthless souls. A penny?"

"Not worthless enough. I once saw a taxidermied monkey's paw in a curio shop. A single little paw with humanlike fingers and pale-yellow nails. The skin was ebony and there were tufts of hair, and the way it was shaped, with a deformed twist, it formed a terrifying maw, like the mouth of some horrid alien creature. And the mouth was talking to me."

"What was it saying?"

"'Feed me,' it said. 'Feed my paw.'"

"When are we having sex, Victor?"

"I can fling your leg over my shoulder and have your breast in my mouth in fifteen minutes."

"I have to warn you. You'll be bitterly disappointed."

"I doubt it," I said. But damn if she wasn't right.

CHAPTER 25

THE MANNEKEN PIS

Connie Devereaux dropped her desiccated claw onto my knee and gave a squeeze. "You are such a darling. Why I could just eat you alive."

"I don't doubt it, Connie," I said and we both laughed and laughed.

We were alone in her parlor, sitting side by side on a love seat, sharing a convivial drink made for us by dear Reginald before he sullenly backed out of the room. My bag was beside me on the floor, two crystal bowls on the coffee table were filled with sweet bundles of cash, and Connie's blouse was coming undone, giving me a view of her liver-speckled flesh and the shriveled tops of breasts stuffed like limp jack-in-the-boxes into her black lace bra. It was all I could do to stop myself from gagging, and that was before she leaned over and bit my earlobe, hard.

"Yikes," I said. "What sharp teeth you have."

"That, my dear boy, is a warning."

I pulled at my ear. "Is it bleeding?"

"Give it time. The police have come asking questions."

"McDeiss?"

"That was one of the names, yes. A big mass of a man. They do grow them big in Philadelphia. How did they know of me? Have you been indiscreet?"

"I am the very soul of discretion," I said, "but there has been a leak. I'm on it, though. I'll plug it one way or the other."

"See that you do. All the kerfuffle has troubled me greatly. I have told the Congressman that I might have to turn off the spigot. And in any event, he hasn't been very solicitous lately. He isn't returning my calls, and neither is that lackey of his, that Tom Mitchum person, who always looks like he just came from a funeral."

"The Congressman has to be extra careful these days."

"I understand. With the papers linking him to a murder, it is a trying time for all of his supporters. And how unfortunate that the link was through you, Victor darling."

"It couldn't be avoided."

"Isn't that what Admiral Kimmel said of Pearl Harbor before they took his stars? But because I can't so easily contact my congressman anymore, I must send my messages through you. Can I trust you to be a reliable go-between?"

"Yes, Connie, you can trust me as much as any politician."

"Now you're being funny? Good. Drink up, Victor. Maybe we'll play some today."

"Oh, I won't be much fun. Isn't Heywood around? His pectorals are so much bigger than mine."

"They are, aren't they?" She sidled closer and rubbed my chest through the suit jacket. "My heavens, Victor, I can feel the bones beneath your flesh. You have the chest of a sparrow. You should work out more."

"I would if it wasn't such work."

"Muscles are very becoming in a man, and Heywood certainly is becoming."

"Becoming what?"

"Oh, you. But today is his day off and I'm lonely."

"You have Reginald to keep you company."

"I'm getting tired of Reginald."

"I think we're all getting tired of Reginald. So what is it you want me to pass on to the Congressman?"

"That I am growing impatient."

"With what?"

"Oh, he'll know. My Heywood is little more than a clenched muscle in both the chest and the head. He doesn't have your charm."

"Few do," I said.

"But he satisfies me, Victor. Oh, does he satisfy me. And so I keep him on. If he failed to satisfy me, I would drop him like a dead trout. You tell the Congressman that I am not feeling satisfied and he is beginning to smell like a rotting fish."

"And what is it that will satisfy you, Connie?"

"Just let him know that if a certain bill doesn't pass out of his committee and soon, I might have trouble rustling up enough ready cash to fill your bag. And tell him that I like Mr. Bettenhauser's smile. It does something to my stomach. I have the urge to nuzzle the war hero's neck. Did you get all that?"

"Oh, yes, I got all that."

"Good," she said, giving my leg another squeeze. "Now, Victor, tell me about yourself. What do you like? Do you want to know what I like?"

"I suppose you're going to tell me."

"Everything," she said.

When I managed to leave that room with my bag full, my pants still on, and the faint vestiges of my remaining virtue still intact, Reginald was standing stiffly by the house's front door, a disapproving mannequin in his pin-striped suit. His perfect blue tie was tied with a perfect double Windsor. The pack of purebred fur balls swam like a school of piranhas about his shiny black oxfords. He eyed my bulging bag like I was taking out the afternoon sewage.

"Perky boss you've got there," I said.

"I hope you remembered everything," said Reginald. "We wouldn't want you leaving anything behind."

"I didn't bring a hat."

"That's not what I was referring to."

"You don't approve of me, do you, Reginald?"

"Your powers of observation are startling."

"Where are you from? I'm having a hard time placing the accent. London, is it?"

"The outskirts."

"The outskirts of merry old London. God save the Queen and all that rubbish. Pubs and pints and shepherd's pie, bangers and mash, fish and chips, rotting teeth. I like your tie. What is it?"

"Lanvin," he said, as if it meant something.

"Get that at Boyds, did you?"

"And that thing around your neck, did you pick that up at Walmart?"

"Target, actually. I've gone upscale. Let's say we swap."

"I wouldn't be caught dead in such a thing."

"Don't tempt me. You know, it's funny, your virulent disapproval, because I think we're pretty similar."

"Don't flatter yourself, Victor. Someone like you, with your greasy little bag, you have nothing in common with me."

"Greasy? Why, I might be insulted if you had actually grown up on the outskirts of London, where the taste in accessories is oh so refined. But I don't think the air is so rarefied in Northeast Philly, where you were born and raised, you sly little fraudster, you."

"Am I supposed to be impressed with your research?"

"I grew up only a few miles west of you, actually. Abington."

"The suburbs," said Reginald, with a slight sneer. "Poor little rich boy."

"Not me. The part I grew up in was as far from sunshine and roses as you can get. At root we're pretty similar, kids who went to law school because there was nothing else for us to do and who are now just trying to work our schemes without getting pissed on." I leaned close enough to make him draw back slightly. "And you're pissing on my head, Reginald."

"I don't know what you're referring to."

"Of course you do, you little guttersnipe. It's a dangerous game you're playing, trying to use the cops to thin the competition. See, I know your type; I am your type. And you wouldn't be here if you weren't after something bigger than a sycophantic position in this horrid old house. My guess is you're making a long play for the whole ball of Devereaux wax."

It was just a guess, the flimsiest of feints, but the way he held his head perfectly still, the way his eyes blinked and his lips hardened, told me that I had hit on something. Maybe not everything, but something, and that was opening enough.

"Good for you. I admire ambition in a man, and no one deserves to have her fortune stripped from her withered hands more than that old bag. And who better to take care of it than her dutiful lawyer. But if I get one more drop of your piss on my head, Reginald, then you're through here."

"You don't have what it takes to interfere."

"Maybe I'll take your play for my play, you little pissant. Oh, you may coo in her ear, but I know enough to know that cooing doesn't plant her turnips. If you were able to satisfy Connie the way she dreams of being satisfied, then she wouldn't need Heywood, and she wouldn't be coming on to me like a freight train. So far I've demurred as politely as a schoolboy—I prefer my meat a bit more undercooked—but have no doubt that if I put my mind to it, I could overcome the revulsion and crank into her like Paul Bunyan's big blue ox. I'll screw her upside and down, downside and up, night and day and fast and slow and hard and true, until her tears are flowing. And in the midst of all that raw rough stuff she so much loves, I'll whisper sweet nothings into her ear about trusts and estates and powers of attorney, and the next thing you know I'll be standing at the doorway in pin-striped Dior with a blue Lanvin tie, listed as the executor on all her estate documents, and you'll be back to trolling for fender benders on Roosevelt Boulevard to pay your rent. Are we clear?"

"Yes, we are clear," he said through clenched white teeth after a long moment during which he let the truth of it soak into his skin. His accent was no longer tinged with Brit, but pure Philadelphia and flush with hate.

"Now give me your Lanvin."

"My what?"

"Give me your tie. We're swapping," I said as I began to untie my own. "I want to be ready when the call comes. You can have this."

"I don't want that."

"Tough," I said. "You'll wear it and you'll like it."

I pulled the tie from beneath my collar with a brisk yank and held it out to him.

Reginald stared at it like it was a dead possum hanging from my hand. He looked back up at my face and leaned away as if I were indeed a strange and fantabulous creature, huge and blue and horned, and ready to chew off his face.

"You're going to keep your mouth shut and your eyes open," I said, "and you're going to let me know anything that might interest me. Especially if it involves the Congressman or that murder investigation. Do you understand?"

"Yes," he said.

"Yes, Babe the Blue Ox, sir."

"Yes, Babe the Blue Ox, sir," he said.

"Now give me the fucking tie."

First slowly, and then with sudden angry jerks, each spasm a perfect metaphor for exactly what he was, Reginald loosened his Lanvin.

CHAPTER 26

PARTY HAT

Ever get the certainty that you are missing something? You pat your pocket for your wallet, for your phone. Everything is where it should be, but you still feel the gap, the nagging sensation of incompleteness that gnaws at the soul like an itch.

I was scratching my neck when it came to me.

"So nice, and certainly unexpected, to see you again, Victor," said Timothy in the atrium at Boyds. "I must say, your diplomatic bag does you more than justice. It makes you seem almost—how should I put it?—diplomatic. And that tie, a Lanvin, is it not?"

"So it is, Timothy."

"Have you been shopping without me?"

"Let's say I acquisitioned it on my own."

"Well done, Victor. Things are looking up for you, stylewise at least. So, what are we after today? A scarf perhaps? A few perfect pieces of Brioni hosiery? Or have you finally come to your senses and decided to cast away that shapeless navy-blue tent in favor of a suit more becoming?"

"Becoming what, Timothy?"

"Becoming a man of import, Victor. A man to be reckoned with."

"And that depends on the suit?"

"What else would it depend on?"

"Character? Intellect?"

"Are we here to joke, Victor, is that it? Are we here to clown around? Because if so, then your current suit is more than adequate—one could even say, perfect. Now, we don't normally carry red foam noses in stock, but I could order one just for you."

"Armani?"

"Party City."

"Well, that might have to wait, and so will the suit. What I'm looking for now, Timothy, is a hat. Something with a snappy brim. Something like a fedora."

"Does that mean you want a fedora?"

"I'm not sure."

"Yes, well, I've grown accustomed to that with you, Victor. Tell me, why this sudden and cracked impulse to buy a hat?"

"I've found myself in a new line of work, and I have some strange urge to dress the part. The formal shoes are unusable at the moment, fortunately, but the bag is perfect. Still, I feel like I'm missing something. My new line is the realm of politics, where I meet in old-style steak houses and drink hard liquor laced with absinthe. The kind of line where I slip through the shadows and say things like 'Hello, friend, do you by chance have a minute for a few words off the record?'"

"Oh, I see. It's like that, is it?"

"Yes, it's like that."

"Politics is a dirty game, Victor."

"Dirtier than selling rags at Boyds?"

"No. Now I could sell you a fedora, yes, in all manner of color, made of all manner of material. But with the normal fedora's wide flat brim you would look like a hood from the 1930s, hardly the image you should be conveying."

"It sounds about right to me."

"But it has no sense of irony, Victor, and politics without irony is insufferable."

"And politics with irony?"

"The same, alas. With headgear, Victor, you must choose carefully. Nothing says as much about a man's life goals as a hat. A man in a beret wants to be Camus. A man in a baseball cap wants still to be a child. Neither can be taken seriously. So tell me, Victor, what is it you want to be in this world?"

The third and most difficult of Timothy's questions. What did I want to be? Gangster, ironist, existentialist? Lawyer, bagman, thief? I was so busy playing the role that had landed on my head I had lost my own sense of direction.

"I . . . I don't know, Timothy."

"Isn't it time to find out? But until you do, let's maybe go with something that fits what you truly are now, something young and sharp, with a limp sense of humor. How about a trilby?"

"Isn't he the senior senator from Rhode Island?"

"Learn your terms, Victor. A trilby is a fedora with a narrow brim and low crown. I happen to have one in a gorgeous rabbit-hair felt with a gray band, which would fit your face perfectly. And trust me, that is not an easy thing to find, considering your face. But you can't just get the hat, Victor."

"No?"

"Oh, no. Alone the hat would look like a peacock feather taped onto a chicken. Do you perhaps have a raincoat?"

"It's not raining."

"It doesn't matter."

"I like umbrellas."

"We sell them, too, but this has nothing to do with the weather. Think of something tan and fitted with a belt rakishly tied in the back. With your bag and a jaunty trilby and a coat such as that, Victor, you will be a specimen to be reckoned with, I promise you that."

"A specimen? Like a virus on a slide under a microscope?"

"It is politics, isn't it?"

"That it is."

"And how will you be paying?"

"American Express," I said.

I was wearing the coat and the hat when I returned to my office to find Maud sitting in my waiting room, legs crossed, arms crossed, smoke rising like a thin blade from her cigarette. It felt, in its strange way, as if the hat and belted raincoat had somehow summoned a member of the Brotherhood. And was that an expression of amusement on her face at my new look?

My secretary, Ellie, a sign on her desk stating THANK YOU FOR NOT SMOKING, lifted her hands in helplessness.

"There's no smoking in the office," I said.

"With that getup?" said Maud.

I tossed the hat onto the top of a file cabinet, where it spun for a hopeful turn before skidding off the metal onto the floor.

When we were situated in my office proper—me behind my desk and Maud, still smoldering, in a client chair—I leaned back and waited. She was a hard mark, that Maud, her eyes squinted to hide her impatience. She was one of those women so quick and competent that she was continually furious to be required to slow down for the rest of us. Just by looking, you could see the strength of her bones, all flats and angles, a bizarre yet sturdy geometric figure. She scared me, but I kept a level expression to keep from letting on.

"What are the rules?" she said, finally.

"Are we talking chess?" I said.

"This conversation."

"A lawyer's office is a little like a confessional in Vegas. What you say here stays here."

"Forgive me, Father, for I have sinned."

"I don't doubt it."

She looked around for an ashtray that wasn't there and then squeezed the cigarette to death with her fingertips before placing the corpse in her purse. "I need your help."

"You need the help of a fool with a bag?"

"A little harsh, that, I admit."

"Maybe accurate, too."

"That goes without saying."

"You're forgiven."

"I didn't ask for forgiveness."

"And yet here you are."

"I need the help of a lawyer."

"I don't doubt it. Apparently, one of your gang is being followed by the police. I got picked up just for talking to you."

"Next time go out the back. I need a lawyer who can help me with a delicate situation, and Stony suggested I come to you."

"How delicate?"

"There's a girl involved."

"Funny how in delicate situations there always seems to be a girl involved."

"This one needs help."

"What's the problem?"

"Immigration."

"Is she legal?"

"Would there be a problem if she was legal?"

"I could give you the name of a good immigration lawyer."

"I don't need the name of a good immigration lawyer. I have nothing but the names of good immigration lawyers."

"And all the good immigration lawyers have told you it's hopeless?"

"Nothing to be done."

"You must be pretty desperate to seek help from the likes of me. Did she do anything criminal, this girl?"

"Beyond overstaying her visa?"

"Yes, beyond overstaying her visa."

"No."

"And no one else in the Brotherhood can help?"

"This is federal."

"Ah, yes, now I see. I'm not good enough for your club, but I'm plenty good enough to put myself and my contacts on the line for some girl I've never met."

"She's not just some girl."

"They never are, Maud, are they?"

"No."

"You stuck me with the check," I said.

"Funny how that happened."

"You're not even sorry."

"I don't traffic in regrets."

"You're not even telling me how wonderful she is, how raw her deal is, all the good I'll be doing."

"Would any of that matter?"

"No."

"You might have a future after all."

I looked at her closely. Strong and wary, she'd be a bad enemy and a good friend. I had enough of the former and too few of the latter.

I took a pad and pen out of my desk and leaned forward. "Okay," I said. "Tell me what I need to know."

The girl's named was Lyudmila Porishkova. She had slipped into the country on a tourist visa and, after developing a taste for filter cigarettes, American football, and hamburgers, had decided to stay. It's not so hard to stay hidden in the shadows, and all would have been fine except someone at the job she worked, a travel agency where she helped book tourist trips to the fleshpots of Belarus, had notified Immigration. Lyudmila had just been promoted from travel-agent trainee. Nothing ruffles feathers like a promotion. The immigration cops arrested her in the midst of booking a week's sojourn to Minsk for a bald-headed computer programmer from Cherry Hill.

I knew how it would go if I played it straight, like a lawyer. I would have called what contacts I had, made an appearance at the Immigration and Customs Enforcement office on Callowhill, schmoozed with the agent in charge of Lyudmila's case, shared drinks with the supervisor at his favorite bar in the Tenderloin, a joint with bored go-go dancers and pictures of busty burlesque queens in the bathroom. I might have even headed out to the ICE's contracted detention facility in Lords Valley to talk to the detainee herself. I would have run through the motions, and dutifully kept my hours, and written my letters, and made my petitions, and appeared on Lyudmila's behalf before the immigration judge, all the while knowing there was nothing to be done. See, Maud would never have come to me if any old lawyer could have done the job. The hearings had gone as could be expected, the deportation order had been signed, Lyudmila's exit chute had been dusted and greased. Lyudmila was on her way out, never to be allowed to return, unless . . .

"I need something," I said into the phone after Maud left the office.

"Victor, sweetie, that's not how it works," said Melanie Brooks. "I call you when I need something, not the other way around."

"You've given me a job to do."

"Yes, and you're being paid well to do it."

"But I need your help to finish it up."

"Don't be wearying, Victor."

"I'm starting to get a whole new appreciation for Colin Frost's pernicious habit."

"What is it you want?"

"There's a woman named Lyudmila Porishkova who is being held for deportation by Immigration in Philadelphia. I need her released."

"Let me think about it. Okay, I thought about it. No."

"Melanie."

"The Department of Homeland Security is very touchy and very expensive."

"That's why I called you."

"Did you talk to the sister?"

"Yes."

"And you received the register?"

"I've begun working my way down it already. It's going to be expensive."

"If you need the bag replenished, we'll set it up. Stay on the register and off the sister. Do you understand?"

"Oh, I understand."

"Don't be naughty, Victor. It's for your own good. Now do you have any news for me?"

"The police are interviewing the Congressman in a few days about Shoeless Joan."

"We know."

"I expect he'll lie, so it will help if I have an idea of what lies he tells them. I was picked up by the police yesterday and expect to be questioned again."

"I'll get the information to you as soon as I can."

"I'll say what I can to cover him, but I won't cover for a killer if it comes to that."

"Of course not."

"And don't think I'm not going to protect myself. I'm going to protect myself at all costs, and everyone should know that."

"It's assumed, Victor. I must say, it's like you were born for this business. Anything on Bettenhauser?"

"Not yet, but I have a lead that I'll be able to follow if you can get someone to talk to someone at ICE."

"How are you doing, Victor? Are you enjoying yourself?"

"Entirely too much."

"And dressing better, also, if the receipts from Boyds are any indication."

"I'm thinking of getting some new suits, too."

"Let's not get ahead of ourselves. My partners continue to be impressed despite the problem with the newspaper. If this all works out, we're thinking of promoting you from temp to full-time contract employee. That would require you to deal with some very impressive people. And impressive people don't like unimpressive suits. But until then—"

"Be a good boy and do as I'm told."

"You always were the cleverest one in study group. Not the smartest, mind you, but the most clever. Now what was that name again?"

"Lyudmila," I said. "Lyudmila Porishkova."

When I hung up, I leaned back and propped my shoes against the edge of my desk. If I'd had a cigar, I would have lit the thing and polluted the whole of my office with its choking stench of arrogance. Timothy had pointed out that I still didn't know what I wanted to be in the world, but even so, just then I was feeling pretty good about things.

Someone was coming after me, sure, and I was being set up hard for a murder, sure, and none of that was salutary, sure, but they don't come after the pilot fish, do they? And it wasn't like I wasn't playing the game like a master myself. Here I was, letting others do the hard work for me, while I sat behind the scenes like a fat duck in a still pond. I had Duddleman investigating the Jessica Barnes murder without my fingerprints on anything she did. I had Stony Mulroney working to get me in good with the local union.

I had Reginald acting now as my snitch in the Devereaux manse. And now I had Melanie, my ostensible boss, working to save some poor Russian immigrant from the feds so that I would end up owed a favor by a personal friend of the mayor. It had taken me a while, but eventually, like a girl with bouncing braids maneuvering the shifting space between double-Dutch ropes, I had found my rhythm. If just then I had been gripping a lit cigar in my teeth, I would have pulled it from my mouth, blown one large circle, and then sent a series of smaller through the ever-widening hole.

There wasn't much to being a bagman, I was learning. It was just a matter of knowing the rules.

CHAPTER 27

THE BRIGGS MULRONEY RULES FOR ASPIRING BAGMEN

It is not enough to pick up the money and lay it down again. It is not enough to run your errands to the letter. As with every worthy piece of corruption, there is an art to it all.

"My father, may he rest in peace, he taught me the trade," said Stony Mulroney, "and the rules that went with it. Are you drinking that or watching the ice melt?"

We were at the table at Rosen's, just the two of us, in the otherwise empty establishment. Stony leaned forward in the booth, his hat on the table next to my new trilby, his glass half-full, his cigarette lit, his sharp voice whetted to a knife's edge. I lifted my glass, swallowed an oversized gulp, winced. This was not a Sazerac, but an old-fashioned concoction of bourbon, sugar, and bitters over a single cube of ice. It tasted like hard cases and backhanded deals and the moist environs of the Sternwood conservatory.

"In the old days, before Hump showed up in our fair town with his Sazeracs," said Stony, "this is what the old men drank when they discussed their murky trade. My daddy brought me here back in the day when I was just a boy, brought me here to meet the crew. I can still see all the old scarred faces, beneath dark fedoras with snap brims and feathers in their bands. They all knew Frank, they all screwed showgirls from the Latin Casino, they all drove Cadillacs. In a town of nobodies they were somebodies, and this is what they drank. It seems right to drink the old drink, given the nature of our enterprise today."

"Enterprise?"

"Order us both another," said Stony. "Maybe two, to be efficient."

"You in a rush, Stony?"

"A man the size of me is bound to die young and leave an impressive corpse; I don't have time for half measures. And neither did my father. In his world there was a way to do a thing, and he passed the way of it on to the rest of us. Now, since you've stepped into our world, for your felonious edification I'm going to give the way of the bag to you. Eight sturdy rules in inverse order: the Briggs Mulroney Rules for Aspiring Bagmen. And don't take notes."

"Is that one of the rules?"

"That's just common sense."

And then he laid them out for me, one by one, each illuminated with legends of the old days, when dinosaurs with cigarettes and cruel hats roamed the streets. And here they are for your own sweet edification, illuminated with stories of my own: the rules of the game, as passed on from Briggs Mulroney to Stony Mulroney to Victor Carl to you.

Rule Eight: A bagman's tools are twofold: greed, to fill his bag, and fear, to keep his grip.

The handoff is to be smooth, quiet, like something out of a spy novel. The instructions in the letter are explicit. An envelope, folded into a newspaper, passed like a football on a Statue of Liberty play: look left, handoff right. The recipient is a union leader with a sterling reputation for integrity; it is as important to us as to him that this reputation be maintained. He insists we keep our distance. The deal is as simple as dirt.

I stuff the envelope with the stuffing from my bag and use a rubber band to keep the envelope inside the paper. I spot him walking toward me on the street. I know him from his picture in the paper. As he approaches, I turn my shoulder. We brush up one against the other and, quick as that, in the crook of his arm, the paper now rests. He moves on, I move on, the deal as neat and clean as an obituary.

When it's done, I turn and watch him go. He walks away from me with calm, unhurried steps. He deftly slips the paper from his left arm to his right. He turns a corner and disappears from view. This job couldn't be easier.

A few minutes later I step into a Starbucks, order an overpriced coffee, black, let it burn the roof of my mouth as I look for a seat. I find one at a small table, across from a man reading a newspaper. I place my bag on the floor, toss my hat onto the table, sit down heavily.

"I actually like the coffee," I say. "It's the rest of it I hate, the whole grinding Seattle vision crap that pisses me off."

"Okay," says the man at the table without looking up, letting me know how welcome the disturbance is.

"I'd pay more, actually, if they put it in one of those blue paper cups they give out at Greek diners. You know what I mean? 'We are happy to serve you.' I'd pay more if they just stopped being so stinking precious. And you want to know something else? In the whole damn book, there's only one boring character. Ahab, Ishmael, Queequeg, Stubb: great, great, great, great. Not to mention the whale.

But upright Starbuck? Yawn. They should have named the place Stubbs. I'd go to Stubbs for coffee any day. Starbuck was a scold and a prig."

The man looks up now, jaw muscles working. "What are you doing?" he says.

"Did it go off okay, our little switcherooni? I felt like I was in a 1930's movie. I could even see the camera pans and the cuts as we approached. 'Get the paper,' says the director. 'Now the hand.'"

"This defeats the whole purpose, you fool," he says, wrapping his paper and standing.

"Don't make me shout after you as you rush to the door," I say calmly. "That's a scene that's not so easily forgotten."

"What do you want?" he says through grinding teeth.

"To stop pretending to be what we're not. I'm the guy who brings the money. You're the guy who gets the money and delivers on his promises. I'm the guy you face if you don't deliver. And later, when it goes as we both hope, we get to do this all over again. The raw truth is quite bracing, isn't it? I've always thought meeting face-to-face is so valuable."

"I have to go."

"Well, if it can't be avoided. But we'll see each other again, I'm sure."

I give him a quiet toast with my coffee as he storms away. He trails anger like a cloud, causing a few glances in his direction. Bad form. I take a sip of the coffee. It is a bit cooler now and I can taste the dark bitterness of the roast. I have to admit, despite it all, I do like the coffee.

Rule Seven: The street is our stage, the bag holds our tricks, and we never reveal our secrets.

Outside the Immigration and Customs Enforcement building on Callowhill Street, I'm in full battle regalia: beige raincoat despite the sunny skies, heavy brown diplomatic bag, my gray trilby. When I catch my reflection in a storefront, it's like Inspector Gadget is on the loose.

"Did you get the time right?" says Maud, standing next to me. She is tall in her heels. Bright-red lipstick marks the filter of her cigarette.

"I got the time right."

"Someone is late."

"It's the federal government."

"That's right," she says. "How much did it cost?"

"Plenty."

"I'll pay whatever it is."

"It's covered."

"Don't be a fool."

"A hundred thousand dollars," I say.

"Well, if you're covering it."

"Yeah."

"How did you do it?"

"A single phone call."

"To whom?"

"Oh, Maud, you know better than that. Let's just say I had one Monopoly card and I played it."

"For me?"

"For Lyudmila. Poor little thing. It feels good to do good."

She stares at me sideways before a mordant laugh kicks the smoke out of her lungs.

We're surrounded by families of all colors and shapes waiting outside the office. There are chairs inside, but there is no smoking and so we are all outside in a choking cloud of nervous hope. The door opens and a young man walks through it to be enveloped by his family. An older woman is hugged by her son. A couple hurries out, arms around each other.

And then: a tall, lovely woman with bobbed black hair and lips like ripe peaches. She steps out slowly, hesitantly. Her heels are spikes. She towers over the waiting families. Maud drops her cigarette and twists her shoe to kill it. The woman steps toward Maud, and Maud steps toward the woman until they are face-to-face, staring one at the other, not embracing in a grateful hug, not touching in any way, but staring stares alone that could rip the clothes off lesser figures.

Before they walk off, side by side, still not touching, but leaning one toward the other as if from some accelerated gravity, Maud comes over to me. She raises her eyebrow as if to say it is all just a little thing, but even the act itself is an acknowledgment of its falsity. And then she leans forward and kisses me on the lips and it is as startling as being kissed by a cobra.

"See you Thursday," she says.

Rule Six: No matter the size of the cake, the bagman always takes his cut.

"We've got such plans for the organization," says Hanratty, leaning back at his desk. He is big and bald and wears a blue-and-yellow tracksuit with three thick lines down the side. Scattered about the office are racks of basketballs, peaks of neon traffic cones, bags of soccer balls. The envelope remains untouched on his desktop. "We're spreading out, expanding our footprint and offerings. There are so many kids we still need to reach."

"The Congressman has always been supportive of your good work."

"We know that, and are quite appreciative. But things are in flux."

"Flux?" I say.

"An organization like ours, it has two choices: we grow or we wither. And our mission is too important for us to wither. We can't do business anymore as if nothing in the future will change. As our footprint grows, so does our influence. We've been speaking to Mr. Bettenhauser's people."

"Ah, I see."

"He is quite interested in our work. It meshes very closely with the services he has performed in his own community the last few years."

"He's quite a guy, that Bettenhauser."

"And so, as we contemplate the political stances we will take in the future, we are required to think of not just our current footprint, but of the footprint we envision for next year and the year after and so on."

"And so forth."

"Exactly."

"Quite reasonable," I say.

I reach forward and take hold of the envelope on the desktop. I open it, thumb the cash, raise my gaze just enough to catch Hanratty's expectant smile. The son of a bitch is as good as licking his lips. I take out a significant portion of the bills, put the wad I extracted into my jacket pocket, and then slap the slimmed-down envelope back onto the desk.

"How's that?" I say.

"What the hell?" says Hanratty.

"Don't worry, we're going to take care of your growth plans. I'll talk to the Congressman about increasing the donation check we make out to you guys. Buy yourself a few more soccer balls. Heaven knows, the one thing this great country of ours needs is more soccer balls."

"But what about . . . ?"

"What, you want more?" I grab the envelope again, riffle the remaining bills, take another significant sliver, slip it with the other in my pocket, and toss him what remains in the envelope. "We good now?"

"No," says Hanratty. "Fuck, no, we're not good. Where the hell's Colin?"

"Colin's gone. It's a new day, pal. Here on in, you'll be dealing with me. My understanding was that everything was based on old understandings. Fine, I'll go along to get along. But now you're telling me you've been talking to Bettenhauser's people. And so what we have is not an understanding so much as an auction."

I reach over and grab the envelope, take a few more bills to stick inside my pocket, weigh what's left as if I'm judging the weight of a piece of fish, then toss it back.

"This should do for an opening bid," I say as I stand. "Now go see what the war hero and civics teacher is willing to give you in cash, because that's all that matters, isn't it? Everything else has to go through the accountants first. My guess is that your new best friend, Bettenhauser, intends to play his first campaign straight. My guess is all you're going to get from him is a pat on the back and an 'Attaboy.' In that case, that thin little envelope is more than enough to buy your ass."

"Hey, pal, let's not get hasty."

"Too late, I couldn't be in more haste. Now if by chance Bettenhauser does give you more, you just let us know and we'll take back what's left in the envelope and find some other community organizer a little more grateful to accept our thanks for supporting our run. Otherwise, your mouth stays shut except when it's kissing Congressman DeMathis's ass. And if you're a good boy, and you do all you can to help the cause, after the election maybe we'll have another talk about cooperation and gratitude. Understand?"

Hanratty stares a moment, grumbling under his breath.

"What's that you say, fuckface?"

<u>Rule Five</u>: Never buck the Big Butter.

"And so what did you tell our friend Detective McDeiss, Connie?" I say into her shriveled little ear. I'm getting sloppy on her gin. My arm is around her neck. Her geriatric leg, with its gnarled knob of a foot, is slung over my lap. My job is to keep the old bag happy in the worst way, and this is the worst way.

"What could I have told him?" she says. "You didn't tell me anything in the first place."

"See?" I say before spilling a wave of gin into my mouth. "I'm cleverer than you give me credit for."

"Oh, Victor. I give you nothing but credit. Why, I couldn't stop talking about you to the nice detective. And he had so many questions. He asked me about a hammer he received from a reporter and whether you had mentioned it. He was trying to get what he could out of me, and he had the physical presence to do it."

"Big, isn't he?"

"My God, yes. Such a man. I almost swallowed my tongue when I saw him coming up the walk."

"Now I'm getting jealous."

"Oh, Victor, his advantage is only in bulk, in size, in raw, rugged masculinity."

"And what's my advantage?"

"You have such nice neat hands."

"Are you doing this on purpose?"

"Kiss me, Victor," she says, puckering her desiccated mouth, like the blood-red sucker of a leech. "Kiss me hard."

"If I kissed you, you'd stay kissed, you little minx."

"Oh, you are bad."

"But propriety forces me to restrain myself, though it is harder than I ever imagined. So, did you tell him anything, our virulently virile McDeiss?"

"Nothing, nothing at all. I know how to keep secrets. All I said was to talk to my lawyer."

"Which lawyer?"

"Why, Reginald, of course. Now this is getting tedious. Are you going to kiss me or do I need to call in Heywood?"

"I have an appointment," I say, uncoupling, "and I'm sure Heywood will treat you with all the raw disdain you deserve."

"Victor, you naughty, naughty boy. One day we are going to dance. Did you relay my dissatisfaction and concerns to the Congressman?"

"I did."

"And?"

"He's working on it."

"Oh dear, he sounds like the repair shop working on my Rolls. You see the bowls on the table?"

"Yes."

"They are empty."

"I noticed."

"And they'll stay that way, Victor, until I get something more than empty assurances. We all have our urges to feed, our dark desires to satisfy. And I mean to have mine satisfied. On your way out, please call in Heywood. Heywood, at least, knows how to get paid."

"And how is that, Connie?"

"He delivers, sweetie. That's what it's all about. Do you know how to deliver?"

Rule Four: Politicians rise and politicians fall; make sure you don't fall with them.

There's an Escalade circling, looking for a parking spot. I grab hold of Duddleman and pull her close, like we're making out, as the car passes for a second time. She smells like lilac and coconut. For verisimilitude, I kiss her. She tastes like youth and argyle sweaters and earnestness. I have the sudden urge to discuss Kierkegaard, that wily Dane.

"I'm glad to see you, too, Kip," she says, still in my fake embrace.

"McDeiss got the hammer, I heard."

"He almost put me in jail for not telling him how I got hold of it. But then he started in talking about you."

"What did you tell him?"

"That I'd never met you. He didn't believe me, but he let me go, so I was free to head up to Lancaster to find out what I could on our Jessica Barnes."

"And?"

"Nada." She pushes me away. "I trudged all through that stinking city, and I didn't find a single thing. I even got hold of Jessica's drunken mother."

"How was she?"

"Drunk."

"Husband?"

"Disappeared. No one knows where he is."

"Did you try the local bars?"

"I went to his regular haunt, a dump called the Starting Gate. He hadn't been there since the murder. He's lurched out of sight."

"And you showed everyone the picture of the Congressman?"

"No one recognized him, neither friends nor family. I also showed the photograph around at shops, restaurants and motels, anything near her home and a few places downtown. Nothing. If they did tryst up there, then they did it in absolute secrecy."

"As you would expect from a politician."

"I can tell you from experience, Victor, that he's not that careful. And I also have to tell you, from what I know, she's not his type."

"What is his type?"

"DeMathis likes the young and ambitious, the over-educated, the easily captivated. He likes to tell stories, give advice, remind you who he is. He needs to be adored, and Jessica Barnes wasn't the adoring type. She might have been pretty enough for him, but she wasn't a woman to be awed by power or position. And she was devoted to her husband, even though he lost his job and drank too much. I can't see her and the Congressman hooking up." She pauses a moment and looks down at her hands. "She was too good for him."

"You developed a pretty detailed portrait."

"I wish I had known her," she says.

"I think you have the first installment of your story. The truth behind Shoeless Joan."

"It's too late. The police released the victim's name two days ago. Jessica Barnes's story has already been written in the dailies."

"But not like you'd write it. It would take a hell of writer to do her justice. A family shipwrecked by the Great Recession, the unemployed husband drinking away his frustrations, the sick daughter, the woman trying to find a way out, only to be found dead in Philadelphia."

"It does sound like a story," she says. "Except for the daughter thing. There was no daughter."

"Of course there was."

"No, Victor. She didn't have any children. She couldn't. That was something the mother blathered on about between swallows and smokes. There was a medical issue. Jessica couldn't have kids."

I turn away to face the row of parked cars and the long line of red lights indicating all the taken spaces. Was there no daughter? Had Jessica Barnes been feeding me a line, parading a sick girl across the marble table between us, all in a successful effort to get me to raise my offer? Had every step of our meeting, from her hesitant entrance to her raw red hands, been part of a con? Had I been played like a sucker by a pro?

The very thought is delicious and I so want to believe it. But even as I let the hope rise to the surface of my consciousness, I know it to be false. And suddenly I understand exactly what the smear of blood is that Jessica Barnes had given me.

"There is a daughter," I say while still looking out at the long line of parked cars. "Adopted, or just given to Jessica Barnes to care for without the papers."

"Are you sure?"

"Jessica's mother didn't tell you to protect the little girl. She's with Jessica's husband somewhere, hiding out. My guess is they fear the daughter's next."

"Why would Jessica be killed because of her daughter?"

"That's the question. Find the daughter and you'll find your story."

"But Kip, I don't know how."

"If it was easy, any old reporter could do it, but you say you're not any old reporter. So use your especial talents, your smarts, your charm. Deconstruct the problem and find a solution on the slant. But I'll give you another lead. The little girl has a condition, something to do with excess copper in the blood. She isn't allowed to eat shrimp. There's a doctor treating her, with a name like Patticake or something. The doctor might get you a lead."

"How do you know all this?"

"Everyone has something to teach you, Duddleman, if you can bear to stay quiet enough to listen. And now I want you to listen to this. Whatever you're trying to learn, someone wants to keep hidden in the worst way, as Jessica Barnes found out. Be careful, and if you get scared, pull out."

"I won't get scared," she says. And that scares me.

Rule Three: Hard liquor keeps the bile down.

"He stares me down and grumbles under his breath like a surly teen, and so I say to him, I say, 'What's that you say, fuckface?'"

"And what does the blubberer say to that?" says Stony.

"Not a thing, not a damn thing. But he sure as hell grabbed hold of the envelope before I could take anything more out of it."

And they all burst out laughing, my new best friends, the Brotherhood of the Bag, barking their guffaws as Stony bangs on the tabletop. We are at Rosen's, of course, and the table is full of empty glasses and empty hats and ashtrays piled with spent cigarettes.

"Which surprised the hell out of me," I say, "because on the dumber-than-he-looks prop bet, I would have taken the over on Hanratty in a blink and lost my hat."

More laughter, peals of it, and I join in, my face reddening with hilarity.

"That's rich," says Miles Schimmeck.

"Indeed," says Hump.

"Aubrey," I call out to the surly bartender. "Five more Sazeracs."

And Maud just smiles like a proud mama, holding her cigarette in front of her, squinting as the smoke rises like a scar across her face. It's her doing, the welcome wagon at Rosen's, she is the one who has brought me into the club. I now bear the mark of her trust, and here on in I will be her responsibility.

Stony might be my new best friend, but Maud is the Sweetheart of Sigma Chi—*the blue of her eyes and the gold of her hair are a blend of the western sky*—and I am in love.

Rule Two: Everyone has a price, and every price is less than you think.

"I'm wondering," I say, "if you saw what Mr. Bettenhauser said in the press the other day."

"He's a war hero," says the man sitting across from me, speaking in a voice like the pebble-grain grip of a Smith & Wesson. His name is Thompson; he sells guns and shills for the NRA. The word on Thompson is that his support for the Congressman has been wavering, despite the envelopes he's pocketed in the past. It's startling how fickle the bought can be; it's enough to erode my faith in humanity. Thompson avoids my hard gaze by looking into the drink I paid for. "A lot of our members are veterans."

"Congressman DeMathis has the utmost respect for veterans," I say, "and his record on veterans' affairs has been spotless. I'm referring to Mr. Bettenhauser's statement on the Second Amendment."

Thompson looks up. Jowly and fair-haired, with a bristling crew cut, he raises his chin. "Was it in the paper?"

"Not yet. Bettenhauser made it at a fund-raising event that he thought was off the record."

"Then does it concern us?"

"Does the Second Amendment concern you? Does the right to shoot the stuffing out of hairy little varmints concern you? Does the vision of federal ATF agents swarming your store and rifling your records and hassling your customers concern you?"

"Is that what he's calling for?"

"He said, and I quote here, about the recent school shootings, that—and here it is, the quote—that, quote, 'Something needs to be done,' unquote."

"He said that?"

"Yes, he did. And I agree with him. Something does need to be done."

"What are you thinking?"

"A demonstration," I said. "Something grand and forceful. You know the drill. Signs, shouted slogans, a show of passion for our constitutional protections. Maybe even a waving American flag to demonstrate love of God and country. Bettenhauser's speaking to an environmental group at a hotel next week. It would be a perfect place to rally in support of the Constitution. Remember, the surest way to lose your rights is to take them for granted."

"Who said that? Reagan?"

"Sure," I say, taking an envelope from my bag and passing it across the table. "Saint Ron of the Bushmaster .223. Now here is enough to pay for the wooden posts and the paper and paint and the costs of organizing and putting the notice on your website, along with a small amount for your trouble. Think you can muster twenty to twenty-five?"

He waits a bit, making whatever calculation he needs to make to satisfy his scruples, before sliding the envelope into his lap. "That won't be a problem."

"More would be good," I say.

"I'll try."

"No violence."

"Of course not."

"But enough sign shaking to show the passion."

"What about the press?"

"We'll take care of the press," I say, "as well as today's bar bill. Another Maker's Mark?"

"Any questions?" said Stony as we finished another hard round of Old Fashioneds. "Anything not clear to your satisfaction?"

"Right now nothing is clear except the queasiness in my stomach," I said. The Briggs Mulroney Rules were becoming a muddle of hard liquor and secondhand smoke, but I suppose that's the way of it in the lower strata of politics. Maybe the lower strata of everything.

"Wait a second," I said, shaking my head and feeling my brain slosh about in my skull. "Wait one stinking second. What about rule number one? You didn't tell me rule number one."

"Rule number one," said Stony, "is the only rule you really need to know."

"Well, don't hold back now."

He raised a finger and lifted his chin. "Rule One: It doesn't matter a whit whose bag he carries or whose ass he wipes, a bagman works only for himself." When Stony ended the recitation, he lowered his gaze from the heavens to my beady eyes. "And don't you be forgetting that one."

"Don't worry, that one's in my DNA."

"My father used to tell me that it doesn't take a genius to carry a bag, but you need to be quick not to let go. The reports I have been getting show you to be quick enough."

"Reports?"

"Oh, Victor, my boy, you don't think we'd let you roam around our fair city with a bag of cash without keeping tabs. We can't have you skewing the rates for the rest of us."

"And I'm doing okay?"

"You're doing just dandy. And I might have a gift for you."

"For me? What ever could you have gotten for me, Stony?" I picked up my drink and gave it a swirl that matched the swirling of my stomach. "Other than a dose of Maalox."

"How about the goods on our friend Bettenhauser?"

"You got the goods on our self-righteous son of a bitch?"

"Come for a ride with me tomorrow and I'll spell it out for you. And bring your bag, boy, I've been building up quite a tab."

"I don't doubt it."

"Another round?"

"I drink another round, I'm going to get awfully stupid."

"Splendid," said Stony as he raised his hand. "You're slipping into the role like a pro."

CHAPTER 28

POLITICAL FAVORS

It wasn't all Briggs's Rules and underhanded payoffs, it wasn't all ugly hats and hard liquor. There were other distractions in the bagman game. Politics and sex: they go together like gin and tonic, like chipped steak and cheese, like syphilis and insanity. Let's just say one without the other would be beside the point. And as Stony pointed out, I was slipping into the role like a pro.

"Is that what you want?" I whispered into Ossana's ear. My voice was soft as a breath, a conspirator's sigh. "Is that the way you like it?"

It was later in the evening of our meeting at the Franklin, where we'd talked of dark secrets and monkeys' paws. She was laid out beneath me now, slim and pale, arms raised, copper hair tossed, neck turned, breasts rising with each breath above delicate ribs, legs still clad in those red fishnet stockings attached with black straps to a lace belt. I grabbed the inside of her knee and lifted her leg, I cupped a breast, I reached for her neck with my teeth. And all the while she was silent and complacent. There was no urgency in her, no quickening.

"I'm going to devour every inch of you," I said with a soft growl, and her eyes stared out with neither fear nor passion nor defiance.

It hadn't been like this with her clothes on; with her clothes on, it was like she could barely wait to get mine off. She was all urgency and rush and sharp teeth, grabbing and loosening, laughing, hurrying to meet some deadline of her own desire. I struggled to catch on, to catch up. "Whoa, Nellie," I said as she ripped at my shirt, buttons popping like popcorn in hot oil.

And then there I was, fully on board, yanking at her skirt, pressing my face between her cotton-covered breasts, feeling the power of ancient desire crest over us both. There is a moment when blood washes the newness off the thing, when the nervous hesitations fall away like iron shackles undone and all that is left is the raw wanting and the act itself. And we were there, both of us, I could feel it in her pulse, her breath, the pull of her teeth on the flesh of my breast.

I threw her on the bed and she laughed as I kissed her deep, and her shoulders rose as she reached her arms around my neck to kiss me back. We were on the precipice of pure abandon and then, like a switch, she turned.

And now I rubbed and kissed, caressed and stroked, and yet the deeper I reached, the less I found. She was pale and stretched and lovely and distant, as distant as a cold white star. I played rough, I played soft, I was silent, I bayed in my wanting. I was all manner of contradictory things, and none of it seemed to matter.

"Are you okay, Ossana?"

"Yes," she said.

"Has something happened?"

"No," she said.

I rose to my knees and stared down at her as she lay sprawled beneath me. Her soft skin glowed in its pallor, her red hair swept across her face and neck, her delicately lined palms were raised above her head like a bored go-go dancer at a second-rate club. The birds on her wrist meandered.

"Don't stop," she said, her voice now as flat as the gaze from her prairie eyes.

I grabbed her arm and pulled it to the left and it lay where I left it.

"Keep on," she said.

I shifted her red-clad leg, her other arm; she was a stuffed rag doll, amenable to my every whim. This was not what I'd expected, this pale passivity. This was not what lived in my feverish imaginings when all the possibilities had spurted through my perverted soul. And yet, and yet, my God this was beguiling, too.

She was passive as a corpse with blood-red stockings, and I couldn't get enough.

"Do you want a cigarette?" she said.

"I'd rather put your breast in my mouth."

"Still?"

"Oh, yes," I said. We were back in my apartment a few days after the first attempt—sadly, sans the red stockings, which I rather liked—trying again and ending with the same peculiar result.

"I thought you'd be plotting to get rid of me by now, shuffle me off to Buffalo."

"Oh, I'm plotting all right."

"You're not disappointed?"

"Puzzled."

"I'm a puzzler, I am. I even puzzle myself. My psychiatrist says I revel in being an enigma."

"So open up, tell me those deep dark thoughts of yours."

"Oh, Victor, isn't it enough to know they're paralytic? I want to forget them, not share them. That's why psychiatry doesn't work on me."

"Then why do you keep going?"

"It's like a form of yoga. I lie to her to empty my mind."

"Is that what sex is, a way to forget?"

"No, that's what alcohol is. Sex is what I use when the alcohol doesn't work."

"And thus . . ."

"Yes. Isn't it romantic?"

"We'll work on it."

"How chivalrous, Victor. You want to save me with your lance. But maybe I don't want to be saved."

"Tough."

"My sweet hard-boiled boy. You should wear your hat when you say that."

"You think?"

"Absolutely."

I rolled out of bed, headed to my living room, put on the hat and the beige raincoat with belt tied behind, grabbed my briefcase. Back in the bedroom, Ossana was sitting up now, one of her long legs bent at the knee and tilted over the other, her soft, full breasts pointing in opposite directions. When she saw me in my getup, her eyes brightened.

"The dashing bagman," she said.

"You bet I am."

"Now what are you going to do?"

"Take my cut."

"As long as you don't take off the hat."

"Don't worry," I said, moving onto the bed, crawling forward on my knees until I was straddling her, my hips over her pale hips, the trail of my raincoat covering us both.

"You are such the grimy political fixer," she said, her eyes widening with electricity that hadn't been there before.

"You bet I am, sister, and it's time to take your stinking payoff."

And I gave it to her, yes, I did. And there was no death this time. I'm not talking *la petite mort* the French go on about—oh, those overly dramatic French, experts in food, fashion, and fornication (and what do we get, fantasy football?). I'm talking the death of will I had seen in her eyes. She didn't turn into a corpse in the middle of it, passive as I had my way with her. This time she was a willing participant, and oh was she willing.

"You were like a different person," I said after, as I rubbed my nose between her breasts.

"Was I?"

"You know it, too."

"I stopped getting in the way."

I flicked a nipple with my tongue and looked up at her. She was staring at the ceiling. "So if it wasn't you, who was I having sex with?"

"An abstract interpretation of myself, a Rothko painting."

"Rectangular fields of color?"

"Yes. Black. Or blue. Or both, with a single line of red."

"Fishnet red."

"You liked?"

"Oh, yes. And if you were a Rothko, what was I?"

"You were a Jasper Johns."

"A flag?"

"And a hat. And a trench coat. And a bag."

"So it wasn't me you were screwing, it was the costume."

"My psychiatrist says I have a problem with intimacy."

"Your psychiatrist is a hack."

"Of course she is. I wouldn't dream of going to anyone who wasn't."

"You know, Ossana, I'm more than just a bagman."

"Don't ruin it, darling."

And there it was, now out in the open, the sad truth I was only just beginning to learn. We like to think we are in control of our destinies, that our tools toil in service to our ends. The Crusader wielded his sword to glorify God, but how long was it before the sword wielded him? And who among us are not slaves to our smartphones?

The bagman carries his satchel of sour political crimes all around the town, selling bits of his soul with each transaction designed to keep someone else's power flowing. How could he ever have expected that the bag wouldn't soon be lugging the man?

CHAPTER 29

POLLS

Have you seen the latest polls?" said Tom Mitchum in a hotel suite high in a tower just off the Parkway. He was standing at the window, looking out over his boss's fiefdom, his jacket off, his suspenders tight. "The numbers aren't pretty."

"Maybe your pollster could jazz up the charts," I said. "Add some color, use a better font."

"What Tom is trying to say," said the Congressman, giving me the stare and speaking slowly, as if I were a Frenchman, "is that we've lost ground despite your much-appreciated efforts."

"I'm doing what I can with the tools I have," I said.

"Do more," said Ossana DeMathis, standing in the corner with a drink in her hand. I turned my chin toward her and kept my eyes flat. That was how we were playing it, per her instructions, like nothing more than business associates, and since she was higher up in the organization, her instructions held. But there was a harshness in her voice I didn't like, a sense of overweening authority. I don't mind taking orders from someone I'm screwing—sometimes I actually like it—but I prefer it to be in bed.

I had been summoned to the suite to give a report on my activities. Politicians just love their hotel suites. Parked by the door was a service cart, with the leavings of a meal scattered across its linen-covered surface: half-eaten club sandwiches, a gnawed pile of bones, an empty bottle of Perrier. I hadn't been invited to the party portion of the afternoon. I wasn't the kind of employee you lunched with; I was the kind of employee you instructed to enter the hotel through the rear entrance. As for me, my only thought on looking around the room was that politics would be so much simpler without the politicians.

"So where are we on your efforts?" said Mitchum. "Tell us about your progress."

My progress?

I could have waxed about my descent into the shadowy netherworld where the gears of politics and money brutally mesh, about my journey into the inferno with my guide Stony Mulroney, about how Maud had ferried me across the River Stinks, and about how I'd finally found a world where the grit and grime matched the darkness at the root of my soul. Oh, I could have gone on and on, and bored them all to tears, but no one in that room, including me, was interested in metaphysics. And so instead I told them about the labor leader, about my run-in with Hanratty, the community sports organizer, about the ward leaders I had reached, the election judges, the opinion makers and local columnists.

"I've gone through the list Ossana gave me," I said. "We're right on track. And I'm setting up an anti-Bettenhauser demonstration that should move the needle on those polls of yours."

"What kind of demonstration?" said the Congressman.

"Tom told me what Bettenhauser said in response to the most recent school shooting. I paid the local NRA guy to picket Bettenhauser's environmental speech next week."

"You should have cleared that with me first," said Mitchum. "I'm not sure it's so wonderful to emphasize that Bettenhauser is pro–gun control and pro-environment at this point in the race."

"It's all in the packaging," I said. "We have to make sure the news reports show him as a divisive figure, an anti-gun crazy and a climate-change crazy at the same time. A daily double for your base."

"What does someone like you know about our base?" said Ossana.

"More than you would think," I said cheerfully. "One could say my whole career has been nothing but base."

"Maybe I should follow up with a speech about the need to reach across the aisle and build consensus," said the Congressman. "That always goes over well."

"Let's wait until after the primary to start reaching for the middle," said Mitchum. "How are you set for financing, Victor?"

"That's a problem," I said. "I told you about Mrs. Devereaux's unhappiness. She's cut off the spigot until you can convince her that her priorities are being looked at."

"I'll talk to her," said Mitchum.

"That won't do it. She wants to talk to the Congressman himself. What is it that she's after, anyway? She made it sound pretty specific."

"That's not your concern," snapped Ossana. "Just do what you need to do to keep her happy."

"I don't know if I'm man enough to keep her happy," I said. "I think six matadors and a stable of bulls aren't man enough to keep her happy."

"She is a feisty one all right," said the Congressman. "You find anything on Bettenhauser?"

"I've got a man on it who says he's found something interesting. I'll get you the details when I can."

"We don't want the details," said Mitchum. "We need deniability. Any dirt you find, give it to Sloane."

"Sloane? You trust that dirtball?"

"I trust his unabashed desire for a story," said Mitchum. "He'd eat dog shit if it got him the front page. Just make sure it's the dog shit we want him to eat."

"All right. Tom, Ossana," said the Congressman. "Why don't you leave Victor and me alone for a few moments?"

"You don't think it's better if I stay?" said Ossana.

"No, I don't," said the Congressman, with a straight razor in his voice. He sat there without looking at his sister, and I spied something on her face just then, a stain of anger that was more real and intimate than any emotion I had seen spill across her face in our nights of wanton sex. The emotion was so raw it was hard to look at, like I was stealing something. I turned my face away until she stalked out after Tom Mitchum and slammed the door behind her.

"My sister is . . . quite protective of me," said the Congressman.

"It must be nice. I'm an only child."

"In some ways you're lucky. I've been questioned about the Shoeless Joan murder by that Detective McDeiss. The police know you met with her."

"Yes."

"How did they know that?"

"Somebody led them to me."

"Who?"

"I don't know."

"Damn inconvenient. I refused to answer any questions, but McDeiss promised he'd be back with an immunity offer to make me talk. Is there anything I need to know?"

"Just tell the truth."

"He'll want to know what she was blackmailing me with."

"Yes."

"Did she say anything when you met with her?"

"No."

"Nothing about her secret?"

"No."

"Did she give you anything?"

"No."

"You're sure?"

"Yes."

"Good. Good. Hopefully, they'll solve the thing before he gets back to me. Now this is what I really wanted to talk to you about." He leaned forward, twisting one hand in the other. "Have you heard from Miss Duddleman? She doesn't answer my calls, she's not at her home when I stop by . . ."

"I don't want to be the one to break it to you, but maybe she's moved on."

"She couldn't, not so easily. You don't know what we were together. She wouldn't just go off without telling me, or at least having a scene of some sort."

"She does love her scenes."

"I want you to find her for me, Victor."

"I don't know if that's such a—"

"I can't work, I can't function. I don't care about the job, the election, anything. I want you to tell her that. Have you ever been in love?"

"You're married."

"What does that matter?"

"She's half your age."

"She makes me feel half my age. I'm not asking for your permission, Victor, I'm asking for your help. You're the only one who can get through to her. Find her. Talk to her. Make sure she's okay. Tell her I am desperate to see her, to touch her. Tell her that I love her."

"You want me to tell Amanda Duddleman that you love her?"

"If that's what it takes for her to return my calls. If she doesn't want to see me anymore, I'll have to accept that. I'll move on. But, Victor, I need to know."

"Okay."

"You'll talk to her?"

"Yes."

"Thank you."

"But don't get your hopes up. She's an independent one, that Duddleman."

"I know. I know. It drives me crazy."

"No arguments on that."

On the way out of the suite, bag in one hand and hat in the other, I was stopped by Ossana with a palm on my chest. She pulled me into a bedroom, closed the door, kissed me hard. I let her, but I didn't join in the party.

"I guess he doesn't know about us," I said when my mouth was free.

"No, of course not. No one can know."

"I understand. I wouldn't want to ruin your reputation."

"Oh, Victor, you're hurt. How charming."

"I'm not hurt, I'm just trying to figure out your whole screwy family."

"Don't be impertinent. What did my precious brother want?"

"It's private."

"It's my brother, there's nothing private between us."

"Except me fucking you."

"Don't be crude."

"I thought that's what you liked. If you want to know what he asked me, ask him."

"But you can't tell me."

"No."

"You have rules."

"Yes."

"You can screw me, but you can't confide in me."

"Precisely."

"Lawyers."

"Trained to infuriate," I said, putting on my hat.

CHAPTER 30

THE GOODS

I'm in Stony's car for a stakeout," I said.

"The black Lincoln," said Hump.

"What else would I drive?" said Stony.

"And Stony's wedged between the steering wheel and the seat like a great suited Buddha. I see these two huge thermoses, one green, one silver, each the size of a rocket ship."

"What on earth were you doing in Stony's car for a stakeout?" said Maud, sitting back, the smoke from her cigarette failing to mask her incredulity. Rosen's was quiet, neat and empty, except for our corner banquette table, which was covered with empty lowballs, overflowing ashtrays, hats, always hats, and the usual choking cloud of smoke. The Brotherhood was in session.

"Because of his other line," I said. "His investigation line."

"Stony has an investigation line?" said Miles Schimmeck. "The man hasn't spied his own pecker in twenty years."

"Just because I haven't seen it doesn't mean I don't know where it is or how to use it," said Stony.

"He told me he took a course," I said.

"In using his pecker?" said Miles.

"Investigations, you ninny," said Stony.

"Did he try to sell you a new bathroom, too?" said Maud.

"Yes, actually."

"Don't take him up on that."

"'Twas just that once," said Stony.

"When it comes to toilets," said Hump, "once is enough."

"So these two huge thermoses, right?" I said. "And I'm thinking, that's a crapload of coffee. There's no way we can drink that much in a single night. And then he tells me, he says—"

"'Only one of them thermoses is for the coffee,'" said Hump.

Our laughter rose sharply and lingered until it devolved into a fit of coughing. Liquor was swallowed, empty glasses were slammed on the table, cigarettes were lit, more Sazeracs were ordered.

"You don't got to tell me about them thermoses," said Hump. "Stony and me, we had business together one night in Atlanta."

"A contractor on the lam who ate the salad and disappeared," said Stony. "I brought in Hump to make my point."

"Stony said it was easier to drive than to fly. Longest damn drive of my life."

"That was a four-thermos drive," said Stony.

"Well?" said Maud to me.

"Well, what?" I said.

"Did you find what you were looking for?"

"I might not be great at toilets," said Stony, "but I always get my man."

He had left the school with a glance behind him, like he was skipping out for a bout of truancy. The kind of look you give before you hide behind the trees and pull out a doobie. But he wasn't a kid planning on stoning away his afternoon; he was Tommy Bettenhauser, AP civics teacher and congressional candidate, sneaking out for something else.

"Hold on to your hat," Stony had said, and off we went.

We trailed him from far behind, so far behind I was sure Stony would lose him. "Pour me some coffee there, Road Dog. From the green thermos." And I did as we jerked from lane to lane, and Stony only spilled some of it on his tie as we kept moving.

"Road Dog?"

"Another of my daddy's rules," said Stony. "If you forget a name, just hand out a nickname. No one ever forgets a nickname. You look like a dog I once saw on the side of the road. Ergo."

"You forgot my name?"

"Well, you have two first names. How the hell am I supposed to remember which is which?"

"Ergo."

"That's right, ergo. Now keep your eyes peeled. I don't want to lose him."

He drove us through the wilds of West Philly, all the way east into an old industrial section, which was on its fifth bout of redevelopment. I looked left and right, peering past the van ahead of us, all the time looking for Bettenhauser's car and seeing nothing. I had severe doubts about Stony's technique—he seemed constitutionally unable to keep Bettenhauser's blue Prius in sight—but he kept moving forward, until he parked on the left side of a busy one-way street and waited for a truck to pass us by before pointing down and across the road.

A blue Prius. And Tommy Bettenhauser, stepping out. Being greeted with a hug by a pretty woman with thin arms and pale-blonde hair.

"Well done," I said.

"Hand me the camera in the glove compartment."

It was a digital SLR with an absurdly long zoom lens. Stony turned it on, unlocked the lens, zoomed it out, and started snapping.

"Who is she?" I said.

Click, click.

“Do we know the relationship?” I said.

Click, click.

Arm in arm, Bettenhauser walked with the woman toward the open front door of a row house not far from where he’d parked. Halfway in, he looked back over his shoulder as if searching for ghosts.

Click, click.

The door closed behind him.

“And now,” Stony had said, “we wait. Do me a favor, Road Dog, and hand over the silver thermos.”

“What did you get out of it, your little surveillance?” said Maud.

“Photographs,” said Stony. “A lovely couple, all hugs and kisses. Printed out in grainy black and white to give the snaps a nicely sordid quality. Nothing spells vice like black and white.”

“I got to give you credit there, Stony,” said Miles Schimmeck. “You always had an eye. Who are you slipping them pictures to?”

“They’re not mine to slip,” said Stony.

“Stony told me I ought to give them to the press,” I said. “That I should let some daring reporter do the dirty work so I could sit back and let the scandal rage without my fingerprints.”

“Too iffy,” said Miles. “Some editor with scruples might spike the whole thing.”

“An editor with scruples?” said Maud. “I heard of one once.”

“He was riding a unicorn,” said Hump.

“Aubrey,” called out Stony. “Five more.”

“Give them to the wife,” said Miles. “That always delivers the biggest bang. And then you get the leaving-the-race-for-the-good-of-the-family speech, which never fails to crack me up.”

"The wife angle works unless she's a regular Patti Page," said Hump, "who decides to stand by her man."

"I hate that standing-by-their-man nonsense," said Stony. "There ought to be a law against that."

"It was Tammy Wynette," said Maud.

"Who the hell cares?" said Miles.

"Mr. Wynette."

"One copy to the wife, another to the newspaper, a third to some TV weather-chick looking to be taken seriously by the news director," said Miles. "Cover all your bases. That's old school."

"What's new school?" I said.

"Just give it to a PAC," said Maud.

Miles and Hump and Stony grumbled at the suggestion even as they nodded in acquiescence.

"Let those fat bastards turn it into a commercial," said Maud. "Let them blast it twenty-four-seven over the airwaves until the public can't bear the sight of it or him."

"That way," said Hump, "it don't even need to be true."

"And your boss can pump up all self-righteous," said Miles, "and deny he had anything to do with it."

"It's too damn easy," said Stony. "The Big Butter takes all the art out of it."

"It's a crime, what they done to the business," said Miles. "Before them we was like Briggsy said, princes of the city. Now it's scraps from the scrap heap for us if we're lucky. It ain't the same as it was."

"What is?" said Hump.

"Me," said Miles. "I'm the same. I got the same hair I had when I was sixteen."

"Just not as much of it," said Stony.

"I got plenty still," said Miles, serious as all hell as he rubbed a hand over that precious comb-over. "One thing I always had was a good head of hair."

Aubrey brought over the drinks and there was quiet as the barman laid them one by one before us. Stony raised his glass in a toast and we joined in.

"To Miles's hair," he said.

"To Miles's hair," we said back.

"Long may it wave," said Stony.

We assented, we drank, Miles Schimmeck looked around, wondering what all the fuss was about.

"My hair, it ain't wavy," he said.

"Sure it is, Miles," said Hump. "It's waving good-bye."

"A bunch of stinking kidders," said Miles before he took a long inhale from his cigarette. "Hey, Hump, remember a few years back, one of your ward boys was having a problem with his landlord. His family was staring an eviction in the face. Out on the street in the middle of the winter."

"I remember."

"Turned out this guy's landlord was having trouble with a court case. One slim envelope in the right hand and everyone's problem was solved. And we got a record turnout in that ward the next election. That's the way the game used to be played. That's the way the city used to work."

"Anyone in my territory had a problem," said Hump, "they went to their ward leader, who came to me."

"And we took care of things for each other," said Miles.

"Indeed."

"But not no more," said Miles.

"We don't matter like we did," said Maud. "When the Big Butter can pour Wall Street money into any race it chooses, the little guys get forgotten. Why waste capital on a single worker here or a single family there when there are batches of television ads to run?"

"It's the new American way," said Hump, "and it counts us out."

"Stop your whining and look alert," said Stony. "We've got company."

And there he came, walking past the rows of empty tables, pointing at Aubrey the barman as if Aubrey were a dear personal friend he was spotting from the red carpet, sucking his teeth and sauntering toward us as if we were his bestest pals in all the world. We snatched up our drinks to fortify ourselves as he came closer. With orthopedic shoes, schlumpy jacket on a schlump of a frame, thick tie, ink-stained fingers, yellow teeth, he was a form of life even lower than the lice crawling through his thinning hair.

Harvey Sloane, ace reporter, and like a rocky-road addict, always looking for a scoop.

CHAPTER 31

PRESS CONFERENCE

"Well, well, well. What have we here?" said Sloane as he reached our table. "Never has there been such a disreputable contingent of political rascals meeting in this fair city since Frank Rizzo drank alone."

"Didn't I tell you to stay the hell out of Rosen's?" said Stony.

"In case you haven't heard, Mulroney, it's a free country. But don't worry your three chins about it, I didn't come for you. If I need to talk to you, I can just rattle the Dumpster behind police headquarters. No, I came for your pal Victor."

"Lucky me," I said.

"Last time we spoke, Victor, your precise words were, and I quote, 'I'm nobody's bagman.' And yet you've been bouncing around town with a bag stuffed with money and a god-awful hat. And now here you are, yukking it up with the rest of these ticks on the body politic."

"Tick tock tick," said Maud.

"So, Victor, care to change your previous denial?"

"Go to hell."

"The atmosphere in here has turned," said Maud, crushing out her cigarette and standing. "I need fresh air."

"Give my regards to the mayor, Maud," said Sloane, "and tell him that we're looking into that courthouse deal you sold him on.

Tell him it's like a rotting goat head the way it stinks, and that the maggot crawling out of the eye has got your name on it."

"It's a clean deal," said Maud.

"Sure, as clean as the rest of this foul little gathering."

"What's the problem?" said Miles Schimmeck, grabbing his hat and sliding around the booth after Maud made her exit. "I showered last week."

"I'll stop the presses on that, Schimmeck. You know our latest exposé of Traffic Court has your name in it. Better get a lawyer."

"I got me a mouthpiece," said Miles. "Victor here."

"Did I ever tell you what happened to my father?" said Stony.

"Over and over," said Miles.

"Then you know when the wretches of the press show up, it's time to go."

"You're abandoning me to this?" I said.

"Indeed we are," said Hump, grabbing his hat.

"Like rats leaving a sinking ship," said Sloane.

"And with a song in our hearts," said Stony. "'Taps.' Try to stay off the front page, Road Dog."

I watched the three men crush out their cigarettes, grab hold of their bags, set their hats in place. They hustled out of the restaurant like they were each wearing sunglasses, and the farmer's wife was chasing them with a knife.

Sloane watched them leave with a raised eyebrow and then slid into the banquette across from me. He cleared a space at the table for his little memo pad, leaned forward, paged forward, rubbed his teeth with a forefinger.

"You're in the shit, Victor," said Sloane.

"That's what you came to tell me?"

"Truth is, I came to help you, unlike those creeps you're drinking with, who will end up burying you if they have their way. You might not know it, but I'm the best friend you've still got."

"If that's true, I am in the shit."

"I hear you might have something for me."

"Is that what you heard?"

"Victor, sweetheart, it's just you and me now. We can cut the adversarial act we put on for your friends, *capiche*? Don't be coy, give it up to Papa."

I knew what he was after: the photographs Stony had snapped of Bettenhauser and the blonde. It seemed the most ordinary of things to pull the envelope from my diplomatic bag and slip it across the table. After all, what came more naturally to a bagman than pulling out an envelope and slipping it across a table? And yet I wondered how he knew about the photographs. Something in me smelled a rat, though I suspected, even then, that the rat in that deal was sitting across from Sloane.

"I got nothing," I said after a long moment of thought. "Sorry."

"You sure?"

"I'm sure. Where'd you hear I had something for you, anyway?"

"A little birdie. Well, not so little."

"If something comes up, you'll be my first call."

"That's wise. I am so looking forward to some new scandal to grab all of our attentions. But until then, we're stuck with the old ones, so I wonder if I can get a comment on some scuttlebutt that's been scuttling around police headquarters. I'm going to tell you what I heard and then I'll take down your comments word for word." He poked the memo pad with the point of his pen. "Ready?"

"Knock yourself out."

"I heard you are more than a person of interest in the murder case of poor Jessica Barnes. I heard you have become suspect number one."

"Where did you hear that?"

"I have my sources. Any comment?"

"No comment," I said.

Sloane wrote it down dutifully. "Here's the story that's being spread. You made a payoff to this Jessica Barnes at a bar called the Franklin, a payoff to keep her from spilling on the Congressman."

I tried to keep my head still, tried to keep my gaze from wavering.

"You gave her an envelope filled with money and then, when she left the bar, you left right after. The story then goes that you followed her, you called out her name, caught up with her, led her into an alley. And there, you killed her through repeated and savage blows with a hammer to her face."

Something rolled into my eye and started it to stinging. I tried to blink the stinging away, but my efforts failed. I blinked harder.

"You killed her for the money, so they're saying, and you killed her to keep her quiet, and you left her to bleed to death in that stinking alley. And after you killed her, you put the cash in your pocket, ditched the hammer and her shoes, and went home to put on your tuxedo so you could party with the governor."

I tried to stay still, still as a statue, but my hands tightened, one in the other, until the knuckles cracked, and my face twitched like an electrified monkey.

"Any comment?" said Sloane.

"No comment," I said.

"No gasps of disbelief?"

"Gasp," I said.

"No protestations of innocence?"

"I'm Jewish," I said.

Sloane smiled as he wrote it all down.

"Can we go off the record?"

"Sure, pal," he said before closing his pad. "Off the record."

"You told me once you wanted to get it right, so I'm telling you, off the record, that this is all the purest of bullshit. Jessica Barnes and I might have shared a drink at the Franklin, but after that it's a lie, all of it. And if I find out who is spreading this goddamn lie, I'm going to wring his stinking neck. And if you do the spreading, the chicken neck I'll be wringing will be yours. They say when the head pops off and falls to the ground, the chicken keeps running around in circles while the blood spurts. *Capiche*?"

"So you're denying it."

"On the record now?"

"Yeah, sure." He opened his notebook. "On the record."

"No comment."

He stared at me and then closed his notebook again.

"I've spent enough time on your front page," I said. "I know how the headline will read if I start responding to all these lies: BAGMAN DENIES STEALING FOOTWEAR OFF CORPSE OF SHOELESS JOAN. So I'm not going to give you a denial, I'm not going to give you anything you can run with other than the off-the-record knowledge that it's all bullshit."

"Fair enough," said Sloane. "Are you sure you don't have anything else you want to give to me off the record?"

"I'm sure."

"Pity," he said, stuffing his memo pad in his jacket and standing. "If you could give me something splashy to put on the front page, anything at all, I could take the heat off of you. And Victor, trust me when I say you could use the cooling off."

As he walked away, I turned my attention back to the empty glasses and butt-strewn ashtray and tried to gauge my exact position. It was as if the ashtray were a giant rock, the empty glasses were hard places, and I was caught in between. The game was trying to figure out how to keep the whole thing going long enough to collect a few more paydays before I got ground to dust.

"Oh, by the way, Victor," said Sloane, who had stopped his egress to get in one last shot. "Just so you know, the police found the murder weapon."

"Good," I said, without surprise and without looking up at him. "They'll do their tests and know I had nothing to do with it."

"They did their tests," said Sloane. "It was a hammer, and the bloody handle is lousy with your prints."

My chin rose suddenly as if jerked by a rein. Sloane was staring at me with a sly smile on his ugly face.

"Any comment now?" he said.

"Fuck off."

"The funny thing is," he said, "you finally gave me something to print."

And then I was left alone at the table, stewing in a toxic mix of fear and anger and disgust as I tried to figure how my fingerprints could have ended up on the bloody goddamn hammer. After enough stewing and figuring, I reached into my bag, took out my prepaid phone registered to Jack Herbert, and sent a text to Duddleman:

NEED TO TALK, IMMEDIATELY!

I had just pressed "send" when someone approached. I tossed the phone into my bag as if I had been caught at something, looked up, and saw him standing there, tall and imperious, Aubrey the barman, with his circular tray.

Those sons of bitches, once again they had stuck me with the check.

CHAPTER 32

TEXTUS INTERRUPTUS

When you're up against it, and the ground beneath your feet is avalanching away, sometimes the only thing to do is dance.

I raise her bare leg and nibble at the arch of her foot, nuzzle the hollow behind her knee, leave a trail of kisses down the inside of her soft white thigh. She tastes of soured candy corn and kaleidoscopes.

I wasn't sure I liked Ossana DeMathis—there was something distant and dark in her manner, something defiant, even if it was unclear what she was defiant about, and she had treated me like a British manservant in her brother's hotel suite, and that had pissed off the raw American in me—but I sure did like dancing with her, horizontal and naked as a mole rat. When she showed up at my apartment in a long diaphanous skirt, with spiky heels and a hesitant twitch of her painted lips, as she apologized for her sharp words, I didn't hesitate. Having sex with Ossana, I felt like a serf drinking the nectar from some royal fruit banned from the common folk; it was sweet, yes, with just the right amount of electric tang, but, even better, it was ecstatically forbidden. She was connected and aristocratic and haughty, she was a delicious prize of this political world that I had fallen into, and, famished for success as I had been, I couldn't get enough of her.

I suck the diamond hanging from the lobe of her ear, hard and cold, just like she, and then run my tongue down from her neck, circling each nipple, where I can't help but linger, and then down into the soft pillow of her belly, and then down again. She tastes of fire, she smells of pure wanting, my wanting. I bury myself in her, and her legs rise this time on their own, as if on a string, and her thighs press against my skull so that I can hear the pulsing of my own blood.

I was following JFK's lead, asking not what my country could do for me, but whom I could do for my county. The "whom" was Ossana, red-haired Ossana, pale-skinned Ossana, green-eyed, thin-legged, and small-wristed Ossana, with nipples like soft red berries that released their juice to tongue and tooth, Ossana, yes, Ossana, that Ossana, cold, aloof, and all-too-willing Ossana.

I pull myself forward, kiss her hard, feel her fighting not to respond even as I can feel the tremble of her jaw.

This was how she liked it, Ossana, hard and active from above, Ossana, even as she lay passive beneath. Again, at the start, she had taken the lead and raised the pitch, but in the middle she took off my hat and tossed it aside and then became lost to herself, Ossana.

I remain propped above her pale, thin body with my arms outstretched, kissing her lightly, massaging her still mouth with my lips and tongue and teeth as I dip with the relentless rhythm of a bassist, feeling the vibration of her body as if my desire were a string within her plucked over and again.

That hat depersonalized me. With it I was just a political tool, a sharp shard of her brother's power. She could respond to power, make cruel love to power, even if it was power twice removed. But without the hat I was someone real and distinct and for some sad reason that drove her to the vanishing point. What I had learned of Ossana was that in the middle of sex with someone real, she dissolved into the moment and became less than herself. Sex for her was like a drug or a long skein of drinks, a place to hide. And when I asked if she was okay, she languidly placed her arms around my neck, and when I asked if she wanted me to stop, she pulled me close and breathed her soft exhortations in my ear.

I turn her over, approach her from the side like a wrestler, lift her with one hand as I sweep her legs beneath her with the other. Like this I can only see the shapes of her, the arched torso, the thin arms reaching forward, the thin wrist turned, the slivers of neck beneath the brilliant swirl of copper, the line of her calf. She is all the more alluring in parts. We are equal now, both symbols to each other, and I rise above her, working hard, sweating hard, working it hard, as if with her laid out like that before me I can somehow screw myself tighter and ever tighter into consequence.

And the buzzing I hear has to be the buzzing of my blood, the buzzing of my desire, as regular as the pounding pulse in my brain. On and off, on and off like a . . .

Oh, crap.

"I have to get that," I said.

"You're kidding, right?"

"No."

"You're taunting me now."

"I will if that's what you want," I said. "But I have to answer this."

It wasn't my regular phone; my regular phone was an emissary from the regular world, a place of struggle and travail, which I could happily exile far beyond the fertile walls of this moment. But the other phone, the Jack Herbert phone, was a lifeline I couldn't ignore. I left the bed with a grunt and made my way to the bag. I glanced back to see the expression on Ossana's face. She was no longer a bunch of disparate parts, she was a whole and she was appalled, as if in the middle of sex I had pulled out a corned beef sandwich.

At least it wasn't a complete loss.

I grabbed the phone and found the text.

YOU WONT BELVE WHT I FOUND!! UNION TRANSFER, 2ND FLR TIL MIDNIGHT.

It was already after eleven. I sent Duddleman a quick reply and dropped the phone back into my bag. When I returned to the bed, Ossana was on her back, the pale lovely length of her covered with a sheet. I sat beside her and leaned down to kiss her. She turned her head and so I kissed her neck.

"I have to go."

"I feel like I should be insulted."

"This is business. Your business."

"What kind of business?"

"I can't tell you, but I have to go. You wouldn't want me to slack when it comes to your brother."

"No, I wouldn't want that."

In the bathroom I slipped off my condom and showered the sex off my skin. As she watched languidly from my bed, I dressed quickly, putting on a suit.

"Will you be here when I come back?" I said into the mirror as I tied tight a narrow black tie.

"Do you want me to be?"

"Oh, yes," I said. "There are terrible things I still intend to do to you."

That twitch of her lips. "Don't be full of empty threats, Victor."

Before leaving the apartment I put on my coat and my hat. Then I stopped in the kitchen, opened a drawer, and pulled out the envelope Jessica Barnes had given me. My next lead for the intrepid Amanda Duddleman.

CHAPTER 33

UNION TRANSFER

Union Transfer is a rock club on Spring Garden that I knew of but till then had successfully avoided. Crowded all-night venues for obscure rock bands, where I could skulk in the back and feel out of place as hipsters hopped and twirled before the stage and shouted out the lyrics to songs I had never heard before, were no longer my kind of place. They were fine in the late nights of my early adulthood, but my life took on a different cast once I embarked on the downward trajectory of my failed career. Now I preferred quieter places with cleaner undertones of desperation that better matched my mood.

Yet here I was, making my way through the crowd loitering at the door, fresh young folk with cigarettes and beers, far cooler than I had ever been, who looked to have just rolled off their couches and into the night. It might not have been my type of place, but it surely was Duddleman's, and I liked that she had asked to meet me there. It meant she was getting back to herself.

The crowd made way as if for a leper as I walked up to the ticket window.

"One," I said.

The woman inside, all tattoos and piercings, with bright, pretty lips, didn't bat an eye at my suit and tie and trilby. "Fifteen dollars."

"Who's playing?"

"Why?"

"I just want to know."

She looked at me as if she had heard it before, heard it all stinking night. I gave her the money and examined the ticket. I guess with The Who and The Guess Who already taken, WHY? was the only band name left.

Just inside the door was an anteroom where T-shirts and ice cream and CDs were being sold, and then beyond that was the main space, large and open and steampunk in design, with lights darting here and there, the room dark, bouncing, mobbed, loud, chaotic.

The band of the night was onstage, the lead singer mixing rap and song over the heavy bass line. The young and the earnest were pressed to the front as the singer exhorted and the crowd shouted back and the lead guitarist tore it up. I walked into the least crowded area in the room, just in front of the soundboard. Behind me was a rise leading to a bar area with scattered tables. Above me a metal balcony ringed the room, every inch of rail leaned on by patrons looking coolly down at the stage. In the rear, behind the balcony, was a set of bleachers upon which a gang of carousers stood and shouted. I spun around as I searched. I didn't spot Duddleman, but she was there, somewhere.

Within the pressing, hypnotic four-four beat, I made my way to a stairwell on the far side of the room. I had to maneuver past stoned dancers, around couples making out, through a horde that barely shifted to let me through, as the singer shouted out his mystifying lyrics, and the music throbbed, and the ceiling lights spun.

Just as I reached the stairs, I saw someone watching me, his eyes uneasily trained on mine.

He was thin, with a sparse beard, wearing a loose flannel shirt, just another weaselly face in the weaselly crowd, but this face stared at me as if I was somehow familiar to him.

And then he backed away before turning and disappearing into the waves of sound and the writhing mob.

It didn't come to me just then, or as I climbed the stairs, but when I reached the second level, I took a moment to grab a spot on the balcony rail and look down, hoping to catch sight of the man again. And I did. I caught the check of his shirt as he pushed his way hurriedly toward a doorway by the stage. He stopped for a moment and looked behind, as if he were being chased, as if he were being chased by me. And suddenly I placed him.

The skinny wretch I had caught rifling my apartment, standing among the wreckage, holding onto my bag as I came out of my bedroom, before some other wretch knocked me into next week. One of the bastards who had placed my prints on the bloody hammer and then buried the hammer in my drawer.

I leaned forward and looked close and saw him grab at another man whose back was turned. He said something to the man and then they both turned and looked up at the second floor, not at me, and not at the bleachers, but at someplace behind the bleachers, as if something back there was of more concern to them than the likes of Victor Carl. They rushed off, escaping out of the room, but not before I recognized the second man, too, the son of a bitch. I recognized him right off, and as soon as I did, I grew scared, very scared, and not just for myself.

I tore away from the rail and fought my way through a bobbing throng to the back of the second level, behind the bleachers. It was an empty space dimly lit and filled only with the shrieking guitar, and the solid wall of bass, and the singer shouting words like nonsense all in time to the beat, the steady, steady beat.

Each second that passed drove the desperation until it nearly clogged my throat. I shouted for her, but my shouts were lost in the darkness, lost in the music, and with every beat I became ever more certain as to what had happened, and what I would find, hoping all the while I was wrong, so wrong.

And then I saw the shape of a leg, just peeking out behind a table in a far corner of the space, one long thin leg, stockinged in black, with no shoe.

CHAPTER 34

REDHEAD

When I returned to my apartment in the early morning hours, everything was different, everything was cleaner.

My hate, for instance, was no longer diffuse and general, but hard and glowing, sharp as a scythe. And my purpose was now as directed as a missile; suddenly I had answers to Timothy's three questions, answers as cold and hard as my hate. And my profile, too, was cleaner, for I no longer wore the hat, that ludicrous gray trilby that made me look like a lothario pol from the fifties. I had tossed it into a garbage can outside the rock club, letting it nestle amidst the empty bottles, half-chewed sandwiches, and vomit, where it belonged.

Well, not everything was cleaner. My apartment itself was utterly trashed. I had straightened it from its earlier ransacking, put the crap back in the proper crap drawers, stitched up what daggered couch cushions could be saved, turning bad side down so that the scars were hidden, and replaced those that couldn't be sewed. It had almost seemed good as new, but not anymore. All the drawers again were pulled open and emptied, all the cushions again were slashed, the floor again was strewn with my crap.

And in the middle of this unholy mess, curled on a chair and wearing nothing but one of my starched white shirts, the shirt open just enough to uncover the ruby point of a single breast, was Ossana, her lips ripe and swollen, her hair a red swarm, her long legs bare and pale and pulled up beneath her, her green eyes so heavily ringed with mascara they appeared bruised.

I looked around at the ruin of my apartment, so precise a representation of the ruin of my political dreams, and kept my expression matter-of-fact, as if finding my apartment in such a state were no more remarkable than finding a fat man at McDonald's. Everything was now on the table. Good.

"Looking for something?" I said.

"A cigarette. I was desperate. I remembered too late that you don't smoke. What took you so long?"

"An unexpected tragedy. There's been a murder."

"I'm sorry to hear that," she said without an ounce of sorrow. "Anyone I know?"

"Just a reporter."

"In that case."

I walked over to the easy chair where she sat, leaned over, reached down and cupped her breast with my hand, put my jaw on the top of her head, smelled her scent, warm and rich with still an undertone of sex. "Have you been in touch with your friend Colin Frost? How's his rehab going?"

"Quite well, from what I hear," she said. "He should be out soon."

"Won't that be a party."

"Why are you bringing up Colin? Are you worried he'll take your job once he's out?"

"Which job is that, working for your brother or working on you?"

She shrugged my chin from her head and pulled my hand away. "Don't be crude."

"I thought that's the way you liked it." I took a handful of her hair and brought my mouth close to hers. "Hard and crude and impersonal."

Her lips twitched into a cruel smile. "I do like it better when I can't see your face."

I leaned forward, brushed my lips across her eye, and then put my mouth at her ear. "Who are you imagining when you can't see my face? Colin?"

"Are you obsessed with Colin Frost, Victor? My God, you sound jealous."

I kissed her neck. "It's just that I thought I saw him tonight."

"Impossible. The facility he's in is very secure. It doesn't allow its patients to just up and leave as they will."

"Prudent policy."

She bent her head back, exposing her long pale neck. "I've been waiting."

I had the bright vampiric urge to take a bite, a large one, a real mouthful. Instead, I let go of her hair, looked at my hand, pulled a strand of red from between my fingers. She turned her head to face me as I put the strand into my shirt pocket and I stared into those eyes, so wide, so green, green as jade, so accomplished at hiding what was behind them.

"I'm sorry you waited for nothing," I said, "but I'm no longer in the mood. A bloody murder tends to do that to me. Not to mention the hours I was held for questioning by the police, and then the hostile interrogation by Detective McDeiss. But at least my absence gave you the opportunity to look around my apartment. For cigarettes, I mean."

"Sometimes I just have such an urge. Did you take the lock of my hair as a keepsake?"

"Something to moon over on full moons. It's not here, you know. It was when they first came up here looking for it. But they missed it. That's the problem with hiring drug addicts to do your dirty work. I think you would have been clever enough to find it—I'm sure of it, actually—except it's not here anymore."

"What are you talking about, Victor?"

"Let's not be coy when just a few hours before we were screwing like unhinged rodents. I'm talking about the proof Jessica Barnes gave to me. You asked for it, your brother asked for it, Melanie Brooks asked for it, even Detective McDeiss pressed me for it. Everybody so desperately wants it, but I don't have it anymore."

"That's too bad. It would have been useful to have."

"How far does it go, you shilling for your brother? Is screwing me part of the job?"

"We all have unpleasant duties."

"Don't we," I said, and then I leaned forward again and kissed her. And she kissed me back, with a bit of urgency in her tongue now, the kind of urgency that would have boiled my blood just a few hours before. I made it seem like it was hard to pull away, I made it seem like I wasn't ready to vomit into her mouth.

"The reporter who was murdered was young and bright and idealistic," I said, "and remarkably pretty. She was getting her life together. Her future would undoubtedly have been brilliant."

"You sound like you were a little in love with her."

"I liked her, very much, actually." I backed away to get a gander at the whole of her. "But it was your brother who was in love with her."

"My brother has his unfortunate infatuations," she said a little too quickly. She pulled her legs further beneath her. There was an expression of distaste, as if she had eaten a rotten clam, but there was no shock or puzzlement, no wondering what was what.

Maybe there had been a bulletin on the radio. Maybe she had been texted the news by her brother. Or maybe she had peeked at my phone while I was in the shower and gave the order herself. Maybe she was a pawn in someone else's game. Or maybe she was a murderous bitch who needed to be put down. Maybe she was a damsel in distress. Yeah, that was it, and I was Richard the Lionheart back from the Crusades.

"The reporter was looking into the Shoeless Joan murder," I said. "And wouldn't you know it, she ended up shoeless herself. It's become a dangerous business, this whole thing, and I have to tell you, Ossana, I have the strange feeling that I might be the next one to lose my footwear."

"Don't be dramatic, Victor. It doesn't become you."

"Neither does death. That's why you didn't find what you were looking for. It was too hot for me, too damn dangerous. I gave it away."

A twitch and an impatient tightening of her lips. "That was imprudent of you. To whom?"

"To someone with very explicit instructions on what to do with it if anything happens to me."

"That's the best you could do?"

"I'm not clever enough to have devised something richer."

"What ever am I going to do with you?"

"Keep me alive," I said. "Keep me employed."

And those words, like an incantation, magically eased her concern. I was still on a line, her line, her brother's line, on the line of this whole political world of easy money and easier virtue. She stood up, lifted her arms in the air and stretched like a cat. She took a step forward, placing her arms atop her head so that I could see the flock of birds fluttering on her wrist.

"You still want to work for my brother?"

"I still want to be paid by him."

"At least you're true to form, I'll give you that. I love men without surprises."

"I know where I've been, I'm not going back."

"But there is something different about you, Victor, a new taste I can't quite put my tongue on."

"I'm seeing everything more clearly."

"Even me?"

"Especially you."

She took another step forward, and another. She lowered her arms onto my shoulders and tilted her head so that her green eyes stared up into my own. "And what do you see, Victor?"

"That you were right about your darkness being darker than mine."

"You don't know the half of it." She pulled my head close and kissed me, tried to slip her tongue through my unmoving lips, was checked by my teeth. "Oh my, I see why you like it like that. It's like kissing a dead man, what could be richer? Are you going to fuck me now?"

"No."

"I'll be anything you want. Cheerleader. Corpse. A cheerleader's corpse."

"No."

"Frightened?"

"Terrified."

"I'll keep my eyes open, I promise."

"That would only make it worse."

"And if I told you I had nothing to do with the reporter's murder?"

"It wouldn't matter."

"I had nothing to do with her murder."

"It doesn't matter."

"But you do believe me."

"No."

She pushed herself away and turned, but not before I caught the beginnings of the smile she was trying to hide. "Oh, how cruel you are, to think me capable of such a thing."

"But not as cruel as you."

"No, Victor, that's right," she said, sloughing the shirt from her shoulders, baring the line of her back, the double question mark of her ass. As she began to walk away, she turned her head and flashed that smile like a punch to the jaw. "You could never be as cruel as me."

"My God," I said, in admiration of her body, her balls, the anarchy that glowed like a bonfire in those bright-green eyes. "This political line is rougher than I ever imagined."

CHAPTER 35

THE BAD WIFE

The night was sleepless, tortured and fat.

With my heart racing, I tossed and turned and bashed my fist against my forehead, unable to stop thinking about Amanda Duddleman and Jessica Barnes, about Ossana's body, about my own brutal culpability. The night seemed to last for a week and through it all I tortured myself, remembering the two women I had wanted to help, both ending up bloodied and dead. I tried to fix on exactly what I should have done instead of what I did, I juggled the possibilities until they smashed like eggs on the floor about me. It was impossible and useless and I was unable to stop going through it all over and again. In the midst of the dark turmoil, the sky outside my window became smudged with gray, and my heart slowed, and weariness snuck up on my thoughts like a thief and began to pull me down to sleep without my even knowing it. And just at that moment the phone rang.

It is always just at that moment that the phone rings.

"Who found her?" said the voice on the line. There were no niceties, no preliminaries, which was a relief. I didn't want any damn niceties just then. I sat up, scratching at my eyes.

"Melanie?"

"Who found her, Victor?"

I checked the clock. Five forty-five. "Give me a minute to get myself together."

"Did you find her?"

"Yes."

"I should have been your first call."

"They can check these things now. Do you want them asking why I called you instead of the police?"

"Then I should have been second."

"They would have checked that, too."

"But there are things I can do. Jesus, this is a bloody mess."

"Yes."

"What do the police know? Do they know about her relationship with—?"

"Yes."

"Dammit. How?"

"I told them."

"Victor."

"They would have found out sooner rather than later. You think Duddleman didn't tell a friend, tell all her Barnard roommates? She probably had it posted on Facebook under her relationship status. Whatever her generation is, it is not discreet. It didn't make sense to hide it up front when it would have tumbled out in a few hours anyway."

"We should have been consulted."

"Calm down, Melanie. If I had called you, the police would be at your door right now asking why."

"We need to meet."

"Okay."

"The Congressman's house. Do you know where it is?"

"Yes."

"Seven."

"Tonight?"

"This morning, Victor. And don't make me wait."

Congressman DeMathis's gerrymandered district was shaped like a writhing snake that had swallowed a gopher. The district had the tip of its tail in Lancaster, its distended belly in one of the more rural Philadelphia suburbs, and its shovel-shaped head sticking into a small fashionable part of the city proper. More than once the district had been referred to as an abomination during the redistricting deliberations, but those who decried its shape didn't have the votes to abort it, and so the hideous creature was birthed into this world to do its damage. Congressman DeMathis lived in a fashionable stone house in the fashionable part of the city that had been included in the district by State Senator DeMathis purely, it was said, to allow him to run for the congressional seat. I tended to doubt that story; was it really believable to imagine such a craven act on the part of a public servant?

"Oh, it's you," said Mrs. DeMathis, who startled at seeing me at the red front door. "Well, don't just stand there, come in."

"Thank you," I said.

She looked at me for a moment after I stepped inside. "Your eyes are so bruised you look like you've been in a fight."

"I didn't get much sleep."

"I made some coffee. How do you take it?"

"Black," I said.

"Good for you. My husband is still getting ready. Let me pour you a cup."

I followed her into a kitchen swathed with granite and dark wood cabinets. The coffee she handed me in a flowered teacup was hot and bitter and quite good, with hints of vanilla and hazelnut. You notice the little things when the big, wide world has collapsed around you. You notice the little things because that's all you have left. Mrs. DeMathis, in a dress and heels—imagine that at seven in the morning—poured a dash of bourbon into her cup, and then another dash, leaving just enough room for a splash of caffeine. She wasn't embarrassed in the slightest at having me see her doctor her coffee so early in the day. She brought the cup to her thin lips and swallowed like an asthmatic swallowing a breath of fresh air.

"So what brings you scuttling here so early in the morning, Victor? Something horrible, I assume."

"Yes, ma'am."

"Involving my husband?"

"Yes."

"Will it be public?"

"Most likely."

"So which of his scandals is about to break? Money or sex? I hope it's money."

"It's not money," I said.

"Too bad. I suppose then I should brace myself for all the hullabaloo that comes with the usual sex scandal. You and his other people should know I've already decided I won't stand by his side at the press conference. That is so Pat Nixon in her cloth coat, although, lucky her, that was only about money. No, I couldn't bear all the knowing looks as I stood there in silent support. *'Oh, you poor thing. How can you stand it?'* Remember sad little Dina McGreevey? At least my husband sticks his crooked thing only in women." She took another sip. "So, so many women. It's just that it is dispiriting when the little indiscretions, with their wide eyes and pert breasts, start talking to the press, giving all the details. The way he touched, the way he kissed, the promises. *'Oh, we were so, so in love.'* Like that Rielle Hunter with Oprah. It's enough to make a whole country puke."

"Don't worry," I said. "No one's talking."

"No? And yet still you're here. Then it must be worse than I imagine. What has he done now? My God, what has that man done now?"

"You need to prepare yourself, Mrs. DeMathis. And you need to know exactly where you and the Congressman were for all of last night."

"You sound worried, Victor. You sound like somebody died. Last night." She took another swallow and stood with the cup just below her lips. After a moment the cup began to shake. "Wait. Just wait one minute. There was a report on the news, a young girl murdered at a rock club of some sort. Is that it? They said she was a graduate of the Ivy League. Pete does like them young and overeducated."

"Where were you and your husband last night?"

"I was here," she said, "in my usual stupor. The life of a politician's wife is every bit as exciting as my parents threatened. But Pete, I don't know. I went to bed alone, I woke up alone, and he was in the guest bedroom as usual when I rose. What did he do, Victor?"

"Nothing, I'm sure."

"Well, I'm sure as hell not sure. I'm not sure of anything. I know what he is capable of. Every sick perversion—things that would melt your soul—every unimaginable cruelty. If you only knew what he has put me through. If you only knew the humiliations. That man is a beast, and I hate him, I hate him, I hate every foul piece of his being."

She pulled her cup back as if to throw it at the wall before gaining her composure and draining the coffee-laced bourbon. It seemed to settle her just a bit, the alcohol. Then in one quick motion she threw the cup and saucer at my head.

I ducked just quickly enough so that the pottery flew past before shattering on the dark wood cabinets and falling to the countertop and floor. I looked behind me at the mess, and the gash in the cabinet door.

"Nice woodwork," I said. "Rosewood?"

"Maple," she said, restored to an eerie calm. "Stained black. Oh, I think someone is at the door. Are we expecting anyone else?"

CHAPTER 36

MORNING TOAST

The Congressman's eyes were dull and unfocused, the exact opposite of the political stare at which he was so proficient. He sat in a red wingback chair in his wood-paneled study, still in a robe, his jaw unshaven, his hair mussed, his gaze lifted to some spot far in the horizon. He had been hit in the head with a fastball up and in; I could almost see the mark of the seam on his forehead.

"We have to get ahead of this, Congressman," said Melanie. "We can't let this turn into a Chandra Levy."

"Chandra Levy?" he said, his voice as unfocused as his gaze. "Do I know her?"

"I've no doubt you would have, given the chance," said Melanie. "What should he do, Victor?"

"Tell the truth," I said.

"Let's think of something else," said Melanie. "In this business the truth only gets you into another business."

"The police know about the relationship," I said. "They'll be coming today, asking all kinds of questions. And don't doubt that they'll have done their homework. He can either refuse to say anything, which is an admission of guilt, or he can tell the whole truth and hope the police do their job and solve the damn thing quickly, taking the heat off."

"What are the odds of that happening?" said Melanie.

"Good," I said.

"What makes you think that?"

"Because the lead detective is McDeiss."

"The one who hasn't yet solved the Shoeless Joan case?"

"He has more leads on this one. My guess is he'll solve them both together, and solve them fast."

"Are there any suspects?"

"Me," I said. "But he'll find others." I leaned forward, putting my hand on DeMathis's knee to get his attention. It was my turn to stare. "What we need to do, Congressman, is figure out if the truth is something you should be revealing. Melanie and I are both lawyers, this conversation will be privileged. Nothing you say can be repeated without your assent. So with that out of the way, let me ask you: Were you involved in Amanda Duddleman's murder in any way?"

"My God, no. No. Why would I? How could I?"

"Jealousy," I said. "And with a knife."

"You don't believe that I . . . You can't believe that . . ."

"What I believe doesn't matter," I said, which was a lie. What I believed mattered a hell of a lot. I was going to make sure it did.

"Let's start with the easy stuff," said Melanie. "Where were you last night? Were you home?"

"I think so. Yes."

"No," I said. "You weren't." I turned to Melanie. "This is what I mean. Any lie he tells will be as obvious as a slap in the face."

"Let's give it another go, sir," said Melanie. "I know you're a member of Congress and it's hard to overcome your first instinct, but let's try to tell the truth. Where were you last night?"

The Congressman, disheveled and disoriented, put his face in his hands. They must teach this in congressman school, how to take a distraught pose so that the audience can't see your lying eyes. There was a pause and there was a sob. I leaned back in my chair. There are moments in life when I fervently wished I smoked—after sex, while drinking Sazeracs at Rosen's, while sitting on the toilet in a gas station bathroom—and this was another.

"I was out," he said finally.

"Where?" said Melanie.

"Just out."

"With who?"

"Alone."

"You can do better."

"No," he said. "I can't. I had a couple of drinks at a bar on Locust early in the evening—you can check that out—and then I went looking for her."

"For who exactly?"

"For Amanda."

This is where I would have let out a long exhale.

"She wasn't answering my calls. She wasn't answering my texts. I was calling and I was texting and she wasn't answering. So I went out to find her."

"Where did you go?" said Melanie.

"To her house. I banged on the door, I walked around to look into the back windows. I rattled a window and called out her name. I was crazy."

"Crazy how?" said Melanie.

"Crazy angry. Crazy with desire. Crazy in love."

"I'm getting a sense of your possible defense," I said.

Melanie gave me a look that meant 'Shut up,' and said, "And then?"

"And then she responded to one of my texts. She told me she was going to some club to see a band she liked. Some rock club. So I went."

"You went to the club?" I said. "Union Transfer?"

"Yes."

"Did you buy a ticket?"

"They wouldn't let me in without one."

"And you a congressman. Imagine that. And you gave your ticket to the bouncer."

"Yes."

"When was this?"

"About eleven or so. I searched the place for her. It was like a sea of Amandas. A thousand young girls who looked just like her. Every time I was certain I spotted her, I'd grab hold, but it turned out to be some other girl. And the looks in these girls' eyes. It was a humiliation. I tried to ask if anyone knew her, but the band was loud, and no one could understand me, and the kids were dancing like nothing mattered but the music, like I didn't matter. I was in the middle of someone else's nightmare. Then I looked up and I saw her, on the rail, looking down at me, her face cold."

"What did you do?" I said.

"I charged up the stairs and I grabbed hold of each of her arms in joy, so happy to see her. And she shrank away as if . . . as if I were attacking her. 'Amanda,' I said. 'What are you doing here?' And she said, with that same cold expression, 'I'm seeing a show.' And I said 'Let's get out of here.' And she said, 'No.' And I said 'Why not?' And she said, 'We're through.' We're through."

"What did you do?"

"I shook her. I shook her and shouted, 'What are you saying?' And she shouted back, 'Go away, Pete. It's over. I know.' 'Know what?' I said. And I admit I squeezed her arms, and I admit I shook her. I was hurt and angry and desperate and I shook her. And then someone grabbed me by the neck and pulled me away."

"Who?"

"Some kid."

"Did you know him?"

"No. He was skinny, bearded, in some flannel shirt. Just a punk. She must have been with him, but it made no sense. How could she be with him? She was ambitious, she'd gone to Barnard. I'm somebody, I have money. It didn't make sense. But when he pulled me off her and pushed me away, I realized what I had been doing, how I had been acting. Crazy. Like a crazy man. And I looked at Amanda and tried to apologize, and all she did was shake her head at me before she turned away."

"And that made you angry," I said.

"It made me sad."

"What did you do?"

"I left," he said.

"After you killed her?"

"I didn't kill her."

"But you loved her."

"Yes. My God, yes, like a sickness."

"Then how could you leave her? She rejected you, humiliated you. How could you leave her without doing something, anything?"

"Because when she shook her head at me and then turned away, I saw something that horrified me."

"What?"

"I saw myself. The way she saw me. The way that kid she was with saw me. The way all those girls I had thought were Amanda had seen me when I accosted them. I saw myself, what I had become. My God, I am a United States congressman and I was acting like a pathetic fool, not just with her but in every part of my life. In the way she turned from me, I saw myself, and I couldn't get away from the sight fast enough."

"And then what?"

"I drove around, for hours, and then came home, ashamed, and fell asleep in the guest room. And I woke up into this nightmare."

"And that's the truth? All of it?" I said.

"Yes, I swear."

"You might have to, at that."

"What should I do with the police?"

"Tell them everything, just like you told us," said Melanie. "Help them any way you can. When they make a statement, they should be glowing about your cooperation. Can you do that?"

"Yes."

"Now go take a shower. Comb your hair, put on a suit. Today's an important day, Congressman. Today is the day you save your career."

"Okay," he said. "Yes. Right. I can do that."

Melanie and I watched him stand unsteadily and shuffle toward the door. It wouldn't take him long to get dressed and all spiffed-up, it wouldn't take him long to don his suit of power and play his role. Maybe the son of a bitch could squeeze out of this.

"What do you think?" I said.

"Pathetic."

"You don't think he killed her, do you?"

"He doesn't have it in him. At heart he's a coward, that's what makes him such a useful politician. Show me a coward and I'll show you a vote."

"So can he do it?"

"Do what?"

"Save his career."

"Oh, Victor, the moment he opened his mouth I knew he was toast. By this time next year our Congressman DeMathis will be selling Italian water ice out of a cart. But until then, he's still our baby."

CHAPTER 37

OBLIGATORY DINER VISIT

The man in the booth fed like a lion devouring a hyena, with great resolve and entirely too much satisfaction. Watching him eat from across the length of the old Oak Lane Diner on Broad Street, with its stainless-steel walls and bow-tied counterman, it almost seemed he was in a good mood, which confused me; for a moment I wondered if I was staring at the wrong man. Then he raised his gaze from the pile on the plate before him, saw me standing by the pies, and scowled like he had found a cockroach in his food.

I didn't wait for an invitation before crossing the floor, placing my bag on the bench seat across from him, and scooting in beside it. "Thanks for waving me over," I said.

"The first meal sets the tone for the entire day," said Detective McDeiss. "That's why I prefer to eat alone."

"You want to stay undisturbed, don't follow habits so regular that every cop in the division knows where you'll be. I have a gift for you."

"I am a public servant. I can't accept your gifts."

"You'll accept this," I said, taking out an envelope and passing it across the table. He stared at it for a long time before carving out a piece of ham steak, sticking it in the yolk of his egg, and then dipping it in his grits. He held the concoction in front of him and cocked an eyebrow.

"Money?" he said. "To buy your way out of a murder rap?"

"No."

"Too bad." He put the ham, yolk, and grits into his mouth, letting his eyes flutter for just a moment as he chewed and swallowed. "I would have loved busting your ass for attempted bribery."

"It's a sample of hair to be matched up with that blood smear I gave you in the club, the one Jessica Barnes gave to me."

"Whose hair?"

"The Congressman's sister's."

"And why do I want to match it up?"

"Because it's as close as I'm going to get to a sample of the Congressman's DNA. Your forensics people should be able to determine if there's a link."

"And if there is, what then?"

"Then I might be able to tell you what this all is about."

"Take a stab at it now. We don't even know who the smear is from. It could be the blood of a goat."

"Right now it's all just supposition and surmise. Amanda might have found the connection, but they killed her before she could tell me."

"They. The same 'they' you told me about at the club."

"That's right."

"You calmed down any?"

"No."

"It was a thing to see, wasn't it?"

"No."

"The way you were acting, red-faced and crazy, Armbruster thought you had gone off the deep end."

"What did you tell him?"

"That you didn't have a deep end, that you were all shallows."

"You got that right."

"Armbruster came up with the idea that it was guilt that was getting to you, like you were hearing heartbeats beneath the floorboards."

"I don't think Armbruster likes me."

"He doesn't. But when I reminded him that you were a lawyer, that put the end to any idea of you actually being capable of feeling guilt." He stared at me for a moment before buttering his toast and smearing a dollop of grape jam atop the butter. "Still, Armbruster couldn't help but wonder why you were so damn upset."

"She was a good kid with a future."

"They're all good kids and they all have futures."

There was something gratifyingly bitter about his words, like it was getting to him, the whole damn job. And for a moment we both remembered the way she'd looked, Amanda Duddleman, with her throat slashed and her head cocked weirdly and her sweater pulled up into the wound to stanch the blood so that it didn't pour out copiously enough to grab someone's immediate attention. The second I saw that shoeless leg, I knew that she was dead, but still the grotesque sight of her was like a kick in the gut, the kind that keeps kicking.

McDeiss took a bite of his purpled toast, swallowed it down with the rest of his coffee, signaled to the waitress for another cup. He sliced through the rest of the ham as he waited for the waitress to come over with a pot.

"Thanks, Shirley."

"Your friend want anything?"

"He's not a friend," said McDeiss, "and he has to be on his way."

"Too bad."

"Sure is."

When she had moved on to the next table, he started dumping in the sugar and the cream.

"I sent Armbruster down to check out the rehab facility you told us about," he said. "They assured him that Colin Frost was on location the night of the murder, that he hasn't left the facility since he was brought in three weeks ago. That's their firm policy for the first month. No exceptions, and their security is very tight. He would have had to sign himself out to leave and he didn't."

"They're wrong."

"Someone's wrong. And Miss Duddleman's editor had no notes on her research. There was nothing on her person or at her house regarding anything of great interest she might have found."

"They must have taken her notebook after they killed her."

"After Colin Frost, escaped from his rehab, killed her."

"That's right. You saw the text."

"Yeah, I saw the text."

He shoveled a few more forkfuls of his breakfast into his maw while staring out at me from beneath his brow, mopped his plate with another piece of toast, washed everything down with the coffee.

"Look, Carl, I don't blame you for kicking at the wall when you saw her, but you can't be accusing everyone and his brother willy-nilly and expect to get anywhere. You threw nine suspects under the bus within the first two minutes of our arrival last night. The Congressman, his sister, his chief of staff, the widow Devereaux and her in-house lawyer, an entire law firm, the law firm's secret client, a drug addict, the drug addict's pal."

"Give me time and I'll give you ten more."

"That's what I'm talking about. We talked to your congressman yesterday morning. He says he didn't do it. He says he was there, and that's been verified, but he says he left before it happened."

"Do you believe him?"

"We don't disbelieve him at the moment. And he seems cooperative enough. Why don't you emulate him, give us everything you know, and stay the hell out of it while we do what we need to do?"

"From what I can tell, all you're doing is collecting corpses minus their shoes."

He stared at me a bit more and then pushed his plate away. "You're killing my appetite."

I looked down; the plate was as clean as if polished.

"How did your prints get on that hammer again?" he said.

"I told you the story. After that break-in, I found it in my apartment. Colin must have planted it when he was searching for Jessica Barnes's proof. But before he planted it, and after he knocked me out, he must have put my prints on it."

"Yes, that is what you told us."

"And your tests will show that the blood wasn't wet when my prints were made. I gave the hammer to Amanda to give to you so you would have the hammer for your tests without linking it to me."

"Quite a story."

"You don't really think I—"

"I don't think; I follow the evidence."

"I liked her and I tried to help her. I liked Jessica Barnes and I tried to help her, too."

"Remind me never to ask for your assistance." He looked at me, a spark of compassion in his eyes. "Maybe you ought to have some coffee. And a little something sweet. Their pies are mighty fine."

"I used to think criminal law was rough. I used to think dealing with mobsters and hit men and felons of the worst stripe had prepared me for whatever crowd I fell into. That politics would be a piece of layer cake in comparison. How naive could I be? What a stinking craphole. Something needs to be done about these people."

"And you're the one to do it?"

"I'm the man with the bag. I know their secrets." I stood from the table, grabbed hold of my attaché. "Don't worry your little self about it, Detective. It's only two murders. Nothing to sweat about in the great scheme of things. But while you're sitting on your ass enjoying your morning coffee, I'll be out on the streets, following in the footsteps of a ghost."

CHAPTER 38

DEAD PRESIDENT

"What the hell do you want?" came a voice from inside the house.

We were standing at the still-closed front door of a stone twin on Queen Street in Lancaster, about an hour and a half west of Philadelphia. You know you're getting close when you pass the cows and the silos, the square Amish buggies with the red triangles affixed to their bumpers, the National Christmas Center with its walk-through Nativity scene. You know you're there when you pass the Dutch Wonderland amusement park, and the windmill where they sell shoofly pie. Now we were in a neighborhood of narrow alleyways and heaving cement and houses cracked by age. I assumed there was a genteel part of Lancaster somewhere, but this certainly wasn't it. On the other side of the street from the small twin was the Woodward Hill Cemetery, overrun, creepy, with a dead president interred.

"Mrs. Gaughan?" I said.

"Who wants her?"

"We're here to tell her we're sorry for her loss."

"You just did, now go away."

"And we have some questions."

"She isn't talking to any more reporters."

"We're not reporters," I said.

"Then why the hell would I talk to you?"

"I'm a lawyer," I said. "And I'm here to help."

It's the hoariest line in the book, usually the start of a bad joke involving a judge, a shark, and two dancing girls, but every now and then it opens a door. Just a crack, maybe, but enough for an overweight bagman with a black suit and matching fedora to stick a shoe in the gap to keep it from closing.

"A lawyer, huh?" said the woman, whose one bloodshot eye appeared in the crack. With a surfeit of suspicion she eyed Stony, with his black stomper wedged in her door, and then me. "You're not the first to come around looking for a payday. Do I know you? I think I know you."

"You don't know me," I said.

"Oh, I've seen your picture somewhere," she said, and I didn't doubt it.

Stony took off his hat and swept it in front of him with a low bow. "May we come in, Mrs. Gaughan? I think you'll be wanting to talk to us."

"Are you a lawyer, too?"

"Heavens, no, dearie. I'm a man of principle." He reached into his jacket pocket and pulled out a pint. "And a man with a bottle, too."

"Is that all you've got?"

"It's still early."

"What are we drinking to?" she said.

"Your daughter," I said.

"Oh Christ," she said, opening the door wide. "In that case don't be skimpy with the pour."

Mrs. Gaughan had been pretty once, the way a Roman ruin had been pretty once, but, like the Roman Empire itself, the structures of her face had now collapsed, leaving it pulpy and red. She was bundled like a sausage in her faded housecoat, and she wore a pair of fuzzy slippers with open fronts to ease her blue, swollen toes.

She told us the story as we sat in her disheveled kitchen, three glasses, one hat, and an ashtray on the tabletop. They were estranged, this mother and her only child. Jessica was ungrateful, headstrong, too independent for her own good. In the last few years, after she married that Barnes, who couldn't keep a job, they barely spoke. And when Jessica discovered she couldn't have a baby, that made it even worse. Like Jessica was jealous of her mother, because the mother had been able to do the one great thing that Jessica never could. Sometimes Jessica needed reminding who was who, and Mrs. Gaughan was just the one to do the reminding.

In the time it took her to tell us this, she smoked four cigarettes and finished off the bottle. She drank her liquor without ice and without water; she liked her alcohol neater than her life. And through all the talk, she ignored me completely. But she liked Stony, she understood Stony, they were having a party together, her and Stony, as she told us how miserable a daughter Jessica had been. That was the thing about Stony, he could draw it out of anyone, he just had that ability. It was one of the reasons I had brought him along.

"And so you've got no grandchild to keep you company in your old age," said Stony.

"Good thing, too," said Mrs. Gaughan, glancing my way. "It's not like I was going to raise it, with her gone and her husband as worthless as tits on a nun. Been there, done that, and it was no picnic, believe me. Maybe we ought to get another bottle, Stony, make a day of it."

"We get another bottle," said Stony, "we'll be making a night of it."

"If you insist."

"Oh, you sly fox, Melinda," said Stony.

"So what do you think happened to your daughter, Mrs. Gaughan?" I said.

"What do you mean what happened? Someone killed her. That's why you're here, right?"

"That's why I'm here."

"You ask me, it was that lawyer down in Philadelphia that did it. The one she was down there meeting. That ugly one in the tuxedo."

"Do you know why she was meeting him?"

"For something bad," she said. "For something awful, and she a married woman. But it had to be something like that if he killed her over it."

"I don't think he did it," I said.

"How do you know?"

"Because I'm that lawyer."

"You?" She lowered her chin, staring up at me through iced eyes. "I knew I recognized you. I thought you were here to sue somebody. I thought that's why you were getting me liquored up, so I'd sign your fee contract."

"Would it have worked?"

"If Stony here bought another bottle, maybe. Though I signed two already, just to cover my bases."

"And who would you sue if you had the chance?"

"The one who killed my daughter."

"And you think that's me."

"The papers do."

"And the papers are never wrong."

"You came all this way to tell me you didn't do it?"

"No, ma'am, I came all this way to show you a photograph."

"Dr. Patusan is seeing patients all day," said the office receptionist, heavy and pretty with limp brown hair. She sported a lovely smile behind her desk as she blew us off. "He won't have time to talk to a lawyer."

"It won't take long," said Stony. "What's your name, sweetheart?"

"Nadine," she said.

"Ah, Nadine. What a pretty name. Reminds me of a song I used to know. I'm Stony and this here is Victor. Now that we're all on a first-name basis, can't you perhaps squeeze us in for just a little meet-and-greet?"

"What is this about?"

"We have some questions about treatments for a childhood condition, something I believe is called Wilson's disease. We understand that Dr. Patusan is the local expert."

"We do have some patients, yes." She looked through her book. "The doctor's schedule is very tight and there are patients waiting, as you can see. I could give you fifteen minutes a week from Wednesday."

"A week from Wednesday?"

"Or a week from Friday, if that works better. Does that work better, Stony?"

"Why don't you pretend we're drug salesmen with a bagful of gifts," he said. "Then he'd see us with alacrity for sure."

"You're not pretty enough to be drug salesmen," she said with a smile.

"Oh, now, Nadine, there you go, cutting us to the quick."

I looked around the waiting room as Stony tried his sweet talk on Nadine. Scattered about were kids and their mothers on colorful chairs, side tables piled with picture books, a little play area with plastic toys and a plastic playhouse, a bulletin board full of photographs of smiling kids. It hadn't taken long for me to diagnose the daughter Jessica Barnes had told me about, with the excess of copper in her blood; the web will diagnose anything for you, even a hangnail. And it hadn't taken much longer to find those few doctors in Lancaster who routinely treated Wilson's disease. Dr. Patusan was the closest thing to Dr. Patticake. Duddleman had surely found it as easily as I had.

"We have questions about one of his patients," I said. "We won't be long."

"Are you a parent of the patient?" she said.

"Heavens, no," said Stony. "Victor and I are both still looking."

"Oh, I see," she said, with another sweet smile aimed at Stony. "But then, of course, Dr. Patusan would not be permitted to talk to you at all. You see, the HIPAA privacy rules are very strict. None of us can say anything about a patient to anyone who is not a parent or a guardian. There are no exceptions."

"No exceptions?"

"None. And the penalties are quite severe."

"I'd like to show you a photograph," I said. I put the picture I had shown Mrs. Gaughan on Nadine's desk. "This is a friend of mine and I wonder if she was in this office a few days ago looking for Dr. Patusan."

The receptionist looked at the picture just long enough to recognize it before pushing it away. "Yes," she said, her smile not as bright, "she was here."

"And did she get a chance to talk to Dr. Patusan?"

"He wasn't in that day. He was at a conference."

"I see. This woman, her name was Amanda Duddleman."

"Yes, that's right."

"She was murdered a few nights ago."

The receptionist's face registered a good amount of shock, which I was expecting, and then her gaze lifted just a moment to a spot over my shoulder, and then she caught me catching her and she stared at me for a good long moment.

"I'm sorry," she said. "I didn't know."

"Yes, it is a tragedy," said Stony. "She was a fine girl, and all we're trying to do is trace her steps a bit. Now you say she was here when the doctor was out. Did she come back?"

"No," said the receptionist.

"How long did she stay?"

"Not long."

"And what exactly was she asking for?"

"I don't remember," she said.

As they spoke, I turned around to see what Nadine had looked at as soon as she learned that Duddleman had been murdered. The bulletin board, plastered full of photos. I walked up to it and gave it a good close look. All the smiles, all the bright dresses and baggy baseball uniforms, all the fabulous children with their brilliant futures. But it wasn't the photographs, so many that each overlapped another in order to fit on the board, that most intrigued me. It was the one empty spot where the cork showed through. I stood at the board and gently pressed my fingers over the spot and waited as Stony and Nadine continued their chatter. I didn't have to wait long.

Nadine came up beside me, pulled a photograph from the top of the board, placed it over the gap, pinned it to the cork.

"We don't want to get anyone in trouble," I said softly enough so that no one else could hear.

"And that's why you're here?" said Nadine just as softly. "Not to get anyone in trouble?"

"She was a sweet girl, Amanda. Like you. She came in here, you gave her a photograph, she ended up dead that night, and the photograph wasn't on her anymore. They killed her for it."

"My God."

"You don't have to tell me anything," I said. "And I won't get you involved with the police, I promise."

"The police?"

"Yes, of course. There's a murder investigation."

"I could lose my job."

"I understand," I said.

"My family depends on this job."

"I understand, I do. All I need is for you to do me a favor."

I have always found cemeteries comforting. No matter the *Sturm und Drang* we're forced to suffer in our lives, we all end up in the same peaceful place, with fields of grass and tottering stone markers that detail the bare bones of our existences. We're born, we die, maybe we procreate, and there it is; the rest, as we say in the law, is dicta. And yet, there are always lessons to be learned in a cemetery.

Just then I was sitting in a car, inside the cemetery gates, not far from the august grave of James Buchanan, another son of Pennsylvania who became enmeshed in the brutal game of politics. I couldn't help but ruminate on how the arc of Buchanan's career seemed so closely to mirror mine. An unpromising start, a disappointing romantic life punctuated by a failed engagement, and then a swift, seemingly inexorable ascension to sparkling heights followed by an ugly, precipitous fall. Of course, James Buchanan's height was the presidency of the United States of America and mine was the role of bagman for a second-rate congressman, and so, yes, there was that difference there, I admit. And Buchanan was supposedly gay, and he liked to tend to the White House tulips, and he presided over the disintegration of the Union, so maybe we weren't as close as I imagined, though I do like tulips. But still, I felt a kinship. Buchanan is generally considered one of the worst presidents in the history of the Republic, and if there is one thing I can always relate to, it is failure.

"If you weren't in politics, Stony, what would you be doing?"

"Nothing," he said.

"You'd be dead?"

"No, I'd be doing nothing on a beach somewhere, sipping piña coladas and slapping the rumps of local wenches."

"Wouldn't that get boring?"

"Not if you do it right. I did have a dream, once, but my father wouldn't have allowed it."

"Old Briggsy was tough, was he?"

"As horsehide. It was this game or no game for me, and so here I am."

"What was the dream?"

"Oh, it's silly, Victor. Spilt milk grows sour."

"Tell me."

"It wouldn't have amounted to anything anyway."

"Go on."

"I always wanted to sing."

"Folk?"

"Opera."

"No."

"Oh, yes. And I wasn't terrible at it, either. For a time even, in my youth, I worked as a busboy at Victor's in South Philly. You know it?"

"With the singing waiters?"

"That's the one. Every once in a while I'd put in an aria or two."

"Wow, color me impressed. Let me hear."

"I'm out of practice."

"Oh, come on now, don't be shy."

And so he sang, Stony Mulroney, with his eyes closed and one arm waving in the air like a flag atop La Scala. He sang something sad and sweet and all in Italian. Gad, it was awful.

"Even when I was young," he said, after he had finished, as I was cleaning the rotten notes out of my ear with a finger, "my voice wasn't a thing of beauty. My father was right about where my true talents lay. I was made for this game and no other. It's the vicious simplicity of it that I take to. Politics is a blood sport, and the goal is to make damn sure it's the other guy with the knife in his neck."

"Is that another of Briggs's Rules?"

"Oh, no, Road Dog, that one is all mine. From hard experience. What about you? If politics doesn't work, it's back to the law with you?"

"I always wanted to be a lawyer; it's just that I can't afford to pursue it as a hobby. What kind of car did you say she had?"

"A Honda, old and gray."

"Like that?" I said, indicating a car pulling quickly out of an alleyway and heading onto Queen Street.

"That's the one," he said, starting the Lincoln.

I paid close attention to how Stony followed the gray Honda as it speedily made its way first through the twisty streets of Lancaster and then through a bucolic grove of trees before landing on the main avenue out of the city. As we passed through a gauntlet of outlets and fast-food joints and the aforementioned amusement park, he kept the Honda close, letting other cars and a truck slide between us, but never so many that we couldn't keep track of who we were following. His technique was spot-on. It was amazing what you could learn from the inside of a matchbook.

When Mrs. Gaughan turned off the main road into a piece of farm country, Stony slowed his pace and fell farther behind. We passed a series of fields, horses leaning their long necks down to pick at the grass, an Amish buggy. Finally, on a rural road called Irishtown, she slowed down her hurried pace and pulled into a drive beside a small farmhouse close to the road.

Stony turned into another driveway, about sixty yards back, and set the car behind a thick, twisty oak in full leaf. The aged two-story farmhouse where Mrs. Gaughan had parked was in front of a much larger, more modern structure. The farm family that lived there had built a new house for itself but kept the old one for guests or renters. The ramshackle old place, set in the middle of nowhere, was as ready-made a place to hide as could be found in America.

Dressed neatly now in slacks and a blouse hanging loose, her hair done, her shoes shiny, Melinda Gaughan climbed out of her car. She had played the part of the soused ruin to perfection, our Mrs. Gaughan, had lied with aplomb, but her reaction to the picture and subsequent lie of never seeing Amanda before had convinced me that the rest of her story was just as unreliable. And so the question was how to get the truth out of her.

I had asked Nadine in Dr. Patusan's office to do me just a small favor in exchange for my going away. It is amazing how much people will do to just get me to go away. I didn't ask for the name of the child in the photograph she had given to Amanda Duddleman, I didn't ask for any information she wasn't by law allowed to give. All I asked was that she review the file and then call Mrs. Gaughan and tell her that one of the tests her granddaughter had taken showed an anomaly and that the doctor wanted her to make a new appointment immediately to have it checked out. That was all. And then we waited outside Mrs. Gaughan's house, waited with two thermoses.

I slipped out of the car with Stony's camera, and under cover of the oak I focused the long zoom lens on the house. There was something in that photograph Nadine had given to Duddleman that had been dangerous, something Duddleman couldn't wait to show me, something Amanda Duddleman had died for. I was going to see what it was even if I had to wait all day. But I didn't have to wait all day.

The front door of the small house opened and a little girl burst out, four or five, in jeans and a T-shirt and small white sneakers. She ran down the steps and spun around a spindly tree in the front yard and shouted something. A moment later Melinda Gaughan and a man in his thirties walked together down the steps, talking quietly, sadly. The grieving mother, the grieving husband, the daughter who doesn't understand her own sadness.

I focused the camera on the girl, young and smiling, with pale skin, swinging around the tree. Click click. I took some of the mother and the husband but focused mostly on the child. Click click. It felt wrong somehow, but I kept pressing the button. Click click. It was evidence, something I could use to convince McDeiss to save the little girl's life. But I didn't need any photographs to be convinced myself about what was what. One look was all it took.

Click click.

CHAPTER 39

THE OPPOSITION

I filched the memory card from Stony's camera. Slipped it from the bottom while I was out of the car taking photographs of the little girl in Lancaster.

I felt a slash of guilt when I snatched it—I considered Stony a friend, my shiny new friend, and he had been nothing but the supportive guide through my whole sordid political journey—and yet I stole the card anyway, yes, I did. I even covered it up by pretending to take a few shots after I had palmed the thing. Fake click fake click. Before she up and left the family, my mother repeatedly told me I was an ungrateful wretch.

And yet I was not without my reasons.

The moment we returned to the city and Stony let me out of his car, I hightailed it to Goodrich Camera on Fifteenth and slid the memory card across the counter. "I need some pictures made," I said to the good-looking blond kid at the counter. "Could you tell me how many snaps are on the memory?"

"Just a minute," he said before taking the card in the back room. He returned a few moments later. "You have sixty-two."

I had taken about ten, and I guessed there were about as many of Bettenhauser. What were the other forty-two? "Print them all," I said. "Eight-by-tens. And I'd like all the files transferred from the card to a disk. Can you do that?"

"For the price of the data disk, sure. Want me to clear the card when I do it?"

"Absolutely," I said. "And could you deliver the disk on your way home, someplace right in the city?"

"No, we don't do that."

I opened my bag, pulled out two Franklins, slapped them on the counter. Without saying anything, the kid pocketed the hundreds before pulling out a square envelope big enough to fit a disk and sliding it across the counter. I started writing an address on the envelope.

"How soon can you do the transfer?" I said.

"I could do it right now, if you want. Anything you want."

"That's fine." After I finished filling out the envelope, I wrote a Lancaster address on a slip of paper along with the words "From your pal Mulroney," signed my name, and put the slip inside. "Make sure you deliver this tonight."

"If you want to wait, I could print up all the photographs for you right now. I'll put you at the head of the queue."

"That's all right," I said. "I'm already late for a picket line."

Even as my political career crumbled beneath me like a stale banana scone, I could still admire my handiwork. There they were, my little grassroots activists, snarling traffic in front of the Hilton, their hate-filled eyes brilliantly illuminated by the lights of the news crews. They formed a rough line of about thirty or so, all of them shouting and jeering for the cameras, singing paeans to the Second Amendment, brandishing their signs like pitchforks. I CARRY A GUN BECAUSE A COP IS TOO HEAVY. IT'S NOT ABOUT GUNS, IT'S ABOUT CONTROL. HEY TOMMY BETTENHAUSER, I'LL KEEP MY GUNS, YOU KEEP THE CHANGE. And the ever-popular outline of an M16 with the stirring motto COME AND TAKE IT.

As I walked between the shouting line of demonstrators and the hotel, I spotted among the picketers our man Thompson, shaking his sign and shouting so fervently the tendons in his neck bulged. I gave him the barest of nods. It was in neither of our interests to have me in any way connected to this patriotic demonstration of love for God and country. I elbowed my way through a corridor of police before I headed into the Hilton to see Tommy Bettenhauser blather on about avoiding an environmental holocaust.

"Our environment is changing, and there are no good answers," said the candidate in front of a group of the tweedy and the earnest, handwrought silver-and-turquoise jewelry on the men, little black ponytails on the women—or was it the other way around? "But in the midst of these wrenching climate swings, we can't even stand together on the same street corner and agree on whether the light is red or green."

The difference between Congressman DeMathis's crowd and this crew, listening like eager puppies to every platitude, was the difference between duck confit served with foie gras on a crystal platter and a jicama, beet, and fennel slaw picked up at Whole Foods. The room was the same dreary kind of place in which I had seen the Congressman speak, but the wine I grabbed was sour and cheap, and the hors d'oeuvres laid out on the tables ringing the room were mostly crudités. Is anything cruder than crudités? As Tommy Bettenhauser droned on, I looked around desperately for something hot and butlered, preferably in a puff pastry.

"And the answer isn't to just cut the difference," said the candidate, "call the light yellow, and feel righteous in our moderation. Because an untruth, even a moderate untruth, will still lead us in the wrong direction. We need to look plainly and honestly at the condition of our world, but, sadly, our leaders are often led astray. The problem with our politics is not stupidity, or venality, though heaven knows both are alive and well in the US Congress." A fervent bout of laughter, as if Bettenhauser had suddenly morphed into Seinfeld. "No," he continued over the laughter. "The problem with our politics is politics."

With that profound thought, as obvious as saying the problem with death is all that dying, I turned to a woman standing next to me in a sweet summer dress, all flowers and pleats, that modestly showed off a sharp little body. She was staring at the candidate with eyes squinted and sincere, eyes that said, *I care; I really, really care.* No matter how pretty they are, and hers were very, sincere eyes always scare the solemnity out of me.

"Is there anything to eat other than the wilted vegetables?" I said.

"They're organic," she said.

"I don't doubt it, and I'm all for organic. I was just hoping for something organic that mooed or blatted. Goat, maybe. I could go for some organic goat on organically grown skewers."

She turned and looked at me, like she was observing some invasive species of fauna, and then I got the smile I'd been mining for. "There were some egg-roll things a bit ago."

"I hate it when I miss the good stuff. I'm Victor."

"Carrie," she said. "I'll elbow you if I see a tray."

"That would be so kind. I'm not sure I can take all this pabulum on an empty stomach."

"When did everything we see and hear, everything we read and think and shout, get infected with politics?" said the candidate. "Politics has become a screen through which too many of us see the world. The lives we then end up inhabiting are cramped and sour, where everything exists solely to outrage us or give us an opportunity to gloat, where the world is a barren zero-sum game in which every vile act to support our side is not just allowed, but required."

"Peace and love," I said.

"Are you not a fan of our Mr. Bettenhauser?"

"Our? What did you do, pull him out of a cereal box?"

"Something like that, yes," she said with a smile.

"I'm no different than the rest of our countrymen when it comes to politicians, interested only in what they can do for me. Right now all your Mr. Bettenhauser can do for me is get me fed. Was there any shrimp? Did I miss the shrimp?"

"No shrimp," she said.

"These low-rent campaigns give me the shingles. If you're going to buy my vote, at least buy it with meat."

"A prime rib would do it?"

"A prime rib would get all three of my votes."

"We'll have to get you a slab of beef, then, posthaste."

"Carrie, are you asking me out?"

"No."

"I can tell you that this type of politics is not a prescription for perfecting our democracy or healing our world," said Bettenhauser, continuing on with his speech as if all the yobs in the room really cared. And surprisingly, glancing around, it looked like they did, including pretty little Carrie. I thought of maybe actually listening to what he was saying, but thankfully that deranged idea fled and I searched around for something other than the sour wine to drink.

"It is, instead, pure poison. And that's why I am here asking for your vote. Not because I have the solution to all our problems—trust me when I say I don't—but because I pledge to bring a new perspective to Washington, where up is up, down is down, and facts are treated with reverence, not disdain."

"Well, that's original," I said. "Everything good as long as you elect me and not the other guy."

"Quite the cynic, aren't you, Victor?" said Carrie.

"Trust me when I tell you it is well earned."

"I have found the worst cynics are actually secret idealists. Cynicism is merely a defense of a bruised heart."

"Or an empty stomach," I said.

"Isn't your cynicism heavy, Victor? Don't you just want to put it down sometime like an overstuffed backpack and take a breath?"

"Then what would I have?"

"I don't know. Find out."

"Would I have to eat quinoa with my tempeh?"

"Yes," she said.

"There's not enough ketchup in the world."

"I don't know if we can heal the damage we've already done to our earth," said Tommy Bettenhauser, "or if we can prevent further erosion of our environment. But I do promise to bring a fresh perspective to climate change, and every other problem facing our country and our world, a perspective where myths hold no sway just because we want to believe them, where clear evidence is accepted as the starting point, and where solutions are reached based on sound science, sound policy, and what's good not just for our own political party, but for the country as a whole."

"Now he's going to talk about changing the world," I said.

"Are you sure?"

"Oh, yes, they love that. It so inspires the young to empty their meager little wallets."

"Together," said Bettenhauser, "have no doubt that we will change the world."

"Good call," she said.

"It didn't take Einstein."

"How fortunate for you."

"We will change the world," said Bettenhauser, "because we have no choice. That is every generation's fate. But I believe that it will take a new kind of political vision to change our world for the better, and that's what I promise to bring to Washington."

"Hear, hear," I said, clapping with the rest after he finished the speech.

"So you were actually moved," said Carrie, looking at me searchingly.

"No, I'm calling out to the waiters with the trays. Here, here, bring them here."

"Would you like to meet him, Victor? The candidate, I mean."

"Yes, please, that would be jimmy."

"Come then," she said, taking hold of my hand. Her touch was warm and dry, and I felt a frisson full of possibility. "I'll take you to him."

After Carrie led me to the scrum surrounding Bettenhauser, she left it up to me to patiently wait for an opportunity to introduce myself. When I saw an opening, I called out his name. He turned and grabbed my hand and bathed me like a babe in the impersonal warmth of his version of the political stare.

And then he recognized me and recoiled as if I were syphilis.

It should have been a sobering moment, to make another man recoil like that, but I had to admit I liked it. *Recoil, you son of a bitch,* I thought. *Let the whole damn world recoil when it sees me coming, just like I recoil every morning when I shave.*

"It is nice to meet you, Mr. Bettenhauser," I said, in my sweetest tone. "I'm Victor Carl."

"Of course you are," he said, eyeing the big brown diplomatic bag I had brought with me. "I recognize you from that scene at the Governor's Ball and then your photo in the newspaper. You work for DeMathis."

"I work for myself, mostly. I enjoyed your speech. 'The problem with our politics is politics.' And all along here I was thinking it was the politicians that were screwing things up."

"Yes, well, we're out to change that. But thank you, Victor, for your support. We'll take it from any quarter we can get it."

"That's good, because a quarter is about all I've got to give. But do you perhaps have a few moments to talk?"

"I'm awfully busy. Why don't you call the campaign office and we can—"

"It would be worth your while to talk to me tonight, Mr. Bettenhauser," I said in a voice as flat as slate. Sometimes you take all the humanity out of your tone, and the point is made.

"Yes," he said. "Of course. Let me finish up here and I'll make some time before we leave. While you wait, why don't you grab something to eat."

"Where?" I said.

CHAPTER 40

PARTY CRASHER

It didn't go as I had planned with Bettenhauser. Nothing in politics had gone as I had planned. You would have thought life would have taught me long ago that plans are written with vanishing ink on tissue paper swirling down a toilet, but about some things I am dim as dusk.

Yet Bettenhauser had unwittingly clarified the precariousness of my position and forced me to count the betrayals like a banker counting his coin. I knew it wouldn't be long before all that treachery came to a head, and I had immediately taken precautions. Still, when I opened the door to my apartment and walked into a wall of smoke, I was startled that betrayal had breached the barricades so quickly. Within the shadows I saw his unmistakable silhouette, sitting solidly in a chair amidst the scattered ruin of my things, his hat still on, a cigarette glowing like the tip of Satan's nose.

"Late night, Road Dog?"

I felt a flash of danger in the calm of his voice, but I tried not to show it. This was Stony, my good pal Stony, and I didn't want him yet to know all that I knew. When I was sufficiently calmed, I switched on the light and looked around at the mess; I hadn't cleaned the apartment yet from Ossana's ransacking.

"If I had known you'd be coming," I said, "I would have tidied up the place."

"Oh, no need to clean on my account. I have lived in hovels that make this look like the Royal Suite at the Four Seasons. Where were you all this time?"

"Meeting with Bettenhauser," I said.

"Ah, sleeping with the enemy."

"Not quite, but almost with the enemy's wife. I didn't know Mrs. Bettenhauser was so attractive. I was hitting on her during the whole of her husband's insipid speech without realizing who she was."

"Now that would have been a scandal worth having; that could have swung the election all by itself. You don't mind me barging, do you?"

"Not at all. Friends, right?"

"Friends indeed."

"In fact," I said, "I was going to give you a call to tell you what I learned tonight. I didn't give the Bettenhauser photographs to Sloane, because I had some questions, and Bettenhauser gave me the answers. It turns out that the woman he was hugging was not an illicit lover but someone he helped off the streets and who is now running one of the charities he sponsors."

"Maybe true, but that doesn't mean he's not giving her his charitable best, daily, over and again, if you catch my drift."

"Yes, except it turns out that the specific woman in the photograph would be more interested in Mrs. Bettenhauser than Mr. Bettenhauser, if you catch my drift. And it was Mrs. Bettenhauser who clued me in after her husband called her in to the meeting. I'll check it out, but Mrs. Bettenhauser's eyes were so full of sincerity that I believe her. Which means the photographs wouldn't have damaged, but instead bolstered, Bettenhauser's campaign. It's a good thing I didn't give the photos to the press."

"In that case," said Stony, "a very good thing."

"But you knew all this already."

"There are so few surprises in our game."

"And yet for some reason you wanted me to give the photographs to Sloane, even brought him in to meet with me at Rosen's. Who are you working for, Stony?"

"Don't be forgetting your rules, now. Rule One: a bagman works only for himself."

"Yes, the rules, your daddy's precious rules. Here's the thing that surprised me. I liked Tommy Bettenhauser more than I thought I would. He is as sickeningly sincere as his wife. Sincerity is nothing you want in a lay, but an interesting trait in a public servant. After our talk he went out and spoke with the pro-gun demonstrators who were picketing his speech, a little protest I had set up. He didn't turn them around, but he spoke civilly and they spoke civilly back. It was a revelation, a glimpse of what we as people could be. It turns out that Tommy Bettenhauser is a conviction politician."

"You're being played, Road Dog. The only difference between a conviction politician and a convicted politician is evidence. The memory card from my camera is missing. You wouldn't know where it might be? I would have tossed the place to look for it, but someone beat me to it."

"Ossana DeMathis."

"A redheaded demon, that one. Remember the story of Odysseus being lashed to the mast so he can't succumb to the Sirens' call? Only a fool goes to bed with a demon."

"Is that another one of Briggs's Rules?"

"That's just sheer common sense, which you seem to have misplaced lately. Where is my memory card?"

"Not here, not on me."

He reached into his pocket, pulled out a gun, laid it on his thigh. It wasn't a flagrant gesture, just a simple restatement of things.

"Maybe I should frisk you just to be sure," he said.

"It wouldn't do you any good."

"So where might it be? And no blustering."

"I left it at a camera store so they could print up the pictures."

"Hand over the receipt."

"It's just pictures of a little girl," I said. But I knew it was more than just pictures of a little girl. It was the thread that would unravel everything, a red thread, coppery and bright, like the hair on that little girl, who looked so much like Ossana DeMathis they could have been clones. Once I saw her spinning around that tree in Lancaster, I knew Ossana would be coming after me like she had come after Jessica Barnes and Amanda Duddleman. I just didn't know how or how soon. Stony, with his gun, was a pretty good answer.

"I've been told to clean it up," said Stony. "All of it."

"And that includes me."

"Rule Seven."

"A bagman never reveals his secrets," I said. "What would your father say if he saw you here with a gun?"

"He would understand. You know what a bagman's pension is? Information. I decided to cash in my pension before it disappeared, which it will, sooner than you could ever imagine." He waved his gun languidly. "The receipt, Road Dog, and don't make me ask again."

I took out my wallet. My fingers felt like sausages as I fumbled about while trying to fish out the receipt.

"I'll just have it all," he said.

"You're going to steal it from me?"

"Rule Six."

I actually laughed as I tossed him the wallet. He looked through it quickly and found the receipt. "Goodrich Camera," he said before stuffing the whole thing in a pocket. "I'll be there when it opens. Now let me have your phone."

"Oh, no, not my phone," I said flatly.

"Oh, yes, your phone. Tasks hard the man who holds the gun."

"Who is that? Chandler?"

"Mulroney."

When I pitched the phone to him, he quickly thumbed around to see if there was anything of concern.

"No texts this evening? Excellent. And no calls in or out. You're not very popular. Such a shame, Road Dog. If we get through this, I'll work to expand your social circles."

"Are we going to get through this?"

"I am," he said with a hearty grin. "We'll see about you." He laughed, bright and easy, a laugh that smoothed my jagged nerves like a shot of whiskey. "But unless you go off and do something half-cocked, like try to run from me, it should all work itself out. Now come on, we can't stay here, the state this place is in."

He pushed himself to standing and waved the pistol at me again before sticking it in his jacket pocket, the gun barrel aimed now at my chest.

"Pretend you're a stray dog and let me take you home. Oh, and bring along the bag."

CHAPTER 41

A BAGMAN'S CANTATA

What was your father?" said Stony. "What did he do?"

It was early afternoon the day after my abduction. We were now in the basement of the Briggs Mulroney house in the Mayfair section of Philadelphia, a modest fully detached stone structure, perched on a rise above the street. You would have thought, with all I had heard about the late departed pater Mulroney, there would have been a historical marker on a post outside:

HERE LIVED BRIGGS MULRONEY, LEGENDARY PHILADELPHIA BAGMAN, WHO HAD THE CITY COURTS AND CITY COUNCIL IN HIS BACK POCKET FOR MORE THAN TWO DECADES. "HE MADE STRONG MEN WEEP."

Stony sat calmly in a spindly wooden chair set in front of me, his heavy black shoes flat on the cement floor. His jacket was off, his suspenders were thick and red to match his socks, his shirt cuffs were rolled, his hat was still in place. It wasn't hot in the basement, but even so, great drips of sweat fell from his temples. Resting on one wide thigh was an envelope fresh from the camera store. In his left hand was a cigarette; in his right hand was the gun.

"My father cut lawns for a living," I said.

"Now there's a job, yes. Fresh air, summer sun, working with your shirt off, the smell of clean sweat and freshly mowed grass.

And clients so appreciative to come home to a smooth emerald carpet, where before was a sprouting mess of weeds." He took a long draft from his cigarette and let the smoke sit in his lungs as a drop of sweat rolled down his cheek like a tear. "I would have liked that, I think. I could have sung my arias beneath the roar of the mowers."

"We all make our choices," I said.

"Not all of us," he said, tilting his head low as he looked down at me.

I was sitting splat on the cracked cement floor of that basement, my wrist handcuffed to a cast-iron pipe sticking out of the stone wall. To my right, teetering like an old drunk, stood a rusted water tank slowly leaking into a puddle at its feet. Beyond that was a single glass window high on the wall. Thoughtfully set within my reach was a large silver thermos.

"You maybe chose to give up the fresh green grass for the stunted tundra of the law," said Stony, "but what choice was there for Briggs Mulroney's son? I was like a prince, raised under the stick and shelter of my father's expectations. How does one abdicate from that? And so here I am, with just a spit shine on my shoes and a bag in my hand, struggling to make my way in a compromised world."

"Willy Loman with a gun."

"And why not? For what is a bagman, really, but a salesman at heart, selling access, selling power, selling other people's integrity? Those with money have wants; public servants want money; all I do is make the sale. I'm like a little Irish sprite spreading happiness. So why, I ask, must I ply my trade in the shadows, behind Dumpsters, away from prying eyes?"

Stony had left me alone for a few hours that morning when he went off to pick up my photographs, and in that gap I had tried desperately to effect my escape. But the cast-iron pipe was affixed so firmly to the wall that all my heaving and shaking did nothing except scrape raw the skin of my wrist. And my pathetic shouts for help came to naught. When a mouse made a quick appearance from behind the water heater and stared at me for a moment, I wondered if I could induce it to nibble the handcuffs in two. That might have worked if I were tied with a rope. That might have worked if it weren't a mouse. But despite all my shouting and yanking and pleading and tears, still there I was, trapped in the basement as Stony sang the sad ballad of his life.

"It gets old fast, Road Dog, carrying the bag. I've gotten old, fast. How many years do I have left? Ten, fifteen at the most before my heart explodes in my chest. Am I not to drink champagne from the slipper of a slim nineteen-year-old? Am I not to bake like a beached whale on the sands of some tropical paradise? Am I destined to die as I lived, in this house, bound by these braces, clutching to the death this stinking bag?"

"The sad lament of the aging bagman," I said. "You're making me sick to my stomach, Stony."

"Use the thermos if you must. But I have my dreams."

"And to reach for them you sold me out."

"I sold you out?"

He put the cigarette in his mouth and tossed the envelope from the camera store, spun it hard so that it would have nicked my face had I not knocked it down with my free hand.

"Take a gander," he said, a line of spite now in his voice. "Take a good look at the reason why you won't ever be rising from this basement, at least not in one piece. I'll have to chop you up and bag the bits to get you out."

The envelope was already open. I tilted it so that the photographs I had ordered from Goodrich Camera spilled onto the floor. I went through them as best I could, sliding through the pile one by one. And in the middle I stopped, picked up a photograph, stared at it for a moment before looking up at the sweating figure sitting across from me.

"Oh, Stony," I said.

"And now you know."

"Now I know."

"It was not what I was intending."

"Oh, Stony," I said again, and strangely, even as he had me cuffed to a pipe on the floor of his basement, even as he was threatening to cut me up and stuff me into black plastic garbage bags, I couldn't help but feel a great heaving pity for him. I knew now why he was sweating, why his emotions were veering madly across the landscape: he had been swallowed by his crimes and had lost himself.

Along with the photographs of the girl in Lancaster, and the photographs of Bettenhauser and his charitable friend that I had already been given, were photographs of me, yes, snaps of me. There I was making my way through the town, there I was walking with Ossana, there I was captured through a diner window breakfasting with McDeiss, there I was passing my envelopes to this labor leader and that community organizer, there I was stepping with my bag into the Devereaux mansion. And let's just say the angles weren't flattering.

He had been spying on me, my friend Stony Mulroney, and based on the photograph of me entering Boyds to buy a tuxedo, he had been shadowing me even from before we first met. There were photographs of Duddleman waiting outside my apartment and then later talking with me before going up my stairs, pictures that nearly broke my heart. But even the Duddleman pictures were not the saddest, no.

The saddest pictures were the photographs of a woman walking out of a bar on Eighteenth Street, walking out of the Franklin, photographs of Jessica Barnes leaving her meeting with me. But Stony's camera didn't stay at the bar, waiting for me to emerge. Suddenly it was following Jessica, down this street and that street, until, in a close-up, she was looking with fear on her pretty face as someone approached her. And then the full pan of the girl and two men who were approaching, Colin Frost and the skinny bearded kid, the same ones who would kill Duddleman.

"You told them where she was," I said. "You told them where she was going."

"I thought all they wanted was a bit of a talk."

"Oh, Stony."

"I didn't know it would end in a murder," he said with a crack of despair in his voice. "It wasn't I that wielded the hammer, believe that. It wasn't those two blaggards either."

"Who, then?"

"Your demon lover, Victor. How does that feel, to know you were slipping it to her that did the hammering? But I wasn't a part of it, I didn't know."

"You're as much a part of it as they are."

"Not without the evidence, see? Oh, Road Dog, if it were only the photographs in that envelope, we'd be having a different conversation now, wouldn't we? I would have already burnt the pictures and smashed the memory card. You'd be none the wiser and I'd be off scot-free. After that I would only keep you here until the deed was done and then we'd leave again as best of friends."

There had been a high level of fear eating at my liver from the moment I saw Stony in my apartment, but now it was like someone had jacked one end of a wire into fear's brain and the other end into a socket.

"What deed?" I said.

"And after all the dust had settled, and all the crimes were over and done with, I would have invited you down to my eventual redoubt on the Yucatan, and we'd have swallowed daiquiris on the beach together and screwed twenty-peso whores and laughed about the old times when all we could stomach was something as hard as a Sazerac."

"What deed are we talking about, Stony?"

"It was the clerk at the camera store, a pretty young thing behind the counter, who laid your perfidy bare. She told me about the other clerk, the one who received two bills to deliver a disk from a Mr. Carl. I suppose she was hoping for more of the same from me, the little conniver. And that right there put a crimp in all our plans. It took me all morning to find him, but I did. And after some encouragement he told me where he delivered the disk. Like a knife in the heart."

"They're going to do something to the girl in Lancaster? When?"

"It was you who set the timetable."

"What are they going to do?"

He stood suddenly, too angry anymore to sit. He began to pace, growing more agitated with each step of those heavy black stompers. The sweat beaded on his forehead now, as from a fever.

"What they tell me is nothing," said Stony. "I'm merely a bagman to them. 'Take the money and shut up,' he says with his affected little snivel, and so I do, and I do. But in the end it wasn't them, it was you who betrayed me. By sending that disk to McDeiss, you as good as put my head on a pike. How could you do me like that?"

I looked at my hand, at the handcuff, at the pipe to which I was chained, and then back at Stony.

"I should kick you in the head for what you did," he said.

"You don't want to do that."

"Oh, but I do," he said. "I really, really do."

And so he did.

In the moment before I closed my eyes, I saw the big black sledgehammer of a shoe come at me like a bounding panther. And then, in the darkness, a bright light exploded as the blow landed just above my jaw and sent me spinning until my other cheek slammed into the basement wall and my wrist jerked, excruciating, in its cuff. My face felt like a smashed ceramic mask, and a bell was ringing in my ear.

When I opened my eyes again, even as the pain was diffusing through the whole of my head, Stony was back in the chair, breathing deeply. He took his hat off and wiped his forehead with a sleeve.

"That was curiously satisfying," he said.

I could barely hear him over the ringing. He lit a cigarette, took a luxurious inhale, lifted his jaw as he blew out the smoke. I reached my free hand to my face and it came away slick with blood.

"Now what?" I said, trying and failing to keep the hate out of my voice.

"The plan was a simple one," he said, eerily calm, as if the violence had taken something sharp out of him. "I would let this little game of ours play out, pocket the money, go on as I've been going on as I set up my departure. I had enough if I sold the house, collected a few debts, twisted what I could out of those I had bought in my years lugging the bag. Maybe even put the squeeze on the old lady, and the runt keeping the Big Butter's eye on her. And then I'd be off, ahead of the inevitable indictment. Now it's too late. Thanks to you, I'm already on the run. Now the only way I collect anything is to make her happy, our demon dream."

He took another inhale, examining me carefully as I lay sprawled and bloody on the cement floor.

"She wants your shoes," he said.

"Take them."

"You know that's not enough."

"You're not a killer, Stony."

"You're right, I'm not, and that's what makes this so difficult. I was stepping over the line with my payoffs and schemes, yes, but at least I always knew where the line it was, and my farthest step was never too far from the straight and the narrow. That was fine when I was answering to the small-money boys, but when you sign up with the Big Butter, the money smothers you in zeroes and suddenly the whole of your soul is in the bill of sale. The line that was firstly here is suddenly there, and then over there, and then so far away it can't even be seen from where you were before. And now here I am."

"Don't cross it, Stony."

"It's already crossed. That's the problem. I'm already on the other side. I want to be more than this. I want to be better than this. And yet they have dragged me into the mire."

"You did it to yourself. Let me go and we'll start to unravel the damage."

"I want to. Believe me." He locked his eyes on mine. "Do you believe me?"

"Does it matter?"

"My father, he always told me to be courageous, yes, and that's the ticket here. But is it more courageous to stand up to them, or to step over my pathetic hesitations by putting a bullet in your throat?"

"Not the second thing, the first thing."

"I'm confused, Road Dog. And sad. And angry. I'm an animal caught in a trap, and there is only one way out."

"You kill me, Stony, and you'll regret it today, tomorrow, for the rest of your life."

"Maybe so, but what choice do I have?" He pushed himself to standing and staggered toward me. "It won't be the grand retirement I had planned, but what I end up with will be something. I can't run away with nothing. My father made of me a bagman, isn't this just the inevitable next step?"

"No."

"Yes, no, what does it matter in the end? In the end all that matters is the doing, and the time for the doing has come. Open up, Road Dog, it's dinnertime."

CHAPTER 42

LIKE HOFFA

When the gun fired, and it did fire, like the crack of the devil's whip, accompanied as it was with a hint of smoke and the scent of sulfur, it wasn't pointed in my direction. At the moment Stony was aiming his black automatic at my open mouth, we were both interrupted, him from killing me and me from dying, by the sound of the basement window being smashed: a crash and a tinkle accompanied by a stone clattering and skidding on the floor.

With the alacrity of an overweight nip-addicted cat, Stony whirled and fired.

He missed the window. The bullet hit the stone wall and ricocheted into the water heater, where the old thing started pissing for real, two nice steady flows, one right onto my head, as if the bullet had killed not an intruder but the water heater's prostate. I scrabbled as best I could out of the thin, steaming stream.

"Damn, Stony," came a deep voice from on high, "you done killed that water heater."

Stony wheeled around again and shot twice reflexively, splintering the ragged wood of the empty stairwell.

"Aw, now you've gone and murdered the stairs. What's next, the boiler?"

Stony cocked his head. "Hump? Is that you, Hump?"

"Indeed. You going to try to shoot me if I come on down?"

"Hell, yes."

"Then aim for my head. That way I know you'll miss me but good."

"What the hell are you doing here, Hump?"

"We aim to pull you out of the shithouse, boy. You ain't making nothing but mistakes lately. You still okay there, Victor?"

"I'm a little wet," I said.

"The bladder is always the first to let go. We're coming down now, Stony. You stay calm and put away the gun."

"I will, surely I will. Just as soon as I kill Road Dog here. Do you know what he did, Hump? Do you have any idea how badly he betrayed me?"

"Let's not quibble about who betrayed who," I said.

"He turned me in to McDeiss," said Stony. "Gave the copper enough evidence to string me up good and tight. And after all I did for him. Why, Brutus was a loving son to Caesar compared to what this little bastard has been to me. I deserve my justice."

"Since when is any of what we do about justice?" This was a different voice calling down the stairs, hard and sharp with a tobacco-stained roughness. "Put that thing away, now, before you shoot yourself in the ass. We're coming down."

Climbing down the stairs bravely were a pair of low heels attached to a set of stick-thin legs. Stony aimed the gun at the stairs as Maud descended, but there was something so implacable about her manner, and her face when it appeared was so calm and unalarmed, that her very presence made the gun seem absurd. Behind Maud came Hump, hard and hatted, his black raincoat swirling about him like a superhero's cape. Hump went right to the water heater and turned off the water so that the scalding stream eased and then stopped. Scuttling down behind the two, breathlessly catching up, was Miles Schimmeck.

The Brotherhood was in session, and the conclave was not a total surprise, since this time it was I who had called them to order.

In the middle of my meeting with Tommy Bettenhauser, when it had become clear that there was no affair and that anyone who had done any research to that effect—like, say, Stony—would have known the truth, I realized I was being abjectly betrayed. Stony had come into my office that very first day with every intent to betray me. He was working for someone else, had been working for someone else even before Bettenhauser announced, which meant he wasn't working for Bettenhauser. There was only one player big enough to have bought Briggs Mulroney's son so early in the game: the Big Butter. I wasn't sure yet why, but I was sure it wouldn't stop with a few misleading photographs. I was being set up, I was being made a fall guy, and Stony, sometime soon and for whomever the hell was paying him, was going to send me falling into a grave.

So even as Mrs. Bettenhauser spoke about the sexual predilections of the woman in the grainy black-and-white photographs, I acted to protect myself.

"Can I borrow your phone, Carrie?" I had said.

"My phone?"

"Mine is out of power."

She looked at her husband, looked back at me, made it clear that she was not so pleased with the idea. "Sure, I suppose."

"Thank you," I said, galloping forward despite her hesitance. In the corner, my back shielding my work from prying eyes, I texted a message.

ITS VC. BEEN BETRAYED BY STONY. NEED HELP!

And who did I text it to? Well, who did I have? McDeiss? He would just laugh and tell me he told me so. Melanie? Who knew which side she was on. The Congressman? He had his own problems, and whatever was going on, his sister was tit-deep in it. Duddleman? Already dead. Timothy from Boyds? He'd just try to sell me an overpriced Trussini for my corpse. No, I had no one to go to with my pathetic plea for help, no one other than—

"Who wants a cigarette?" said Maud, taking out her pack.

"Don't mind if I do," said Hump.

"Stony?"

"I suppose if you're twisting my arm."

"Is it menthol?" said Schimmeck. "I prefer menthol."

"You don't get a choice, Miles, I'm not a fricking Wawa. And anyway, smoking a menthol is like smoking a can of deodorant. You, Victor?"

Soaked and still bleeding, still in pain, still scared out of my wits, I looked back and forth at the four of them, nonplussed by the calm. "I . . . I don't smoke," I said.

"Oh, yes, that's right," said Maud before handing out the cigarettes, inhaling deeply as she lit hers, and then tossing the lighter to Hump. "Being handcuffed to a pipe and having a gun pointed at your face is one thing, but a cigarette, now that's just asking for trouble."

A swarm of laughter, like a swarm of bees, flew around my head. One by one they lit their cigarettes and stood together, smoking, bonding, like an ancient tribe over the nightly fire. And I felt, just then, the stirrings of a love, true and grateful, for all of them, minus that son of a bitch Stony Mulroney.

"You might as well light up, Road Dog," said Stony, "since I have to shoot you after this smoke."

"You're not going to shoot Victor," said Maud.

"Thank you," I said.

"But that's why I brought him here," said Stony. "That's why I have this gun. I'm going to shoot him dead, and then I'm going to shoot him again just because."

"Tell him, Hump."

"You can't be shooting Victor in the basement," said Hump.

"Thank you again," I said.

"Too messy," said Hump.

"What?" I said.

"The blood will end up splattering on the plaster and pouring onto the floor," said Schimmeck. "Linoleum is one thing—it cleans up nice—but cement just soaks up the stain. You'll end up with a crime scene you'll never be able to clean. When the cops come, and they will come, if Victor did what you said he did, then it will be like an announcement of the murder."

"Oh, don't you be worrying about that," said Stony. "By then I'll be gone."

"But we won't," said Schimmeck. "You kill Victor and they'll be on us like bears on honey. We don't need that kind of heat right now."

"Then what do I do?" said Stony. "I've got to kill the man."

"We understand, Stony. We do," said Maud. She took a long inhale and blew a thin stream. "And truth is, I don't think we could stick him with any more checks at Rosen's, so what happens to him is not our concern. But this shooting-in-the-basement thing just isn't going to cut it."

"Just do the usual," said Schimmeck. "Drive him out to Hog Island, find a boggy strip of marsh, and make him start digging."

"You gots to go deep though," said Hump, "or the body starts rising. We had that problem in New Orleans, arms and legs sticking out the swamp like stunted trees. Not good. Don't know if Victor is up to digging deep enough. You work out, Victor?"

"Just looking at him," said Maud, shaking her head sadly, "my guess is no."

"That's a problem right there," said Hump.

"Hump, aren't you carrying for that new parking lot going in on Sixth Street?" said Schimmeck.

"I am," said Hump.

"When are they pouring?"

"They been. Got the basement almost formed."

"There you go, Stony," said Maud. "I'm sure Hump could reserve a corner for you."

Stony lifted the gun. "Then I'll kill him here and take him there. It's as simple as pain."

"Don't forget the blood," said Hump. "Better to kill him on scene."

"Will that work?"

Maud shrugged. "It's worth a try."

"You want to do it right," said Hump, "get a barrel."

"Barrel?" I said.

"A metal barrel, the kind they start fires in," said Schimmeck.

"You stick him in a metal barrel," said Hump, "fill it with concrete, then roll that down into the foundation."

"That's what they done with Hoffa," said Schimmeck.

"Do I get to shoot him first?" said Stony.

"It's neater if he goes in alive, so they say," said Schimmeck. "Try to make him climb in himself and then hunch down. Put a gun to his head, and a lunkhead like Victor will do anything."

"I will not," I said.

Stony pointed the gun at my head and said, "Shut up."

I shut up.

"Then when you pour in your cement," said Miles, "they struggle, but quietly, see, and eventually they breathe it in. They say the cement fills the lungs nicely."

"That sounds a bit cruel to me," said Stony.

"At least it's not a cigarette," said Maud.

They laughed and laughed.

And then came the footsteps.

They weren't trying to be soft or unheard, the footsteps from the floor above us. There was no furtive creeping. Just a single set of heavy, assertive steps, a man's footfall. And the laughter died, cackle by cackle, as the Brotherhood, one by one, heard the steps. And they each looked up, first Maud, then Hump, then Miles Schimmeck, and finally Stony, tossing away his lit cigarette and pointing his gun at me as he put a finger to his lips.

Step-by-step, closer and closer. McDeiss? The Congressman? Colin Frost, out to kill another? Aubrey, bringing a tray of Sazeracs? I couldn't imagine who the hell it was, but I sensed, rightly, that something fierce was bound to follow in the footsteps' unerring wake. The footsteps stopped at the door to the basement and we were engulfed in a cold, smoky silence.

And then a voice called out, ragged as a chain saw and hearty as a pirate: "Lower your hats and raise your bottles, you deadbeat beans. I'm coming down."

CHAPTER 43

THE COMEBACK KID

The man who appeared was a colossus, with ham hands and a jaw like a slug of whiskey. He was old, sure, but one of those old men who have held onto their size and aura of ferocity. He wore a gray suit, a beige raincoat, a fedora the size of Pittsburgh. His ears were great sprouts of cauliflower, his mangled nose looked like it had been sacked by Gaul. I didn't recognize him, of course I didn't, I had never seen the like of him before. But Stony's face grew curiously pale, like it was Hamlet's ghost who had come down that stairway for him, and I guess, in a way, it was.

"Hump," said the old man, with a nod. "Maud. Schimmeck, you twit." He put those ham-sized fists on his hips, looked around at the mess in the basement, including me—still cuffed to the pipe, still bloody, now sitting in a puddle—and thumbed his fedora higher on his head. "What the hell happened to my water heater?"

"Are you . . . ?" I said. "You couldn't be . . ."

"Who were you expecting?" said the old man. "The Batman?"

"I thought you were dead," I said.

"Dead?"

We turned to look at Stony, who had stayed silent and pale.

"Did you tell this sopping piece of meat I was dead, laddie?" said the old man.

Stony's head sagged and his gaze hit the floor. "Not exactly. I left some wiggle room."

"You sure as hell implied it," I said. "What was all that stuff about his going off to greener pastures?"

"I was talking about Shannondell," said Stony. "His retirement community in Valley Forge."

"Oh, I understand, all right," said Briggs Mulroney, the one and only. "It's a hard thing living in a shadow as grand as my own. It wasn't until my father was buried deep that I myself began to roar. But no, I'm not dead, just shacked up with a young piece of quaff in that Shannondell. Quite the lively place, actually. I've got an art exhibit next week." He stuck out a thick, squat finger and swept it at the rest of the Brotherhood, like a machine gun wiping out an entire troop. "And all of yous beans is coming."

"What are you doing here?" said Stony.

"Maud called me in, said you were in the middle of a situation. She was right, as usual. First off, give up the gun."

"I'm taking care of things myself," said Stony.

"Not with a gun. Rule One: we carry bags, not guns. Too many things go wrong when the bullets fly."

"I thought a bagman always working for himself was Rule One," I said.

He turned and looked at me like I was a patch of mold growing on the wall. "Every rule becomes Rule One when you screw it up."

He reached out his hand and snapped his fingers, once, twice, and then waited. Stony seemed to deflate with each snap, until, with the hesitance of a child, he stepped forward and put the gun in his father's huge paw. The old man slipped it into his jacket pocket.

"Christ, look at the water heater," said the old man. "What were you shooting at, rats?"

"I'm in the crapper, Pop," said Stony.

"You was always in the crapper, even as a kid. No matter how much we banged on the door, we couldn't get you out." He looked at Maud and shook his hand like he was shaking dice. "Of course, then at least he was being productive. So what is it now?"

"I got caught up with the Big Butter."

Briggs Mulroney nodded sadly. "What did I tell you, you dumb squirt? The Big Butter is always fatal."

"But the only butter left is the Big Butter," said Stony. "The world's changing."

Briggs's head snapped toward his son like a chain had been yanked. "Don't let it," he growled. "How deep are you in?"

"Up to my neck."

"What do they got on you?"

"They have me on a murder rap."

"Ah, Christ, who'd you kill?"

"I didn't kill anyone. There was a woman I was supposed to tail. I didn't know what was going to happen, I swear. But they have me as an accessory."

"Accessory?" said Briggs, with a spit of disgust. "That's a handbag or a belt. A pair of socks. Accessory we can work around, or I'm not Briggs Mulroney. I'll make calls."

He took out a cigarette and lit it. The others tossed what shortened butts they still held and lit new ones. They stood in a circle, the five of them, Briggs and his son, Hump and Maud and Miles Schimmeck, silently smoking, like the pure purpose of the world spinning around and all of humanity scurrying to and fro was for that very moment, in that foul, soggy basement, when they could grab a second of respite to light up a cig.

"Does he want one?" said Briggs, thumbing toward me.

"Doesn't smoke," said Hump.

Briggs raised an eyebrow and shook his head. "That's smart, it might kill him."

General laughter at my expense.

"It would do a better job than Stony, in any event," said Schimmeck.

"Shut up, Miles," said Stony. "He'd be dead now if you degenerates hadn't stuck your noses in."

"And then where would you be?" said Briggs. "So far inside the crapper you could only breathe when they flushed. Okay, what's the play?"

"There is no play," said Maud.

"There's always a play."

"Not here," said Hump. "Not now."

"Who's the lead on the case, and how much will it take?"

"It's McDeiss," said Miles.

"Oh, crap," said Briggs, as if that settled that. "How the hell can you trust someone you can't buy?"

He stood there for another moment more, smoking and thinking. Briggs Mulroney smoked in black and white. He held his cigarette between thumb and two forefingers, and shriveled it an inch with each inhale. He twisted an ear as he thought. Finally, he looked up at his son.

"How does the beach sound?" he said.

"The beach?" said Stony. "For real?"

"For every fucking day of the rest of your fucking life. You might be better off in prison. But I know a guy who knows a guy who's got a plane. I got a scam going down in Panama and you're the perfect guy to screw it up. Grab your coat and let's get out of here."

"What about me?" I said.

Briggs stopped and looked at me, a complete afterthought. "You was the bean in the papers."

"That's right."

"Didn't anyone ever tell you to keep your fucking face out of the papers?"

"Actually, yes."

"Do you still need to kill him?" said Briggs to his son.

"Not anymore."

"And you, paper boy, you'll keep your fucking mouth shut?"

"Yes, sir," I said.

"Let him go."

Stony hustled over and fumbled in his pocket for the key. "I wasn't going to do it," he said softly.

"Sure you were," I said.

"Maybe. But I wouldn't have been happy about it."

I rubbed my wrist when I was finally freed, and scrabbled to standing to get out of the damn puddle. "What is she doing with the girl?"

"I don't know the details," said Stony. "I was just the hired help. But something, for sure."

As he started to walk after his father, I said, "Stony. My wallet."

He stopped, came back, and popped it out of his pocket. "Sorry."

"Let's go, boy," said Briggs Mulroney before tossing down his cig and starting up the stairs. "Time to ride into the sunset."

"So long, suckers," said Stony.

Briggs was halfway up the stairs, stooping so as not to bang his head, when he stopped, turned around, and pointed.

"Don't forget my show," he said. "Next Wednesday. I'm working in clay now. Horses."

"We wouldn't miss it," said Maud.

"And make sure you buy something, too, you beans," he said, and then he turned and disappeared up the stairs, Stony dutifully disappearing behind him.

And that was how a dead man named Briggs Mulroney saved my life.

Wet and bloody and smelling rank, I looked at Hump and Schimmeck and the luminous Maud, and my heart opened to them. I owed my life to them, each of them, and my indebtedness felt surprisingly rich.

We all want to be the heroes of our own stories. We all want to use our wits and wiles and outsized physical gifts to save our own damn lives. But I learned early and hard that I am not James Bond, that in the tightest of spots I would always be dependent on the beneficence of others. It is a frightening state of affairs, true, but it is not a terrible way to go through life. And I felt just then that I needed to say something, to let them know how I felt. But what could possibly convey the multitude of emotions that were flooding through me? And then the words came, as if formed by gratitude's own sweet lips.

"A stinking barrel?"

CHAPTER 44

PUBLIC POLICY

She was waiting outside my apartment when Maud dropped me off, sitting in a black-and-white illegally parked in front of a hydrant. Before I was halfway up the front steps she swooped out to intercept me, her figure as short and squat as the hydrant itself, in full uniform with gun weighing down her side.

"You've got to be kidding," I said.

"Why don't we avoid the meaningless patter," said Officer Boot, "and just go where we have to go?"

"But meaningless patter is the basis of our entire relationship. What would we have if we didn't have meaningless patter?"

"Nothing. That's the point."

"So you want to go deep."

"If that means silent, like a submarine, then yes."

"Where is he?"

"The Roundhouse."

"Tell him I need to shower and change, because he won't want to see me the way I am. And then I'll meet him there."

"No, sir."

"No what?"

"You can shower and change, because I can smell you from here and I don't want you fouling up my car. While you're at it, you can fix up that wound on your cheek, which, I must admit, gives your face the dashing air of a violent meth addict. But my orders are to deliver you personally, and personally it will be."

I had learned before that there was no arguing with Officer Boot. Resigned to a trip to the Roundhouse in the back of her squad car, I primped for the ride. The view in the mirror as I shaved was more unpleasant than usual; the left side of my face was swollen from Stony's kick, the right side was scabbed from the wall. And my wrist, my poor damaged wrist, was raw as sushi. I patched myself as best I could before I put on a suit and tie, hoping to hide the damage.

"What the hell happened to you?" said McDeiss in the interrogation room.

I put a hand up to my raw, scabby cheek. "I got kicked in the face by a pony."

"You should get that looked at."

"You're looking, aren't you? You get my gift?"

"Yes, I did," said McDeiss. "I wanted to thank you for that. It was—how should I say—out of character for you to be so generous with information."

"And that's why you sent Officer Boot to haul me in?"

"We still have some pressing questions."

"Dry cleaning helps." I looked around at the green walls, the large mirror, the locked door. In this place, time no longer belonged to me. I was going nowhere, this whole investigation was going nowhere, even as I knew the case was going somewhere deadly fast. The whole reason I sent the photographs to McDeiss was to get him up to speed, but he apparently hadn't made the leaps I'd hoped he would make. This was my moment to get him to start doing what I needed him to do, and fast. I leaned forward and slapped the table.

"What have you done about the photographs?"

"Well, for one, we've got an APB out for Colin Frost. We checked at the rehab clinic and he's not there."

"Surprise, surprise."

"And neither is another patient, one Jason Howard, whose description matches the second man in the photograph. Coincidentally, this Howard also matches the description of the man you gave us after the Duddleman murder. We're looking for him, too."

"Now what about Ossana DeMathis, are you looking for her?"

"She wasn't in the photographs."

"But she's the one behind the killings, she's the one behind everything. She was the one with the hammer."

"The hammer with your fingerprints on it."

"You're not getting it," I said. "What about the girl?"

"Red hair, playing around a tree. I thought they were just snapshots. What about her?"

"Are you protecting her?"

"From what?"

"You're not getting it, not at all."

"That's why I dragged you here. Let's start at the beginning. Where did you get the photographs?"

"From a card I swiped from a camera."

"Mulroney's camera, according to the note you scrawled on the envelope."

"That's right."

"Any idea where that scum is?"

"No," I said.

"Armbruster just called from his father's old house. There was a mess in the basement. Handcuffs on a pipe, bullet holes through a water heater and in the wall. Stains that looked like blood. Do you know anything about that?"

"No," I said.

"What's with your wrist?"

I looked down at my left arm. Blood had soaked into the shirt cuff. "My digital watch exploded."

McDeiss leaned back and stretched out his arms. "That's the Victor Carl I know and loathe. Tell me about the pictures of Tommy Bettenhauser, candidate for Congress."

"They don't matter, they're a sideshow. The girl is the story. You need to get somebody up to the Lancaster address I gave you, to protect the girl. The girl's the reason for all of this, and Ossana now knows where she is. Did you check out the blood smear and the hair I gave you?"

"There's a preliminary match," he said. "The blood and the hair are of the same family."

"Aunt and niece," I said, nodding.

"Tell me why that is so damn important."

"It's why they killed Jessica Barnes, because she had the girl and was about to spill about the link. And why they killed Amanda Duddleman, because she was getting close to the truth. And why the girl is in danger from Ossana DeMathis."

"What is it with you and her?"

"I know a demon when I screw one."

"Ahh, I see."

"See what?"

"It's personal."

"You bet it's personal, as personal as blood, but not in the way you think. It's personal because she's a killer and I think that little girl is next on her list. I sent you the photographs and gave you the address so you would do something, and fast. I thought the pictures would be a spur in your ass."

"You know I'm a little slow, right?"

"I've noticed."

"Maybe you better explain it to me slowly."

I took a deep breath, weighed the little girl's welfare against any dubious claims of privilege I might have had, and then told McDeiss a story.

Once there was a girl who was rabidly devoted to her brother, a randy frat boy with political ambitions. At one point, when the brother was serving in the august House of Representatives, a baby was born, probably to one of the brother's paramours and, for fear of scandal, it was given away to be raised by a family in Lancaster, home of presidents. All was well until the Great Recession hit and the family fell into hard times and the adoptive mother felt she had no choice but to try to blackmail the Congressman with evidence of the child's existence. Her proof was a smear of blood on a card that showed paternity. She was paid off by the brother's noble bagman, paid off exceedingly well, actually. All would have gone as it was supposed to go, except that the sister, with that crazed devotion to her brother, and in order to protect his career from continuing blackmail demands, murdered the woman before she could get home to the child, stealing the money to pay off the killers and setting up the noble bagman as a murder suspect. Later, a young reporter, who happened to be the Congressman's lover, finally tracked the girl down, even getting a photograph as evidence from a doctor's office. But before the reporter could pass along this newly discovered information to the noble bagman, the sister made sure the reporter also was murdered. And now, the sister intended to do something horrid to the little girl to finally end any threat the girl may present to the brother's precious political career.

McDeiss listened to this all with the patience of a cat, taking notes now and then, asking a few questions to clear up this detail or that inconsistency. And when my little story was over, he leaned back and shook his head.

"It doesn't add up," he said.

"What doesn't add up?"

"The motivations. They don't make sense, or at least enough sense. The devoted sister? Who the hell is that devoted? What other evidence do you have that she was involved?"

"She sort of admitted it to me."

"Sort of? Is that pillow talk?"

"No, more like fuck-off talk. And Stony sort of confirmed it for me."

"And you believe that fat piece of corruption?"

"Yes."

"Based on what you've said, even if Frost and this Howard did the killings, as the photos suggest, the person behind them might just as easily have been the Congressman, or the Congressman's wife, or the Congressman's chief of staff."

"Or maybe it was the Congressman's bagman," I said.

"It makes more sense than the sister. All you have pointing to Miss DeMathis is that she might have a motive, but the motive is weak tea. And now you want us to run a police operation out of our jurisdiction to protect a girl who as far as we know has no connection to anything."

"You have the DNA test."

"And we know the blood is hers?"

I stared for a moment. "If I didn't know better, I'd think you've been reached."

"By common sense and self-protection, yes. It is the policy of the Philadelphia Police Department not to arrest congressmen, or their immediate family, without any proof of guilt, and your sort-of confessions and counterintuitive suppositions are not proof. Do you have anything else?"

I scraped my skull until it hurt. "No."

"So there we are."

I looked into his passive face and felt something in me deflate. "You're not going to arrest Ossana DeMathis," I said.

"Someone with a higher pay grade than me will ask to question her, but that's as far as it will go."

"You're not going to protect that girl."

"Someone with a higher pay grade than me will confer with the Lancaster police."

"That's not good enough."

"Get more evidence, and the Department can do more."

"I thought getting evidence was your job," I said, standing. "I'll be in touch."

I was at the door when he said, "Carl?"

I turned around and raised an eyebrow.

"You're going to do something stupid."

"Character is destiny."

He nodded sadly at all the sad stupidity in the world, and then said, "You want company?"

CHAPTER 45

RUNNING MATES

I brought the thermoses, McDeiss brought the surly.

"What do we expect to happen exactly?" growled McDeiss.

"Sunset," I said.

"When you said you were going to do something stupid, I didn't realize you'd be so literal about it."

"We're just here to wait and see what there is to see," I said.

"More like wait and wait."

"What did you think, I was going to put on a costume and a cape and swing into action?"

"At least then I'd get to arrest somebody."

"Who?"

"You, for a crime against spandex."

We were in Lancaster, sitting in my small Mazda, parked behind that wide leafy oak on Irishtown Road. With a pair of binoculars, I was keeping an eye on the front door of the house where Stony and I had seen the little red-haired girl. McDeiss, wedged into the seat next to me, his head rubbing the roof, his knees chest-high, was letting loose an endless supply of pained sighs.

"I thought with all your experience you'd be more patient on a stakeout," I said.

"Is that what this is? It feels more like a waste of good vacation time."

"You're the one who said you could only do this off duty."

"And you're getting paid?"

"I'll keep track of my hours and submit a bill, if that's what you're asking."

"To whom?"

"I wish I knew. You want more coffee?"

"I've had enough caffeine. What's in the other thermos?"

"You don't want to know."

For a long time there was no action at the house, no evidence of anyone inside, and I wondered if my tour in Stony's basement had given Ossana time to play it out without my interference. But then, just as I was about to do something reckless, Mrs. Gaughan appeared, Jessica Barnes's mother, lugging a bag of groceries with a stuffed teddy bear sitting on top. She looked around and failed to spot anything suspicious, including us. The screen door closed behind her, along with my doubts about who was inside.

"Don't worry about wasting your time," I said. "I have the feeling that whatever's going to happen is going to happen soon."

"What is going to happen exactly?"

"I don't know, but something." I paused a bit and looked at his surly mien before saying, "And when it does, I'll be glad you're along."

"But not until then."

"No, until then you're just a complaining pain in my ass." I sat quiet for a moment, letting a thought or two burble. "You want to hear something funny? A prime political fixer who lunches at the Union League said I had the common touch. Can you believe such a thing?"

"I don't know anyone more common than you."

"What's your great ambition in life? Head of detectives?"

"No."

"Chief of police?"

"God, no. Last thing I need is a bunch of sycophants dancing around my desk like some troupe of modern dancers. I've worked hard all these years to avoid a management position and I aim to keep succeeding. No, sir, all I ever wanted was to be a homicide dick."

"You're lucky. My life can't ever live up to my ambitions."

"Penny-ante bagman isn't high enough?"

"That whole common-touch thing got me to thinking. Maybe if this political thing worked out just perfectly, when the Congressman finally left office I could run for his seat. United States Congressman Victor Carl. Why the hell not? Can't I mug for the cameras? Can't I suck up money from rich widows and tell the mob what it wants to hear? Lower taxes, higher benefits, a flag pin on every lapel. And after a few terms of getting my smile on the Sunday shows, maybe I'd run for Senate and from there, who knows? Nab a VP slot? Go for the big seat itself?"

"You're kidding me, right?"

"Why someone else and not me?"

"And then what?"

"Well, you know what Nietzsche said."

"'God is dead'?"

"That means there's an opening."

He laughed at that.

"I'm cursed," I said, "with unbridled ambition."

"And yet you've done so little with it."

"Thank you. But when your ambition is so wrought that you're never satisfied, it takes a load of pressure off. Every spot on the ladder is equally disappointing because it is not the rung above. Which means I've perfectly fulfilled my potential; I've reached as high as I'll ever get, the point of not good enough. Does that look out of place?"

"Yes, it does," said McDeiss.

It was a Lincoln Town Car, black and sleek, making its way toward us on the dusty road. We had already been passed by pick-ups and vans, old beaters and a muscular Camaro with a blown muffler, but this was the first Lincoln Town Car, maybe the first in a decade.

"It's Ossana, coming for the girl," I said.

"Paying a visit? Saying good-bye?"

"She's not that innocent. She'll be with Colin Frost and that other murderer, that Jason Howard, and whatever she intends, it won't be good."

It wasn't a surprise when the Town Car stopped right in front of the house we had been watching. For a moment the car remained idling, quivering not so much from the churning of its engine as from anticipation. I kept the binoculars tight to my eyes. McDeiss took out his gun and pulled back the slide to slip a round into the chamber.

The rear door opened, and I could just see a leg step out, a long shapely leg in a shiny high heel, the shoe red, the leg itself dark as coffee. An instant later the whole red-clad figure appeared in the circle of my binocular vision. She clutched a stack of blue-backed legal documents in her hand as she made her way to the house.

"Damn," I said.

"She looks familiar," said McDeiss. "Who is she?"

"Her name's Melanie Brooks."

"I think I know her."

"She's a lawyer in the firm of Ronin and McCall."

"I've never heard of them. What are they? Criminal?"

"Undoubtedly."

"Who is she representing?"

"She does errands for the Congressman, but she's working for someone else."

"Who?"

"I don't know."

"What's she doing here?"

"It won't be too long until we find out."

And it became clear a few moments later when Melanie Brooks came out of the house holding the hand of the little red-haired girl.

The girl was looking behind her all the while that Melanie was leading her to the car. And following the two of them with frantic hands was Mrs. Gaughan, staggering behind as if lurching after a disappearing dream. The girl stopped and turned around and tore away from Melanie. She ran to Mrs. Gaughan, who slowly collapsed to her knees, an old ruin finally going to ground, and hugged the girl tight as misery.

"Melanie, Melanie, you Machiavellian minx," I said.

"That the girl?" said McDeiss.

"That's the girl. Melanie, Melanie, Melanie," I said, with a true sadness in my voice, certain now that she had gone the way of Stony. "What have you done?"

What she did, when Mrs. Gaughan completed her desperate hug, was to gently lead the girl into the backseat of the Lincoln in order to whisk her to someplace awful. Awful, I was sure, in the primary definition of the word: terrible, dreadful, appalling. There was a moment, between the hug and the car, when the girl looked around at her surroundings and, in my solipsistic gaze through the binoculars, it appeared that she was looking around for someone to save her, looking around for someone like me.

Without a word we watched as the Town Car turned around in the driveway and headed away from us, up Irishtown Road. Mrs. Gaughan stared after it with a broken gaze, a woman who had already lost her daughter and was now losing something just as precious. Without a word we waited a moment longer until Mrs. Gaughan began the long walk back to the house. Then I pulled out from behind the tree.

I kept the Mazda as far behind as I could, obeying McDeiss's terse commands while the Town Car wended its way across the long rural roads. "Slow down. Speed up. Give it more room." Not surprisingly, he was better at the whole follow-without-being-seen thing and I deferred to his hard-won expertise.

"Crap," he said after the Lincoln had made still another turn. "They spotted us."

"How can you tell?"

"The way they took that turn, hard and without a signal. Close on in."

Suddenly our discreet following turned into a chase. I hit the gas, felt my tires slip before they engaged. The car screeched into a turn, I passed one of those buggies like a maniac, the car screeched again as I turned the other way. On either side of us were fields plowed straight as a comb's teeth, silos and houses huddled within stands of trees, a rusty metal harvester pulled by three horses. There was a moment when I thought I'd lost the Lincoln, that the car had used its brawny power to escape, but McDeiss calmly directed me until there it was, ahead but in sight as it veered off onto a busier road called Old Philadelphia Pike.

It was harder to get close now, with a bunch of cars between us and the Lincoln. The black car weaved desperately to lose us in the traffic, but McDeiss acted as a lookout while I weaved just as desperately. The buildings on the side of the road thickened and turned quaint, and the traffic slowed to a crawl. We moved in a processional through a touristy spot called Bird-in-Hand, with antique shops, and restaurants promising authentic Pennsylvania Dutch cooking. A lean man with a straw hat and gray beard lifted a box of apples.

Melanie wasn't after antiques or apple dumplings, I knew that, but where she was headed remained a mystery until, not far away and to our right we saw a small single-engine plane rise with twists and turns.

"Her plane's probably waiting on the runway," I said.

"I'm going to get on the horn to the local police now," said McDeiss.

"And tell them what?" I said. "Whatever Melanie did, she has the law on her side. That's what those blue-backed documents were all about. Let me find out from her what's really going on."

"You need to catch her first."

"I'm trying."

It wasn't easy keeping track of her in the slow-moving jumble of traffic, but the kitsch on the sides of the road eased and the traffic accelerated and McDeiss caught a glimpse of the long black car taking a turn just past a gas station ahead on the right. I heaved past a long furniture truck and veered in front of it to follow with a right of my own, onto the road that led straight to the airport. And on that small airport road, with a pizza place on one side and a machinery shop on the other, I saw the Lincoln careening to the right again.

I took the right right after, sped through a small parking area, then jagged to the left when I saw the black car sitting on a wide piece of asphalt bracketed by a shed on one side and a low hangar with a prop plane facing out in the other. And in front of the black car, waiting on the airport runway, was a small blue-nosed jet, an engine with the word "Honda" rising over its narrow white wing.

I jabbed my Mazda beside the Town Car, leaped out to grab hold of the handle to Melanie's door, and yanked it open.

In the backseat the child was crying and Melanie sat with her arm around the girl's shoulder, her face shot full of terror. But when she registered who had thrown open her door, something changed, brightened.

"Victor," she said. "Thank God it's you."

CHAPTER 46

AIR FORCE NONE

I had gotten it wrong. Spectacularly. No surprise there. To put down everything I had gotten wrong during my miserable descent into the mire of politics, I'd have to write a book.

I was standing between Melanie and McDeiss, newly clued in to the truth of what was actually happening, when the door to the plane disengaged from the body and dropped down, slowly down, revealing a set of bright-green stairs. The girl was still in the car, McDeiss was getting antsy, killers were still on the loose, push was coming to shove, and climbing down these stairs now was the Congressman's wife.

"Victor?" said Mrs. DeMathis. "I didn't expect to see you here. The situation must be more dire than I imagined."

I stepped forward so that we could talk privately. "Melanie explained the situation to me," I said. "I'm just a little surprised that you're the one who has come for her."

"I don't strike you as the maternal type?"

"No, actually, you don't. And certainly not with a child born of your husband's illicit affair. I would think you'd want her as far away from you as possible."

"What must you think of me."

"Yes," I said. "What must I."

"And you brought that insistent detective all the way from Philadelphia just to be sure my intentions were honorable."

"I wasn't willing to let it go."

She smiled. "My goodness, Victor, are you ever in the wrong game."

"So what exactly are your intentions?"

"At first, when I learned of the child during a drunken spat—where he sweetly used her existence to prove I was the barren one in our family—I contacted the agency just to see if there was anything I could do to help in difficult times. But after two murders, I realized the danger she was in from that insane woman, and my intentions changed. I intend now to take the girl away, to take her somewhere safe, until your detective neutralizes the threat. And then afterward, for as long as she needs it, to take care of her."

"As if she were your own."

"And isn't she? What else do any of us have in this world other than an obligation to her?"

"And your husband will be okay with that?"

"I've made clear to him that he has no choice. Whatever his objections, he'll give way and be grateful for it in the end. I've given my life over to the man still on the plane, and all he has proven over and again is that he is unworthy of it. And you wonder why I drink. But now fate and Ossana's insanity have given me another chance."

"So now you'll use the girl to find some sort of meaning in your meaningless existence."

"And is that so terrible? If I clutch her like a ring buoy in a salt sea, is that so terrible? All she'll know is my warm arms and beating heart, all she'll know is my strength and my love. I've so much to give and now I get to give it to her. Is that so terrible?"

There was steel within her that I had never seen before. Maybe because it was the first time I had seen her when she wasn't drunk.

"No," I said. "That's not so terrible. She's a lucky girl."

"One of us is," she said as she walked past me.

She said something to Melanie before opening the door and climbing into the backseat next to the girl. Melanie had convinced the Orphans' Court to award custody of the child to the Congressman. Now Mrs. DeMathis was going to spirit the girl away and raise her as her own, and it was all legal as sin. I gestured to McDeiss to wait on the tarmac before I climbed the stairs onto the plane.

The cabin of the small jet was tiny, pale and plush, with two narrow seats facing each other on either side of the aisle and another seat facing the door. Congressman DeMathis was sitting toward the rear, his body stiff, his tie tight, his glass three-quarters empty. He didn't react when he saw me. He looked like a guy holding on for dear life as his plane headed nose-first into the ground. His chief of staff, Tom Mitchum, was standing beside him, wringing his hands.

"Dammit, Victor, how did you let it get this far?" said Mitchum. "How could you shovel our money to Ossana? Why would you finance her?"

"You're looking at the wrong bagman," I said. "I haven't given her a cent. Someone else is serving up her salad."

"Who?"

"That's not the question. The question is for whom. Any ideas, Tom?"

Mitchum worked his lips as if trying to pull a hair out of his teeth.

"That's right," I said. "No matter the crime or the cost, let's all swallow our cocks for the Big Butter. Good idea, too, because the way things are shaping up, you'll be looking for a private-sector job in November. Now crawl off the plane and give me a moment with the Congressman."

Mitchum stared at me with something like hate in his eyes, self-hate maybe, before the Congressman gave a little wave of his hand. After Mitchum left, I sat across from the Congressman and leaned forward.

"Where is your sister?" I said.

"I still can't believe it's over."

"We need to find her."

"I'm lost, Victor, drifting in space, and it is brutally cold. What am I going to do now?"

"Take care of your daughter."

"My niece."

Niece? Did that make any sense? The little girl certainly looked enough like Ossana to be her daughter, but then why would Ossana DeMathis work so hard to hide her existence? Who was she really protecting?

"Where's Ossana?"

"I don't know. Who the hell knows? All I know is I'm out in the cold and I don't know what to do."

"Don't expect tears. That's just the way it is with political careers. Like relationships, they all end badly."

He shook his head, as if he were shaking himself out of a trance. "I'm not talking about my career. Why would I be talking about my career? My fund-raising is strong, my positions test well, the people will support me no matter what. It's my seat as long as I want it. And I still want it."

"Where is Ossana, Congressman?"

"I don't know."

"We need to find her before she hurts your niece."

"My daughter."

"I thought you said—"

"How do I get over something like this? You knew her, you understood."

"What are we talking about?"

"Amanda. What else would I be talking about?"

"You're right," I said, incredulous at my own incredulity. "What else."

"I loved her, I saw a future with her."

"As long as you didn't have to divorce your wife."

"Amanda understood my circumstances."

"Whose plane is this?"

"A supporter's."

"Which?"

"Does it matter?"

"Yes, it matters. It matters very much."

"I can still feel her touch, the silk of her skin, the very smell of her. She smelled young and earthy, like fresh lilacs. I can't let go of the way she made me feel."

"Like a politician?"

"Like the man I wanted to be. When I was young, the mother of one of my friends called me "The Senator," because even as a boy I was so accomplished. And I liked it. It fit the vision I had of myself. And so did Amanda. The way she laughed, the way she stroked my chest."

"Where are you taking the girl?"

"It's my wife who has insisted on taking care of her. I suppose it will give her something to do. A friend has a house in North Carolina. We're going to stay there for a bit. Hide from the press, plot the future. I need to gear up for the campaign. It would all be no problem if only I didn't feel so cold."

"This should heat you up. She was betraying you."

"Who?"

"Duddleman. She was murdered in Philadelphia, but she spent the day here, in Lancaster, investigating the Shoeless Joan murder. She was trying to find the key to it all, trying to find the girl."

"My niece."

"Right. Of course. Why do I have the urge to slap you silly? We're talking about the little girl with the liver disease who your sister gave to some adoption agency, who then gave her to Jessica Barnes. The little girl you were so desperate to keep a secret that you hired me to buy Jessica's silence. Duddleman wanted to rise in the journalism game and she was going to do it on the carcass of your career. I admired the hell out of that. I wished her well."

"I don't believe you."

"It's why she died. Your sister—"

"It doesn't change the way I feel."

"Men like you, it's never about the truth of things. It's only about your own precious sense of self. She was trying to be nice, that mother of your friend, calling you The Senator. But she sure as hell did a job on you. Where's your sister?"

"I don't know, I told you."

"Well, you better find out fast. And tie your shoes tight, because I get a sense, Congressman, that she's coming for you next, jilted heart and all."

I left the plane feeling disoriented and disgusted, with myself as much as anything. I couldn't get down the stairs of that tiny plane fast enough.

Mrs. DeMathis was talking to McDeiss and Mitchum and Melanie while holding the little girl's hand. Her name was Calynne; I got it off the legal documents Melanie showed me. Little Calynne, carrying her own little suitcase, was eyeing the plane with a child's wariness. When she looked at me, I could see the fear in her tense smile. I walked over and kneeled down next to her, letting the conversation between the adults twitter back and forth above my head.

"Are you scared?" I said.

"I've never been on a plane before."

"It's fun. Did you ever go to Dutch Wonderland?"

She nodded.

"What's your favorite ride?"

"The Turtle Whirl."

"It's just like that but without all the spinning. And they let you drink soda."

"Really?"

"Make sure you ask for the soda. Mrs. DeMathis is going to take care of you now."

"I miss my mommy."

"Yes, I know. Do you have a picture?"

"My grammom gave me one."

"Good." I took out a business card and gave it to her. It was stupid, I know, it embarrasses me now, but I did it. "Put it with the picture. If you ever need anything, have someone call me. Anytime. And I'll come running. Even if only to get you off the Turtle Whirl."

"Okay."

"Bye-bye, Calynne. Take your medicine."

"I will," she said.

I looked up. McDeiss was staring at me, like I was an ambulance chaser sticking his card in a dead man's mouth. I stood and stepped back. Mrs. DeMathis smiled at me before slowly leading Calynne toward the plane, Melanie and Mitchum following behind.

I watched them all enter, watched as the hydraulic piston slowly pulled the door up, watched until it sealed shut. Then I took out my phone and snapped a picture of the plane before its engines started and the thing pulled away to the end of the runway. The plane turned and paused, began to shake, and, with a shout, up it went.

Damn.

I thought of the man barreling through the sky, the man who would now be acting as Calynne's father. How could I ever have ended up an errand boy for such a creature? I wondered if they were all like him, self-absorbed twits who cared for nothing so much as their own power and privilege, careening off one another, like pinballs in the granite-cloaked corridors, blindly pursuing their little prizes while the country burned.

CHAPTER 47

NIETZSCHE'S SISTER

With the girl safe for the moment, it was time to find a killer, and I was no longer in the mood to chase.

The man behind the airport counter hadn't shaved today, or yesterday, for that matter, and I had the distinct impression he had no intention of shaving tomorrow. The mismatched files on his desk were covered by an unfolded Wawa wrapper holding half a hoagie. When he saw us come through the door, he clicked something off the computer screen, something pornographic and baldly fetishistic, no doubt, and made a backhanded swipe of his greasy maw, loosing slivers of lettuce onto the wrapper.

"What can I do you for?" he said, mouth still full.

"The plane that just left," I said. "Do you know where it's headed?"

"Sure, hold on a sec." He slapped his hands clean. "The HondaJet, right?" He pushed the edge of the wrapper from his keyboard and started tap-tapping. "That's a sweeter bird than we normally have landing here. Usually the jets, even the small ones, end up at LNS. But we're big enough if they're small enough, and that one surely was. I got the flight plan somewhere in here."

"We can wait," I said.

He looked up, annoyed at being rushed, before he started searching through the files on his desk.

McDeiss leaned on the counter, took out his badge, clicked it a couple times on the counter. It took a moment for the guy to notice the clicking and what was causing it. When he did, he stopped his search and looked at the badge, up at McDeiss's face, back down at the badge.

"You're not local," he said.

"Philadelphia," said McDeiss. "Homicide."

"Oh."

"Yeah."

"A little out of your jurisdiction, isn't it?"

"That's why we're asking and not telling," said McDeiss. "You want telling, I can make a call."

"No," he said, with a glance at the door as if a horde of Lancaster cops were about to burst through. "Asking is fine. Just give me another minute and I'll get this stuff for you."

"Don't bother," I said. "I know where the plane is going. I just wanted to know if the jet's destination has been logged into the system."

"It will be as soon as I put in the flight plan."

"Then let's say you don't. There's a kid on that plane who is trying to get away from a stalker. We need to keep her whereabouts as private as possible until the detective here can ensure her safety. I'm a lawyer and I represent the man on the plane, who happens to be the girl's father. He hired the jet to get her out of harm's way. We should help him, don't you think?"

He looked at McDeiss when he said, "I suppose."

McDeiss simply nodded.

"Anything to help the police."

"That's right," I said. "Anything. So here's the play. Let's keep the flight plan out of the computer for a couple of days. And if anyone comes in asking for the information, you can send them right to me."

I took a card from my jacket pocket, slapped it onto the counter along with two of Mrs. Devereaux's hundreds, pushed the bundle forward.

The man turned his head to McDeiss. "Is that what you want, Detective?"

"Like you said, it's out of my jurisdiction."

"I got you." He pocketed the bills and gave the card a quick look. "Victor Carl."

"You think you can remember that?" I said.

"Sure."

"Then that's that." I gestured to the computer screen. "Sorry about disturbing your . . . hoagie."

Outside the office, we stood for a moment and stared at the empty runway. The sun was shining, a light breeze was caressing our cheeks. One could imagine that all was right with the world, but then one would be a fool.

"You might as well have tied yourself onto a Mayan altar," said McDeiss, "and sent her a card offering up your heart."

"That almost sounds romantic."

"Sure, until she comes after you with a knife the size of a marlin."

"My guess is you have Armbruster looking for her."

"Maybe."

"And I know you've been looking for Colin Frost."

"Yes."

"How's the search going?"

"Poorly."

"We need to stop looking for them and get them looking for me. If I spread my card enough places, they'll take the bait."

"And then what?"

"And then I'll string her along long enough to get the goods before you swoop in with your legions of coppers and save the day."

"I might be busy eating lunch when she makes her appearance."

"Eat fast," I said. I looked along the length of the runway and thought about what had happened inside that plane. "Let's take a ride."

We drove the same streets through which we had chased Melanie's car: the antiquing congestion of Bird-in-Hand, the rural byways leading to Irishtown Road. I didn't hide behind the mighty oak this time, just pulled up right to the edge of the property and put the car in park. For a moment I eyed the tree that young Calynne had swung on, so innocent and free.

"Did the technicians give you any details about the DNA they found on the blood and the hair?"

"Just that it was a match, close enough that it was almost from the same person."

"I bet. Do you have a sister, Detective?"

"Yes, actually."

"I wonder what that's like. Because I was an only child, so I missed out on all the sibling stuff. The big brother teaching you the ways of the world. The little brother you can take under your wing and show how to throw a curve. The sister whose room you can slip into in the middle of the night and—"

"Say what?"

"Doesn't every young boy try out his sexual tricks on his sister before taking them out into the big bad world?"

"No they do not," said McDeiss, his voice suddenly aggrieved, like I had just shat on his shoe.

"Well, some do."

"Who the hell?"

"Our friend Nietzsche, for one."

"Well, he had a mustache the size of a rodent, what could you expect? Who else?"

"Think about it. Remember when you said the motive for Jessica Barnes's murder wasn't right? How you wondered why Ossana would be so desperate to hide any evidence of the child?"

"You're not saying—"

"He's a United States congressman," I said. "Who wouldn't he screw?"

McDeiss sat in silence for a long moment before saying, "Every time I think I can no longer be shocked by a politician, I get proven wrong."

"You want to know the funny thing? For a brief, naive moment I thought I'd be the barracuda in the cesspool." I looked off at the house. "Let me go in alone. The grandmother knows me. It should go smoother without your hulking presence."

"Hulking?"

"I just want to tell them that the plane has taken off and the girl is safe, and then drop off my card for when Ossana comes a-calling."

I slammed the door shut behind me and walked up the front path. At the front door I rapped on the wood with my knuckles.

"Oh," said Mrs. Gaughan as if she had opened the door to find a flaming bag of dog crap on her front step. "It's you."

"Do you have a minute, Mrs. Gaughan?"

"No, actually. Carl, was it?"

"Yes, that's right."

"Go away, Carl, now, and leave us be."

"I just wanted to tell you that Calynne has been taken someplace safe."

"Thank God," she said. "Now go away."

"I know you've been concerned and I just wanted to give you an update on her care and to let you know that I'll do—"

I stopped my yabbering when I heard a screen door bang in the back of the house, like someone was running somewhere, running from me. But who could ever want to run away from the mild likes of me? Unsure, I took a step forward, until I was no longer on the doorstep, until I was one step farther into the house. And I saw, on the floor in front of the couch, Jessica Barnes's husband, or the corpse of Jessica Barnes's husband—it was hard to tell—sprawled and still.

That was when I looked to my right and saw a gun aimed at my face.

"Close the door behind you," said Colin Frost, staring at me from beneath heavy-lidded eyes.

I turned and glanced at McDeiss in the car before I closed the door. Mrs. Gaughan took a step back and bowed her head. Colin Frost smiled. They had found me all right, the bastards, just like I had expected, but a good bit sooner than I had expected, which, terrifyingly, made all the difference.

CHAPTER 48

TROPHY

"Move and you're dead," said Colin Frost, with a slur in his voice. It wasn't comforting to see him stagger while his gun was still pointed at my face.

"How's the rehab going, Colin?"

"I'm taking it day by day."

"I'm sorry," said Mrs. Gaughan, her whole body shaking as she backed away. "I tried to warn you."

"You did nothing wrong," I said. "In times like this, always blame the guy with the gun. You know what you are, Colin?"

"Enlighten me."

"You're a bad client."

He laughed; a spool of drool dripped from his lip.

"Right now," I continued, "I'd have to say you're the worst client I ever had, and if you knew my client list, you would be appalled. I've had clients that never paid, that lied to my face, that tried to pick up my secretary, that tried to pick me up. I even once had a client that peed in court, right there at the defense table, while the cop was testifying. From under the table he took out his prick and let loose. On my stinking shoes. But you, high as a circling vulture, with two murders postacquittal and now sticking a gun in my face, you take the prize. Congratulations, and pick up your trophy at the front desk. Worst client ever."

"And you don't think you had it coming?"

"What did I do other than pull every trick in the book to win your case before making sure you ended up in rehab. I gave you a chance to clean yourself up, to make something of your life."

"All while stealing my job and tapping my piece."

"Your piece? Ossana?"

"What did you think?"

"I was just filling in," I said with a shrug. "Someone had to."

"How'd you like it?"

"Not much, either one."

"Now maybe you understand."

"Now maybe I do."

"I hope you came alone, because if not, Jason's going to have to take care of it, and he gets so sloppy. The good news is, out here no one comes running at the sound of a gunshot. Out here a gunshot is as natural as the rain."

So that was the slamming screen door I heard, not someone running from me but the murderous Jason Howard, the skinny kid in the beard who had done in Duddleman and was in on the killing of Jessica Barnes, running out to take care of McDeiss. I had maintained a kernel of optimism even in the face of Colin Frost's gun, sure that McDeiss would somehow save the day, but that optimism suddenly popped into despair. Who else would I get killed? Was Mrs. Gaughan next? Christ, I was a plague on the land. It scared me, sure, but it pissed me off, too.

I thought about lunging back to the door to warn McDeiss, but before I could even twitch in that direction, Colin grabbed me by the lapel of my suit jacket and yanked me to the floor. He dropped down, slamming a knee into my chest so hard it felt like I was having a heart attack. I struggled to get loose from the pain, but then he put the muzzle of the gun in my eye, and my struggling froze.

"Thinking of going somewhere?"

"Let him alone," said Mrs. Gaughan.

"Get the hell upstairs, you witch," said Colin.

"Don't hurt him."

"Shut your mouth. If I hear another sound from you, I'll put a bullet in his brain. Now get the hell upstairs."

I couldn't see her, that brave woman. But I could hear her rush out of the room and up the stairs, could hear her footsteps above us.

And then came the flush of a toilet from someplace on the lower level. The washing up in a basin. A door opening. The clackity footsteps of high heels on a rough wooden floor. I wasn't able to turn my head and so I didn't get a sight of her until she appeared in my half sphere of one-eyed vision. The upward sweep of her bare leg, the tight skirt enfolding her thighs, the starched blouse hanging loose and unbuttoned, the breasts cupped in black lace, the chin jutting, the downward-turned mouth, the wide green eyes ringed with dark mascara staring down, down, with pitiless judgment.

Even pinned to the floor with a gun in my eye, even knowing what I now knew of what she had been and all she had done, even then, the sight of her standing over me just like that was sexy as blood.

CHAPTER 49

NO EXIT

With Colin's knee still on my chest and his gun still pressed against my eye, Ossana DeMathis rubbed my bruised cheek with the point of her shiny black shoe. "I'm going to miss you, Victor."

"Going somewhere?" I managed to strangle out of my throat.

"Oh, yes," she said. "It's getting a bit puritanical here to suit my tastes."

"Hell is too puritanical to suit your tastes."

"Maybe so," she said, raising her foot and rubbing her spiked heel roughly across my lips. "One can imagine hell as a locked room filled with judgmental prigs harping on your every act."

"One already has."

"*L'enfer, c'est les autres.* I prefer a more self-indulgent destination. Fortunately, there is always Paris." She turned and walked away. "Put him on the couch."

Right after Colin threw me to the sofa, not far from the sprawled body of Matthew Barnes—alive, I could tell now, from the rise of his chest with each breath—there came a knock on the door. Before I could do the calculation of the cowardice of keeping quiet versus the stupidity of shouting out to warn McDeiss, the door opened and Jason Howard, a gun in his hand, stepped inside. Scrawny and bearded, his neck and arms scabbed, he looked at me as he jabbed the gun into his belt.

"Nothing," he said.

Nothing. It has always been one of my favorite words, a handy description of the bald truth of my existence. And yet those two empty syllables had never been so full of hope than in that very moment, because the word just then meant not the morass swallowing my life but the instrument of my salvation.

"He came alone," said Jason Howard.

"You sure, dude?" said Colin. "He wasn't acting like he came alone."

"I checked the car, I checked around. Nothing."

"Who's out there?" said Colin to me.

"No one."

"You lie like a lawyer," said Colin.

"That's always been convenient," I said.

"I told you I looked," said Jason. He rubbed his arm across his nose. "There was no one there."

"That doesn't mean he came alone."

"Both of you check the windows," said Ossana. "I'll deal with Victor."

She walked toward the couch with one of those sexy catwalk steps, one high heel placed carefully in front of the other, her shoulders back, her chin tilted down. She stood over me for a moment. "Where is she, Victor?"

"Why don't you just forget about her?" I said, softly enough so that only she could hear. "You're going away—good. Go to Paris and avoid all the uncomfortable questions. Take Colin with you if you're lonely. He's a needleful of fun. Just go, but go without her."

"A girl needs her mother."

"Not that girl, and not her mother."

"Your opinion of me has deteriorated markedly."

"You shouldn't have killed Duddleman."

"She should have minded her own business." Ossana took a breath and then fell down onto the couch next to me. She tossed her hair like a frustrated cheerleader and lowered her voice like we were just friends chatting. "It was bad enough she was riding my brother, but then she had to go off snooping. Calynne was decidedly not her business."

"Why did you have the baby, anyway? I don't understand. If you wanted to avoid the scandal, why not just get an abortion?"

"Love, Victor. Have you ever felt it? Have you ever watched it slip away as your lover started chasing ever-younger fauna? His wife couldn't give him the child I could, and I thought a child would win him back. But when he saw what I was up to, he insisted I give it up, he pleaded, he broke down in tears. He said his precious career was on the line and he promised if I put it up for adoption we would be like we were before, like the teenagers we once were, making our own rules, living our own secrets, following no one's conventions but our own."

"Excuse me while I gag."

"Aren't we the fifties' society matron. I listened to him, Victor, and I gave my daughter away, and I hoped. But I should have known better. We no longer could be what we had been. You know he chases these young girls because they remind him of what I was when he first sneaked into my room. That's why politics is so perfect for him. The halls of Congress are filled with the young and the ever eager."

"And they're all named Jessica or Amanda."

"And don't forget Ashley, there's always a fucking Ashley in the wings. At first I was just trying to protect our secret, but now I have a purpose far greater than our love: our daughter. And it was you, Victor, who convinced me to stop deferring my maternal responsibilities."

"Me?"

"Oh, yes."

"Please don't say that. I have enough guilt as it is."

"You were so proud of yourself. Ooh, look at me, Victor Carl, all filled with hate. I hate this and I hate that. So dramatic and self-important. Trust me, darling, when it comes to hate, you don't know the meaning of the word. You might give a good speech, but you screw like a minister. God, I can't look at you without wanting to kick you in the face."

"I want to kick myself in the face, too."

"But I figured if you can show your milky emotions so proudly, why must I hide what I truly am?"

"And what is that, Ossana?"

"A woman free of the shackles of common morality, free to indulge any impulse, free to journey into the darkest depths of her being, free in the only ways that matter. And that's the freedom I'm going to pass on to my daughter. I have so much to teach her."

"I can't imagine."

"Because you are sadly limited. I will make her in my own image. There are so many delicious boulevards for her to tread. Life, love, sex, art, brioche, absinthe, passion."

"Murder and incest."

"Why limit ourselves?"

"What do you do with the shoes?"

"The shoes?"

"Do you keep a collection?"

"Oh, those. Surprisingly, they're not for me. What would I want with Jessica Barnes's little working-woman shoes? They're for Colin."

"That Colin is such a pill," I said.

"Where is she, Victor? It is time for me to collect my daughter."

"Like a debt?"

"Yes, exactly. And don't doubt my sincerity on this. Tell me or die, it's that simple."

"It's not that simple, because I don't intend to tell you a thing, and I don't intend to die. Ever, actually, but that's another sad debate."

"Your intentions don't matter when we have the guns," said Ossana.

"Well, here's the thing," I said. "I don't intend to tell you where she is, because you're a sick puppy who killed the only mother that little girl ever knew. You are the last thing that girl needs and I won't be a part of putting you together. And I don't intend to die, because right now the police detective I came with, a man named McDeiss who has been looking for all of you, is gathering up the Lancaster police for an assault on this house."

"McDeiss is here," she said, her voice suddenly loud enough for Colin to hear.

"Where?" said Colin.

"Check the windows," said Ossana.

"He's bluffing," said Jason Howard, still looking out the side. "I told you, there's nothing out there but corn growing. What do they do with all that corn?"

"Soda," said Colin.

"Corn soda?"

"Quiet down," said Ossana before leaning toward me, caressing my face with her long slender fingers, slipping her tongue into my ear.

"Oh, Victor, Victor," she whispered, "you poor little innocent. There's no one out there, and there is no one coming. You must understand that a very influential man is very much convinced that my brother will provide him something no one else can."

"Who is he?"

"It doesn't matter. All that matters is that he wants what he wants and he's willing to do what he must to get it. Calls have been made up and down a long and complex chain. The Lancaster police won't be charging in with guns drawn. Oh, no. Instead, they're going to help a distraught mother find her darling daughter."

"Not if McDeiss has his way."

"Your precious detective might be incorruptible, but he works for someone who works for someone. Everyone at some point has to follow orders."

"Except you."

"That's right," she said. "Where's my daughter?"

"Go to hell."

"I'm going to miss your little pout, Victor. And the hat, especially the hat."

She stood up and kissed the top of my head. As she walked away from me in that same catwalk stride, she said to Jason Howard, "Kill him."

"I don't think you should count on your benefactor to save you this time," I said.

She stopped, turned around, put up a hand to halt whatever Jason Howard was intending to do. "You have something to say?"

"Just a little story you might find interesting. I was asked to get the goods on Bettenhauser, your brother's opponent in the upcoming congressional race. And I was guided in the search by an operative who was being ordered around and paid by the same rich bastard that you think is going to get you out of this jam. And together we found a neat little scandal that by all appearances could have ruined Bettenhauser before he even got out of the gate. But it turns out it wasn't a scandal at all; rather, it was an example of Bettenhauser's civic magnanimity. If I had given it to the press, it would have greatly boosted his chances at the expense of your brother. Which was just what the rich bastard intended to happen."

"What are you getting at?"

"That the man you're counting on to protect you has hedged his bets, has already put Bettenhauser in his pocket, and no longer has to stick his neck out for a murderous bitch like you."

"Uh-oh," said Jason Howard, still peering out the window and now pulling the gun out of his belt. "We've got company."

CHAPTER 50

ATTICA

And then the kid pulls the gun out of his belt and says, 'We've got company.'"

I took a sip of my drink—hard rye and bright bitters in a stolid lowball rinsed with absinthe—and winced at the alcohol and the memory as I looked around the table for effect. We were at Rosen's, of course, drinking Sazeracs, hats on the table, briefcases by our sides, cigarettes burning in mute defiance of the laws of man and nature. It was late afternoon and the place was empty except for the group at our round table and an old lady with a pillbox hat drinking vodka alone at the bar.

"What did you think right about then?" said Hump.

"Well, I'll tell you, Hump," I said. "First I thought McDeiss had saved me, hallelujah. And then, when Colin pointed his gun at my face again, I thought I was dead."

"And how did that make you feel?" said Maud, sitting back with her arms crossed as usual, the smoke from her cigarette rising in a line before it curlicued into chaos.

I thought about it for a moment. How did I feel when Colin pointed his gun at my face for a second time—or was it a third time—and it seemed, finally, that he was going to end it all and take my shoes? I felt fear, of course, a blind terror that rises in times of mortal peril as naturally as a sneeze. But there was something else, too, something that tasted bitter and sweet at the same time.

"Relieved," I said. "So it had come for me at last. About stinking time."

"I'd be shitting, I would," said Miles Schimmeck, crushing out a cigarette. "Right in my pants."

"What you got to live for anyway, you little muskrat?" said Briggs Mulroney. Yes, Briggs Mulroney, swollen-eared, hulking Briggs Mulroney had worked out a deal with the powers that had sent him scurrying, and had come out of retirement to carry his son's bag just long enough to personally instruct a surprising new trainee.

"I got plenty to live for," said Miles.

"Tell me one measly thing," said Briggs.

"Cigarettes."

"What else?"

"Sazeracs."

"What else."

"More cigarettes."

"Try something that ain't killing you."

"I got plenty, I do," said Miles, looking around at the rest of the table. "Don't I got plenty?"

"Sure, Miles," said Maud. "You've got plenty."

"Aubrey," yelled out Briggs Mulroney. "Miles ain't the only one needs something to stay alive for. Another round for all of us."

"Truth was," I said, "I didn't have time for a metaphysical wrestling match just then, because at that moment, with his gun still in my face, Colin tells Jason to check out the back, and that's what the kid does. He bolts out to the back of the house, we hear the screen door slam, and the next thing you know—crackatooey—the bullets are flying out there like angry bees."

"Damn," said Hump.

"Apparently, Jason just barreled out of the back of the house, saw a line of cops, and thought the best way forward was to fire wildly in panic."

"Guns are for amateurs," said Briggs, "like I was trying to tell Stony. Once it starts raining lead, it never stops cheap."

"How is our boy Stony doing?" said Maud.

"Already blistered with sunburn," said Briggs. "I'm told he looks like an overstuffed salmon. I've the sense none of this will end well for him."

"It didn't end well for the kid with the gun," said Hump. "One word you never want written in the same sentence with your name in the papers is 'riddled.'"

"Or 'indictment,'" said Maud.

"Or 'gonorrhea,'" said Miles. "I should know."

We all looked at Miles.

"What?" he said.

"Go on, Victor," said Maud.

"When the kid went down, there were a few shots rattling around the inside of the farmhouse, which caused me some concern," I said. "And the next thing you know, I hear McDeiss's sour voice coming out of a loudspeaker. 'We don't want any more trouble.' 'We don't want anyone else getting hurt.' 'Come out with your hands up.' That kind of thing."

"Does this ever work?" said Lyudmila Porishkova, smoking impassively. Tall and stylishly dressed, she was sitting between Maud and Briggs, who was teaching Lyudmila his rules for aspiring bagmen so that she could take over the police route. Imagine that.

"No," said Maud.

"But I suppose they need to try," said Hump, "before they level the place."

"And that was when Ossana came up with her brilliant idea," I said.

Aubrey appeared at the table, a magician emerging from a puff of smoke. In his left hand he was balancing a tray of drinks: five Sazeracs and a shot of vodka. Lyudmila hadn't yet developed a taste for rye, but it would surely come. I gulped down what was left of my current drink, my third, and felt the burn and swoon of the alcohol. The killed drinks stayed on the table, along with the dead cigarettes and empty hats, creating a tableau of corruption and degeneracy that was surprisingly cheerful.

Briggs lifted his glass. "To the Brotherhood of the Bag and its newest member."

There were hurrahs to Lyudmila, and clinks of glass, and swallows followed by hacks and coughs and the inhale of tobacco, with a couple of swear words thrown in for effect.

"How the hell did I ever end up back here?" said Briggs, shaking his head.

"Bad parenting," said Maud.

"So, Victor?" said Miles. "What was the sister's idea?"

I took a moment, sipped my drink, looked around the table, catching each of the gazes one by one. I had to be careful here, I had to do this right. It had been a brutal afternoon, horrific enough that it still felt like a wound. But I wasn't here just to pass the time and weave a story or two like any common pub-crawler. Oh, I was here to pass the time and weave a story, sure, but all of it had a purpose behind it, and I had to be sure to keep my eye on the purpose through the whole of the telling. I lowered my gaze and ran my finger across a stray bit of condensation on the table, leaving a smeared trail.

"She told us we had to get out of there, and the only way we were going to get out of there is if the police escorted us out," I said. "She had thought the Big Butter could save her when the time came, but I clued her in that the Big Butter had hedged his bets with Bettenhauser and that in all likelihood she was on her own. So she decided she was going to go play it differently, she was going to go all *Dog Day Afternoon* on McDeiss's ass."

"Dog Day Afternoon?" said Hump.

"You know," I said. "Al Pacino in the bank? Chants of 'Attica!'? The whole sex-change thing?"

"Sex change?" said Lyudmila.

"Al Pacino's boyfriend wants a sex-change operation," I said. "That's why Al Pacino was robbing the bank."

"I must be thinking of a different movie," said Miles Schimmeck. "What was the one where Al Pacino holes up in a house and the wife gets raped over and over?"

"That was Dustin Hoffman."

"I could never tell them two apart," said Miles.

"So Ossana DeMathis came up with the ridiculous idea to turn it into a hostage situation?" said Maud.

"And worst of all," I said, "she decided the hostage she'd use to get out of her impossible mess would be me."

"Isn't that one of your rules, Briggs?" said Hump. "Never become no hostage?"

"If it's not, it should be," said Briggs.

"I didn't volunteer, Hump, but that didn't matter to the two of them. They had a quick huddle, and next thing I know Colin's got his arm around my neck and his gun at my head and he's dragging me out of the house and down the front steps, keeping me in front like a shield."

"What did terrorist, he ask for?" said Lyudmila.

"What they always ask for," I said. "A way out."

"I just want to leave here without any trouble," shouted Colin to the row of cops, hidden behind tree and car. His voice was a shriek that left one of my ears ringing; the gun was jammed into the hinge of my jaw just beneath the other. Colin gripped my neck so tightly with his arm that I had to grab at the thing just to breathe. "All I want is for you to guarantee me a safe exit. You do that, no one gets hurt."

An electric whine came from a distant loudspeaker before McDeiss's voice could be heard, stretched and roughed by the amplification. "Let's start at the beginning, son," said McDeiss. "How many are you?"

"There's just me," shouted Colin. "Just me and four hostages."

Four? I thought.

"Four?" said McDeiss.

In the midst of the terror I tried to count, fumbled about in my mind, and came up short, until Colin explained it to us all.

"I got Victor here, who will be the first to get it, I promise you that. And inside, bound so they can't get anywhere, is an old lady, the dead lady's husband, and the Congressman's sister."

Ahh, yes. Now I saw it. Ossana, Ossana: how dark are your ways, how persuasive is your visage. Ossana. But the panic had twisted her reason. There was no way she could get away with it. No way in hell. Was there?

"Is anybody hurt?" called out McDeiss.

"The husband's been coldcocked. The rest are just shitting scared."

"Will you release some of the hostages in a show of good faith?"

"I don't have any good faith to spare," shouted Colin. "I don't have any faith at all. But you let me go and I'll leave two of the hostages behind when I make my run. I'll just take Victor here, and the sister."

"Where are you going?" said McDeiss.

"That's my business. But if you don't want a dead lawyer and a dead politician's sister on your hands, you'll let me go."

There was a long moment of silence. I wondered if McDeiss was thinking that neither result would be so tragic. I began to slip through sheer gravity out of Colin's grip. I bent my knees to increase the slippage before Colin yanked me back up and slapped my head with the gun. A sharp white light edged like a knife into my vision.

"Don't get frisky," he whispered into my ear.

"What kind of car do you want?" said McDeiss finally, through the loudspeaker.

"Something big and fast. A pickup with power. And no tricks."

"No tricks," said McDeiss.

"Or Victor here gets a bullet in the brain."

"It will take some time," said McDeiss.

"Not too much time, because I'm getting antsy. Twenty minutes, no more."

"I can't get you anything in twenty minutes."

"This area is lousy with pickups. Twenty minutes, or the hostages start dying one by one, one by one by—"

All I saw was a cloud of red in front of me before I was pulled to the ground in a strange quiet, pulled down to the ground by a lifeless arm around my neck, sent off-balance and dragged down by gravity and death. I landed atop a dead sack of something, lying now in a puddle of something, and in the confusion it took me a moment to realize the dead sack of something was Colin Frost, and the puddle of something was the spreading stain of his blood.

I sat up amidst the gore, feeling weighed down by the horror and the blood, and looked for the army of police running my way. A sharpshooter somewhere had killed Colin, I was sure. The police had taken him out to save my life, I was sure. There should have been an army of police charging the scene after their success.

Where were they? When were they coming to rescue me? Why were they still hunkered low behind their shelters?

And then McDeiss's voice. "Put down the gun and step out of the house with your hands empty and high."

I turned around, my hands sliding through the blood, and I saw her in the doorway, standing high in her heels, her shirt now modestly buttoned. Her copper hair swept across her impassive face. Her long pale arms were raised languidly over her head, showing the flighty birds of her tattoo. And hanging from her right forefinger was a small black automatic. She tossed it to the side like it was a bad peach and started walking down the steps, walking right toward me.

"Keep walking," said McDeiss's voice over the loudspeaker. "Don't stop. Keep walking toward us."

But she didn't obey, did she? Obeying was never Ossana's way. Instead of walking to McDeiss, she walked to me, the slightest smile on her bright-red lips, her breasts heaving with some hidden emotion. And she kneeled down and put her hand in my hair, despite the blood and gore, and leaned close with a kindly smile, like she was ministering to the halt or the lame, and she whispered with her sweet, vile voice, sugary and slick, into my ear . . .

CHAPTER 51

THE BROTHERHOOD

"And what she said was this," I said at that table at Rosen's, each member of the Brotherhood leaning forward, eyes wide, rapt at the telling.

I stopped to take a sip of my drink. And then another.

"Don't leave us hanging here," said Schimmeck.

"Amidst the blood and death that she had caused, root and stem," I said, "she leaned her pretty lips close to my ear and in the softest, sexiest of whispers she said—and this is a direct quote, mind you—she said, 'I just saved your life, lover. Now do your job and save me back, like a good little bagman.'"

Maud leaned slowly away from the table, put her cigarette in her mouth, inhaled deeply.

"Eesos Christos," said Lyudmila.

"Indeed," said Hump.

"Now that is a woman," said Briggs before swallowing the rest of his Sazerac like it was a gulp of air. "I could have owned the city with a woman like that."

"And lost your soul," said Maud.

"I'd have rather had the city. Tell me true, now: Is there anyone at this table, anyone, who isn't even the slightest bit turned on?" He looked around at the five of us, tried to detect dissent, then leaned back. "Oh, what a sick pack of bastards we are. Aubrey, my good man, let's do it again."

"Another round and I'll be crawling home," I said.

"Perfectly acceptable way to go home for a maggot," said Briggs. "You think yourself better than a maggot?"

"No, sir."

"So what did you do, Victor?" said Maud. "Did you concoct a story for her?"

"I sold her out," I said. "I told them every stinking thing that happened in that house, that she was the leader, not a hostage, and that killing Colin Frost was her way to stay free. She's a killer and she'd plug me like she plugged Colin if she had half the chance."

"Rule Four," said Briggs, nodding.

"You bet, not that it did any good. While the cops and the DA were figuring out who to believe and whether to charge her, there was some sort of screwup in the paperwork and she was able to just walk out the door, simple as that."

"Imagine such terrible thing," said Lyudmila.

"I couldn't," said Briggs. "Not in a million years."

"There's an ongoing investigation into how it happened," I said. "McDeiss promised to get to the bottom of it and see that heads roll."

"I'm sure it was just slipup," said Lyudmila.

"Mistakes happen," said Briggs.

"By the time they realized she was gone, they looked high and low but couldn't find her."

"Obviously, they didn't look low enough," said Maud with a sly smile. "So what are you going to do now? Remain the loyal bagman for her brother?"

"Victor knows where his bread is buttered," said Miles. "Of course he'll keep hold of the bag."

"He would if he was smart," said Maud.

"But Victor, he is not that smart," said Lyudmila.

"A bagman keeps filling them bags and passing the salad no matter what," said Miles. "That's the code."

"Indeed," said Hump.

"But you were never really one of us, were you, Victor?" said Maud.

"Maybe not," I said. "Look, I'm not weeping for Colin Frost, the worst client I ever had, but I can't just walk away from Jessica Barnes and Amanda Duddleman. And there's something more. The Big Butter needs Ossana to disappear to hide his involvement in murder, but Ossana won't vanish without her daughter. The only sure way to protect that girl is to shut off Ossana's money faucet, which means I need to melt the Big Butter."

"How are you going to do that?" said Maud with a snort.

"The question is," I said, leaning in now, bringing them all close, "how are we going to do that?"

There was a bemused moment of silence, followed by bouts of rueful laughter—not the reaction I was hoping for.

"You're a bit confused," said Hump.

"Since you apparently have us confused with missionaries," said Maud.

"Even when it comes to sex, laddie," said Briggs, "we are not missionaries."

Lyudmila barked out a Russian laugh.

"There's a little girl who needs to be saved from her mother," I said. "If we stand back and do nothing, Ossana will destroy her soul and devour her future."

"You might be right about the girl," said Miles. "But we ain't tree huggers."

"And our hearts don't bleed without a knife stuck into our chests," said Hump. "Pay us and we carry, that's the end of our story."

"We're bagmen, Victor," said Maud, "and that's all we are."

"You're more than that," I said.

"No, we're not."

I sat back and looked around the table and saw something they didn't see. Sure, they were bagmen, each of them, carriers of corruption that clogged the free flow of the people's business, but they were also more. In the forgotten neighborhoods of the city, when someone needed something from a politician, it was a bagman who carried the request, along with an envelope, sure, but still. And when that politician needed a passel of votes to keep up the fight, it was the bagman who spread his street money among the voters like a Santa Claus two months early. If cash was the beating heart of our politics—and who would deny it?—then bagmen were the red blood cells feeding every organ, every cell, keeping the whole thing alive and in fighting trim. In a world where politics had lost its meaning amidst a welter of lies and stratagems and think tanks full of one-way hacks, bagmen were the last direct link between the politicians and the people.

And they were going the way of the dinosaur.

"All right, forget about the girl, or the justice of the thing, or how it will feel to put a psychopath where she belongs. Let's think about ourselves, for a moment."

"Now you're talking," said Miles Schimmeck.

"How's your business been, Miles?"

"Lousy."

"And it's only getting worse, because the Big Butter is making you irrelevant. What can you do in a courthouse that the fancy lawyers dropping fat pats of butter into every judge's pot can't do better? What can you pass out that the one percent can't top tenfold? The Big Butter is buying the courthouse stone by stone, leaving you with dust."

"I get along," said Miles.

"Not for long, you won't. What can you do with your little envelopes, Maud, when the Big Butter can buy City Council for less than a rounding error on its expenses? You can buy a voter here or a councilman there with your envelopes, sure, but the Big Butter can buy television stations, pack the legislature, and bury anyone who gets in its way."

"It will swing back."

"Hell it will. You're hiding in the back alleys while the Big Butter spreads its graft, legal as a newborn. And the Supremes in Washington say it's all sweet and lawful, that the Big Butter has the constitutional right to put its cash on the line anywhere, anytime, without conditions. Listen, when your competitor gets big enough to buy the Supreme Court, you're screwed. And the Big Butter has bought it, believe it, and you are screwed. It's not swinging back, it's never swinging back. All it's swinging is a wrecking ball. You've known the city's been for sale all along, your whole existence is based on that fact, but now you're shit out of luck because the Big Butter is bidding ten times higher than you ever could and raking in all your chips."

"Man's got a point," said Hump.

"Tell me, Briggs, how's your boy doing?"

"He's a chunk of seared beef on a brittle third-world beach."

"And it was the Big Butter that set him on the road to that tropical hell. Stony saw the writing on the wall and decided to sell himself to the highest bidder, but after the Big Butter burned him to the nub, it tossed him to the dirt as casually as you toss off a cigarette butt. And don't get any ideas that the Big Butter doesn't have the same plans for you."

"What about Rule Five?" said Miles.

"Fuck Rule Five."

"They're too strong to fight," said Miles.

"Oh, they're big all right, but that just means they've got more to lose. The Big Butter who crapped on Stony is the same Big Butter who's protecting Ossana DeMathis. He's dirty and arrogant and he thinks he can sit safely back while his minions shit all over our city just to gain some political advantage for himself. The hell with that. We're going to find out what he's after and snatch it from his jaws. How much fun would it be to bring him down to size and kick him in the balls?"

"You don't know what you're getting into, laddie," said Briggs.

"Sure I do. I've been fighting the Big Butter my entire career. And yeah, I lose more than I win, and when I lose, I end up on my ass. But I just get up and do it again with a song in my heart. The sons of bitches want to buy the country; well, fuck them. Maybe I can't take them all down, but I'm taking this one down, and I'm going to grin like an orangutan when I do it."

"My God, Victor," said Maud, "your eyes are positively glowing."

"Want to feel joy in this life? Burn down a bank."

"What's your plan, laddie?" said Briggs.

"I don't have a plan. All I have is hate and step one: find the bastard."

"And how do you propose to do that?" said Maud.

"That's where you come in."

CHAPTER 52

THE BIG BUTTER

The mystics say the way to truth is through suffering and madness, which is an eerily accurate description of the road to Montauk.

By the time I hit the final leg of my journey, taking the scenic way out on the Old Montauk Highway, with windows down and the fresh salt air whipping my tie, I had already scaled the majestic heights of the Verrazano, suffered the traffic and insanity that skidded by the Five Towns, and felt the edge of my class resentment sharpen keenly as I drove slowly, within a line of trucks and convertibles and black European monstrosities, through Westhampton and Southampton and Bridgehampton and East Hampton, with their neat lawns and exclusive bistros, their obscene castles and airs and pretensions. The sky was clear, the breeze was up; it was a bright, sunny day in Richberg.

The two-lane road I now was on was rustic, rough. The farmers' stands selling peaches, corn, and early tomatoes had petered out after Amagansett, and there was only the occasional outcrop of lavish estate between me and the Napeague Beach to my right and then the great swells of the Atlantic.

About a hundred miles from my destination, my phone had started jangling to life every five minutes or so. It was Melanie. I kept pushing the red button on the phone's screen, declining her calls. She had undoubtedly tracked my location with some illegal technology and caught me rushing ever closer to the tip of Long

Island. She was smart enough to know exactly where I was heading. She wanted to know what the hell I was up to and I wanted not to tell her.

I wasn't going to Montauk for the beaches, which were supposed to be lovely, or the views of the Sound and the ocean, which were supposed to be spectacular, or the restaurants, which were supposed to be stocked with the freshest bounties of the sea. No, I was going east for something far richer, rich enough to strangle your heart.

I was going to Montauk to take a bite out of the Big Butter.

The Big Butter sits on the rooftop aerie of his bungalow, staring out toward the inlet that leads to the Sound. The afternoon sun pounds his floppy face; the frightening brightness of the falling star fills the lenses of his gold-rimmed sunglasses.

His thighs are grossly thick, his fat feet lay flat in leather slippers, his swollen fingers grip a crystal lowball half-filled with a single malt, the primary flavor of which is its expense. Except for his sunglasses, a gold necklace, and the sandals, he is naked. What need has the Big Butter for clothes? He is swaddled by his money; it embraces him like a mother's arms. It protects him from the elements, from thwarted desire, from small-time lawyers practicing in distant outposts like Philadelphia.

Sometimes when he sits naked up here, glistening with sweat and oil under the sweltering sky, one of the girls will climb the metal stairs to the roof and kneel between his thighs and give him a blow job. But the current girl graduated from Wellesley, so that is out.

His bungalow is no bungalow, at least by common standards. It is a cantilevered masterpiece of glass and steel perched on the side of a rise in the middle of Montauk. The angled planes of the house provide every room a view of the ocean or the lake or the Sound. The structure has been featured in magazines. It is very important that it has been featured in magazines. Five bedrooms, six bathrooms, five fireplaces, one pool, one graduate from Wellesley who won't suck his cock. For five point five mil you'd think the bungalow would at least come with a graduate from Vassar.

He knows I am coming. He has undoubtedly been told by Melanie that I am getting close. He knows I'm coming and he is not afraid. He has almost a billion dollars. Did you hear me? Almost a billion dollars. If almost a billion dollars cannot protect him from small-town lawyers with venality in their hearts, then what can?

Maybe a billion dollars. And don't you worry, he is working on it. Prisons, that's his new ticket. He is readying an aggressive move into prisons. Whatever the worth of the poor as consumers, once imprisoned they become exponentially more valuable as a natural resource. With enough money invested, with the right powers bought, fortunes can be extracted. It is like fracking the lower classes.

The only crime is that he hadn't thought of it before.

How did I track him down, the Big Butter, this vile mix of flesh and coin? I didn't; the Brotherhood did, using my brief and disastrous career as a bagman for a map.

First Hump found the link between Enrique Flores in old Chicago, the first of my bagman meet-and-greets, and a congressman named Louis Steinberg, a former associate of Flores's who had mystified pundits and pollsters by coming out of nowhere and winning his district's primary against better-known opponents.

"How much of the vote did he get?" I said.

"Fifty-one percent. In a four-way race."

"Funny how that works. I suppose anything more would have been unseemly."

"Indeed."

Briggs Mulroney had gotten drunk with an old colleague in Washington, a fellow handler of the bag who worked within the hungry maw of the House of Representatives, and learned that DeMathis and Steinberg sat together on the Ways and Means Subcommittee on Select Revenue Measures.

"Word is," said Briggs, "a proposal by DeMathis up for consideration in the subcommittee had been facing stiff opposition and then, magically, the opposition just melted."

"It's magic all right."

"Apparently, our pal Steinberg had a change of heart and brought the rest of the Democrats on board."

"What's the proposal about?"

"What do you think it's about, laddie? What do you think the whole damn game is about?"

It was up to Lyudmila to explain the specific bill to me in her charming Russian accent.

"In simple terms that you might comprehend, Victor, there is opinion from Internal Revenue Service about specific tax loophole. It is loophole concerning offshore corporations and transferred dividends, very complicated and very stupid, but it eliminates tax under certain specific conditions. It means nothing except to a very few, but to the very few it means so very much. IRS, it is trying to close loophole. Subcommittee said not so fast and now wants to keep loophole open."

"Who benefits?"

"Not you, Victor. You don't benefit. Or me. Or average Joe Stalin in street. Who benefits is someone involved in tax-avoidance scheme that buggers the imagination."

"You mean beggars the imagination."

"Maybe you are right. Maybe I am using wrong word. I was talking of tax scheme so sophisticated that it takes your imagination and bends it over chair."

"Lyudmila, I stand corrected."

"I have former client who is in tax department of some crazy bank in New York, Sacks of Gold or something. I used to book him special number-one trips to Belarus. He owes me favor. And so he did research on this very loophole. It turns out there are three corporations taking this loophole and ramming their money through it over and over until it bleeds, yes?"

Yes. Of course. Taxes, taxes. It was almost wearying in its inevitability.

The intrepid Miles Schimmeck paid a visit to the rehab facility in Virginia that had found a spot for Colin Frost at a moment's notice and then allowed him to slip in and out at will during his stay. Miles sweet-talked his way into filching the names of the facility's most important donors.

"Quite the list," he said. "I'm going to hit them all up for my favorite charity."

"What's that, Miles?"

"It's called GOOMS—Getting Oodles of Money for Schimmeck."

"How's it doing?"

"Not as well as I hoped."

I took everything we had and turned it over to Maud.

"Who knew," said Maud, "that the number on a plane's tail is as distinctive as a fingerprint?"

"Maybe the guy who took the picture," I said.

"The owner of our little jet, Potter Transport, is a wholly owned subsidiary of something called Avia Acquisitions Four, which is owned by a holding company called National Capital Trust Two, owned by another shell corporation the name of which has fled my memory."

"There must be gangs of lawyers sitting in offices all over the country," I said, "churning out corporate names whose only purpose is not to be remembered."

"I went down to the Delaware Division of Corporations in Dover to put everything together. It got so complicated I wanted to smash my cigarette into someone's eye." Inhale, crackle, long exhale. "But in the end I drew up a diagram of all the names I had and all the corporations I'd found. It looked like a spiderweb. And right in the middle, presiding over everything, like the spider itself waiting for some helpless little bagman to fly into its web, is a name, one of the very names of the donors Miles had given me."

"And you have an address?"

"What do you think?"

"I think I'm ready to step on a spider."

The Big Butter made his money in commodities. Or was it drugs? Finance or car parts? Real estate or derivatives or dog food, it doesn't matter. He made his money on his own, dug it out of the dirt with bare, bloody hands. Or he inherited his money from a father who never gave him an ounce of love. Or he stole his money in a stock scheme that still confounds the authorities. Truth is, none of it matters. The how gets swallowed by the how much. He could buy a basketball team if he wanted to, but who the hell would want to. He is no longer a man with a history; he is a number.

And his number is bigger than yours.

His name is Norton Grosset, but that is a vestige, like his appendix or coccyx, a name used only for legal matters and corporate documents, a name the banks require he scrawl on the fat checks that purchase bodies, carnal and legislative both. Norton Grosset is the name of a little boy teased on the schoolyard, a fat kid who couldn't get a date in high school. But the present has slayed the past and sucked its bones. Now he is the Big Butter, now he gets his picture taken with over-the-hill pop stars at charity balls in Manhattan, he meets young princes at charity polo matches in the Hamptons, he plays golf with aging golf pros at charity outings at Shinnecock and Olympic. He is so popular with charities it makes him want to vomit.

The Big Butter doesn't just sit naked in the sun, he sleeps naked, too. Even in the winter. Even with the windows open. Even when the girl of the moment is in the city carousing with her college friends and he is forced to sleep alone. He is worth almost a billion dollars, and that is enough to keep him warm at night, at least until the next divorce. It will be his fifth, and his new lawyer has told him the prenup is shaky. What would he be with only half of almost a billion dollars?

Cold. When the number is all that matters, the number is all that matters.

He shivers and takes a drink from his glass. He tastes the peat. Ah, the peat. What the hell is peat anyway? Is it scarce? Can he corner the market? Can he be the Peat King? He will have his people look into it. Prisons and peat, they go together like nickels and dimes. The bottle set him back two grand, but no matter how cold he becomes thinking of the sordid squander of his failed marriages, the price of the bottle is enough to warm his blood.

He knows I am coming and he is not afraid. I am small-time, I am in it for the shakedown, I can be bought with a pocketful of spit. He can read the want in others as if printed in block letters on their foreheads and he has read me clear. I want what everyone else wants, a piece of the swaddled bloated creature he has become. An arm, a cheek, a meaty thigh. Every cause is worthy, every child is deserving. Think of the children, the little children. No matter how much he gives, still they come begging, pleading, never satisfied. Well, fuck the little children. They are vultures, all of them, and he is certain I am just another of the kettle, out to pull from his corpus my own strip of his flesh.

And he isn't wrong.

As I got closer to the tip of the island, the phone rang ever more insistently.

Melanie. Decline.

Melanie. Decline.

I couldn't turn the phone off because I was using its GPS to get me where I was going. But I was also enjoying evidence of Melanie's growing worry. It meant I was getting ever nearer to something big, something huge. Close, maybe, to the very truth of things. But what I didn't know was that I was getting close to the truth of Melanie herself.

I thought I had Melanie Brooks flat figured out. I believed she had followed the route of an entire generation before us and sold her youthful idealism for mounds of cash. I could admire that; it would have been my preferred career path if I had evidenced any idealism in my youth and I could have found someone to pay me for abandoning it. With Melanie so easily understood, I thought I knew who stood at the center of this story. Me, thank you. Or maybe Jessica Barnes and Amanda Duddleman. Or Ossana DeMathis. Or her brother, the corrupt congressman. Or Bettenhauser, so new to the scene and already bought and paid for. Or maybe the man in Montauk who had done the buying and toward whom I was racing.

But I was wrong about Melanie. Yes, she had transformed, but not in the way I had imagined. And now, when I think back on all that happened, I think Melanie—and her shocking transformation—is the beating heart of this story. If you understand her, you begin to understand the price we all are paying. I wonder now what she would have said to me if I'd had the temerity to answer her calls. I wonder if then she would have spilled the truth.

Except I didn't answer her calls. I wasn't in the mood to be harangued or dissuaded. I was on a mission.

Melanie. Decline.

Melanie. Decline.

Sloane. Yikes. Accept.

"It's all set, Victor," he said. "It's running tomorrow, everything, and we're ready to publish on the website right away when you give us the word."

"But you'll hold off like you promised until I give the word."

"Sure, pal, like I promised. But don't keep us waiting too long."

"And you'll clear me of everything?"

"You'll be smelling so sweet they won't notice the shit hanging off your ears."

"Did you get the cover?"

"Not yet. We need an image that wows."

"You pay for pictures, right?"

"Extra for the cover."

"Hold tight and I'll see what I can do."

"Will you want the credit?"

"Hell, no, just the check. Give the credit to Jack Herbert."

"Who's he?"

"Some guy I used to know."

When I hung up with Sloane, I checked the GPS. Seven minutes to go. Seven minutes before I'd be face-to-face with the force behind my political rise and fall, the force behind the dance of death we all had suffered through. Seven minutes before I finally had my moment with the son of a bitch. I could barely wait. The phone rang.

Melanie. Decline.

From his rooftop deck, the Big Butter can see a car making its way toward the house. The car is old, battered, unclean. It belongs in Montauk like lobster Newburg at a bar mitzvah. He takes another sip of his drink as he hears the car pull to a stop across the street, a car door open and slam shut again.

He could go downstairs to greet me, but he doesn't want to greet me. The girl will bring me up, and I will gape at her fresh Wellesley loveliness, and I will understand the base truth of the world: he is fucking her, and I never will. He could put on a Speedo to make himself more presentable, but he doesn't want to make himself more presentable. Lawyers scuttle around in their suits, but higher species face the world in the raw.

As he hears footsteps rising up the metal treads of the outdoor stairwell, and the tinkle of conversation between me and the girl, he reaches to the table beside him and from the humidor chooses a thick Cohiba from Cuba. He snips off the pigtail at the foot, flicks a lighter to life, brings the flame to the head, pulls and blows and pulls again as a thick cloud of smoke envelops his face. The puffing of his cheeks sounds like the repetition of a prayer. How much, how much, how much. It is not a matter of whether he can buy me suit and soul—he has bought better men in better suits while pissing in their ears—it is only a matter of the how much.

He takes the cigar from his mouth and blows a rich plume of smoke. When it comes to the game of how much, no one plays it better than the Big Butter.

And then suddenly there I am, standing before him. He notes my cut-rate suit, the way my shirt collar chokes my neck, the cheap sheen on my tie, the thick soles of my heavy black shoes. But the bag, he notes, the bag is superb. Maybe, if time permits, he'll shit in my bag. He can see my eyes dart hither and yon, trying desperately not to gawp at his proud stretch of naked flesh.

"You don't mind if I don't get up, do you?" he says.

"God, no," I say.

"You've come all this way, so I suppose you have something to get off your chest."

"I want to know why."

"Are we talking physics or metaphysics?"

"I'm talking you and your money and a tax loophole that has become so terribly important that you ended up financing two murders, had me chained to a basement pipe with a gun to my face, and now threaten the future of a little girl. How can you justify such a thing? How dare you?"

"It must be gratifying to hate me so. It must delight your soul."

"It keeps me warm at night."

"I prefer Charlotte. Sit down, Victor."

"I'll stand."

"Sit down. Have a cigar. Have a drink. We've met before, remember? At the Congressman's reception. You impressed me then and I've heard good things about you since from the suits at Ronin and McCall. I'm sure we can come to some sort of accommodation."

"I don't want an accommodation. Didn't you hear? You're responsible for two murders. Your henchman had me chained to a basement pipe with a gun at my face. I only want to see you burn."

"I don't burn, I tan. Sit down, put up your feet. The cigars are from a factory just outside Havana. Quite exclusive. I have them flown in from Britain. Here, I'll clip the tip for you. And I've brought out the good single malt for the occasion. You've never tasted anything so fine, trust me."

"I'll choke on it."

"You might want to, but at two thousand dollars a bottle, the Scotch goes down too easy to choke on. Sit down, Victor, and let me tell you a story."

CHAPTER 53

HAYM SOLOMON

Let me tell you a story," said the naked man with a cigar.

I intended to stand there, curled like an accusation, and hurl expletives and anger. I intended to make a stand. But something about the scene, the splendiferous view of Lake Montauk and the Sound beyond, the sun and sky, his slow, ripe voice, something about his dreadful nakedness next to the stunning beauty of the young woman who had led me through the house and up the metal outdoor stairs, her tight tan skirt shifting like a prowling cheetah with each upward step, something about all of it dulled the loathing in me. I was suddenly weary, not just from the long eastward drive, but from my entire life of grasp and fail.

And so I sat. And out of habitual politeness I took the cigar he proffered, and leaned into the flame he produced, and took hold of the glass of whiskey neat he poured.

"This is a story of Washington," said Norton Grosset. "I'm speaking not of the city, but of the man himself, George, with his face on the dollar bill, yes?"

We were sitting side by side as he told his story, each of us staring across the landscape toward the bright blue of the Sound, which, thankfully, meant I could avoid the view of his roasting flesh. He seemed to delight in his vile appearance: boils, pustules, toenails out of a Japanese horror film, lips like eels.

"The story happened during the War of Independence," said Grosset. "The British were on their hind legs in Yorktown, and Washington, camped with his army in Philadelphia, was desperate to head down to Virginia and finish the Limeys off."

Grosset spoke in a slow growl, a voice from a different era, an unhurried voice designed to send chills up the spines of chairmen of the board.

"Washington saw a way to win the war and forge a new country. But there was a catch, see. He needed twenty thousand dollars to make the march, see. Yet he was broke, and so was the whole damn country. Broke. Not a penny to be had. The enterprise was teetering. Think of it as a start-up in its death throes. Nothing sadder than that, let me tell you. Résumés flying out the door, employees stealing whatever they can carry: computer monitors, chairs. And the smell. It has a smell, failure, like potato chips and dead squirrels."

"I hate that smell."

"So what did Washington say? He didn't say, 'Too bad.' And he didn't say, 'Hell, we'll march on down for nothing,' because let me tell you, no one does anything for nothing. You get me, Carl?"

"I get you."

"So what Washington said instead was this: 'Send for Haym Solomon.' How's the cigar?"

"Thick."

"Legend has it the dimensions of this particular cigar were designed to approximate the penis of Che Guevara. The cigar master went to every bordello in Havana to make a model based on the descriptions from Che's favorite whores."

I pulled the cigar out of my mouth and stared at it.

"Smooth?" said Grosset.

"Quite," I said before taking another mouthful of smoke.

The sky was high, the sun was hot, the cigars were phallic, the Scotch whiskey tasted like money pure on the tongue, oily with hints of oak and breast. The woman who had led me up the stairs to the rooftop deck with that animalistic ass, a woman named Charlotte, had spoken in such glowing terms—*Norton is so brilliant, such a clear thinker, it's a magnificent opportunity to work with one of the leading*—that it was obvious she was sleeping with him, which somehow made the view all the more precious and the taste of the whiskey all the more rich.

"Who was Haym Solomon?" I said.

"He was a Jew from Philadelphia, like you, but not like you at all, because Haym Solomon understood money."

"I understand money," I said, failing to keep the pout out of my voice.

"You understand that you don't have enough, yes, but everything else, its rhythms and harmonies, its magical abilities, the way to get it to spread its legs, all of it is a mystery to you. But not to Haym Solomon. He was in finance. That's right, a one-percenter. Those hippie wannabes who are allergic to showers would be occupying him if they had a chance. More Scotch?"

I looked down at my glass, realized it was empty, let him pour me another.

"And what did this Haym Solomon, this moneyman, this one-percenter do when Washington came begging?" said Grosset. "I'll tell you what he did. He came through, that's what he did. He found Washington his cash, and Washington made it down to Yorktown, and he cornholed that Cornwallis with his pretty white wig, and we won the war. Hurrah."

I lifted my glass. "Three cheers for the Jew from Philadelphia."

"Three cheers indeed. Haym Solomon is why your teeth are pearly and why you didn't get buggered in grade school. You see the point here, don't you, Carl? It's fun to mock us, we know that—fat cats who tip poorly and piss on the poor—but you need us, too. Your cell phone, your Facebook, every aspect of your vaunted modern life, we financed it all. Every dollar that gets made gets made because of us. Every dollar we pull in, we make twenty for the rest of the world. We're underpaid. And still you despise us for it. Why is that?"

"The pissing-on-the-poor part might be a clue."

"You think we have it easy, don't you? You think it's all tea cakes and young tits and holidays in the Hamptons."

I looked around at my surroundings. "It's not?"

"Do you see any tea cakes? But there's also envy and spite, bitterness and rage, all directed at us for one reason, and one reason only: because we risked what others didn't have the courage to risk and we've reaped our rewards. You know why we buy politicians, Carl? To even up the odds. The mob would tear us apart if they had their way, and then where would the country be? Twenty dollars created for every dollar we rake in, remember that. Take us down and what do you have? Not just bedlam, but depression, spreading slicks of poverty, a great march in reverse back to the mud."

"So you're the last bastion of civilization."

"We built this country and rebuilt it over and again. Vanderbilt, Carnegie, Rockefeller, Morgan. And yes, Noyce and Gates and Jobs. You live in our handiwork, yet your hatred is like a snake twisting around our necks. How would you like to suffer it?"

"If it comes with the house and the Scotch and Charlotte, I'd take it, and without complaining like a diapered baby."

"We'll have to see about that," said Grosset. "You've accused me of horrible things: thuggery, aiding in the delinquency of a minor, murder. I would be appalled if I even knew what you were talking about."

"You paid for all of it."

"What I paid for was an equalization of the political process, which is perfectly legal, as the Supreme Court will tell you. My payments were a simple exercise of my First Amendment rights. How my agents pursued my goals was their prerogative. I was never informed of the nuts and bolts of their activities. They were independent contractors, you see. Just like you were an independent contractor."

"I didn't work for you."

"Of course you did. You knew you were working for someone; did you truly expect it to be anyone other than me?"

I swirled the glass, drained it, and winced, not at the bite of the alcohol so much as at the bite of self-recognition.

"More Scotch? Here, let me pour a few extra fingers. Is that enough? Oh, maybe just a bit more. How is the cigar holding up? Can I get you anything else? I'm sure I can. As you may know, one of my independent contractors went rogue. I am not pleased about what happened to those women. It is a rotten way to do business and he has been dismissed. But the fight is not yet won."

"The fight for the loophole."

"Exactly."

"All this for a loophole."

"Why not?"

"Isn't that cruelly venal, even for the likes of you?"

"Not if it's worth enough. Think of all the businesses I can nurture with the taxes I'll save. Twenty to one, Carl. Once that ratio becomes clear, you can't avoid the responsibility. It is my patriotic duty to raise the populace from their pallid little lives."

"And we are so grateful."

"But to get it done I need someone new to handle my political affairs."

"Some other political hack to be your bagman."

"Someone like you."

I stared at the amber sloshing in my glass. "You're offering me a job."

"The reports on you were glowing. 'Clever and effective,' they said. And I can see both qualities. DeMathis will lose, Bettenhauser will win. Someone needs to keep his money flowing. Washington said, 'Send for Haym Solomon.' I am saying, 'Get me Victor Carl.'"

"Why not Melanie?"

"I've detected in Melanie an agenda of her own. And Ronin and McCall have a peculiar affection for the niceties of the law. I need someone who will go the final mile for me, someone I can trust, because I would pay that someone extravagantly."

I looked at the tip of my cigar, smoke rising inexorably from the ash. "I like that word."

"I thought you might."

"How extravagantly are we talking?"

"Extravagantly enough so that one of the burdens of the job would be to feel the hate of the masses."

"I always wanted to be rich," I said with a touch of sadness in my voice. He was trying to buy me, of course. He was doing his best to justify it, peddling some crap rationalization for all he was worth, but in truth, he had to justify nothing. All my life I had been waiting to be bought.

I put the cigar in my teeth and swirled the smoke in my mouth. It tasted dark and mellow and sweet with the sweat of those who picked the tobacco, those who cured it, those who rolled it. It tasted of limousines and houses in the Hamptons and girls like Charlotte. As I stared through the smoke toward the bright blue of the Sound, it was as if I were staring across some mythical sea over which the promise of this very country lay. There, yes, just there, on the far shore. Lurking beneath the waves were deadly shoals, I knew, and perched on outcroppings of rock and sand were Sirens who had called thousands to their deaths, yet still I had spent my life staring across the gulf with futile longing. To hell with the past, I had spent a lifetime beating the oars to find my future there. And now this man, this gross tub of larded greed, was building for me a bridge to the other side.

"Well, Vic, what do you say?" said Grosset with all the confidence of his bank account. "Do I have myself a bagman?"

CHAPTER 54

PETER PARKER

When I emerged from Grosset's Montauk bungalow with both my bag and my future sealed, the sun was low in the horizon and Melanie Brooks was leaning on my car, ever fresh and put together in her patented red dress. I walked slowly down the pale pebbled drive to the car parked on the far side of the curbless road edged by weeds, and took a spot on the hood next to her. We both stared at the house to avoid staring at each other.

"How'd you get here so quickly?" I said.

"The airport's just a mile and a half away. I figured whatever was going to happen, I needed to get here as fast as I could. Did you shoot him in the gut?"

"No."

"How could you miss?"

I turned my head to find the wry smile, but it wasn't there, like she was actually disappointed that I hadn't come brandishing a gun.

"Did he offer you a job?" she said.

"Yes."

"Did you take it?"

"No."

"He pays quite well."

"He thought my refusal was a negotiating ploy and tried to give me a figure, but I wouldn't let him. I told him the number would just give me indigestion."

"And you said no."

"I would like to say I turned down his offer on principle, but that would be a lie. The only pure principle I stand upon is to never turn down money on principle."

She narrowed her eyes, like she was looking for something in my face. "Then why?"

"Because I know a chimera when I don't see one."

"He'd come through," said Melanie. "As he likes to remind us, his word is his bond."

"Oh, I think his bond will be higher than that," I said. In the distance we could just make out the faintest rise of a single siren, and then a second.

"There must be a fire somewhere," said Melanie.

"There's no fire," I said.

"So you didn't rush all this way to shoot him in the gut, and you didn't rush all this way to become his bagman. What did you rush all this way for?"

"To personally serve wrongful death lawsuits I filed on behalf of the families of Jessica Barnes and Amanda Duddleman."

"Jesus, Victor, you are a peach."

"Truth is, the joke's on me. If I had known he was going to offer me extravagant wealth to carry his bag, I might have played this thing differently. I might have gone out of my way not to go out of my way in finding answers. Who knows all I wouldn't have done for his money. But he didn't find me and make me an offer, so I didn't let two murders slide. And here I am, forced to make my money the old-fashioned way, by suing the bastard."

"My poor baby. How'd he take it?"

"His reaction was a little raw."

As the sirens grew louder, we could make out the flash of red and blue coming ever closer in the dimming Montauk sky.

"Who's coming for him?" said Melanie.

"McDeiss."

"Does our detective have the goods?"

"Oh, yes," I said. "I was there when he got them."

I had known someone was running Stony for the benefit of the Big Butter, and I'd assumed it wouldn't be Melanie—she's smart enough to avoid the real hard-core muck—and so the question had been who. And then Stony mentioned the snivelly little voice of the guy giving him his orders and I immediately knew who the bastard was. So after that scene of blood and death in Lancaster, McDeiss and I went to pay a visit to Mrs. Devereaux. When we told her all of what her dapper in-house lawyer was involved in, and let her know how implicated she might be by his crimes, she was so horrified that she slapped Reginald's face once, twice, three times before McDeiss grabbed the little vixen away. Connie always did like her stuff rough. And that spurt of violence was enough to break Reginald. Out it all spilled: How Grosset had hired him to be his conduit for illegal money. How Grosset had pushed him to hire Colin Frost to get rid of Jessica Barnes, because she was blackmailing his boy DeMathis. And how Grosset, even as he hedged his bets by buying Bettenhauser, had urged Reginald to give Ossana DeMathis anything she wanted to keep a crucial vote on Ways and Means in his stable, which meant hiring Frost again to get rid of Duddleman. It was enough for McDeiss to get an indictment, and for me to file my lawsuits, and for Sloane to get his story, and for Norton Grosset to be laid out like the roasted suckling pig that he was.

"You want to get a drink and tell me about it?" said Melanie. "And maybe catch a little dinner on the firm?"

"You're not going inside that house to fight tooth and claw for each of your client's constitutional rights?"

"I'd rather murder a plate of oysters."

"Can we at least see the show first?"

"Dinner and a show," said Melanie. "Dearheart, you do know how to woo a girl."

The first one out of that bungalow, with the cop sirens growing louder, but before the cop cars themselves had turned the final corner and crested the final hill, was Charlotte, lovely young Charlotte, with her long legs and high boots and a hastily packed bag, clothes leaking from the opening like regrets. On my way down the stairs, after having slapped the envelope containing the complaints and the summonses onto Grosset's ample and naked belly, I had confided to sweet Charlotte that it might be time to head on home. I figured that anyone brutally ambitious enough to sleep with Grosset was ambitious enough not to go down with the listing ship. Now she darted from the house with her head down but eyes alert, scanning the street for trouble. She stopped when she saw me and gave the briefest of nods. I couldn't help myself from giving her the "Call me" sign. Without responding she turned away from the rising tide of sirens and hurried up the hill to some sort of safety.

"Nice-looking girl," said Melanie. "She going to call?"

"Not a chance," I said.

A moment later, the garage door started rising.

"What does he drive, a Beemer?" I said.

"Remember who you're dealing with."

"A Porsche then?"

"That's for the low-level quants who do his bidding. Norton drives a Lamborghini."

"Fast?"

"It will make any cop cars chasing look like they're going in reverse. At least until he hits a tree."

As the driveway door continued to rise, the sirens grew ever louder. Inside the garage, we could now make out the red snub-nosed front of the sports car. The car rumbled and shook in place, like it was scraping its hooves on the garage floor.

Two cop cars, one after the next and each with lights flashing and sirens screaming, made the turn at speed, leaving a gap between tire and asphalt as they crested the hill. The garage door rose. The sound of angry engines and excited sirens swirled around us as the cop cars thumped back down onto the roadway. When the garage door was high enough, the Lamborghini spun its wheels into smoke before it charged madly out of the garage.

And then it was all a matter of sound and fury:

The sirens still rising.

The roar of the Lamborghini's engine as the sleek monster leaped forward.

The shriek of a cop car's brakes as it jammed to a stop at the mouth of the driveway.

The bang-crash of too much money slamming nose-first into too much authority, sending both Lamborghini and Impala spinning, squealing into the street amidst shards of glass and fiberglass and steel that flew about like bats before clattering onto the road.

"Oh my," said Melanie in response to the violence, as if something sexual had just come over her. "I do so love a smashup."

When the cars had spun to a stop, engines still roaring beneath the cloud of sirens and smoke, the gull-wing door of the sports car opened and out stumbled a still-naked Norton Grosset, golden sunglasses askew. As he began to run, leather sandals slapping on the ground, saggy roasted flesh flopping like a sack of live fish on dry land, he looked back at us with terror in his eyes.

It was a ludicrously slow sprint, ungainly and wholly ineffective, and Grosset wasn't twelve strides down the street before he dropped to his knees and gasped for breath. The first cop to reach him didn't even have to run. A few moments later Grosset's hands were cuffed behind his back and he was being yanked to standing.

"Melanie," he called out, as he was being pulled to his feet. "Victor. Look at what's happening. Police brutality. Take notes on what they are doing. I need a lawyer."

"Yes, you do," called back Melanie, not uncrossing her arms, not budging off the car.

"Make them take these cuffs off of me."

"I'd like to, Norton, but I don't actually represent you. I represent a number of your corporate entities in which there are minority shareholders. In these circumstances, I perceive representing you in a criminal case would constitute a conflict of interest."

"Victor," he called out.

"I represent the Barneses and the Duddlemans," I said.

"I need help."

"If you cannot afford an attorney," I said helpfully, "you can have one appointed for you."

"I'll remember this."

"I hope so," I said before taking out my phone and snapping away. Tomorrow's cover of the *Daily News*. I felt like Peter Parker.

While we were having this pleasant little colloquy, McDeiss climbed from one of the cop cars, shook his head sadly as he looked at the naked figure of the raging, flopping Norton Grosset, and then spoke softly to one of the uniformed cops.

"Take him inside and get him dressed," the uniformed cop called out.

"Thank God," said another of the uniforms.

After Grosset had been led unsteadily back into his house, McDeiss put on his hat and ambled over.

"You have time to do what you needed to do?" McDeiss said to me.

"I did. Thank you."

"Don't thank me. I didn't slow down a whit for you. It just took a bit longer than I thought to tidy up the package."

"Detective McDeiss, I'd like you to meet Melanie Brooks, an old classmate of mine."

"We met at the airport," said McDeiss. "And didn't you cross-examine me once in court?"

"It's good to see you again, Detective," said Melanie.

"She cross-examined you?" I said.

"And pretty damn well, too, if I remember it right," said McDeiss. "You get anything out of Grosset?"

"He said he didn't know anything about any murders, but then later told me he was not pleased about what happened to those women."

"I'm going to need a statement," said McDeiss.

"Did you get her?"

"We're running her down now. Your pal Reginald had been using Grosset's money to pay off a credit card that she'd been using under a false name. He showed us the statements, we tracked the purchases. She's in a motel in North Carolina, not ten miles from the girl."

"You ever figure out how she got away?"

"We're still working on it. Heads will roll, I promise you that. We've been hearing strange rumors that Briggs Mulroney is back in town."

"Imagine that," I said.

"I thought he was dead," said McDeiss.

"From what I understand, Mr. Grosset's arrest wraps up this whole case," said Melanie, "from the shooters to the woman behind it all to the man who financed the killing."

"Apparently, yes," said McDeiss. "As neat as could be hoped for."

"What about Congressman DeMathis?"

"From everything we know, he wasn't involved in any crimes," said McDeiss. "At least any penal crimes. His sister shielded him. It's up to the voters to decide on his future."

"DeMathis? Bettenhauser?" I said. "Does it really matter?"

"You still carrying DeMathis's bag, Carl?"

"It turns out I'm not suited for the political game," I said. "The shoes never really fit."

"Good decision." McDeiss adjusted his hat and looked to the side so that he didn't have to look at me. "Against all odds, you have too much character for it."

"Don't be nice," I said. "It's unbecoming."

After McDeiss left, I turned to Melanie. "So you practiced criminal law before joining Ronin and McCall."

"I dabbled."

"You played me for a dupe from the start."

"You ended up with a new tuxedo, those darling shoes, and some thick checks, so quit complaining. You want to get out of here and suck down whole beds of oysters?"

"Yes, please," I said.

And that's what we did.

CHAPTER 55

THE RED DRESS

It was at a seafood restaurant on the inlet to Lake Montauk, facing the Sound and, beyond that, the great heaving expanse of the American continent, where I learned the bitter truth about Melanie Brooks.

We sat on the deck and stared into the setting sun over plates full of fried calamari, fresh Montauk Pearls, spicy tuna rolls, over skeins of cocktails from the restaurant's fancy menu, too many cocktails to count, black-cherry cosmos for Melanie and something called a Perfect Storm for me, made with vanilla vodka mixed with blood-orange and cranberry juices, which tasted suspiciously like a Sea Breeze. We laughed and ate and got amiably soused. And as the sun swelled over the peaceful Sound, I turned down a lucrative job offer for the second time in a matter of hours, which, for me, was a record.

"Are you sure, Victor?" said Melanie. "We could use someone with your talents at Ronin and McCall."

"As a lawyer?"

"No," she said.

"I'll give you the name of a crackerjack bagman if that's what you want, but what I told McDeiss holds. Here on in, I'm only lawyering."

"That's too bad." She took hold of an oyster shell, squeezed a spurt of lemon onto the bivalve, and speared it with her little fork.

"There's opportunity," she said before lifting her chin to let the raw oyster slide down her throat. Her eyes fluttered with pleasure; it was only the second time I had ever seen Melanie's features exhibit some sort of sensual delight.

"Is that what got you into politics, opportunity? Because I've been wondering. The Melanie Brooks I knew in law school would have sooner spit in Norton Grosset's face than run his errands. What happened?"

"You don't want to know."

"But I do," I said.

Melanie picked up what was left of her cosmo and downed the remnants with a quick swallow. "I'm almost drunk enough to tell you. Let's just say I had enough of losing to a rigged game."

"We did okay today," I said.

"It's sweet how you still have such faith in our system."

"Why not? Norton Grosset is behind bars, tomorrow's paper will be full of his misdeeds, and I'm going to get rich off his carcass."

"No, you're not, Victor," said Melanie with the sad certainty of a mortician's accountant speaking of taxes and death. "Grosset's lawyers will get you recused at the first hearing. You're too involved. They won't let you keep the cases."

"So I'll get a referral fee."

"Don't count on that, either. Grosset's money is sheltered six ways from Sunday. It's his game and it's rigged. You should have shot him in the gut after all. And, Victor dear, you knew it was hopeless even as you were rushing up here with your precious indignation."

I closed an eye and took a long look at what was left of the sun through my reddish drink. "Maybe I did," I said. "But at least he's headed to jail. And Ossana's about to be caught. Those two deserve each other."

"Two peas in a pod," said Melanie, though we soon learned they wouldn't be podding in prison together.

Ossana was holed up in a seaside motel in North Carolina when Armbruster and two cars of cops approached to serve the arrest warrant. *Knock knock. Time to go to jail, you sick murderous puppy.* It had been a routine affair, until the bullets started flying. Ossana finally let loose the full anarchy in her heart, even clipping Armbruster in the shoulder, before, with the final bullet in her gun, she achieved that which she had been seeking from the first: defiant self-obliteration.

"But it doesn't matter what happens to Grosset," said Melanie. "When one falls, twenty rise. It's a Medusa's head."

"You want to know the truth, Melanie? I'm so sick of it I don't give a damn anymore."

"That's their plan, dearheart. If enough people figure it's not worth the fight, well, that means they just have a freer hand to get what they want."

"And what's that?"

"More."

"More what?"

"More everything. Money, sex, power, real estate, peasants to carve and devour at their Thanksgiving tables."

I couldn't help but laugh. "My God, Melanie, aren't you the bitter little fruit."

"I'm in the belly of the beast, Victor."

"More like at the breast."

"When the corruption of a system is irreversible, there are only two choices: capitulation or revolution."

"Who said that, your boy Machiavelli?"

"No, me."

"And I guess we know which one you chose."

"Do we? What about you, Victor? Where do you stand? Are you for the sincere and the deranged protesting at city hall?"

"I'm for myself, always and forever. I don't want to change the system, I just want to beat it."

"Our occupying friends want to beat it also," she said. "To death."

"Because they're true believers. The only thing I believe for sure is that I have too much doubt to throw bombs. I am constitutionally able only to sabotage myself."

"You should get out more. A few years in Legal Aid will change your tune. Remember when we were in law school and I used to worship Clarence Darrow and Thurgood Marshall?"

"Defenders of the damned and dispossessed."

"I have new idols now." She picked up her empty martini glass and turned it upside down among the other empties on the table. "Do you know of La Malinche, the slave woman who toppled the Aztecs? Or Mir Jafar, the Indian prince who betrayed the corrupt Bengal Empire? Or Ephialtes, who doomed the Spartans at Thermopylae?"

"All a step down from Thurgood Marshall, don't you think?"

"Different times demand different role models. History tells us that every sweet piece of carnage has had its inside man. Someone needs to know the names."

"Melanie?"

"You want to know what I learned from Machiavelli? 'He who wishes to establish a Republic where there are many Gentlemen, cannot do so unless first he extinguishes them all.' I think we should order more oysters."

"I don't like that word."

"Oyster?"

"Extinguish."

She grabbed herself another shell. "You're paralyzed by your aspirations, Victor. You always have been."

"Don't forget what we are, what we've sworn to uphold."

"Robespierre was a lawyer, too, dearheart. The thing I love most about freshly shucked oysters is the way you can almost feel them squirming as they roll down your throat."

As I watched Melanie swallow whole another Montauk Pearl, the true change in her became manifest. It wasn't the straightened hair or the thinned cheekbones or the startling red dress. The real difference in Melanie Brooks was that her sincerity had been twisted, by what we the people have done to our politics, into something virulent and dark, a nihilism waiting for the right moment to leap and tear at the corruption, even if it meant tearing out a hundred thousand throats. It made me shiver, and made me feel ashamed.

"You know how farmers used to burn their fields after the harvest to rid themselves of the unneeded stalks?" said Melanie Brooks—sincere-and-committed Melanie Brooks, always-the-best-of-us Melanie Brooks—staring out now at the setting sun in a way that the light reflecting in her eyes matched her crimson dress. "All it takes is a match. Look at the sunset, look how gorgeous the light is as it spreads across the whole of the horizon. Like the landscape is igniting into a great field of fire."

First thing I did back in Philadelphia was throw away the shoes.

ABOUT THE AUTHOR

SIGRID ESTRADA

William Lashner is the *New York Times* bestselling author of *The Barkeep*, *The Accounting*, *Blood and Bone*, and seven previous Victor Carl novels, which have been translated into more than a dozen languages and sold across the globe. Writing under the pseudonym Tyler Knox, Lashner is also the author of *Kockroach*, a *New York Times Book Review* Editors' Choice. Before retiring from law to write full-time, Lashner was a prosecutor with the Department of Justice in Washington, DC. He is a graduate of the New York University School of Law as well as the Iowa Writers' Workshop. He lives outside Philadelphia with his wife and three children.